BLACK MAJESTY

Book Two – Wild Harvest

by

CHRISTOPHER NICOLE

BLACK MAJESTY

Book Two — Wild Harvest

by

CHRISTOPHER NICOLE

Severn House Publishers

New edition published 1987
This first world edition published 1985 by
SEVERN HOUSE PUBLISHERS LTD of
4 Brook Street, London W1Y 1AA

Copyright © 1985 F. Beerman BV

British Library Cataloguing in Publication Data

Nicole, Christopher
    Wild harvest.—(Black majesty: bk. 2)
    I. Title II. Series
    823'.914[F]   PR9320.9.N5

ISBN 0-7278-1161-4

Typeset by Spire Print Services Ltd., Salisbury, England

Printed and bound in Great Britain by
Butler & Tanner Ltd, Frome and London, England

This is a novel, but the events it relates are history. Henry Christopher, born 1767, died 1820, whose name became Henri Christophe, was a Negro slave who fought his way to power as the Emperor Henri I of Haiti. With his great compatriots, Pierre Toussaint l'Ouverture and Jean-Jacques Dessalines, he created a black nation capable of matching itself against the two foremost countries in Europe: England and France.

The quotations in this book are taken from *The West Indies: Their People and History* by Christopher Nicole.

Christophe was every white man's conception of the noble savage. Over six feet tall and built to match, he had the natural grace that both Toussaint and Dessalines lacked. He was as intelligent a man and as brilliant a soldier as the one, and as illiterate and lion-hearted as the other. He was born in one of the British islands – both Grenada and St Kitts have been awarded the honour – and although sold to a Frenchman at an early age, he preferred to retain the English spelling of his name until his coronation. His personality attracted legend, and there are many conflicting stories of his youth.

CONTENTS

8

Prologue

'Sail ho,' came the shout from the main top. Christopher Hamilton ran to the larboard rail of the brig to gaze at the vessel approaching them out of the Atlantic.

Tall, powerfully built, sun-browned and wind-burned, Kit Hamilton looked every inch of what he was, a sea captain whose trading routes lay through the magical islands of the West Indian chain and across the warm waters of the Caribbean Sea. At thirty years of age he possessed all the confidence of health and strength, allied to a mastery of his profession; his blue eyes could be as warm as his ready smile. Yet, in repose, his face, handsome enough, too often settled into the deep-etched lines of a man who had looked on too much tragedy for a single brief lifetime – and on this voyage, the firm lips had been turned down more often than they had flared with amusement.

Rogers, the first mate, and Ducros, the Frenchman, stood at his shoulder, as the captain levelled his telescope. '*The White Ensign*,' he said. 'A Britisher. And signalling us to heave to.'

'She'll be after men,' Rogers growled, looking over his shoulder at the fluttering Stars and Stripes. For in this year of 1792 the Royal Navy was reluctant to recognise that the infant United States merchant marine had any rights at all, and often impressed men from the very decks of American vessels, claiming that they were merely rebellious Englishmen, in reality.

'Great Britain is at peace, at the moment,' Kit said. 'And we've no choice, Mr Rogers. Heave her to, and break open the gangway.' His helplessness made him boil with anger. But, when confronted with the guns of a frigate, there was nothing a trading brig could do. He preferred to turn back and study the shore to the south of him, the unbroken line of trees, with the backdrop of the mountains . . . and the yellow sand beach, on which the rollers ceaselessly pounded.

Hispaniola! In this western, French half of the island, where the colony of St Domingue had thrived, and become the richest of all the Antilles, he had grown to manhood. In every way. His family came from St Kitts, one of the British islands some distance away to the south, but his mother had been a Mortmain, a daughter of the richest of French West Indian families. Thus, when his father had fallen foul of the British Government in his opposition to the infamous Stamp Tax, and had been forced to flee to the already rebellious American colonies, it had been natural for Jeanne Hamilton to take her two children and seek a refuge with her famous and powerful cousin, the Sieur of Vergée d'Or. Vergée d'Or Plantation, supposing anything was left of it, lay behind those trees.

Philippe de Mortmain had lived virtually as a king. As a king he had taken his pleasures as he chose, as a king he had tortured and executed his black slaves as he chose, as a king he had brooked no opposition to his decrees . . . and as a king he had chosen his bride, his beautiful half English cousin, Richilde Hamilton. Kit could only marvel at the strange workings of Fate. By then, *he* had long fled the horrors as well as the majesty of Vergée d'Or, enlisting in the Continental Army to fight for George Washington, and more important, to fight with his cousin, Alexander Hamilton, another refugee from St Kitts and her sister island of Nevis. Unable to regard black people as slaves – on Vergée d'Or, one of them, Henry Christopher, had been a friend – Kit had chosen to make the United States his home, and under Alexander Hamilton's patronage, had prospered. But Richilde had remained, the queen of Vergée d'Or, mistress of everything she surveyed . . . and yet slave herself, not only of her husband, but of the society over which she ruled.

Undoubtedly she had rebelled as well; she was his sister. Yet he knew none of the truth of the matter. When the blacks, led by the fanatical obeah man

10

Boukman, and guided by the wise, wizened hand of the coachman Toussaint, had finally risen against their white tormentors in a mayhem of murder and destruction – only a year past – Richilde had miraculously survived, while Vergée d'Or, Philippe de Mortmain, crushed in his own sugar mill, and his family had been torn apart. Save for Annette de Mortmain.

Annette! Kit's fingers tightened on the rail. She was in Cap François at this moment, awaiting his return. She was beautiful, and she was his betrothed. He knew what had happened to *her*. She had been raped and beaten, had staggered into the safety of the French-held seaport half naked . . . and worse. Part of her brain had closed, and would open only in seething madness against anyone with a black skin. His betrothed! He had arrived too late to influence events in any way, and to an awareness that not only honour, but common humanity, demanded of him that he make her his wife: only he could save her from true madness. As if he, or any *man*, could possibly save Annette.

And he had more than just Annette to consider; now he must attempt to save his sister – if that, too, were at all possible.

'Boat approaching,' Rogers said.

'Well,' Kit said, 'give him a whistle, Mr Rogers. We'll show our manners.'

'But will he show his?' muttered Ducros, retreating against the far rail. The Frenchman had all of his nation's antagonism towards the British. But he was a courageous man, or he would not be here at all. He had been an overseer on Vergée d'Or, and he could have no doubt that any blacks who were surely hidden in those trees would remember his face. Yet he had volunteered. Which was more than Etienne de Mortmain, that other survivor of the revolt, had been prepared to do. Etienne had fled from Vergée d'Or to the safety of Cap François even before the blacks had surrounded and assaulted the Great House, with all his family

11

inside. He had appeared to have adequate reasons for his cowardice; he claimed to have ridden for help. But he had point blank refused to return to seek his lost cousin.

The boatswain cooeed, and the crew gathered in the waist as the naval officer came on board. To Kit's consternation he realised that it was the captain of the frigate himself. Now the small, slight figure in the splendid white and blue uniform saluted. 'I seek Captain Hamilton.'

Kit hurried forward. 'I am he, sir.'

The Britisher frowned. 'You? By God! I had heard there was youth here, but you . . .'

'I have powerful and prosperous friends, sir,' Kit said. 'And I have sailed these waters for better than ten years.'

'My apologies, sir. My tongue ran away with me. Edward Pellew.'

They shook hands.

'I would have a word with you, sir,' Pellew said. 'In confidence.'

Clearly this was no press-ganging operation. Kit showed his guest down into the small aft cabin, placed the decanter of brandy and two glasses on the table, raised his eyebrows to Rogers as the door was closed upon them.

'Your health.' Pellew drank.

'And yours. I am interested to discover how you knew my ship.'

Pellew smiled. 'We keep a list of all vessels regularly trading in these waters. I know something of your history, Mr Hamilton. You seek your sister?'

Kit leaned forward. 'You have news of her?'

'No, sir. Save that she is reputed to be held by the blacks.'

Kit studied him. 'You claim to know something of my history, Captain Pellew. Therefore you must know something of hers as well.'

12

'It is not my business to pry, Mr Hamilton.'

'Yet you must be aware that after my sister escaped the blacks, last August, together with her cousin, Annette de Mortmain, my betrothed . . .' he would not have this man be unaware of a single aspect of the situation, even if he also no doubt knew of Annette's affliction, '. . . and gained the security of Cap François, she was discovered to be pregnant. It was naturally assumed that the child was by her husband, Philippe de Mortmain, who had been murdered in the revolt. When the babe was born, it was discovered that was not the case.'

Pellew gave a delicate cough, and drank some more brandy.

'The child,' Kit said evenly, 'was therefore allowed to perish. I was not there at the time, so I do not know what my sister felt or said. I do know that a few nights later, when she had regained her strength, she disappeared from Cap François. It was supposed that she might have taken her own life, but it was later discovered that she had swum along the coast until she was beyond the perimeter established by the French troops, and then come ashore and walked into the forest, apparently wishing to be re-united with her . . . with the blacks.'

'She sounds an intensely strong young lady, of both mind and body,' Pellew observed. 'May I be so bold, Mr Hamilton . . . you say you were not in Cap François when this tragedy occurred. But the way you say it suggests that, had you been there, you might have insisted the babe should live.'

'I would have insisted that, sir, yes.'

'The child of a rape? A mulatto bastard? At a time when everyone with even heavy colour from the sun is suspect and hated?'

'Times like this will pass, Captain Pellew. The babe would have been my nephew.'

'I see,' Pellow said, clearly not seeing at all. 'This is

13

not a point of view held by a large percentage of your own countrymen,' he remarked. 'Much less the French here in St Domingue. I am sorry to press this point, sir, and I trust you will not take offence, but as I will explain in a moment, it is very necessary for me to be sure of your motives. Dare I suggest that the fact of your sister's return to the forest, and indeed every other fact about this case, raises two rather . . . well, unpleasant possibilities? One, that she has, after all, chosen a rather unfortunate way of committing suicide, and has already been torn to pieces by the blacks; two, that the rape was not a rape at all, and your sister has merely sought to rejoin her . . . ah, lover. The father of her child.'

'There is a third possibility, Captain Pellew,' Kit said, evenly. 'That my sister might actually have chosen to live with a people who have been ill-used for too long, and now have sought only their freedom, rather than conceding to their oppressors, who seek only to return them to slavery.'

They stared at each other, and Pellew flushed. 'Would you agree with that point of view?' he asked.

'Very probably,' Kit said. 'In fact, sir, I believe your second conjecture to be right, and that my sister does have a Negro lover, but . . .'

'And you can sit there?' Pellew demanded.

'I was going to say, sir, that fact does not necessarily mean that my point is not also correct. As for my sister's private affairs, if I am right in thinking that I know the man to whom she has returned, he is, or was, my friend, regardless of his colour. I hope that one day he will again be my friend.'

'I see,' Pellew said again. And half shrugged, as if to indicate that clearly the Hamiltons were totally beyond his understanding. But he was looking quite contented with the situation. 'Then would *I* be right in assuming that this expedition has not been mounted with the intention of regaining your sister by force?'

14

'Look around my ship, sir,' Kit suggested. 'Do we look armed and equipped for a military campaign?'

'No, indeed. And that relieves me greatly,' Pellew confessed. 'So, you go to speak with your sister, and discover if she is well, and what her intentions are.'

'That is correct.'

'And you anticipate being welcomed by the black leaders?'

'I believe they will treat me fairly,' Kit said. 'Because I have always treated them fairly.'

'That is splendid,' Pellew said, apparently having done a complete volte face. 'I wonder, sir, if His Majesty's Government could make a request of you?'

Kit frowned at him.

'I also would speak with these people,' Pellew said. 'But I have as yet been unable to do so. You will understand, sir, that over the past year my ship has been on patrol on this coast, and we have of course endeavoured to rescue such planters and their families as we might. This has no doubt encouraged the blacks to consider us their enemies, though we were simply playing a humanitarian role. The result is that whenever I land, St Domingue could be a desert island.'

'And *you* wish to speak with the black leaders?' Kit was incredulous. 'May I ask why?'

Pellew looked into his brandy glass. 'St Domingue is too great and fertile a country to be permitted to become an empty jungle, Captain Hamilton. Do you not agree? And France, sir, well, it is the opinion of most neutral observers that France is daily slipping further into chaos. You have heard the news from Paris?'

'Some of it, sir.'

'Yes,' Pellew said. 'Well, sir, I can tell you that since the mad French declaration of war on Austria and Prussia, things have deteriorated. On the approach of the Duke of Brunswick's army, last month, Paris seems to have gone wild. I have heard terrible stories of what

15

happened here last year, but I can assure you, sir, that they do no more than match the tales of what happened in Paris last month. And there was no colour or slavery question involved there. The whole world seems to be entering a prolonged period of anarchy and brutality.' He sighed. 'But we were discussing St Domingue.'

'Which Great Britain would like to annex, if it can be done without provoking a war,' Kit said thoughtfully. 'I have heard it said that England has always coveted Hispaniola, that Cromwell, indeed, sent his commanders to the Tower of London because they took Jamaica instead, in 1655.'

'I implement my country's policies, Captain Hamilton. I do not make them. But, as I have said, here is a great and fertile land, daily descending further down the scale of human savagery. France no longer controls it. As for the blacks, well . . .'

'But you wish to speak with them, and enlist their support, perhaps. May I ask what you will say to them? You can hardly offer them freedom, when Great Britain herself is the mistress of a dozen slave-holding islands.'

'I have heard that some of the black leaders are quite intelligent,' Pellew remarked. 'I may not be able to offer them freedom, but I can offer them a better life than the existence they now maintain. I can offer them, too, a final solution to their hatred for the French.'

Kit's head came up. 'You seem to forget, sir, that I am half French myself.'

'And half English, by birth. The whole having become American. That is where your loyalties should lie, sir. Does the United States have designs upon St Domingue?'

'Of course not,' Kit said.

'Well, then . . . I do promise you, Captain Hamilton, that my government means no ill towards those French who remain in Cap François and Port-au-Prince. They will be evacuated, to wherever they wish to go. There is even talk of compensation, for the loss of their plantations, should Great Britain become mistress of the colony. Now, sir, what could be fairer than that? When compared with the miserable existence they are presently forced to tolerate?'

'And of course,' Kit said, 'the Royal Navy would supply the one weapon the blacks need to force the French to surrender Port-au-Prince and Cap François – a naval blockade to prevent supplies from entering those ports.'

'Indeed, sir. But I would beg you to remember that it would be the Royal Navy seizing Port-au-Prince and Cap François upon a French surrender, not the slaves. And would not *that* be more preferable than to have those cities, and their inhabitants, forced to surrender to Jean François? I think I am correct in stating that he claims to be the blacks' general?'

'You are correct,' Kit said.

'Well, sir, that may well happen – and soon. If things in France are as bad as they seem, Cap François and Port-au-Prince may run out of food and munitions even without a blockade.'

Kit got up, walked to the stern windows to look out at the coastline, as his ship bobbed gently on the calm sea. The man spoke sense, of course. There *was* no future for any Frenchman, in St Domingue, ever again. Hanging on, as Etienne Mortmain was doing, waiting for a counter-revolution to re-establish him, as Philippe de Mortmain's heir, in control of the vast wealth of Vergée d'Or, was merely to perpetuate the madness. And Richilde, her black lover suddenly again reduced to the status of a slave? But that was something she would have to resolve for herself, if she would not return with him now. For could he, personally, care whether the colony belonged to the British or the French? He was an American, and he knew one of the two alternatives had to happen – he had no faith in the ability of someone like Jean François, who was a brutal

17

savage, being able to create an independent nation here, even with the patience and intelligence of someone like Toussaint ever available.

'And of course, Captain Hamilton,' Pellew said, gently, 'should the blacks be recalcitrant, and refuse to release your sister, for example, well, once we have discovered her whereabouts, I can promise you the assistance of my ship, and my men, in returning Madame de Mortmain to safety and comfort. Supposing that is what she wishes.'

'The man you need to speak to is Pierre Toussaint, not Jean François,' Kit said sombrely. He went to the doorway. 'I think it is best we use my longboat, and fly the American flag.'

'There, Mr Hamilton,' Ducros said. 'You should see the chateau through the trees. If it still stands.'

The brig hardly did more than drift before the light breeze; the frigate remained three miles farther out to sea, waiting to be signalled. It was early morning, and although there were heavy clouds over the mountains, they had not yet descended towards the shore. It was a beautiful day, with the sun just gaining in heat as it soared into the eastern sky, and the sky itself matching the blue of the sea in calm serenity. And yet, Kit knew as he levelled his telescope, horror was their business this day. Horror was what they anticipated, what they knew they must expect.

'I can see the chateau,' he said. Through the trees, the sun glinted on blackened timbers.

Pellew was inspecting the beach. 'And, as usual, no blacks.'

'Yet they are there, sir,' Rogers suggested. 'We know they are there.'

'What do you think, Ducros?' Kit asked.

The Frenchman hesitated, chewing his lip. 'It is hard to say, monsieur. We understood in Cap François that Vergée d'Or was their headquarters. But we have had

18

no positive information for some time. Since the failure of their last attempt to storm the city, they may have retreated into the mountains. Or they may have not.'

'Then we accomplish nothing by standing here,' Kit decided. 'You'll prepare the boat, Mr Rogers. Make sure the Stars and Stripes are prominently displayed, and also a white flag. Captain Pellew, may I ask you to leave your sword behind?'

'Eh?'

'I do not propose to expose any of my people to murder, sir,' Kit said. 'Therefore I am going ashore with Ducros alone. You have expressed a wish to accompany me, and you are welcome. But the three of us certainly can never fight the entire black army. We succeed here today by talk, and by proving from the outset that we *mean* to talk.'

Pellew hesitated, then unbuckled his sword belt and handed the weapon to Rogers. Kit wondered if he was afraid. If he was, he was too well disciplined to show it. Ducros most certainly was, crossing himself as he climbed down the ladder into the boat, and was clearly regretting his offer to accompany this mad American.

And am I afraid? Kit asked himself. Amazingly, he wasn't. Because he trusted Toussaint, and Henry Christopher. As Richilde had done.

The boat approached the beach, perhaps a hundred yards from where the pale-watered stream debouched into the sand, forming a miniature estuary of drying banks and flooded waterways, before losing itself against the gentle surf. But the water remained clear, and almost white.

On that beach he had become a man, in the arms of his cousin's mistress, Jacqueline Chavannes. He wondered what had happened to that tall, proud, beautiful mulatto, in the turmoil of the last year.

Beyond the beach there was a fringe of trees, empty and silent.

The keel grounded, the three men climbed over the

bow, and stamped on the sand to empty water from their shoes.

'Keep your place in deep water,' Kit commanded the coxswain. 'But be alert. We may return in some haste.'

'I'll be here, Captain Hamilton,' the coxswain promised.

Kit led the way up the beach, the two others behind him. He pushed his way through the trees, to emerge on to the lawn, and face the patio, where Philippe de Mortmain had condemned a man to be torn to pieces by dogs, on the Hamiltons' first night in St Domingue. But there was no grass here now, only trampled earth. And the first skeletons, a cluster of three, black men he thought from the remnants of their clothing. And a crow, still investigating the meal he must have completed over a year ago, casting a disgusted glance at the living men who approached him, and then flapping his wings as he rose from the ground.

They gazed at the burned-out shell of the house. The walls had fallen outwards as the roof had fallen in, and yet the remains of the great staircase still jutted upwards out of the huge hall. Here the main work of exccution had been conducted. They looked at skeletons, of men, and women, and children, many of the bones blackened by the fire, others torn and twisted and chopped away from their fellows, to suggest some of the dreadful things that must have taken place, while skeins of golden hair still clung to shattered skulls – and the white ants lived and roamed in their dreadful habitat.

'These were not men,' Ducros muttered. 'These were beasts.'

Kit said nothing, turned and walked back on to the drive, looked at the scattered skeletons there. Here he felt he could breathe again, as he watched the clouds sweeping lower, occasionally obliterating the sun, bringing the promise of a noontime rain shower. He walked down the drive, looked at the white township.

20

This too had been burned. But the slave village beyond was undamaged. And so, amazingly, was the factory.

He began to hurry, away from his companions, ran into the shade of the great chimney and the huge vats, guided by instinct, and by what Annette had told him. He climbed the ladder to the first of the rollers, and paused, and lost his balance for a moment in sheer horror. Only Philippe de Mortmain's skull remained, clinging to the top of a shattered spinal column. The rest of his body had been fed through the rotating iron drums. But even the skull's expression seemed twisted in the torment he must have experienced before death.

He climbed down the ladder, slowly, regained the ground. Pellew and Ducros waited for him. And the rain began to fall, a gentle patter on the factory roof, a gentle thudding on the dry ground outside.

'You would treat with these people, Captain Pellew?' Ducros asked.

Pellew waited for Kit to speak. But Kit had nothing to say.

'I think we should leave this place, messieurs,' Ducros said. 'It is a charnel house, and there are no blacks. Thank God! They have gone to the mountains, as I said. Let us return to the ship.'

He made his way up the drive, and after a moment Kit followed. He felt the rain splashing on his hat, dampening his shoulders. In time the rain would wash all these bones away, even as it would wash away Vergée d'Or itself.

He checked, because Ducros, fifty yards in front of him and just approaching the trees which lined the stream, had also checked. He felt a sudden lurch of his heart, a constriction of his belly. There, standing in the trees, was Henry Christopher.

He was exactly as Kit remembered him, from the last time they had met, which was several years ago, on the occasion of Richilde's wedding to Philippe de Mortmain. He was better than six feet tall, and had a strong, gaunt face, handsome but reserved. Only his clothes had changed. Then he had been a coachman, wearing the Mortmain livery and white stockings. Now he wore a blue uniform jacket, straining across his shoulders, and ragged white trousers, and a blue tricorne, obviously taken from some dead French soldier. And he carried a sword, and had two pistols thrust into his leather belt. Henry, Kit recalled, had always wanted to be a soldier, and wear a uniform.

'By God,' Pellew murmured. 'By God.'

Kit advanced, slowly.

'Do you not recognise me, Kit?' Henry asked. 'I recognised you, the moment you landed from your ship.'

'You were here, then?'

'My people have watched your ship, sailing along the coast. We knew whose ship it was. We knew you would come to Vergée d'Or.'

'And you let us walk into your trap,' Ducros muttered. 'My God . . .' he turned, slowly looked at the black men, who now stood all around them.

'You have come for Richilde?' Henry asked.

Kit licked his lips. 'We have come to talk.'

'Then come to the General,' Christopher said.

He led them past the village, and the wood beyond, through the deserted and overgrown canefields, towards the distant forest. Now there were more black men, and women, gazing at them. Ducros crossed himself again, and had clearly committed his soul to the Almighty.

The Negro encampment was on the edge of the trees. Here was surprising industry, men sharpening weapons, others even attempting a form of drill, women cooking over the open fires, children playing, dogs growling at one another. Wooden huts gave it a suggestion of permanence.

And here too was Jean François, standing in the

doorway of the largest of the huts, surrounded by his bodyguard, who were in turn dominated by the squat, bull-like man, who gazed at the whites with hungry eyes. All wore the suggestions of a uniform, like Henry. But Jean François had also made epaulettes for himself, and, playing the general, wore no weapons.

'Kit Hamilton,' Henry said.

'Do you remember me, Jean François?' Kit asked.

'I remember you,' Jean François said. 'You will address me as "Your Excellency". You have come for your sister?'

'I have come to see my sister,' Kit agreed. 'But this gentleman is an English sea captain, and he has come to talk. With you. And with Toussaint, Your Excellency.'

'Toussaint?' Jean François gave a bellow of laughter.

'He's not dead?' Kit asked in alarm.

'He is gone,' Henry said, quietly. 'He has fled to the Spanish side of the island.'

'But why?'

'He sought to dispute my orders,' Jean François said. 'Just as Rigaud and his brown skins sought to dispute my orders. No one disputes my orders, white man. You . . .' he pointed at Pellew. 'You have something to say to me? Say it.'

Pellew hesitated, and then went forward.

'While they speak, I will take you to see Richilde,' Henry offered. 'Come.'

He led Kit through the growing crowd of black people, who stared at the white man with dull interest.

'I am sorry Toussaint has gone,' Kit said.

'So am I,' Henry agreed, without turning his head.

'And Jean François . . .'

'He is my General,' Henry reminded him and halted.

Kit lowered his head and entered another hut, another large hut, almost as large as Jean François's headquarters. Inside, he gazed at the bodies lying on the floor, several of them bandaged against wounds, but the majority ill, he estimated, of fever and festering sores. Kneeling beside one of the sick people was Olivier, the Vergée d'Or dispenser. Richilde knelt at his elbow.

She wore a shapeless white gown, and her head was concealed beneath the bandanna of the Negress. The bandanna completely obscured the rich, curling brown hair which had always been one of Richilde's peculiar treasures, but on the other hand it left another of her treasures, the softly beautiful face, exposed. The face was not as soft as Kit remembered it. The chin had always pointed, the nose had always been a delightful retroussé; in between, the mouth had flattened from the perfect rosebud of her youth, and he suspected that the green eyes would now suggest marzipan icing rather than lush tropical foliage. Yet the beauty remained, and of body as well, for the gown was pulled tight as she knelt, and outlined shoulder and breast and thigh, strong and muscular, but voluptuous and appealing as well.

Above anything else, both face and body gave an impression of strength. Richilde had always been strong, in body and mind. She had needed that strength to survive marriage to Philippe de Mortmain, and she had needed it even more to survive the revolt, the horrors to which she had been exposed, and which had driven her cousin Annette mad. Those had perhaps been passive strengths. Her true strength had been demonstrated in her decision to return, where, despite all, both her love and her sympathies lay.

She looked up as the two men came in, gave Henry a quick smile, and then frowned incredulously as she saw her brother, hastily stood up, drying her hands on her skirt. 'Kit? But . . .'

'He has come under a flag of truce, as an American,' Henry explained. 'And with an English officer. He wishes to speak with you.'

She licked her lips, waited.

'I think you should go outside with him,' Henry said.

24

Richilde walked to the door, ducked her head, stepped into the open air. She hesitated for a moment, and then walked into the trees. Kit glanced at Henry, who nodded. Then he followed his sister. But what a strange, upsidedown world this is, he thought, that I should need a black man's permission to speak with my own sister.

'Is that what they make you do?' he asked. 'Tend their sick?'

She turned to face him. 'It is what I *wish* to do. It was what I did even before the revolt. Nobody has made me.'

He made a gesture, at their surroundings. 'You left Cap François, to come back to *this*?'

She raised her head. 'I came back to Henry.'

'The man who raped you? Who murdered your family?'

'He did not rape me,' she said. 'In the sense that Annette was raped. And he never touched any of our family.'

'He led the assault, I have been told. His people followed him. I have just come from the chateau. I have just seen Philippe.' He drew a long breath. 'Now I also will have nightmares. Could you not have had him buried? Have had them all buried?'

'It was Jean François's command that Vergée d'Or should be left exactly as it is. We did not bury the black men, either.'

'And you can live here, with such barbarous savages?'

She met his gaze. 'You say you have seen Philippe. Did you also see my child? Henry's child?'

'Richilde . . .'

'These people acted out of revenge,' she said. 'Out of excitement. Out of a whipped-up religious mania. That was the only way they could risk what they did. But over the centuries, whenever our people, Kit, our white people, have inflicted no less dreadful injuries upon

25

them, it has been done in cold blood. As my child was murdered, in cold blood.'

He sighed. 'I have no wish to defend the planters. I have always loathed the whole idea. But Richilde, for better or for worse, the white people are *your* people. You belong in beautiful gowns and wearing rich jewellery, riding in a carriage and sleeping between linen sheets, eating good food and drinking the best wine. You are Madame de Mortmain. Not some white Negress scrubbing about for roots in a jungle.'

She shook her head. 'I am not coming back with you, Kit.'

'You mean you are *happy*, here?'

She thought for a moment. 'No,' she said. 'I am not happy here. I am happy with Henry. He can make me happy.' A faint flush. 'I have never been happy with a man before. Philippe was a purgatory of nine years. And I think that Henry is happy with me. But *we* are not happy, yet. That remains to be accomplished.'

'Do you know how disgusting that is?' he asked. 'You seek physical pleasure, from a black man? A black . . .'

'Man,' she said. 'With whom I have grown up. A man I know, and who knows me. Do not think Henry a savage, Kit. He is as intelligent as you or I, even if he cannot write his name. That is why he is unhappy. He knows as well as I that this revolt has become dissipated in a senseless civil war. Perhaps that had to happen. It was not planned that way. But then, it was never expected to be so successful. We know that it is a tragedy that we should control so much of St Domingue, and yet be making no effort to form a government, or even any social order. Toussaint might have done those things. But Jean François drove him out. He had driven him out before I returned. When I realised Toussaint was no longer here, I nearly went back to Cap François. But I didn't. And I'm glad I didn't. I don't know who will do it. Henry is too young, and is still too uncertain to put himself forward. Rigaud might have done it, but Jean François drove him out too, and now he lives like a bandit down in the south. But someone must make these people into a nation. Make them realise that they are fighting *for* something, instead of just fighting. Make them realise that freedom has to be organised. I believe Henry may yet be the man to accomplish that. If I stay at his side. And if we can both stay alive long enough. I think that is a more worthwhile thing to do with my life than attempting to play the great lady. Than pretending to be part of a society and a people that I hate.'

'As you say, if you stay alive. You returned to these people, a lone white woman, and . . .'

'No one has touched me,' she said. 'Not even Jean François. Because I came to them. And because, once the frenzy was over, they understood that I had always tried to help them.'

'And if I tell you that everything you have just said is a senseless dream? Do you really suppose France, or England, is going to allow St Domingue to become some kind of a Negro kingdom, here in the West Indies? France is experiencing a revolution, so she can't do anything about these people, at the moment. But the British mean to. That's why Pellew is here.' He caught her hand. 'Richilde, this absurd revolt is only a revolt. These blacks are merely lucky that circumstances have allowed them to remain free for over a year. Circumstances won't allow that much longer. And then they are going to be blown apart by cannon, shot down and hung up. That is as inevitable as night must follow day. There will be nothing you can do about it. Except die with them. Or be returned to some kind of everlasting notoriety, as the white woman who lived with the blacks, of her own free will. Is that what you want?'

'I'm sorry, Kit,' she said. 'I do not expect you to understand. Sometimes I do not understand myself. I think perhaps I died, the night the chateau fell. Certainly I expected to. And next day, I discovered I was

27

still alive. And with Henry. And I suddenly realised that was all I had ever truly wanted, that all my life, certainly since my marriage to Philippe, I had been living nothing more than a sham. I wanted to stay. Even after everything that had happened, everything that had been done to *me*, I wanted to stay. Henry made me go to Cap François. We didn't know I was pregnant, then. And I believe he was right. Of course I did. I'd been brought up to feel that. Perhaps if you'd taken me away with you, last Christmas, I'd have always felt that way. I'm not blaming you. I'm glad you didn't, now. I came back, because I love Henry. There, I've said it. I love him, and I've always loved him.'

'And you think he loves you?'

'Yes,' she said. 'Yes, I think he does love me. But there is more than that, Kit. As I said, I came back, because I thought I could help these people, to stop being savages, to create something. Even to win their war, and their freedom. So Toussaint has gone. And Rigaud has gone. Even Boukman, who at least gave it the sanctity of religion, is gone. But Henry is still alive. And however long he remains, however long he is prepared to put up with Jean François, then I am going to stay with him.'

They stood in a group, to watch the white men receding through the trees.

'A British colony,' Jean François sneered. 'The man must think we are fools.'

'We should have killed them all,' Jean-Jacques Dessalines growled. 'They are white people. We should kill every white person we find, as they kill every black person.' His eyes gloomed at Richilde, and she made herself stand still with an effort – he was the only black man she truly feared, now. She had braced herself for an ordeal, with Jean François, on her return, had feared then, to provoke a confrontation between himself and Henry, had indeed resolved to prevent it by accepting

28

the older man, if she had to. But Jean François had grown, as a man, in her ten months' absence. He was still no more than a coachman. He still had no concept of strategy or tactics, of leadership, other than by browbeating anyone who stood against him. But he had also realised that he *was* the General, that he could not dissipate his energies in either women or wine, as did so many of his followers – and also perhaps that Henry Christopher was his most loyal aide, of whom it would be ridiculous to make an enemy. Thus he had merely scowled at her, and said, 'You ain't tired suffering, Richilde?'

But Dessalines . . . his eyes followed her wherever she went, as much because of her white skin as because she was a woman, she thought. Yet Dessalines had a brain, was well aware that he was the newcomer here, even more than she. If he destroyed her, if he could ever attain that ambition, it would have to be part of a fresh wave of hatred and lust. And it would have to be inspired by the General.

Who scowled at her again. 'They came for you, Richilde,' he said. 'Why did you not go with them?'

'Because I preferred to stay here, Your Excellency,' she said.

'Because you are a fool. All white people must be fools. A British colony. Bah.'

'Yet the British will seek to implement their plan, whether you agree to it or not,' Richilde said.

His frown deepened. 'How they going do that?'

'Suppose they were to take Cap François, and Port-au-Prince? Because they can do that, Your Excellency. The reason you have not been able to drive away the French is because they are being supplied with food and munitions, from the sea. The British have the ships to put a stop to that, and force them to surrender. Then you will be fighting the British. And they have great armies as well as great navies.'

'She is right,' Henry said. 'If we cannot beat the

29

French, it might be better for us to make peace with the British, rather than have to fight *them* as well.'

'Bah,' Jean François said. 'You keep telling us you are English yourself, Henry. And she is English too. So you are afraid of them. But these English are not gods.'

'They are men who live by fighting,' Henry said.

Jean François glared at him, then he snapped his enormous fingers. 'Then we will prevent them. Summon the army. We march on Cap François.'

'Again?' Dessalines asked.

'Again,' Jean François roared. 'And this time we will take it, you black-faced nigger. Summon the army.'

'I did not mean to send you back to war,' Richilde said, when Henry came to say goodbye. 'My God, I did not mean that, Kit will be returning there.'

'Well, like you said,' Henry said, 'we can't fight ships. He will be all right. Maybe this time they will all take to the ships. That is what we want them to do.'

'And if they don't?'

He shrugged. 'We will hurl ourselves against the walls, as usual.'

'As you did before. And you will be killed. Henry, if you were to be killed . . .' her shoulders slumped.

'If I were to be killed, Richilde,' he said, 'then you would go back to your people. Promise me that.'

'Don't you understand that that is impossible?' she asked. 'If you were to be killed, Henry, I should have to die too. I have no people, white or black. I have only you. So come back to me, Henry. Come back to me.'

Even from the sea, the vast column of marching Negroes could be discerned. And long before the brig made the harbour, the afternoon was torn apart by the explosion of the cannon, the rattle of the musketry, the screams of the dead and dying. While now the watchers from the ship could see the clouds of black smoke rolling above the town.

30

'Christ give us a breeze,' Kit growled, as they almost drifted towards the harbour. 'I wonder if Pellew realised he would stir them up to another assault?'

'Englishmen,' Ducros grumbled, and looked out to sea. But the frigate had disappeared, making for Jamaica, no doubt, Kit thought. To report the failure of his mission.

It was dusk before they dropped anchor, and he could get ashore. By now the firing had died down, although it continued in a desultory fashion, and there were still fires burning by the walls. He encountered Etienne, smoke stained and elated, as he hurried towards Madame Ramlie's house. 'Kit!' his cousin shouted. 'Another victory. We have beaten them again. Why, we must have killed hundreds. Thousands of them. Let them throw themselves against our walls. That is the surest way to end the revolt. By killing every nigger in St Domingue. But you . . . did you get ashore?'

'I got ashore,' Kit said.

'And Richilde?'

Kit went up the stairs, knocked, opened Annette's door. She stood by the window, looking out, but turned, her face lighting up as she saw him. 'Kit,' she cried. 'Oh, Kit. Madeleine has just been in. Have you heard . . ?'

'Etienne has told me. You have repulsed another onslaught.'

'We have won a great victory,' she insisted. And looked past him. 'Richilde? Oh, Kit . . .' tears filled her eyes. 'How did it happen? Tell me. It is better to speak of these things.'

'Richilde is not dead.' He took her in his arms, kissed her on the lips.

She pushed him away. 'Not dead? But . . .'

'She wishes to stay with them.'

'With the *blacks*?' She was incredulous. 'She is demented. Quite mad.'

31

Kit sighed, and sat down. 'Her reasoning was fairly cogent. And there was no way I could force her.'

'I hope she rots in hell,' Annette said, speaking in a low, hate-filled voice.

'Well . . .' Kit said. 'Annette, there are going to be other attacks. This war is not going to end soon. My ship is waiting in the harbour. I am leaving tomorrow for Savannah. If you will pack your boxes, we can go aboard tonight. I will talk with Madeleine and Etienne, of course, but if our minds are made up . . .'

'Savannah?' she asked. 'I cannot leave here, Kit.'

'But . . .'

'Not now, when we have won a great victory. And you have not heard all of it. There is news from France. Reinforcements are on their way. A commissioner, to settle with the blacks. Now we'll see. Now we'll have them all hanging. You said you'd stay with me, to make sure that happened, Kit.'

'Annette,' he said. 'You cannot spend your entire life hating. I know what happened to you is the most terrible thing that can happen to any woman. But it is in the past. You must try, like Richilde, to forget it, and look to the future.'

'Like Richilde?' she asked. 'Like Richilde? She's a white nigger. When they hang, she'll hang with them. That's what I'm staying to see, Kit. Her and Henry Christopher, hanging together.'

Richilde waited, sitting beside Olivier. They were again friends. In a different way to ever before. His desire for her was unceasing and unquenchable. If she stooped with her back to him he was immediately pinching her bottom or trying to get his hands beneath her skirt. When she slapped him he merely grinned, and waited for his next opportunity. But he would never attempt to take her by force – he was too afraid of Henry Christopher.

And he was intelligent enough to share many of her anxieties, even if for entirely different reasons.

'They going get beat,' he said. 'They must be going get beat. And we going have too much work to do, Richilde.'

Too much work. She sighed.

'If that Henry does be kill,' Olivier said, 'you would lie with me?'

'No,' she said.

He considered her reply, without offence. 'You have to lie with somebody,' he pointed out, speaking very reasonably. 'Woman must belong to somebody. If it ain't me, you know who it going be? That Dessalines. Man, you ever watch his stick? It big like a tree. He would split you ass to tit.'

'Then I won't lie with him, either,' she said. 'Listen.'

The Negro army was returned. The army. Henry had said he would send a messenger if Cap François fell. Had she wanted it to happen? Presumably Annette and Etienne and Madeleine were still there. She did not want them to be killed, and she could not doubt that the Negroes would kill every white person they found, in the heat of storming the walls. Even Henry would take part in that – he hated Etienne more than he hated anything else in the world. No, she had not wanted Cap François to fall to an assault. And yet she wanted the Negroes to win their struggle. If only the French had sailed away.

And here they were, straggling back through the trees, shoulders bowed, helping such of the wounded as could walk. Dessalines marched at their head, bull face angry, nostrils twitching as if he sought some new enemy to charge.

Dessalines?

Heart pounding, she ran towards them. 'Jean-Jacques?' she shouted. 'Jean-Jacques? Where is . . .' she bit her lip.

'I am here.' Henry was supporting two wounded men, one on each arm. 'I have brought you much work.'

'But . . . Jean-François?'

'He is dead,' Dessalines said. 'Dead,' he bellowed, raising his fists to shake them at the mountains. 'Dead,' he screamed.

She looked at Henry. 'The attack failed?'

'Of course it failed,' he said bitterly. 'They had cannon. We have no cannon.' He dropped the two wounded men outside the door of the hospital, sat with them. 'It was a cannonball blew Jean François apart.'

She could not believe it. Jean François? He had been there, since the day of her arrival on Vergée d'Or. He had been Henry's mentor, and his friend. And she had thought he was her friend as well. Until *that* night, when he had castrated Philippe and then sought her with an angry lust. But that had passed, and in many ways they had become friends again. She had even been able to sympathise with his uncertain gropings towards leadership. And now he was blown to pieces by a cannonball. The first of the triumvirate she would always associate with each other to die.

But was that not the inevitable fate of the other two, as well? Certainly of Henry, if he kept on being sent against cannon, and stone walls.

Toussaint would never have ordered so futile an assault. But Toussaint had quarrelled with Jean François . . . Her heart began to pound again.

'We must have a new general,' Dessalines said, putting into words her thoughts.

Henry Christopher raised his head, and Dessalines stared at him. 'It must be,' he said.

He was claiming the post for himself. And she knew Henry would not oppose him. Henry had too great a respect for those older than himself.

'Toussaint,' she cried.

They looked at her.

'Toussaint,' she said again. 'He only left you because of Jean François. But Jean François is dead. Send for Toussaint. He will lead you. He will teach you how to beat the French. And the English. And he will teach you more than that.'

The little figure limped through the crowd of Negroes.
But it was a small crowd. A much smaller crowd than
when he had gone away.

'This, is your army?' he asked.

Dessalines shrugged. 'They have eat up all the food
around here. They can't stay.'

'They do not want to stay,' Henry Christopher said.

Toussaint looked at the triangles, the half dozen suspended figures. 'You are a planter now?' he asked.

Dessalines grinned. 'They talked of surrender, to the
white people.'

'They came from Cap François,' Henry explained.
'With a flag of truce. But . . .'

'We ain't recognising no more flag of truce,'
Dessalines said. 'They getting twenty-five lashes a day,
and they hanging there, until they die. Black men
should fight, for black men. Not talk, for white men.'

'Cut them down,' Toussaint said.

'Eh?'

Toussaint met his angry gaze. 'If I am to be General,'
he said, 'I will be General. Otherwise I will leave again.'

Dessalines snorted.

'Cut them down,' Henry commanded. 'You are the
General, Toussaint. That is what we wish.'

'Tell me when they can speak.' Toussaint walked
away from them, towards Richilde. 'Well, madame, I
could not believe what I was told. But I see it is true.
Because of Henry?'

'Mainly,' she said.

'But not entirely?' He sat beside her. 'Do you know
how much you will be hated, by your people?'

'How much I *am* hated,' Richilde said.

'And this does not frighten you?'

'Will you make these people a nation, Toussaint?'

'I do not know that is possible.'

'Those messengers, the ones Dessalines has been
flogging, they came from Cap François.'

'So I have heard.'

'From a man called Santhonax. He is from France,

and he represents the National Convention. The new government in Paris. He asks to speak with the Negro General.'

Toussaint frowned. 'Why?'

'I do not know. Those men do not know. But . . . what is to be lost by listening to what he has to say?'

'And suppose he offers peace, madame? Or is that an unthinkable thought, for a white man?'

'If he wishes to speak with you, he must be going to offer something.'

'If we could have peace,' Toussaint said wistfully. 'Peace to make something of ourselves . . .'

'A people,' she said.

He glanced at her. 'Something, madame. Something. I do not know what a nation is. Neither do any of these people. They know only tribal law, and the white man's lash. But as they have fought together, and died together, it should be possible to make *something*.'

Léger Felicité Santhonax was not a tall man; indeed, he was no more than medium height. But he carried himself like a big man, and in his clothes, which were those of a Republican general, with the red sash around his waist to separate his red and white striped breeches from his blue coat, and his plumed bicorne hat, no less than his cavalry sabre and his large paunch, he presented the picture of a *successful* man. And a courageous one, Richilde thought. Where his staff, which included several officers who had been stationed in Cap François before the revolt, seemed to huddle against each other as they stared at the huge mass of Negroes, the Commissioner walked forward, smiling, hands on hips, apparently as unconcerned by the armed black people as he was uninterested in his surroundings, either the sparkling blue of the sea to his left, the looming overgrown canefields to his right, or the tumbled ruin of Vergée d'Or, just visible through the trees in the distance.

A man to be trusted? A man with whom it would be possible to make an honest peace? Richilde thought that his eyes were too small, his mouth too slack. But he was all the hope they had.

He paused, looked at the Negro commanders. She could almost read his thoughts. Contempt, for the raggedness of their makeshift uniforms, perhaps for the idea of slaves wearing uniforms at all. But also a watchful recognition that their swords were bright and sharp, and that now, after eighteen months of trial and error, they handled their muskets with careless ease – he would know that their only powder and ball nowadays came from dead French soldiers.

'Monsieur Toussaint,' he said, and gave a low bow. Toussaint replied in kind. 'Commissioner.'

Santhonax glanced at the two huge black men standing beside Toussaint.

'My army commanders,' Toussaint said. 'General Dessalines, and General Christophe.'

Henry looked at his idol in surprise. A general? For that rank he was even willing to overlook the French pronunciation of his name. Richilde wanted to clap her hands for him.

But Santhonax was now looking at her. 'Madame de Mortmain? I have heard a great deal about you, madame.'

She inclined her head. Today, for the first time in six months, she had taken pains with her hair, and cleaned her nails. But he would still be able to see that she wore but a single garment, and her feet were bare.

'I look forward to talking with you,' Santhonax said, eyes drifting up and down her body as he invested the word *talk* with an entirely new significance. Because, of course, as she had elected to live with the blacks, in his opinion she had to be a whore.

His gaze returned to Toussaint. 'Is there somewhere we can sit?'

Toussaint lowered himself to the ground, and after a

moment Santhonax did the same, carefully folding the tails of his coat over his thighs. Henry and Dessalines remained standing, as did everyone else, including Richilde. She supposed she must get used to this, for the rest of her life. She was the inferior being in this very masculine world she had chosen for her own.

'I cannot offer you peace,' Santhonax said. 'Save you win it for yourselves. But I can offer you honour, and freedom.'

Toussaint waited.

'France, the new France, the France of the tricolour,' Santhonax said, 'would have all men free. But no other country would have it so. Thus France is at war, with all the world. We are at war with Great Britain. Because we too have had to execute our landlords. We have executed the greatest landlord of all, monsieur. The king. So we offer you your place as Frenchmen.'

'To fight for you, against the British,' Toussaint said.

'This is your country, Toussaint,' Santhonax said. 'And the British are certainly coming. A vast armament fits out in Kingston. The British have long wanted St Domingue. And do not suppose *they* mean to free any slaves.'

'But you would set us free,' Toussaint said.

'I have the power to do so the moment you agree to my terms.'

'Then speak.'

'They are that you swear allegiance to France, to the National Convention. That you will restore St Domingue to her rightful place as the brightest jewel in the French overseas empire. You will appoint your own commanders, choose your own tactics, be answerable only to me. And I ask only your success.'

'And the white people, in Cap François and Port-au-Prince, they will agree to this?' Toussaint asked.

Santhonax smiled. 'Those white people are royalist by instinct. They will have to do as they are told.'

Toussaint gazed at him. 'You will open the gates of Cap François, to my people?'

'Once you have taken the oath of allegiance.'

Toussaint looked left and right. 'And afterwards?'

'When the war is won?' Santhonax shrugged. 'There will have to be a . . . re-organisation, of St Domingue. But your people will be free, Toussaint. That is guaranteed by my government. Free, as Frenchmen.'

'I do not trust him,' Richilde said, as Henry came to take her in his arms. 'I do not trust him, or his government.'

'They need us,' Henry said. 'They need us, and we must make sure they go on needing us. Besides, Richilde, how else could we ever get inside Cap François?'

PART ONE

The General

[Toussaint] persuaded his Negroes to go back to work, and in a short space of time had restored a measure of prosperity to the island. This was as well, because the European War came to a [temporary] end sooner than he could have anticipated, and the French government was left in the hands of a revolutionary dictator like himself. At the start of his career as ruler of France, Bonaparte was very much interested in the Western Hemisphere.

Chapter 1

THE VICTORY

In the southern half of the country, the mulatto General Rigaud also held his own, and the British gradually came to the realisation that to conquer Hispaniola was beyond their power. Of the two native commanders they preferred to open negotiations with Toussaint, and it was from Cap François that General Maitland sailed with the last British soldiers in April 1798, having secured from his Negro adversary a promise that the lives and properties of those whites remaining in the island would be respected.

Only the mulattos still questioned the right of the Negroes to decide their own future, but a brief campaign forced Generals Rigaud and Petion to flee the island. However reluctant Toussaint might have been to thrust himself forward, he knew when to take advantage of circumstances. He now turned his attention to the Spanish half of the island, with equal success. Suddenly St Domingue was one country, a black country, ruled by a black general.

'Look,' Kit Hamilton pointed, past the volcanic crater of Saba, rising sheer out of the Carribean Sea. 'Mount Misery.'

They had sailed through the Anegada Passage, leaving San Martin to port, the Virgins to starboard; St Kitts was only a few hours away, if the breeze were to hold.

And there, Madeleine Jarrold would be reunited with her husband and her family. She at the least should have been happy at that prospect, after so long a separation. But she remained as gloomily silent as her brother.

Who now sighed. 'Do you know, I had not thought to see St Kitts again, ever? But then, there are so many sights I had not supposed I would ever see at all. Those black scoundrels marching through the streets of Cap François . . . I was told poor Peynier's hair turned white when he heard what Santhonax had agreed. And those are the men who would rule France.'

'How Richilde must have crowed,' Madeleine said, bitterly. 'Did you see her, Kit?'

'I said goodbye,' Kit said.

'I do not see how you could bear even to speak with her,' Madeleine said. 'Was she triumphant?'

'Quite the contrary,' Kit said. 'She views the future with much concern. She knows it is going to be a long, hard war with the British.'

'The British,' Etienne sneered. 'She will have to worry when *we* return.' He met Kit's gaze, and flushed. 'We will return, Kit. France. The real France. We will return, and when we do there will have to be an accounting. And Richilde will be one of those brought to book. You must accept that, Kit. She is a traitor. Not only to her family, but to her race, her very sex.'

Kit turned away, went down the companion ladder to the cabin. Not that he expected any joy from Annette. But she was his responsibility. He did not know if she had discussed his proposition with her brother and sister, but they had tacitly accepted that it had happened. They had too much to do with their lives, hating and dreaming of revenge, to be saddled with a mad sister.

And did he not have something to do with his life?

She sat by the stern window, looking out at the bubbling wake stretching across the blue of the ocean. When she sat like this, her face in repose, she was again

43

the pretty, quiet girl with whom he had fallen in love ten years before. Almost he feared to speak, to disturb the picture.

'St Kitts is in sight,' he said. 'Old Mount Misery,' pointing his finger at the sky. 'Remember him?'

'I think so.' She turned her head, gave a quick, shy smile. 'Will we stay there long?'

He shook his head, sat beside her. She had screamed and wept when told she would have to leave Cap François – or live there under black dominion. Yet he thought that the voyage, away from the sights and sounds which evoked such powerful memories, had done her good. Dare he believe that she might work her way out of her dementia, then he could be a happy man.

'We shall stay there not a moment longer than we need, to offload Madeleine and Etienne,' he promised, and smiled at her. 'I've a business to attend to, cargoes to be shipped. And I've America to show you.'

She held his hand. 'Will I like America, Kit? Will I?'

'You'll love America,' he said. 'And America will love you.'

She sighed, and rested her head on his shoulder, while he held her close. And wondered. That he loved her, that he *could* love her, he never doubted for a moment. Therefore, that he *would* love her. And yet he had never done more than kiss her lips. Because that he desired her was also undoubted – it was an essential part of his love.

'You will be happy there,' he said, putting his arm round her shoulders to turn her against him, kissing her hair as he did so.

'Oh, I so want to be happy,' she breathed. 'So very much, Kit.'

'It shall be my charge,' he said, and allowed his hand to stroke from her shoulder and across her breast. Immediately he felt her body grow rigid, and then she leapt away from him.

'They cut her,' she shouted. 'Here.' She held her own breasts, one in each hand. 'They cut her. I watched them. I watched the blood. They cut her,' she screamed.

The cabin door opened, and he gazed at Madeleine. She took in the situation at a glance, stared at him in turn. Her eyes were the saddest he had ever seen.

But could they possibly be more sad than his own?

'Get up off your knees,' Henry Christopher said. 'That ain't no work for you, Richilde.'

Richilde let her scrubbing brush lie in the welter of soapsuds on the parquet floor, sat on her heels, used her wrist to push water from her eyes. 'It is work for someone, Henry. If we are going to live in a house, then it must be a clean house.'

He held her shoulders, raised her from the floor. He wore a new uniform, blue coat and white breeches, tan boots and a red sash. He had at any rate achieved the first of his ambitions. Or was it the second, she thought, as he bent his head to kiss her?

And did she really care whether or not the house they had appropriated for their own was a filthy wreck? She was happy. Wildly, irrelevantly happy. She knew that it was a purely physical, irresponsible happiness, sometimes found it difficult to believe that she had really abandoned position and race and even family to be the mistress of a Negro general who had no idea where he was leading his army. But he made her happy.

Thus she made herself work, where everyone about her, men and women, in the euphoria of being masters and mistresses of this once lovely city, had abandoned themselves to eating and drinking and sleeping in soft beds. It had only been with great difficulty that Toussaint had managed to get them to bury the dead bodies hanging from the gallows. She laboured not so much to remind herself that she was different to them, as to remind herself that this had to be a transient phase, that at the very least all the food in Cap François would soon be eaten, all the wine be drunk, and then they would *have* to work.

Toussaint was aware of this too. As he confided most of his thoughts to her, ever interested in her opinions, she understood many of the reasons for his indulgency. He loved his people too much to wish to drive them back to work. He was prepared to allow them this holiday, knowing like her that it must end, that they would have to follow him eventually – and hoping they would do so voluntarily.

Santhonax did not seem interested, as long as *he* also had food to eat and wine to drink, and utterly amoral Negro girls to take to his bed – and the white woman to watch, with his little pig eyes.

So she also worked to stop herself from thinking, of either yesterday or tomorrow. Of what she had been or what she might yet become. Of the family she had lost and the position she had abandoned.

'Well,' Henry said. 'I don't know for how much longer we going to be living here, and that is a fact. The British are here.'

She frowned at him, then ran to the window, as if expecting to see redcoats on the streets. No redcoats, but a great many people, shrugging away their languor as they hurried towards those ramparts overlooking the sea.

There she and Henry joined them, to stare at the myriad ships, perhaps as many as fifty of them, she estimated, standing slowly towards the land, an immense spread of white canvas. Great Britain was called the 'Mistress of the Seas' – with reason, as long as she could command fleets like that.

She glanced at Henry, watched him biting his lip. He must know that he had never encountered any force as formidable as this before.

'A magnificent sight, eh, madame?' Toussaint also wore the uniform of a French officer, had Santhonax beside him as usual. 'But they are your people, are

46

they not?' He smiled, slapped Henry on the shoulder. 'And yours, too.'

'What are we going to do?' Richilde asked. She knew how scarce was their supply of powder and ball, even had they possessed any trained gunners.

'Do?' Santhonax shouted. He was as usual the worse for wine. 'Why, madame, we shall fight them.'

'In due course,' Toussaint agreed. 'But on ground of our own choosing, monsieur. For the time being, we will evacuate the town. General Christophe, you will give the necessary orders.'

Henry hesitated, while Santhonax stared at his army commander.

'Evacuate the town? Evacuate Cap François? Surrender it?'

'Better to surrender it, than die in it, monsieur,' Toussaint said. 'That fleet is quite capable of blowing this town into little pieces. And when they have done that, they will land several thousand men, disciplined and well trained soldiers. There is no way we can oppose them, successfully, on open ground.'

'But . . . do you not mean to fight them at all? By God . . .'

'We will fight them, monsieur,' Toussaint said quietly. 'But we must make them come to us, and fight on our terms.'

'And you suppose they will do that?' Santhonax sneered. 'Come to you?'

'They will do that, monsieur. Those are neither frightened planters nor garrison troops, content to hold a fortified position. They are fighting soldiers, and they have come to conquer St Domingue for their king. They know they cannot do that until they have first conquered us. They will come.' He pointed at the puff of smoke rising from the foredeck of the first warship, at the plume of water where the ball entered the sea, only a couple of hundred yards away from the wall on which they stood. 'Let us make haste.'

His calm certainty left even Santhonax dumb.

47

But . . . abandon Cap François? Richilde asked herself. Back to the forest and the huts and the rain? Back to living like animals? They had been going to build. Or was that just another of their dreams?

She gazed at Henry with wide eyes, but Henry was thinking like a soldier. 'If we are not going to defend the city, Toussaint,' he said, 'let us then burn it, so that the British will not have the use of it.'

Toussaint smiled, and shook his head. 'But they must have the use of the city, Henry. To evacuate their men from, when they realise that they cannot defeat us.'

Redcoats. A very large number of them. Richilde sat her horse on the edge of the rising ground at the rear of the plantation to watch them. Beside her were Toussaint and Santhonax, and Dessalines. But not Henry. General Christophe, as he was now known and as he had accepted the title, was down there amongst the overgrown jungle that was all that remained of Vergée d'Or, seeking to oppose his tactical skill and Toussaint's strategical genius to these most formidable of soldiers. Risking his life, as he had constantly risked his life from the day the revolution had begun.

And thus also risking her happiness, her sole reason for living.

Toussaint handed her his telescope, and she gazed at the British. There were two columns of them, both alike, and yet utterly dissimilar. The first column wore trousers, and tall shakos. They might have been on a parade ground, in the way they marched, ever watched by their sergeants and their mounted officers, with every musket at the same angle on every shoulder, every red jacket buttoned to the neck – almost, she thought, she could see the sweat dribbling down their cheeks, darkening arm pit and between shoulder blade. The second column also wore carefully buttoned red jackets, with the same white cross belts, and maintained the same perfect order, but they were slightly more comfortable, she estimated – they wore kilts instead of trousers, which left their red knees bare, and huge bonnets instead of shakos. The Negroes were inclined to smile as they pointed at the Scots – Richilde remembered sufficient military history to know they were more dangerous than any foe Toussaint's army had yet faced.

Puffs of white smoke rose from the scrub, several seconds before the reports of the muskets reached the watchers. The British skirmishers immediately returned fire, the columns behind them formed square. But the anticipated attack never came, as Henry withdrew his men, slipping silently through the tangled, unharvested canestalks. After several moments the square formed column again, as the British marched for the factory, which stood out like a beacon amidst the surrounding devastation. But this march took them close by the old plantation farm, which in two years' neglect had become almost a forest. Richilde's heart pounded as she watched the black men, wielding machetes, rise from the grass where they had lain concealed until almost trodden on by the marching soldiers. She did not doubt that Henry was down there with them.

All was confusion for several minutes. The British had marched with fixed bayonets, but had not had time to form line abreast before the black men were amongst them, cutting and slashing, yelling and screaming. Orders were shouted, mounted officers rode into the centre of the melee with total disregard for their own safety – and half a mile to the rear the Scots began to run, bringing their bayonets to the charge as they did so.

'Enough, Henry,' Toussaint muttered. 'Enough.'

Henry might have been able to hear him. The black men were suddenly hurrying, back towards the slave village, pursued by the enraged redcoats, but, when those had been brought under control by bugle calls and shouted orders, by volleys of musketry, ineffectual as Henry's men were out of range.

Toussaint watched through his telescope, grunted his

satisfaction. 'It is your turn, Jean-Jacques,' he said to Dessalines. 'Remember my instructions, now. Do not get involved with them too closely.'

Dessalines nodded, hurried off to lead his men.

'We will withdraw,' Toussaint said.

'Where now?' Santhonax had been drinking wine.

'Into the bush,' Toussaint said.

'The bush?' Richilde asked, her heart sinking.

Toussaint smiled at her. 'Do not worry, Richilde. Henry will follow.'

'The bush?' Santhonax bellowed. 'But you've given those lobsters a bloody nose. Now's the time to close, to chase them back to Cap François.'

Toussaint shook his head. 'No, no, monsieur. Now is the time for them to chase *us*, into the jungle.' He slapped a mosquito which had settled on his wrist; dead, it left a splodge of fresh blood which it had just drawn from his veins. 'We will find allies, in the jungle.'

The jungle! How often had she looked at the densely matted slopes from her window on Vergée d'Or? Richilde wondered. That forest had attracted her, as the mountain peaks which rose out of the trees had attracted her. They had been something to explore. To investigate. One day. That had been another dream.

But this dream, like the dream of revolution, had come true. And like the dream of revolution, the reality was too grim to be considered. Here was a world she did not suppose had been invaded by man since the Spaniards had first come here, led by Columbus himself, three hundred years before, to destroy the Indians, Caribs and Arawaks, who had lived here. And fleeing Indians could hardly be described as invaders. This was a world in which the vine and the bush and the insect held sway, in which mankind was totally alien. Even men like Jean-Jacques Dessalines, to whom the West Africa jungles were still a living memory, knew nothing like this.

At least the growth, and the ground, were together too formidable for animal or even reptile life, on any scale larger than a lizard. Only the men, and their women, and children, and dogs, floundered onwards. They cut their way through clinging vines, flogged by low slung branches, tripping through poisonous leaves and bushes which brought their flesh up in agonising blisters, assailed by downpours of tropical rain which pounded on their heads like pebbles – and never knowing when the ground over which they made their way would simply not be there, and their scouts find themselves tumbling down a hundred feet and more over a precipitous slope into a fast running river, or come face to face with an equally unclimbable escarpment, rising sheer above them. They walked on beds of dead leaves which without warning would give way to outcroppings of razor sharp rock to tear at their bare feet. Whenever they halted they were immediately assailed by a host of insects, many of which they could hardly see, but which burrowed beneath their flesh to leave itching, festering sores – these they called *bêtes rouge*, the red beasts. And day or night their skins were smothered in mosquitoes, whirring and humming, pouncing in clusters on the sudden feast of unprotected human flesh which was being presented to them.

Soon it was difficult for Richilde to recall that she had ever had a daily bath, or used perfume, or brushed her hair, or slept in a bed, or protected her body, either from the sun or from prying eyes. Toussaint and Henry obviously worried for her, because she was the madame. But the Negroes suffered equally, especially their women, and even more especially elderly women like Clotilde Toussaint, who was just as used as Richilde to a sedentary life around the plantation, and who worried ceaselessly about her two sons, both just teenagers – she had only been allowed to become Toussaint's wife late in life, in a sudden spurt of generosity by old Thérèse de Milot – but who were both determined to fight alongside their father.

51

Because the Negroes also fought, as the British followed them. The redcoats knew that where Toussaint went, there was the main source of resistance to them, and sweating and cursing, they too hacked and pushed and forced their way through the forest, checked every so often by a fierce rearguard action, allowed, every so often, to catch a sight of their prey, as they staggered onwards, subjected, every so often, to a savage counter attack, planned and devised by Toussaint, and executed by his two faithful Generals, Christophe and Dessalines, who crept past the British outposts to wreak havoc amongst the supply trains before once again disappearing into the forests.

'L'Ouverture,' the Negroes called Toussaint. 'L'Ouverture,' they shouted, whenever he passed by. He was the man who opened the British ranks, for them to enter. And Toussaint was obviously delighted by the nickname, as delighted as he was with the success of his hit and run strategy.

Even if it did not apparently please Santhonax. The fat Frenchman indeed suffered more than any of them, cursed and swore and slapped at mosquitoes, grumbled as his supply of wine ran out, and as he had to live on water and what food could be gathered in the forest, like the rest of them.

'My instructions were to regain control of the colony for France,' he would say. 'Not abandon it to the British.'

'And we will do that for you, monsieur,' Toussaint would reply, with endless patience. 'When we are ready. And when the time is ripe.'

For he was not only waiting for the climate to take effect. He was also working at training his army, firstly in the use of European weapons – many of his counter strokes were intended less to check the British columns than to secure British muskets and ammunition from the dead – and secondly to accustom them to receiving commands, just as he taught his officers to understand the elements of strategy. All based entirely upon the books he had studied, the considerations upon which he had obviously reflected during long hours driving his coach, or sitting on the box in Cap François waiting for his mistress to return from a social call or a shopping expedition.

Richilde was prepared to concede that he was probably as great a natural genius as the world had ever known – and yet, like Santhonax, she could not stop herself from occasionally feeling utter despair. It was not so much the hardships of her new life, the poor quality and often limited quantity of food, the visible deterioration of the milky white complexion she had so carefully cultivated and protected for twenty-six years into a sunbrowned hardness which made her appear almost a mulatto. These things were acceptable and even exciting, as she shared them with Henry, determined never to become a burden to him in any way, equally determined to prove to the black women that even a pampered white *mâitresse* could survive the jungle. And succeeding, she thought, in that they no longer regarded her with frank wonder or cold suspicion, but accepted her as one of themselves, whatever her colour, a development led and controlled by Clotilde Toussaint. The women like Amelia who had tormented her the day after the revolt had begun had long abandoned the army, either in surrender to the British, or to live in some remote jungle clearing, just as such a *mamaloi* as Céleste had also disappeared in the tumultuous days following the revolt, understanding that it was a time for men to do, rather than women to prophesy. If the army, and perhaps even Toussaint himself, continued to pray to Damballah Oueddo and Ogone Badagris, there was no time for any large voodoo ceremonies in this hurried, gypsy existence.

But it was this last point caused her concern. For was the army not also living like a tribe of savages as it conducted a savage campaign?

She would, she knew, have been here anyway, because of Henry. She could now be amazed at the power of an upbringing and an ideology which had kept her living in close proximity with him for twenty-six years, increasingly aware of his love for her, but only able to accept it as her due as his mistress rather than as a cause for pride, and quite unable to suppose that she might be able to reciprocate. She recognised that what had so nearly happened on the night of the voodoo ceremony had been a pure explosion of emotional lust, immediately regretted. Once the scales of prejudice had been ripped from her eyes she knew that there could be no other man for her, under any circumstances. That she dared not have another child for him in these conditions, had to resort to the very effective Negro methods of post sex contraception, was a principal source of her unhappiness.

But beyond Henry, her interest in the blacks, and her sympathy for them, had been aroused by the growing awareness that they were not, as she had always been taught to believe, an inferior race to the whites, but merely a less civilised one, and by her belief that, given equal opportunities of education and freedom, they would be just as capable of creating a nation and a culture equal to any. She had, she supposed, quite neglected to consider the endless centuries during which *her* ancestors had clawed their way out of the primeval swamp, had supposed that in some miraculous fashion the revolution would be followed by a long period of peace, to enable Toussaint to instruct his people in the cohesion and industry they had to display if they were ever to become a nation.

Instead she daily watched them revert more and more to savagery. Living in a jungle, fighting and killing, were impulses that lay too close to the surface of their consciousness. What disturbed her most was that Toussaint himself did not appear to share her concern. That he did dream of a future for his people, as a civil-

54

ised nation, was certain, and from his conversations with her she was equally certain that he even had well laid plans to be implemented when the time came. But beating the British came first, in his estimation. She understood this, even as she understood that they had to be beaten not because they were *there* – or he might have been prepared to sue for peace – but because he was fighting for France, in a partnership which he hoped and believed would bestow great benefits on his people once victory was achieved. Thus, to gain that victory he was prepared to practice the most formidable patience, confident that no matter how long it took, his people would follow him in peace as they were following him in war.

Perhaps, she thought, it is that sublime confidence which most terrifies me. Because there was only one Toussaint, and he was already past sixty. When she looked at his Generals, at Jean-Jacques Dessalines, the most savage of men, or even at Henry Christopher, still uncertain of what he really wanted in life, and still, above all else, the soldier pure and simple, she could not but shudder at what might lie ahead.

But Henry, at least, was hers to control. She hoped and thought. He sat on the banks of the stream along which the army was camped, and watched her kneeling in the shallows to wash her hair. It was evening, and they were high in the mountains, higher than she had ever been in her life before – although the peaks still towered above them – and thus it was delightfully cool, with the rushing water cold enough to bring her flesh up in goosepimples, while even the mosquitoes seemed to find it difficult to struggle up to this altitude.

Her hair rinsed, and squeezed as dry as she could, she commenced to launder her tattered gown – her only garment – using the Negro method of pounding it between stones, as were several other women further down the stream. This worked very well as regards cleanliness, but it played havoc with the material.

'Do you suppose we will ever be able to get some new clothes?' she asked.

'Some day,' Henry said: his uniform was equally tattered.

She sighed. He was a man of very few words. And yet she could feel his gaze on her back, which was worth more than a speech.

'I wouldn't mind if we could stay here for a while,' she remarked. 'It really is a delightful spot. Do you think we could stay here, Henry? Surely the British aren't going to climb this high after us?'

'They coming,' he said.

She raised her head, somewhat chagrined to realise that he had not been watching her after all, but was instead looking past her down the tumbled slopes, at the forest, and at the soldiers who could just be seen, like a line of red ants, toiling up a sharp escarpment. They were several miles away, and several hundred feet beneath them, but, as he said, they were coming.

'So where do we go now?' she asked, turning to look at him.

He smiled. 'These mountains have to slope back down again some time. But you know what I am thinking? It is time we should fight a battle.'

She frowned at him; it was the first time she had ever heard him make a criticism of Toussaint, even implicitly. 'You mean here?'

'It could be here,' he agreed. 'But when they get up here, they done the worst. Down there would be better.' He pointed at the very escarpment over which the British were clambering, with increasing difficulty as the slopes grew steeper and more strewn with boulders. Certainly they did not look in much shape to fight after such a climb.

Yet they were British soldiers. 'Do you think your men are capable of meeting the soldiers, in a pitched battle, yet?' she asked.

Another smile, this time a trifle wry. 'Yet? Or ever?'

She crawled to sit beside him, rest her head on his shoulder. 'Well, then . . .'

'They would fight, behind a wall,' he said.

She raised her head. 'A wall?'

'I saw those men fighting behind walls, in America,' he said. 'Ten men behind a wall can beat twenty outside.' He thought for a moment. 'And if it was a big wall . . .'

'You are thinking of a castle,' she said.

'A castle?'

'Like the fort in Cap François. Or Brimstone Hill in St Kitts.'

'They were both captured,' he said, half to himself.

'By bombardment from the sea,' she said. 'But there is no castle anywhere in the world which can stand up to siege guns.'

'Yes.' Suddenly he was enthusiastic. 'But they must be able to reach. If we could build a castle down there, where those soldiers are now, nobody could drag guns close enough. And no ships could reach us, either.' He snapped his fingers. 'And yet we could watch the ships.'

Which was perfectly true. From where they sat they looked, not only over the forested slopes beneath them, but all the way down to the coast, could even make out the scarred ruin of Vergée d'Or, huddled against the trees fringing the white sand beach, and beyond, the surging blue of the Atlantic. The view from a few hundred feet lower down would be no less dramatically beautiful.

But he was dreaming again. 'It would be quite impossible to build a castle, down there in the jungle, Henry,' she said. 'It would be . . . well, like building the pyramids. It would take years, and thousands of people.'

'The pyramids?' he asked.

'I will tell you about them,' she offered. And saw his preoccupation and perhaps disappointment, at her lack of enthusiasm. 'Anyway,' she said. 'If you *could* build

57

such a fortress, Henry, it would be so impregnable no one would ever dare attack it.'

He smiled at her. 'And *you* don't think that would be a good thing, Richilde?'

Toussaint had noted the British vulnerability, and ordered an attack for dawn. A more determined attack than usual, for he intended to accompany his men and direct them from the immediate vicinity of the battle. But it was still to be a hit and run affair. He instructed Louis-Pierre, the tall serious Negro who was his third General, to break camp at sun-up and move along the ridge – not up towards the mountains any longer – with a view once again to descending to the plains. 'If we cross the mountain,' he said with a smile, 'we shall be fighting Rigaud's mulattos as well as the British.

'Bah,' Santhonax grumbled. 'Are they not also against the British? Have we not sent them messengers inviting them to unite with us in the common cause?'

'Indeed we have, monsieur,' Toussaint agreed with his invariable patience. 'And they have not replied. Until they do, it would be best for us to proceed with caution.'

'Caution,' Santhonax said, standing beside Richilde to watch the army filing down the hillside towards the trees, while the sun plunged into the peaks behind them – it would take them all night to reach their assault positions. 'I have never met a man who set so much store by caution. Is it not true, Madame de Mortmain, that he sought no part in the actual slave revolt, wished only to restrain it?'

Richilde could no longer make Henry out. She turned, to walk back to where she would sleep, her still damp gown clinging to her legs and shoulders. 'That is true, monsieur.'

'Then I cannot understand how he has achieved such authority,' Santhonax said, following her. 'What is needed here are men of spirit. Men like your Henri, eh, madame?'

'Toussaint commands because he is the most capable of command, monsieur.' She knelt, waited for him to go. '*Henry* might win a battle for you, but Toussaint will win the war.

'That is no way to speak of your lover.' He knelt beside her, an absurd series of jerky and uncomfortable movements in so bulky a man. 'He *is* your lover, is he not, Richilde?'

She met his gaze. 'He is my lover, monsieur.'

'A Negro, who was once your coachman.' He grinned at her. 'Or did you enjoy his black stick more than your husband's, even then?'

'Does it matter, monsieur?'

'Of course it matters.' He cast quick glances, left and right, to estimate just how thoroughly they were shrouded in the gloom. Richilde sighed. She knew exactly what was going to happen next – could not decide how firmly he should be repelled. He was, after all, the Commissioner.

'Richilde . . .' He took her hand. 'Believe me, I know much of what you have suffered. I have heard a great deal of this Philippe de Mortmain, a true aristocrat, the sort of man who so nearly brought France to her knees. I can understand how difficult it must have been, your life with him.' A sly smile. 'I have also heard much about the . . . the perquisites of you great ladies. In France it was the pages. Here it was the blacks, eh?' He chuckled. 'Or in your case, it is still the blacks, eh?'

Still she gazed at him, as his fingers began to slide up her arm, and his gaze dropped to her nipples, clearly visible through the thin, damp material of her gown.

'But now, to surrender yourself entirely to a black embrace . . . of course I realise that you are in their power. But it will not always be so, Richilde. When the British are beaten, when I am able to take my proper place as Governor General of St Domingue, and reduce these savages to *their* proper places, then if you wished you could sit at my side. Would you not like that, Richilde?'

59

'My dear monsieur,' she said. 'How could you possibly consider taking me to your bed, when, as you say, I have been impaled upon a black stick, time and again?'

He frowned at her, unsure whether or not she was laughing at him.

'How could you be sure,' she asked, 'that I am not riddled with some hideous disease?'

His frown deepened. 'You are not, madame? Say that you are not. There would be a waste.'

His arrogance was hardly less incredible than his lack of humour.

'Or worse, monsieur,' she said. 'How could you be sure I would not be continually comparing you with the manhoods I have known?'

'Bah,' he declared. 'I fear comparison with no man. I have eight inches. Did you know that, madame? I am renowned throughout Paris. Here, I will show you . . .' he began to release his trousers and she realised that she was dealing with neither a gentleman nor an intelligent savage. He would have to be crushed.

'Spare me, monsieur, I beg of you,' she said. 'I have no desire to investigate your manhood. Or to experience it.'

'You would spend the rest of your life in these conditions? You wish to do that?'

'No, monsieur, I do not *wish* to do that. But I am prepared to do that, if such is the decree of fate. Nor am I a prostitute, merely because I share a black man's bed.'

'And you suppose a savage can know anything of love? Will he not throw you aside the moment he tires of you?'

It was time to end such a ridiculous conversation. 'Henry and I share more than our bodies, monsieur,' she said. 'Certainly we share more than would ever be possible with any other *man*, much less a puffed-up bullfrog from the Parisian gutters.'

He stared at her for a moment, then swung his fist,

rising as he did so. She fell away from him, rolled over to reach her knees again, saw him on his feet above her.

'Bitch,' he snarled. 'Whore. White nigger.'

His boot was carving through the air, and she could only roll again, desperately seeking some weapon to defend herself.

But the sounds of the scuffle had alerted the encampment, and Santhonax was surrounded by black men, led by Louis-Pierre, who gripped his arms.

'Release me,' he bawled. 'I am Monsieur Santhonax. I am the Commissioner. Release me.'

'You have attempted to assault Madame Richilde,' Louis-Pierre said. 'Say the word, madame, and I will have him flogged.'

'Flogged?' Santhonax bellowed. But now he was afraid, and his voice trembled. 'Flogged?'

Richilde reached her feet. She was aware of anger combined with an understanding that this was a situation which had to be faced, or it could become a festering sore running through the black army. And he deserved far worse than a flogging, not so much for insulting her, as for revealing so clearly his true attitude towards the people he pretended to govern.

'Do not flog him,' she said. 'We will put the matter to General Christophe, when he returns.'

Santhonax glared at her. 'Christophe?' he shouted. 'Do you suppose I am afraid of a black savage?'

'That, monsieur,' she said, 'we shall discover tomorrow.'

It was midday before the column of women and children was rejoined by the army, elated with another considerable, if limited, success. Santhonax was there to greet them.

'There has been a mutiny,' he told Toussaint. 'These niggers of yours have dared to place me under arrest.

Me, Léger Santhonax. You must make an example of them, Toussaint.'

But Toussaint had already spoken with Louis-Pierre. 'You have insulted Madame de Mortmain,' he said.

'Bah,' Santhonax said. 'How may the Commissioner insult a mere woman? How may he insult anyone?'

'You may insult whoever you choose, monsieur,' Toussaint agreed. 'Providing you are prepared to answer for it. But you are fortunate. General Christophe is prepared to regard the incident as a personal matter, between you and him.'

Santhonax gazed at the huge young man, licked his lips.

'You have choice of weapons, monsieur,' Henry said, speaking very quietly.

Richilde held her breath. She could have no fears for Henry were he able to come to grips with any adversary, but he knew very little of accuracy with a pistol, or skill with a sword.

Santhonax was still chewing his lip, looking from Henry to Toussaint to Jean-Jacques Dessalines, grinning at him, and then at the black faces which surrounded him.

'I do not fight with savages,' he said, and walked away.

Dessalines gave a bellow of laughter, which was taken up by the watching soldiers. The camp echoed with their mirth. Santhonax checked, and almost turned, as if he would come back to face them, then walked into the trees.

'You have killed him more surely than with a sword thrust,' Toussaint said.

'I did not mean it this way,' Richilde said.

'He insulted you, madame,' Toussaint said. 'He deserved his shame.'

'But he is the Commissioner, appointed by France,' she said.

'Yes,' Toussaint agreed, thoughtfully.

She sat beside Henry in the cool of the afternoon. 'I seem to attract misfortune.'

'You are a beautiful woman.'

'There's a profound thought,' she said. 'But Henry, to have Santhonax hating us . . .'

'Santhonax is nothing,' he said. 'He was useful, because he got rid of the French for us. When we have beaten the English, we shall have no more need of him. We have no need of him now.'

'He has similar plans for you.'

Henry grinned. 'Then we are even. But we are the stronger, would you not say?'

'Men are coming.' Louis-Pierre stood above them. 'Mulattos. General Toussaint wishes your presence.'

It was the young man, Alexandre Petion, accompanied by an even younger man, with handsome, liquid brown features and alert dark eyes, which flickered over the black faces before coming to rest on Richilde, standing with Clotilde Toussaint and several other women.

'My aide,' Petion said. 'Jean Boyer.'

The young man gravely shook hands, but still stared at Richilde.

'We have sought you this fortnight,' Petion said. 'But you never stay in one place long enough to be found.'

'Thus the British cannot find us either,' Toussaint said.

'You run away,' Petion said. 'We stand and fight.'

'And get beat,' Dessalines said, with a shout of laughter.

'And could you meet the redcoats on an open field, black man?' Boyer asked, speaking quietly.

Dessalines's smile faded into an angry frown, and he reached for his sword.

'We need to co-ordinate our strategy,' Toussaint said, resting his hand on Dessalines's arm. 'That is why we have sought this meeting.'

'General Rigaud feels our cause is hopeless,' Petion

63

said. 'The British have offered good terms for our surrender. It is better to accept the inevitable than to spend the rest of our lives fighting a war we cannot win.'

'Those terms do not include freedom for black people,' Henry said.

'Would you rather be dead, than alive as a slave?' Petion asked. 'Things are different in England. There is a great anti-slavery movement there. Certain it is that no English planter dare abuse his slaves like a Mortmain or a Milot. There is even talk of emancipation, one day.'

'One day,' Henry said.

'We would rather be dead, than return to slavery,' Toussaint said.

'General Rigaud wishes the matter laid before Monsieur Santhonax,' Petion said. 'It is for him to decide.'

'Santhonax is a fool,' Dessalines growled.

'I have sent to tell him you are here,' Toussaint said. 'But I do not think he will agree to surrender to the British.'

'They would chop off his head when he went back to France,' Dessalines said. 'That is what they do to those who surrender.'

'It does not matter what Santhonax would do,' Henry said. 'We shall never surrender. We shall not be slaves again.' He looked at Richilde, followed her gaze towards Boyer.

'There is no need to surrender, or even to consider it,' Toussaint said. 'We will beat the British.'

'What with?' Petion sneered.

'With what we have,' Toussaint said. 'We have sufficient.'

Petion stared at him, then decided there was no point in arguing with such confidence. 'My message is for Monsieur Santhonax,' he said again.

'I have sent for him,' Toussaint repeated.

'But he will not come,' Louis-Pierre said, standing above them. 'He is dead.'

'Dead?' Toussaint asked.

'Dead?' Richilde cried, starting forward. 'But how?'

'I found him, madame,' Louis-Pierre said. 'Hanging from a tree. By his own belt.'

In all the violence and bloodshed with which she had been surrounded for the last four years, this was the first time Richilde had actually ever felt complete responsibility for a man's death.

'That is nonsense,' Henry insisted. 'He killed himself because of his guilt. And his shame. He deserved to die.'

'But what of the future?' she asked – even she could feel no real sympathy for such a man. 'He was France's representative.'

Toussaint smiled. 'I will have to be France's representative, until they send someone else.' He watched Petion and Boyer riding away to the south. 'Even if *they* will not willingly acknowledge the fact.'

'France,' Dessalines growled. 'Mulattos. Why do we not settle with them all?'

'Because we must beat the British first,' Toussaint said, with his usual patience.

If only, Richilde thought, she could convince herself that was possible. Her emotions were naturally totally confused. The British were her own kith and kin, by birth and background, even if both her father and her brother had been forced to change their nationality and however she had been brought up as a Frenchwoman. And besides, the soldiers themselves were not slave owners. She doubted if they even hated and feared the Negroes, the way the planters had done. They were merely helpless young men called to do a distasteful job of work in unfamiliar surroundings and for the profit of their masters in England.

Yet it was a job they were doing well. Like the mulattos, she found it difficult to understand Toussaint's certainty of victory. Certainly his hit and run tactics were brilliantly successful, but every such raid cost him as many men as the British, and as the months became years his army also dwindled because of desertions and sickness, usually a variety of fevers which caused men, and women, to waste away as they shivered and groaned. The future became impossible to consider. Even Henry had no idea of how long this desperate, primeval existence might continue. Undoubtedly he enjoyed it. It was a part of his dream, and if she was sure that his dream had encompassed other things as well, even in a very general sense, such as commanding huge armies of brilliantly uniformed men, of building palaces, and even a vast fortress to overlook all of St Domingue, he was young enough to enjoy the excitement of the present while remaining sure the future would arrive, eventually.

She wished she could share his optimism. She was no older – they celebrated their joint thirtieth birthdays after three years in the forest – and allowing for the fact that she was a woman, she was just as strong and, miraculously, just as healthy. When she did come down with a feverish attack, he took her into the forest, cradled in his arms, like a babe, found a clear, cool rushing stream, and sat her in it, up to her neck holding her there for an entire night. Next morning she was half frozen, and as weak as a babe, but the fever was gone.

Then he had made love to her, to restore her body warmth. It was the most tumultuously delicious hour she had ever spent, so much so she had wondered if she might not be delirious. But in fact she found all the physical pleasure she could possibly dream of in any of his embraces, adored his explorations of her which he still carried out in a sort of fascinated wonder. To him she was the greatest treasure in all the world, and even had she not found in him everything she could ever wish or respect in a man, she would have had to respond to such adoration.

She was by now utterly attuned to life in the forest,

66

with feet so hard not even burrowing insects like chiggers could find a home for their eggs in her flesh, and with sunbrowned skin so similarly toughened as to repel even the fiercest of mosquitoes. Her muscles were so firm that she could walk for hours over uneven ground without feeling fatigue, and her digestion was similarly trained to exist sometimes for thirty-six hours without food before being able to indulge in a stupefying meal. She had allowed her hair to grow until it stretched past her thighs, and could be used as an extra garment, which was useful, as she had been forced to do as the other women, and retain nothing more than a piece of cloth wrapped round and between her thighs and secured round her waist, thus leaving both her torso and her legs utterly exposed. But in fact since Santhonax's death she was unaware of any necessity for prurient modesty. She was surrounded by black girls with figures better than her own, and she was General Christophe's woman. He certainly saw her only as a woman, and no longer considered her either as white or as an ex-mistress. And this acceptance she thought extended throughout the entire army, with the possible exception of Jean-Jacques Dessalines. But she was not alone in fearing Dessalines. Sometimes she thought even Toussaint gave a shudder when he considered the savage instincts of his chief lieutenant, who was only restrained from an orgy of mutilation and slaughter, whenever prisoners were taken, by the calm composure of his commander. Richilde could only comfort herself with the reflection that even Dessalines had a most healthy respect for Henry's giant muscles.

But he remained a symbol of everything she feared about the future, everything that prevented her achieving the happiness she could not help but feel was there, dared she reach out and take it. She had no regrets for the past, for either the vanished mistress of Vergée d'Or or the equally lost excited girl who had been surrounded by anxiously eager relatives and seamstresses

67

on her wedding day. If she sometimes missed her family, she would remind herself that she no longer had a family. Etienne and Madeleine and Annette undoubtedly regarded her as the most despicable sort of traitor to her race and to them, and even Kit had revealed a total lack of ability to understand any aspect of her feelings. Besides, she knew that even if in some miraculous way they could all be reunited, *she* would never be able to forgive *them* for murdering her child, whatever their motives.

But it was the memory of them, not less than her fear of Dessalines, which made her so desperate to see an end to the war, and a beginning of a new and better life for the black people. However physically enjoyable they might find their surroundings, she could not allow herself, or Henry, to sink into pure primitiveness. The dream would not dissolve into a perpetual hunger, whether it be for food, or shelter, or sex. On that she was utterly determined.

Thus she knew the depths of fear every time he led his men away to carry out a raid on a British patrol or encampment. And when he was not the first to return . . . She gazed at Louis-Pierre, striding towards her, and her heart constricted.

'The General sends for you, madame,' Louis-Pierre said.

'General Christophe?' she asked.

'All the Generals, madame.'

She hurried, in the midst of a crowd of women and children, all aware that something tremendous had happened. The British had at last realised they were accomplishing nothing by the endless pursuit of an always elusive foe. Thus they had changed their strategy, and instead of flying columns of exhausted men, had established fortified posts at selected places. They were well aware that the Negroes had, from time to time, to descend from their mountain fasts to find and slaughter the wild cattle of the central plains, and accumulate whatever other food they could discover, just as they had always relied upon successful ambushes for their powder and ball. Cut off from all those sources of life, the redcoats had concluded, Toussaint's army must disintegrate. As he could not allow that to happen, he would thus be forced to issue forth from his hideaways and fight a battle on open ground, which was the only favour the invaders asked of providence.

And they had been proved right. The Negro army had waited, and suffered, for two weeks, while the last of their food was consumed, glowering at the Union flag flying above the closest British camp, a large fort containing, Dessalines's scouts had said, not less than an entire regiment, sitting in the woods behind Rio Negro Plantation, daring the blacks to attempt to reach either the canefields or the fishing on the coast. And after two weeks, Toussaint had been forced to order an assault, knowing full well that to have his irregulars charge the disciplined volley fire and glittering bayonets of the soldiers had to be the dream of every British commander.

But now . . . those waiting in the trees had heard no gunfire. Could the British have withdrawn? That was impossible – the Union flag still fluttered in the breeze above the orderly row of huts, behind the sheltering earthworks. She ran towards Henry, who stood, with Toussaint and Dessalines in the open, under the very guns of the fort. Their men stood around them, apparently as bemused as she was.

'Use this.' Henry gave her a piece of cloth to hold across her nose and mouth. Stomach rolling, she walked beside him up to the gateway, recoiled from the stench, stared at the fully uniformed guards who lay at their post.

She clutched Henry's arm. 'Plague?' she whispered.

Henry pointed at the white men's complexions, all tinted a dreadful shade of yellow. 'Fever,' he said. 'Yellow fever. An entire regiment. Dead.'

She turned to look at Toussaint in horror. His face was equally grim, but his eyes were dancing. 'As I promised, madame,' he said. 'We have found allies, in the forest.'

One of the terms on which Toussaint insisted was clothes for his women. Richilde was almost disconcerted to feel the material of a gown on her shoulders, the gentle tug of it across her breasts. Suddenly she was afraid of the future indicated by the restraining garment – the future she had anticipated for so long – as much as by the thought of having to face white men again, even if from a distance.

There were a great number of them, redcoats and blue coats, gleaming buttons and braid, bristling bayonets rising out of a forest of muskets, shakos proudly erect. Certainly they were undefeated, by any human adversaries, still looked a sufficient force to gain any victory.

'But they have lost the will to fight,' Henry said. 'I watched them do that at Yorktown, in 1781. Were Toussaint so minded, we could destroy them all.'

But Toussaint had better things to do, for which Richilde thanked God. His first priority had been the expulsion of the British from St Domingue, not their annihilation, or even their surrender. He sought the fact of victory, not the glory.

And now he had achieved it.

General Maitland saluted the flag, and gave a grim smile. 'You could fly your own, General Toussaint,' he said. 'Or do you look for support from the Directory in Paris?'

'I agreed to fight for them, monsieur,' Toussaint said.

'And you are a man of your word,' Maitland agreed. 'L'Ouverture! You have at the least opened a new world for the black man in Hispaniola. I can only hope, for your sake and the sake of your people, that your French masters understand that.'

'Masters?' Dessalines growled. 'We have no masters.'

'Every man has a master, General,' Maitland remarked. He held out his hand. 'I congratulate you, General Toussaint. I know you will honour the terms of our agreement.'

'Your people will be allowed to embark, unmolested,' Toussaint said.

'And the lives and properties of such French citizens as choose to remain behind will be respected?'

'As long as they do not take up arms against us, monsieur.'

Maitland nodded, looked up at the tricolour and again along the row of black faces waiting by the trees, gazed at Richilde.

'I have with me an American sea captain,' he said. 'Who would like to speak with his sister.'

She waited, suddenly exposed, feeling the breeze fluttering her hem and her hair, feeling too the eyes of several thousand people on her, white as well as black, feeling the immense weight of their thoughts, their imaginations, of what she might be like, of what she might have experienced these last six years, of what she might have suffered. Or enjoyed?

Kit was thirty-four, she recalled, and had become a serious, perhaps somewhat pessimistic man. This much was evident from the cast of his still handsome features. But also an exceedingly prosperous one, as could be told, not only from the cut of his clothes, but from his manner, which denoted more confidence, more aware-ness of who and what he was than even she remem-bered.

Now he shook hands with Toussaint. 'I will add my congratulations, General,' he said. 'I must confess I never supposed you would succeed.'

Toussaint smiled. 'And I will confess, monsieur, that there were times I never supposed I would succeed, either.'

Kit looked up at the flag, obviously thinking much as General Maitland had done, glanced at Dessalines, shook hands with Henry.

'So after all you have become a soldier,' he said. 'And a famous one.'

'It is what I wanted, Kit,' Henry said, simply.

'And is it the summit of your ambitions?'

Henry gazed at him. 'That is for Toussaint to say.'

Kit nodded, held Richilde's hands, kissed her on each cheek. 'You are looking well.'

'I have been living a healthy life.'

'Not all white people have found it so, or I would not be here,' he reminded her.

'But you will have observed that my skin is now brown,' she pointed out.

'It becomes you. Richilde . . .' He hesitated.

She shook her head. 'I will stay here in St Domingue, Kit.'

'With Henry?'

'With Henry. This moment, the ending of the war, is what I have been waiting for, for six years. Now Toussaint and Henry can start to build, and I wish to be here to help them.'

'Will you have another child, for Henry?'

She met his gaze. 'If I can.'

He nodded, and sighed. 'Well, then . . .'

'How is Annette?'

His face seemed to close. 'She is well.'

Her turn to hesitate. 'Kit . . . will you continue to trade with Cap François, after the British have left?'

'If your people wish it.'

'We wish it,' Henry said. 'Like Richilde has said, we need to build.'

'Yes,' Kit said. For a second time he looked at Dessalines, then turned and rejoined the British forces.

'He is an unhappy man,' Henry remarked. 'Because you will not go with him.'

She shook her head. 'Because of Annette,' she said.

Toussaint stood beside them. 'General Christophe,' he said. 'You will take your regiment and prepare to occupy Cap François the moment the British evacuate. I put you in command of the entire north coast.'

Henry saluted. 'And you?'

'The main army will march south. We must finish with Rigaud and Petion.'

'But . . . you mean the war will go on?' Richilde was aghast.

'For a little while, madame. A divided country is no country at all.' He smiled. 'But I promise you, it will be only for a *little* while.'

Chapter 2

THE INVADERS

*Even before the conclusion of [the] peace [of
Amiens, with England, in 1802] an expeditionary
force had been assembled, comprising twenty
thousand of those veterans who had played havoc
with the military reputations of Europe. But as they
were only intended to subdue a parcel of rebellious
blacks, no Lannes, no Massena, was sent to command them. Instead the First Consul gave this per-
quisite to his brother-in-law, Charles Victor
Emmanuel LeClerc, a veteran of the Egyptian campaign. Pauline LeClerc accompanied her husband
– a fine chance this, to see the world – and possibly
the only men in the French armada who had any
doubts as to the eventual outcome of the campaign
were the Generals Rigaud, Petion and Boyer,
included for the sake of their local knowledge. On 3
February 1802 the French fleet, under the command of Admiral Villaret-Joyeuse, dropped anchor
off Cap François.*

Christopher Hamilton dismounted, handed his reins
to the groom, a white boy. As the maid who
opened the front door of the house for him was a white
woman. It was just as easy to obtain white servants in
New York, if one was prosperous, as black.

Which was why he lived here. Besides, New York
was where Alexander had made his headquarters. Offi-
cially he practiced law, but in fact he was steadfastly

pursuing his political career. Since completing his most successful term as Secretary of the Treasury, in which he had managed to place the finances of the infant republic on a firm footing, he had spent a brief spell as Inspector General of the Army, before turning his attention to his real goal, the Presidency itself. In the last election he had been unsuccessful, but his intervention had secured the position for his old friend Thomas Jefferson, to the exclusion of Aaron Burr. Now there could be no doubt that the two men would clash again, when the position of Governor of New York State came up, in 1804. That that was still two years away was irrelevant; the battle lines were being drawn. Thus Alexander needed the support of all his friends and relations, just as he needed the financial backing provided by his interest in the shipping firm, even if he no longer took any active part in that business.

But Kit Hamilton was also a social asset, a romantic if slightly notorious character, rendered more so by the stark tragedy of his domestic life.

'Is the mistress at home?' he asked.

'She is in the garden, Captain.'

Kit nodded, went through the house, and into the rose garden at the rear. It was a small garden, hardly more than a lawn surrounded by flowerbeds, but it was Annette's favourite place. Even on a brisk autumn day she sat here, reading her book, looking up with a quick, shy smile.

'Kit!' She turned up her face for a kiss, on the forehead, squeezed his hand. She loved him. No one could doubt that for a moment. As a brother. Ten years might have passed since that August night in 1791, yet there was still no way of telling when her mind might be engulfed by terrified loathing. But he had assumed the burden of that shattered mind, in the optimism of ignorance, he was prepared to admit to himself, certain that the lively and loving girl he remembered must recover, at least when under his care.

Now he sat next to a thirty-six year old crone, with hair as white as snow, with movements matchingly slow, and yet with a demeanour utterly proprietorial. He was her cousin, her protector, and her man. They lived in conditions of complete intimacy, even shared the same bedchamber – yet he had never touched her body below the neck. That he might still wish to do so apparently never crossed her mind, nowadays, just as that he had once in the past tried to do so had been easily relegated to the level of the nightmares from which she continuously suffered. What agonies of desire he might experience when confronted with her ample figure, what doubtful company he might from time to time be forced to seek to preserve his own sanity, was no concern of hers – he did not suppose she was even aware of such emotions. She concentrated on simpler things.

'I'm so glad you're back,' she said. 'It looks like a storm.'

He nodded. 'Wind's freshening all the time.'

'Did you visit them?' she asked.

'We're unloading a cargo of prime sugar,' he said. 'Some of it from Vergée d'Or, believe it or not.'

She gazed at him, face cold. But he could not cease trying to break through the cocoon of hatred in which she limited her life.

'It is quite remarkable what Toussaint has managed to accomplish,' he said. 'They are actually growing cane again. Not on the old scale, of course. Not yet, anyway. But now that he has expelled the Spaniards from the west, as well as the mulattos from the south, and rules the whole island, they've a lot more space to play with.'

'Does Richilde still walk around with nothing on?'

He smiled. 'Richilde is again the grand lady. She is the head of Cap François society.'

'Living with a black man?'

'They love each other.'

'That is impossible, except in a diseased brain. Presumably she is again a mother?'

He shook his head. 'Although I think she would like to be. Annette . . .' he drew a long breath. 'Why do you not come on a voyage with me, to Cap François? To see it again, to see how peaceful it is, even how prosperous it is again becoming. I know Richilde would be so pleased to see you. She asks after you every time I visit.'

Annette stared at him.

He sighed, got up. 'It was just an idea. A sea voyage would do you good.'

He had turned to go inside before she spoke.

'I will go back to St Domingue,' she said. 'When the French send an army to reconquer it, and hang all the blacks. That is when I will go back. With Etienne.'

'That is not going to happen, my dear,' he said patiently. 'France is at war with all Europe. She has no fleets and no armies to spare for colonial adventures. Besides, why should she? St Domingue is as French as it ever was. Toussaint makes no claim for independence. He is Governor General. He rules beneath the tricolour. He has been recognised by the First Consul. Believe me, Bonaparte must be happy to have at least one of his dominions in such secure hands.'

'It will happen,' Annette said, quietly. 'My family will be avenged. No matter how long it takes, it will happen. And then I will go back.'

'Sail ho, bearing due north,' came the call from the main top.

Kit levelled his glass, Rogers at his elbow, gazing across the sparkling blue waters. February was one of the good months of the year, below Cuba – the winter gales through which they had battled on their way south from New York and down the Gulf Stream were nothing more than unpleasant memories. Now their one concern was the possibility of encountering a British man of war on the hunt for men – it was a situation which daily grew more aggravating to American seamen, and yet which seemed insoluble, while Great

Britain so arrogantly, and so effectively, ruled the oceans.

But this was an unusual place for a British frigate to be. The *Stormy Petrel* had just rounded Cap-à-Foux at the western extremity of St Domingue, and the green of the land was only ten miles away to starboard, while already just looming above the horizon, he could make out the craggy low peaks of the island of Tortuga, where once the buccaneers had held sway, and where now only a few French planters remained, eking out a precarious existence, cut off, despite Toussaint's blandishments, from the mainland of the colony. His course lay between the island and St Domingue itself, with Cap François only a day's sail beyond that. Since their evacuation of the city and hinterland nearly four years before, the British had hardly shown a flag in these waters.

Yet bearing down on them now was undoubtedly a frigate.

And more than one. 'Look there,' Rogers said, pointing.

Kit counted two more sails, and then several others.

'That is a fleet,' he muttered.

'An expeditionary force,' Rogers said, as suddenly the entire northern horizon was filled with white canvas.

'And signalling us to heave to,' Kit said, as he watched a puff of smoke rising from the foredeck of the leading frigate.

'They'll have foul bottoms, if they've just crossed the Atlantic,' Rogers observed. 'If we run for it, they'll never catch us.'

Kit continued to stare through his telescope, his heart commencing to quicken its beat as he realised that he was not staring at the white or red ensigns of the Royal Navy, but at the tricolour.

'Heave her to, Mr Rogers,' he said quietly. 'It can do no harm to discover what they are about.'

A French fleet, he thought. More, as Rogers had accurately determined, a French expeditionary force, launched across the Atlantic in the middle of a life and death struggle with Great Britain. His memory went back all of twenty-three years, when as a boy of fifteen he had watched de Grasse's fleet drop their anchors off Cap François. He gazed up at the yellow varnished hulls, the closed black gunports, the masts towering towards the sky as his jolly boat, Stars and Stripes proudly flying from its stern, threaded its way between the slow moving hulls, on its way to the flagship, as he had been directed. De Grasse had come to secure the independence of the Thirteen Colonies, and also to tweak the lion's tail. What could this immense armament, crowded with soldiers – they thronged the bulwarks to look down at him – and even with women, he observed with surprise, be seeking? It could only be either Jamaica or Canada. And in these latitudes, Jamaica was more likely.

The jolly boat came into the side of the huge three-decker which was named *Bucentaure*. Kit stared at her in total admiration – he had never in his life seen so enormous a ship. Certainly a hasty count of her gunports, taken in conjunction with the huge carronades mounted on her bow and in her stern, convinced him that she could not carry less than a hundred guns. Another calculation, made as he climbed the ladder and stepped through the opened gangway on to the snow-white deck, to the 'cooee' of the boatswain's whistle, and surveyed the cluster of red-pompommed sailors, the two lines of blue coated soldiers drawn up beyond, the crimson sashed officers waiting to welcome him, convinced him that her complement could hardly be less than two thousand men. And again, women, for both forward and on the poop there was the flutter of skirts.

'Citizen.' His salute was returned. 'Captain Duguay, at your service. Welcome on board.'

79

'Captain Hamilton, brig *Stormy Petrel*, out of New York.'

'And bound for Cap François?' Duguay inquired.

'That is my destination, monsieur,' Kit agreed.

'Do you trade regularly with Cap François, Captain Hamilton?'

'I do, monsieur.'

'Then my Admiral would speak with you.' Duguay led him aft, and up the ladder to the poop. At the top a short, powerfully built, and surprisingly young, man waited for them. Duguay saluted. 'This is Captain Hamilton, of New York, Citizen Admiral,' he said. 'Admiral Villaret-Joyeuse.'

Kit clasped the proffered fingers.

'And bound for Cap François?' the Admiral inquired.

'Yes, Your Excellency.'

'Good. Good. I would talk with you, Citizen Captain. We all would talk with you.' He turned, led Kit to the group of men wearing military uniforms who waited further aft. 'General LeClerc, here is a man who may be able to give us information as to our destination. Captain Hamilton, may I present Citizen General LeClerc, in command of the army.'

Again Kit shook hands, again impressed by the youth of the man – he doubted LeClerc was yet thirty. But he was preoccupied with what he had just heard. 'Your destination is Cap François?'

'Kit, by God!'

He turned, gazed at Etienne de Mortmain, more floridly stout than ever, hurrying across the deck towards him, arms outstretched.

''Tienne? But you were in Jamaica.'

'What nonsense,' Etienne said. 'I have spent these last three years in Paris. Preparing for this occasion.' He turned to LeClerc. 'This is the man of whom I have spoken, Citizen General. My cousin. He will be invaluable to us.'

80

Kit glanced from him to Villaret-Joyeuse, and then LeClerc, and then at the ships which composed this immense armament. 'And now you go to Cap François?' he asked, incredulously. 'To recruit blacks?'

LeClerc smiled, deprecatingly. Etienne gave a shout of laughter. 'Not to recruit the blacks, Kit. Never that. To hang Toussaint, and return the rest to slavery.'

Kit could only stare at his cousin in total consternation. 'Hang Toussaint? But . . . he too flies the tricolour.'

LeClerc once again gave a deprecating smile. 'A man may fly any flag he chooses. It is his intentions that are important.'

'And you doubt Toussaint's intentions? He has now ruled for four years, in the name of France. I should have thought that if he intended anything different he would have made it plain by now.'

LeClerc shrugged. 'Who can tell the workings of a black devil's mind, Captain Hamilton? Certain it is that the First Consul, my brother-in-law,' he said with a squaring of the shoulders so that Kit could be in no doubt of his importance, 'intends to restore St Domingue to its proper status. If the blacks resist us, then we shall destroy them.'

Kit allowed himself another glance at the fleet. 'The British tried that, with respect, Your Excellency,' he remarked. 'For five years.'

'The British!' This time LeClerc's smile was frankly contemptuous.

'With whom you are at war,' Kit reminded him. 'Is your entire fleet not a hostage to fortune?'

'You are short of information, Captain Hamilton. Peace has been agreed, between France and England. It waits only to be formally signed, at Amiens. We have naught to fear from the Royal Navy. As for the British adventures in St Domingue, we have them much in mind, believe me, Captain. And have no intention of repeating them. I would have you meet these gentlemen.' He gestured to the other officers. 'Or perhaps you know them already. General Rigaud.'

Kit shook hands with the mulatto, grey and somewhat weary in appearance.

'General Petion.'

A bundle of nervous energy, Kit estimated.

'And Colonel Boyer.'

Incredibly young. But then, so was LeClerc, Kit reminded himself. And of the pair, the mulatto was far the more purposeful man, in his firm lips and hard mouth.

'These gentlemen were born and bred in St Domingue,' LeClerc explained. 'They know the forests and the mountains. What is more, they know Toussaint, and his savage Generals, Dessalines and Christophe. You will observe that I do not treat this campaign lightly. Then there is your cousin, who also knows both the men and the country.'

Kit put up his hand to scratch his head, lowered it again. 'The campaign? With respect, Your Excellency, there is no *need* for a campaign. Toussaint will welcome you with open arms.'

LeClerc glanced at the mulatto officers, then at Etienne, then at the Admiral. 'If you are right, Captain, and my advisers are wrong, why, then, as you say, there will be no campaign.'

Villaret-Joyeuse clapped Kit on the shoulder. 'You'll dine on board, Captain Hamilton, and we will discuss the matter further.'

'But first, the ladies,' LeClerc said. 'Pauline, my dear, this gentleman is an American sea captain, related to Citizen Mortmain.'

Kit was drawn forward, checked in consternation Pauline LeClerc was by no means a beautiful woman – her features too closely resembled those of her brother Napoleon – but she had an extremely well developed figure, as he could tell at a glance, for she was dressed unlike any white woman he had ever seen in his life

before, in what appeared to be a single utterly diapha-
nous garment, which had no shape to it other than an
embroidered gather just beneath the breasts, themselves to all practical purposes quite uncovered, and
which, in the gentle breeze propelling the ship onwards,
snuggled at groin and buttock, wrapped itself round
thigh and calf.

As if in a dream he kissed the offered fingers, and
listened to the somewhat abrasive Corsican tones.
'Why, Captain Hamilton,' she said. 'You are quite
handsome. All the Americans I met in Paris were old,
and ugly. But they were ministers, not sea captains.'

He endeavoured to concentrate on the pert features,
the careful ringlets of yellow hair.

'You should visit America, madame. Most of the
men there are young.'

She glanced at her husband. 'Perhaps we shall visit
America, in due course, Captain. But now, let me see,
you know Citizeness Mortmain?'

'Citizeness . . ?' He gazed at the plump young
woman, with the faintly familiar, doe-like features.

She giggled. 'You will remember me as Louise Ramlie, Captain. We met, oh, ten years ago, in Cap François, when my poor mama was caring for your sister.'

'And now . . .' he glanced at Etienne, who was
puffing out his chest in pride. 'I must congratulate you.'

'And this is Citizeness Palourdes. Colonel Palourdes
is General LeClerc's aide-de-camp.'

The girl, and she was certainly no older than Louise
de Mortmain, gave him her hand with grave expression.
She was in fact by some way the most attractive of the
women, in her demeanour, which was quietly modest,
and in looks, with a perfect heart-shaped face, around
which long black hair made a delightful shroud, and
which contained a straight nose and a wide mouth, perfectly set off by the pointed chin and the serious dark
eyes. Her figure, too, like the others distinctly delineated by the transparent gown she wore, was at once

83

slender – she was above average height – and full, both at breast and thigh. With a spasm of disloyalty to Annette, he realised she was the most beautiful woman he had met in a long time.

'And this, is Citizeness Jacqueline Chavannes,' Pauline LeClerc was saying.

Jacqueline, Kit realised, had to be more than forty years of age, and he had not seen her since two days before Richilde's wedding, which was now nineteen years in the past. Nineteen years during which she had certainly, if apparently temporarily, been sucked into the horror and passion of the slave rebellion.

Yet it might have been nineteen days. Her hair remained the same impenetrable mat of glossy blackness, her face and eyes possessed the same hard glittering beauty, and her figure – she was at once taller and more powerfully built than any of the Frenchwomen around her – was as voluptuously attractive as ever. If she suffered by comparison with Seraphine Palourdes, it was only because of the French girl's obvious youth and innocence.

Nor had her liquid voice changed in any way, either. 'Captain Hamilton is an old friend,' she said. 'We *knew* each other, as children.'

Pauline LeClerc glanced from man to woman, and gave a peculiar smile; it made Kit think of a lizard, about to swallow a fly. 'I forgot,' she said, 'that you are all going home, in a manner of speaking. And now, Citizen Admiral, shall we dine?'

Kit found himself next to Jacqueline, as they slowly descended the companion ladder to the great cabin. 'Perhaps you can explain to me what is truly happening,' he suggested. 'I see you, standing next to Louise de Mortmain, dealing with Etienne as an equal . . .'

'Necessity makes for strange bedfellows,' she agreed. 'We are all people with wrongs to avenge. Possessions to regain.'

'But . . . did your people not fight alongside the blacks?'

'Once,' she smiled. 'Does Richilde still sleep with the niggers?' She smiled at him. 'Because that is what Etienne seeks, you know. To regain Vergée d'Or.'

He was seated on Pauline LeClerc's right. 'My husband intends to make Cap François his headquarters,' she remarked. 'And you trade there regularly. So I will hope to see a lot more of you.' She accompanied her words with a slow gaze, up and down his body, to leave no doubt that she meant exactly what she had said. But such febrile sexuality, such implicit amorality, was too strange for him, certainly with her husband seated beside him – he could feel himself flushing, and looked away in embarrassment. Besides, as the sister of the greatest man in France, she had to be merely amusing herself at his expense.

He found himself staring across the table at Seraphine Palourdes, who met his eyes for several seconds before turning her head to talk with Boyer, seated beside her.

Pauline LeClerc gave a low laugh. 'Believe me, Captain Hamilton, should you enlist my support, all things are possible.'

It was necessary to say something. 'I suspect your husband means to employ me,' he said. 'And will no doubt keep me busy.'

'I do indeed,' LeClerc said, indicating that he had been listening all the while, which merely increased Kit's embarrassment. 'If you are agreeable, citizen, I would have you act as a go-between for us. Will you do that?'

'If it can avert bloodshed, General, and lead to an honourable peace, I will be happy to do so.'

'You know the Negro who commands in Cap François?'

'Henry Christopher? Yes. I know him well.' Kit gazed at Etienne.

'Ah, yes, Christophe,' LeClerc said. 'We have been told of him. I understand he is by way of being your brother-in-law.'

'By way of, General,' Kit said, refusing to take offence.

'Thus you trust him, as no doubt he trusts you,' LeClerc said, giving not the slightest indication that he might be treading on delicate ground. 'But you will understand that I must have guarantees of the blacks' willingness to submit themselves to French rule. Thus my message to this Christophe, which he may relate to Toussaint, is that he should evacuate Cap François with all his force, leaving their weapons behind them.'

Kit looked at him in dismay. 'Do you really suppose Christophe would agree to such a capitulation?'

'It is not a capitulation, Captain. It is a command, issued by the new Governor General of St Domingue, myself. A command which, if these people are as anxious to be ruled by France as you claim, they will be happy to obey. After all, Captain, now that I have arrived, and with an army to protect them, there is no longer any necessity for them to bear arms. Is there?'

Kit sighed. 'I doubt they will agree, until they have some evidence of your intentions towards them.'

LeClerc's eyes were opaque. 'Any Negro found with arms in his hands or on his person, after I land, Captain Hamilton, will be considered as being in rebellion against France, and be hanged. You may tell this brother-in-law of yours that *those* are my intentions.'

Saturday was market day, as it had always been market day, in the past. Thus it was a page from the past, with the differences those of degree. The houses of Cap François might be dilapidated, their gardens neglected, but the city, because of its situation, curving round its land-locked bay, was still beautiful, and in the good-natured hubbub set up by its inhabitants was again *alive*. The soldiers on the ramparts might have black faces, but they wore French uniforms and paraded beneath the tricolour. And Richilde de Mortmain proceeded from stall to stall, followed by her maid, as ever in the past. That this girl was named Aimee, rather than Amelia, that she was free rather than a slave, and that she was utterly delighted at being in the employ of General Christophe's woman rather than resentful at her lowly station in life was again a matter of degree. But what a delightful degree.

The truly apparent change was in the market itself; the goods on display. For while Toussaint had recognised that if he was ever going to restore St Domingue to its old position of being the wealthiest island in the Caribbean it was necessary to re-establish the sugar industry, he was still reluctant to use force to drive his people back to work, and any man prepared to farm had been granted his acre of land. Thus the market was no longer a huge junk stall, but instead displayed produce in every variety, from goats and chickens to baskets of mangoes and pomegranates. A selection from which Richilde made a careful, if wide, choice to the delight of the various traders. She was the best known woman in Cap François, at once because she was white and because she belonged to the commanding general, which meant that she was plentifully supplied with the *assignats* which Toussaint had issued to act as money, basically worthless, but eagerly sought by the uneducated Negroes, to whom money had always been a tangible suggestion of white omnipotence.

But more than her wealth or position, the very fact of her presence reassured them that their new found freedom was not such an impermanent uncertainty as they sometimes feared. They sought a return to normality, even if it was to be an utterly different normality to any they had ever known, and she was the symbol of their goal.

Just as she also sought a return to normality. A ship had been sighted, making its way slowly along the coast towards the port, and had been identified as the *Stormy Petrel*. She had in fact become used to Kit's visits, and treasured them as her only link with the world she had abandoned. That he came at all showed that he was reaching towards an understanding. That he came so regularly when the trade available hardly justified it, indicated he was accomplishing his intention. And that he could come, and take part, however warily and however briefly, in this unique social experiment, encapsulated all of her hopes for the future. Her personality would not permit her to hate on a timeless and unyielding scale. Whatever he had done, he had acted as he had thought best – and he was her brother.

Thus, as he would be here by this afternoon, she planned this night to have a supper party, for Henry's principal officers, and their wives. For part of Toussaint's attempts to restore that all important normality had been a restoration of the civil law as decreed by the new French republic, just as he had sought to diminish the part played by voodoo in his people's lives. He regarded, rightly in her opinion, the West African gods as the products of despair, and as such they were no longer necessary. He himself was a practising Catholic, and if he had attended voodoo ceremonies often enough in the past, as she knew so well, he was now anxious to put that behind him. Indeed, one of his principal sources of concern was that nearly all the ordained priesthood, necessarily white, had fled the country. Nor was he likely to replace them, with France itself sunk into atheism.

His rejection of voodoo had not been universally popular. Many of his aides, and notably Jean-Jacques Dessalines, were genuine believers in the Snake God, and at once feared and resented his derogation. It was an emotion Richilde was herself afraid to consider too deeply; Ogone Badagris touched too powerful a chord of primeval sympathy in her own personality. She was merely happy that Henry was a sceptic in either direction. He was, in fact, the most individualistic man she had ever met, far more so than Philippe, who had had the individuality of wealth, which merely encourages outrageous behaviour. Henry pursued entirely his own path through life, preceded any action with hours or even days of profound and silent thought; deeply personal moods which were disturbing to behold, and which might have frightened her had she not known him so well. For if, knowing him as she did, she could no longer doubt that he had foreseen the Negro revolt for many years – his true reason for never accepting Kit's offer and leaving St Domingue – she also could no longer doubt that obtaining possession of her, as a product of that revolt, had always been his goal, as he had pursued it with such single-minded purpose on that terrible August night.

Nor, in ten years, had his love for her seemed to diminish in any way. Hers for him had certainly grown as she had come to understand him, to *know* him, better than she had ever known anyone in her life. Yet they alone of all the military hierarchy created by Toussaint were not married. Because he had never asked her. The subject had never been raised between them; she did not know if it had ever been raised by Toussaint. Sometimes she supposed it was because she had not had another child for him – and as she was now approaching her thirty-fifth year it was unlikely she would ever do so. And thus she had to suppose that eventually he would – as Santhonax had warned – throw her over for another woman.

But as he had never done that either, and clearly loved her as much as ever, she had to reassure herself that it was simply because he knew, or feared, it would pose her an insoluble problem.

As if it truly mattered. They lived together as man and wife, were so regarded by the society they ruled, and she had as much pride in her Cap François home as she had ever had in Vergée d'Or. It was a large house, and had once belonged to Monsieur Peynier; she had visited it often enough in the past as Philippe's wife. It was thus entirely fitting that the military governor of the city, as appointed by General Toussaint, should have taken Peynier's place. With his lady. And his retinue of servants. Because it was within these walls that the past was most convincingly recreated. Again, these liveried footmen and white gowned maidservants were not slaves, and again they were delighted to have the opportunity to work for their great hero and his beautiful white mistress.

In fact, Henry was a stern master. He was a soldier, with a soldier's outlook, and Richilde often wondered if her servants' lot had in any way been improved. But they were free. There was the vital thing. Even if not one of them would ever have dared look Henry in the face and tell him that he or she was leaving for another employer. There could be no better employer than General Christophe, save possibly General Toussaint himself, and *he* preferred to live in absolute simplicity, out in the country. But he never criticised his protégé's arrangements, or his style.

Certainly she was not prepared to do so. After her years in the jungle, despairing that she would ever again be able to live like a lady, to sleep between linen sheets, to wear proper clothes, to soak in a hot bath and eat with silver cutlery off china crockery, was to make all that had gone before merely a long nightmare. And to share these things with Henry was a source of continual wonderment. With his serious thoughtful approach to life he had undertaken the mastery of those civilised arts as a challenge to be surmounted. His patience was inexhaustible, as his good humour, at least where she was concerned, never appeared to fade, however often she had gently to remove the meat from his fingers and spear it with his fork, or endeavoured to prevent him from blowing his nose on his serviette. But for her it was an unending joy to sleep with him in the enormous tester bed they shared, to reach out and touch him in the middle of the night, to feel that tremendous strength and purpose living quiescent at her side, just as it was for her to interpret the pictures in the books of Peynier's library. Henry was insatiable in his search for knowledge, of people and houses, ships and fortifications, weapons and military history – yet he seemed quite unable to grasp the elements of reading and writing himself. This she put down to male perversity, for that he possessed the intelligence and the application to master so simple an art could not be questioned. Yet it was not something she truly wished to change. Because of it he needed her.

She supposed she had never been so happy in her life. All that had gone before, all the uncertainty of her youth, the groping after some reality in the totally unreal world of Vergée d'Or as created and maintained by Philippe de Mortmain, the horrors of that August night in 1791, of her virtual imprisonment here in this very city, the murder of her only child, the grim years in the forest, had all come together in this utterly unique situation. That it had as yet no permanency, that any progress had to depend upon some return of material prosperity, that such prosperity would in turn depend upon a degree of application lacking in the average Negro, and certainly one who had only recently earned his release from a lifetime of horrifying servitude, were worrying considerations. Even more worrying was the realisation that the entire young nation lived, worked, and played at the behest of the personality of Toussaint, and Toussaint was an old man. But this was one subject on which Henry, usually so willing to consider every aspect of any situation, was totally unresponsive. For all his hard commonsense, his considerable intellectual powers, he regarded Toussaint almost as a god, could not envisage life without his reassuring presence.

In which he was utterly representative of the people he commanded. And of her? She had at least learned to

91

live for the present. And this present *was* utterly happy. Especially when it would contain, however briefly, both of her favourite men. She waited for them at the top of the grand staircase, her heart pounding with pleasure, but slowing in concern as she watched their hurry, their animated and unsmiling conversation.

'Kit!' She embraced her brother, kissed him on each cheek. 'Annette?'

She always asked this, knowing the answer would always be the same.

'Well,' Kit said. 'Well.' He glanced at Christophe.

Who gave Richilde's hand a tight squeeze – he had never been able to make himself kiss her in public, even on the cheek. 'Kit has brought us an ultimatum,' he said.

'A command,' Kit suggested.

'That is better?'

Richilde looked from one to the other, her slowly gathering frown matching her slowly constricting heart. 'An ultimatum? A command? From whom?'

Christophe snorted, flung out his right arm in the direction of the sea. 'There is a French fleet, out there.'

'Anchored off Tortuga,' Kit said.

'But . . . isn't that what we expected?' she asked. 'What Toussaint has wanted?'

Henry chewed his lip, walked past her, threw himself into a chair, long booted legs thrust in front of him.

'I don't understand,' Richilde said to Kit.

'This is a fleet of war, Richilde,' he said. 'An immense fleet of war. Far bigger than de Grasse's in 1780. And it carries an army. Twenty thousand men. It is an expeditionary force. Intended for here.'

'But . . .' She felt like scratching her head. 'We fly the French flag. Toussaint governs in the name of France.'

'They are aware of that,' Kit said. 'But claim to distrust his motives.'

'Distrust Toussaint,' Henry growled.

'They have never met him,' Kit explained. 'When he and this LeClerc come face to face . . .'

'All will be well,' Richilde said. 'I'm sure it will.'

'Before they can meet,' Henry said, 'I am required to surrender Cap François. To disarm my men and withdraw them from the city.'

Richilde glanced at Kit. 'Because the French General is suspicious. But will that matter? It is surely what Toussaint wishes, peace with the French.'

'But is it what the *French* want, Richilde?' Henry asked. 'They do not trust us, but they expect us to trust them. And they will allow me no time to send to Toussaint. My answer must be returned by tomorrow.'

She gazed at his huge, strong face. 'What else can you *do*?' she cried. 'Start another war?'

He chewed his lip, and she felt a pang of real fear.

'You will find it difficult to defend Cap François,' Kit pointed out. 'That is the biggest fleet I have ever seen. And those soldiers have beaten all Europe.'

Henry gazed at him.

'I'm sure Toussaint would wish to make peace, to have peace,' Richilde said. 'He doesn't want another war. No one wants another war.'

'He will trust them,' Henry said, thoughtfully. 'I know he will.'

'Well, then . . .'

'He is too eager to trust people,' Henry said, even more thoughtfully. 'He is too eager to be ruled by the French. You have not heard who is on that fleet.'

Richilde looked at Kit.

'Etienne, and his new wife. And all the mulatto generals.'

'Those men are our enemies,' Henry said. 'Your cousin is my sworn enemy. You expect me to trust *him*?'

'But . . .' she could hardly frame the words. 'Then you do mean to fight, for Cap François?'

He shook his head. 'As Kit says, I do not think we can defend Cap François against a fleet and an army of French regulars. We could not defend it against the British, remember?'

How she remembered. But somehow this was different. The British had planned a straightforward war of conquest, horrible enough, to be sure, but not to be compared with the prospect of a war of *re*-conquest, inspired by men like Etienne.

'We will evacuate the city, like we did then,' Henry decided.

'Which is what this LeClerc is asking you to do, anyway,' Richilde said. 'Can you not then negotiate?'

'I will not negotiate,' Henry said. 'He has come to return us to slavery. I know that. We will withdraw into the bush. But LeClerc will not have Cap François to use as a base. When we withdraw, we will burn the town.'

'Burn the town?' General LeClerc stared at Kit in disbelief. 'That is absurd.'

For reply Kit pointed. An immense pall of smoke hung on the western horizon, only slowly breaking up as the wind struck at it.

'The man is a savage,' Etienne de Mortmain observed. 'An utter savage.'

'A savage would hardly reason so clearly, act so decisively,' Admiral Villaret-Joyeuse remarked. 'He means to fight, and he knows the city is indefensible. Is that not so, Captain Hamilton?'

'He knows Cap François is indefensible from the sea, certainly. Your approach, General, as I suggested, was a little too uncompromising.'

LeClerc stared at the smoke, his fingers curled into fists. 'If he wishes to fight, he will find that we too wish to fight. I promise you that, Captain. And we will not fight these savages in any Christian spirit, I promise you that too.'

Kit sighed. 'It is still possible to avert a war, General. If you can make contact with Toussaint . . .'

'Will he not act as his General has indicated?' asked Major Palourdes.

'He has a mind of his own.'

'Bah,' Etienne said. 'You speak of coachmen, slaves, niggers. You speak of them as if they were men like ourselves. Negotiate with savages? What an absurdity.'

They stared at him.

'Toussaint is no savage, monsieur,' Alexander Petion said, quietly.

'Well,' Kit said, 'the decision must be yours, General. I have apparently failed in my mission.' He smiled, 'I have even failed in my personal mission, which was to trade. If you will excuse me, I will rejoin my ship and make for Havana.'

'Not so fast,' LeClerc said. 'You tell me I must seek a meeting with this Toussaint. He is an acquaintance of yours?'

'I have met him,' Kit said, cautiously.

'Then I would have you act as my negotiator, again.' He gave a brief smile. 'You can hardly be less successful a second time, Captain.'

'I doubt negotiation is really my forte, General,' Kit said. 'Besides, I have a living to earn.'

'You will be well paid,' LeClerc promised. 'And I need you.'

Kit frowned at him. 'You would keep me here against my will, General? I am an American citizen.'

'Who once fought for France, I am told. Come, come, monsieur, is this not a great cause we pursue here? Peace, and the restoration of St Domingue to her proper prosperity? Of your cousin to his estates?'

'In which Richilde shall have her proper share, I give you my word,' Etienne was quick to add.

'Believe me, Captain, we will make it worth your while,' LeClerc said, and looked at his wife.

Remarkably, he wished to stay, at least for a while. He wished to see the outcome of this new struggle, if it were possible to do so. And he felt the necessity to remain at Etienne's shoulder, should the French be victorious, to attempt to restrain his cousin from the excesses of which he was certainly capable. 'Tienne's words on board the *Stormy Petrel*, as they had sailed down to St Kitts, nine years before, kept coming back to him; the thought of Richilde in these people's hands was unthinkable – and it could happen.

But he knew too that he was staying for another, and far less admirable reason: he had nothing to go home to New York for, and a great deal to remain here for. Over ten years he had played the nursemaid, emotionally and even physically, to a demented woman, had restricted his private life and all the demands of his powerfully masculine nature, because of a careless vow, carelessly accepted. Now suddenly the past had caught up with him, and it was possible to lose himself for a very brief season in a world at which he had only just nibbled in his youth, a world typified by the outrageous garments of the French women, the provocativeness of their conversation and the gaiety of their careless approach to life. They were the outpourings of revolution. They were not constrained by centuries of privilege and power and position, but sought only to enjoy each day, each hour, each moment, as it came, and with whoever it might bring.

And it was a world, for him, represented and made sure by the presence of Jacqueline Chavannes.

He watched her on the quarterdeck of the flagship as he conned the huge vessel towards the harbour. By now most of the flames had died down, and yet the smoke pall still hung above the destroyed city, still drifted inland towards the mountains to illustrate Christophe's determined act of defiance. Had it been *his* decision, Kit would have remained at Tortuga, pending the outcome of the negotiations with Toussaint; but LeClerc was determined to take possession of the city, even if it was a burned-out shell.

'You can see the deep water clearly now, Admiral,' he said. 'It is the area of dark blue which stretches in that semi-circle round the bay. Your ships may safely lie at anchor there, providing there is no storm.'

'It is not yet the season,' Villaret-Joyeuse said, perhaps to reassure himself. 'And there are no isolated coral heads?'

Kit shook his head. He left the group of officers, walked to the rail, stood behind her, watched her single transparent garment being flattened against her flesh by the gentle breeze, and knew the most powerful passion he had experienced for many years.

'You are a most capable seaman, Kit,' she said, without turning her head.

'It is my profession,' he reminded her. 'I am not so capable a man, alas. At least when it comes to controlling my heart.'

Now she did turn her head, and he moved to stand beside her.

'I have been told,' she said. 'that your treatment of Annette was gallant in the extreme. Has she not recovered at all?'

'Rather has she dwindled.' But his brain was immediately running off at a tangent. She could only have been told about Annette by Etienne. A man who once would not have deigned to speak with a mulatto at all, much less discussed his family. 'Truly,' he remarked, 'this catastrophe has brought about some strange alliances, as you say. Did you see much of my cousin, in France?'

She gazed at him. 'I an not *his* mistress, if that is what you mean, Kit.'

He flushed. 'I had not considered that. I wondered . . . if you knew his plans. Does he really hope to regain Vergée d'Or? To recreate Philippe's plantation? Philippe's spendour?'

'You must ask *him* that,' she said, quietly. 'I had supposed you sought something different from me.'

'I . . .' He could feel his cheeks burning.

She smiled at him. 'And to he who seeks, it shall be given. Is that not a quotation? I understand the General means to disembark his army this very day, but we ladies are to remain on board, until the land is secured and made safe for us. I am sure you will find more duties to occupy you afloat than on land. LeClerc can hardly mean to commence negotiating with Toussaint before tomorrow.' She blew him a gentle kiss with her lips as she turned away. 'You are invited to dine, with the ladies.'

He watched her glide towards the companion hatch. Too late he remembered that he had not discovered whose mistress she actually was.

Toussaint gazed at the slowly dispersing smoke cloud. His face was expressionless, but that he was angry could not be doubted.

'Is this how you treat the city I gave you?' he asked Henry Christophe. And turned to Richilde. 'I had supposed, madame, that you loved Cap François. That you would prove a restraining influence on this . . . savage.'

Never before had he spoken to Henry in such terms. Richilde caught her breath, could think of nothing to say.

'Cap François is indefensible from the sea.' Henry would not lower his gaze. 'You know that as well as I.'

'And why should we talk in terms of defence?' Toussaint demanded. 'By your own account this LeClerc wished only to treat. He is the representative of the country on whose account we hold this land.'

'He does not wish to treat,' Henry said. 'He has come to conquer. By deceit, if possible. By force of arms, if he must. Etienne de Mortmain will see to that.'

Toussaint gazed at him. 'It is a mistake, it is a catastrophe, for those who hope to attain high office to be influenced by personal hatreds,' he said. 'So the man once had you flogged. That is long ago, in the past. He has suffered more than you for it.'

'He is my enemy,' Henry said. 'He also murdered my son. He is Richilde's enemy as well. I tell you, he has not come to treat.'

'Henry is right,' Dessalines growled. 'Why should we

treat with them? We beat the British. We will beat
these as well. Let us start now. The sooner the better.'

Toussaint stared at him in turn, then at the other
officers, gathered in a semi-circle round the Generals.
'Is that all you know how to do, fight, and kill, and
destroy?' he asked. 'Is that what you would make my
memory?' He turned, walked to his horse, mounted.
'Were I to have no more hope of the future,' he said, 'I
would blow out my brains, here and now.'

Chapter 3

THE WAR

The French victories, in a country such as St Domingue, were largely worthless, as the British had discovered, but they were impressive – some of the Negro commanders surrendered without firing a shot.

There were seven for supper: Pauline LeClerc, Louise de Mortmain, Jacqueline Chavannes and Seraphine Palourdes, two officers of the ship, and Kit. The Admiral and the Captain had both gone ashore with the soldiers and the Generals, and the returning colonists. Leaving their wives to play.

Because that was undoubtedly their purpose. The chattering conversation swirled about Kit's head, as the wine swirled about his mouth before slipping down his throat. He was surrounded by bare shoulders and flowing hair, by scantily covered bosoms and outrageous conversation, concerned entirely with anatomy and past exploits, all overseen and controlled by the glittering personality of Madame LeClerc.

Kit had been seated at her right hand, where she could lean over occasionally to kiss him on the cheek. 'You have no idea what a new face, a new *man*, does to me,' she said. 'Especially after all those weary days on the ocean. I had thought to go mad, more than once. But now, having arrived, it is all worthwhile. That is one of life's great compensations, do you not think, Kit: in time everything is worthwhile.'

'A very comforting philosophy, madame,' he agreed. 'It would enable you to endure a great deal.'

She leaned away to gaze at him, chin resting on her forefinger. 'Why, yes,' she said. 'I suppose it would.'

'Is it a philosophy shared by your husband?' he asked, determined to remind her of her situation, no matter how drunk she might have become. As if she was drunk at all, he thought, no matter how much wine might have slipped down *her* throat.

She made a moue. 'Charles is not a philosopher, alas. He is a soldier, and he dreams. Of great deeds.'

'You mean he has not yet accomplished any?' Kit asked, politely.

For a moment her eyes hardened, as if wondering whether he was poking fun at her, through her husband. Then she appeared to decide that the question had been genuine.

'Alas, no,' she said. 'He accompanied my brother to Egypt, four years ago, and has fought with him in several campaigns since, but always on the staff. This is his first independent command, which is why he is so anxious to bring it to a victorious conclusion.'

'But he is still very young,' Kit suggested.

'They are all very young, monsieur,' she said. 'Lannes, Ney, Bernadotte, Soult, Victor, Junot, even Massena, they are all young. Because Napoleon is himself young. France has suddenly become a young country again, after too many years of being *old*.' She made the word sound almost obscene. 'Thus Charles is old, not to have gained a reputation. But you know, Kit, I did not invite you to an *intimate* supper to discuss my husband. That is the height of bad taste.'

'I suppose I am feeling guilty,' he said. 'That the soldiers should be on shore, preparing to be attacked, while I sit here in comfort.'

'What nonsense,' she said. 'You have played your part. Now let them play theirs. And if you are distressed, Kit, you may be pleased to know that Charles is

101

aware I am having this little party, and who will be attending, and what games we will play. His sole concern is to keep me happy.' She smiled. 'Should he not keep me happy, why, he would not even have an *opportunity* for greatness. Napoleon would see to that.'

For a moment she looked almost vicious. Because, Kit had no doubt, she *was* vicious. But he was more concerned with what she had said, as the stewards were clearing the table, leaving only the cheese and the wine.

And Louise de Mortmain was producing a pack of cards, and handing them to Pauline, who gave them a perfunctory shuffle.

'Are we then to gamble?' Kit asked, a trifle anxiously – he had no doubt that everyone here was far wealthier than himself – but also in some disappointment that the evening should end so prosaically.

Louise giggled, and Pauline smiled. 'In a manner of speaking, Kit.' She dealt the first card, face up, to the officer on her left. 'We are taking our chances on what the evening might hold for us.' The card was the two of Hearts. She now dealt the four of Diamonds to Louise, the seven of Spades to the second officer, the Jack of Hearts to Seraphine Palourdes, which brought an 'Oooh!' from Louise, and then the two of Clubs to Jacqueline.

'A pair,' Louise cried. 'A pair.'

'Of deuces,' Pauline said in disgust. 'Ah, well, the night is young.' She smiled at the officer holding the first deuce, who was licking his lips in anticipation. 'We play aces high, Lieutenant Pinet. So the deuce is the lowest card in the pack. It calls for nothing more than a kiss. A five minute kiss, with no other part of your body touching. Go to her.'

Louise clapped her hands in delight. Pinet hesitated, flushing, then got up and walked round the table. Jacqueline leaned back, her head tilted, and he lowered his mouth to hers.

'I will tell you when to stop,' Pauline said, tapping her fingers on the table.

The two mouths seemed almost to melt. Jacqueline of course had clearly played this game before, Kit realised; her hands remained on the table, lying flaccid. But Pinet, under the influence of that masterful tongue, could not keep his still. They kept moving forward, as he wished to touch her arms or shoulders, only to have them slapped by Seraphine Palourdes, to remind him to keep them behind his back. Kit studied the girl – she was by some distance the youngest person present. But as old as any of her female companions in vice? The evidence of his eyes suggested that. And yet that perfect heart of a face was so innocent, so angelic; indeed, it was almost obscene to suppose she could be the least corrupt.

'Enough,' Pauline remarked. 'Your breeches will not be able to stand any more strain, Pinet.'

The officer straightened, face crimson with passion and embarrassment. Jacqueline's expression had not altered at all

'Well,' Pauline said, picking up the pack of cards again. 'I suppose that will have to do as an *hors d'oeuvre*.' She smiled at Kit. 'Let us hope the evening provides some better entertainment as it goes on.' She dealt him the King of Spades.

'A King,' Louise screamed with excitement. 'A King.'

'Well, well, Kit,' Pauline said. 'Now let us see who will be your Queen.'

She turned over her own card, hesitantly, frowned at the nine of Spades. 'Damnation. But wouldn't it be amusing if it turned out to be you, Pinet?'

That possibility had not occurred to Kit, and he felt distinctly alarmed as she dealt the next card – he had no idea what a King involved, but if the two had been a kiss . . . the card was again a two, this time of Diamonds.

Louise gave a shriek, and Pauline slowly shook her head. 'I do not think it is going to be your night, Pinet.'

Louise herself was dealt the six of Hearts, the second officer the seven of Clubs . . .

'Now there is bad luck,' Pauline said. 'But you can hardly spank yourself, I suppose. Or should we try?'

'They fell on top of each other,' Jacqueline insisted. 'Only the top card showing counts.' She glanced at Kit, and flushed. Clearly she was anxious to discover who would be the next person to be dealt a King. Undoubtedly she hoped it would be herself. Had she not invited him to the supper party? Or had she merely been acting on instructions from Pauline? But had he not accepted, entirely in the anticipation of being able to sleep with her? With her, after the party. Now he was not so sure that that was what he wanted. His excitement began to grow, even as his instincts, lurching through the wine fog which was obstructing his brain, kept shrieking warnings. Warnings which would have to go unheeded, this night, and in this company.

And perhaps, warnings that he had heeded too often in the past.

Still unlucky, Pinet this time received the three of Clubs, while Louise got the eight of Hearts.

'I have a suspicion that you and Montcere *are* going to get together eventually,' Pauline said. 'Even if it is only at the end of a stick.'

Her deliberateness, the way she commented on almost every card, only served to heighten the slowly growing tension in the cabin. Kit reached for his glass, and discovered that it was empty. And the wine bottles had been removed.

Because to become actually drunk would make him incapable?

Montcere had received the Queen of Hearts, to a shout from Louise, and then Pauline was turning over the King of Clubs, in front of Seraphine.

'Oh!' the girl said, and raised her head, to gaze at Kit; little pink spots appeared in her cheeks.

But he could feel a hot flush in his own.

'A fuck,' Louise was shouting, clapping her hands. 'A fuck.'

Kit's head jerked up, as he gazed at the smiling Pauline.

'Well,' she said. 'There is a start. Although *I* am bitterly disappointed, dear Kit. Nevertheless, for this evening I shall have to enjoy you by proxy.'

Seraphine pushed back her chair and got up. Kit also pushed back his chair, uncertain where they were going. Or even what he was supposed to do. Louise could not have been serious. 'What *does* the King mean?' he asked.

'Louise has told you,' Pauline said. 'But it is a free fuck, you see. All the face cards are fucks. But whereas the Knave is designated a rear entry, and the Queen a front entry, the King leaves the first holder, that is you, free to make his choice. Come along, Kit.'

He gazed at Seraphine, who was slowly removing her gown. As he had suspected, it had been her only garment in any event, and now she shrugged it past her shoulders, Jacqueline having obligingly released the ties, and he watched the large, almost perfectly shaped white breasts slowly coming into view, crowned with magnificent, and erect, pink nipples. He thought of Venus rising from the ocean.

'*She's* ready,' Pinet remarked.

Kit tugged at his cravat. But it was more to allow himself to breathe. He felt that he must speak, must appear, at the least, as nonchalant as everyone else. 'You said you play aces high,' he said. 'What can *that* signify?'

Pauline laughed. 'An ace gives absolute rights, except that of permanent injury, on the partner. I love drawing aces. Or even being drawn against one. There is sport. Shall I help you?' She signalled Louise, and between them they pulled off Kit's coat and unbuttoned his shirt. Louise was busy with his shoes, as Pauline unfastened his breeches. Certainly he was ready. He had never been so ready in his life. All his thirty-eight years of repression and self discipline

105

seemed to have exploded in the gigantic rush of desire, and now Seraphine was naked, her belly and her legs as perfectly shaped as the rest of her, her groin a curling mass of black delight . . . he realised that she was the most perfect creature he had ever beheld in his life. And the most innocent? That at the least could not be.

His own breeches were about his ankles, and Louise was shrieking her enjoyment. 'He wears drawers!' she screamed. 'He wears drawers.'

'All Americans wear drawers,' Pauline said, knowledgeably. 'They are all prudes.' Gently she eased the cotton underpants down his thighs. 'Oh, you *are* ready.'

He stood up. Suddenly he was desperate to have it over. And desperate, too, to enjoy this girl, as she seemed to wish it, in one unforgettable embrace. 'Which cabin?' he asked.

Louise gave another shriek of laughter, and to his total consternation he watched Pinet and Montcere pushing back the candles and the cutlery, and watched too, Seraphine climbing on to the table, every movement a picture.

'Now, Kit,' Pauline chided him, gently. 'You'd not rob us of our sport? But it is for you to tell her how to lie.'

And that, Kit thought, is the society which would impose itself on the stately ruins left by the Mortmains and the Milots. Or even on the primitive ambitions of Toussaint and Christophe.

But he had been a part of it. The drumming in his head, seeming to keep time to every movement of his horse's hooves, would alone have reminded him of that. If only other memories could be clearer. But perhaps he did not wish to remember. It had been magnificent, as he had crawled on to the table, between her spread legs, as she had reached for him, her expression serious, and yet sufficiently passionate. As she had kissed him, with opened mouth and wet tongue, to make sure he sus-

106

tained the necessary erection, as that glorious body had moved against and beneath him, legs half in and out of bowls and dishes.

But actual sensation, that of entering her, that of climaxing, that of knowing whether or not she had climaxed with him, was lacking, lost in the drink fog, in the awareness of the people around him, in the hands smacking his shoulders and buttocks, in the laughter . . . and in the growing sense of shame and humiliation, of self disgust. He had made love to the most beautiful girl he had ever known . . . in the most debasing circumstances he had ever known. That other and similar events had followed, as Louise had finally drawn a seven to match Jacqueline's, and had had to submit to a caning on her bare buttocks, and as Pauline had produced a Queen for Montcere's, to end the evening in a riotous, doggy style romp on the deck, had merely confirmed his self contempt. And his confusion, as he had raised his head and seen those splendid black eyes gazing at him, so seriously.

He would no longer be a part of that society. On that he was determined. The question he had to answer was whether he wished any longer to help that society become the ruling society in St Domingue.

'You look terrible,' Etienne remarked, riding beside him. 'You must have had a heavy night. Which one of them did you get?'

He asked the question in a perfectly matter of fact tone – and his wife had been amongst the participants.

'I was drunk,' Kit said, truthfully enough.

'Anyone can tell that.' He watched the horseman galloping towards them. 'Well?' he shouted.

The hussar drew rein in a flurry of dust and sweat and swinging blue sabretache. 'We have seen no blacks, monsieur.'

Etienne peered at the trees, the fields of waving cane. He and Kit had ridden in advance of the main body, which marched behind them, a reconnaissance in force commanded by the General himself; 'Tienne had been impatient to see his old – and as he hoped, his future – home. 'Then we shall go on,' he decided.

He kicked his horse, and cantered forward, and after a moment Kit rode behind him, the hussar at his side. How familiar it all was, even after ten years. But ten years ago he had approached Vergée d'Or from the beach, not this well beaten road. He wondered where Christophe was today. He had no doubt they were being watched, even if no shot had yet been fired on this campaign.

And where Christophe was, there would be Richilde. How his stomach revolted as he imagined Richilde being forced to endure an orgy like that of last night. And they were the women who affected to regard her as a savage.

He looked for the crows, but the crows were gone. As were the bleached bones. The civilising hand of Toussaint had passed over the plantation, and he knew that the factory had recently been used for grinding. But the bones of the house still stood, gauntly waiting.

Etienne dismounted, let the reins lie, walked on to the cracked stone of the front patio, stood with hands on hips. 'Do you know,' he said. 'It is not as bad as I had supposed. There is quite a lot that can be saved. I shall not rebuild on quite such a lavish scale, of course. We have lost ten years' revenue. But still, I can promise you a fine house. And it is good that the blacks have recultivated so much of the cane. We shall be a profit making concern from the start.'

Kit also dismounted. 'Do you really suppose they have been cultivating that cane for your benefit?'

Etienne chuckled. 'Possibly not. But it *has* turned out for my benefit, has it not? I certainly mean to reap it. As I mean to get started on rebuilding Vergée d'Or just as quickly as possible. And living here. I have already written to Madeleine, asking her to find a passage for

Cap François. In fact, Kit, I thought that if you were going in that direction after leaving here, you might give her a berth on your ship.'

'Supposing I am ever allowed to leave here,' Kit remarked. 'And do you suppose Madeleine will wish to come? She does have a husband and children of her own, you know. Besides, what will Louise say? Won't *she* wish to be the new mistress of Vergée d'Or? Supposing Richilde isn't interested.'

Etienne frowned at him. 'I don't think Richilde enters into the matter, Kit. She has chosen to live with a black man, and I understand that she is unlikely to change her mind. As for Louise, well, she is a dear thing, but I will confess to you that I married her during a period of despair, when I doubted I should ever see Vergée d'Or again. Besides, that dragon of a mother of hers . . . but that is in the past. The fact is that she is not really the right material to be the mistress of Vergée d'Or. Madeleine will be happy to come. I have told her that she can bring the children, and I can tell you that she is virtually estranged from that English boor of a husband she has. It is my ambition, Kit, as far as it can be done, to restore Vergée d'Or as it was in our childhood, when we first came here. I meant to discuss the matter with you, in fact. I should also like Annette to return here.'

'Annette?' But what was so absurd about that? Had he not suggested she return often enough? But Annette, part of a society ruled by Pauline LeClerc and Louise de Mortmain?

'I do not see it could do her any harm,' Etienne said. 'This is, after all, her home. And if the chateau is rebuilt on somewhat different lines then there will be nothing in the building to remind her of that night. She is my sister, Kit, and although I am eternally grateful to you for looking after her all of these years, yet the ultimate responsibility must be mine.' He turned his head as another hussar appeared, then half a dozen more, guiding their mounts with some urgency through the tangled rubble and stone. 'What news?'

'Blacks approach,' said the lieutenant in command. 'Armed?'

The boy nodded, led his men towards the approaching troops.

'We'd best rejoin the military,' Etienne decided.

Kit followed him back along the road, wondering if Etienne intended to have a regiment of soldiers stationed permanently on the plantation to protect him. But LeClerc had also taken the news seriously enough, had formed his men into two squares, with the field guns between, and had taken himself and his small cavalry force within the lines of bayonets. Here Etienne and Kit joined him.

'You know these people,' LeClerc said. 'Will they charge, or engage in musketry?'

Kit pointed. 'I do not think they mean either.' For the approaching column of blacks, and it was several hundred strong, was carrying a white flag.

'Well, well,' LeClerc said. 'A pleasant surprise. You'll accompany me, Captain Hamilton.' The square opened, and he walked his horse forward, his aide-de-camp and Kit behind him, together with a trumpeter; Etienne preferred to remain within the safety of the French ranks.

Kit could not help but glance curiously at Palourdes, who would know as well as anyone about last night. But the man's thin features were expressionless as he concentrated on the coming encounter. Presumably, such ability to separate work from play in the mind was an asset for any man. But Kit realised he was discovering a powerful dislike for the unsuspecting soldier, who had the use of Seraphine whenever he chose, games apart.

The black soldiers advanced to within fifty feet of the little group of horsemen, then their leader came forward, accompanied by a single aide, bearing the white flag. The Negro was vaguely familiar – he was tall and thin and sad of expression – but Kit could not remember his name.

'We seek the French commander,' he said, in good French.

'I am he,' LeClerc said. 'Your name?'

'I am Louis-Pierre, General in the army of General Toussaint L'Ouverture.'

'L'Ouverture?'

· 'It is a title given to the General, monsieur,' Louis-Pierre said. 'Following his victories against the British.'

'I see. And your purpose?'

'We acknowledge the flag of France, monsieur. We will not fight against it. We have come to place ourselves under your command.'

'Indeed? General Toussaint has sent you?'

Louis-Pierre shook his head. 'It is our decision, monsieur.'

'Ah. Well, it has been a wise decision. Tell your men to pile their arms, Louis-Pierre.'

Louis-Pierre hesitated. 'We have come to serve, Your Excellency. Not to surrender.'

'If you will serve me, Louis-Pierre, you must first learn to obey me. Now tell your people to pile their arms.'

Another hesitation, then Louis-Pierre turned and gave the necessary orders to his men.

'Call up the guards,' LeClerc said to his trumpeter, who immediately gave a blast on his bugle. The French soldiers formed column and marched forward, one regiment to either side of the blacks, who watched them with interest. But by now all their muskets and swords and spears had been piled, and they had resumed their ranks.

'We await your orders, Your Excellency,' Louis-Pierre said.

111

'Yes,' LeClerc said. He turned to Palourdes. 'Every tenth man will be hanged,' he said. 'Starting with this insolent fellow.'

'You cannot do that,' Kit protested. 'These people came of their own free will, to serve with you.'

'They came to me as a result of my proclamation, Captain Hamilton,' LeClerc said. 'A proclamation which also pronounced that any black man bearing arms would be treated as an enemy. These men came bearing arms.' He gave a brief smile. 'But I am being generous. I am not hanging them all. The rest will be put to work, on rebuilding Cap François.'

Kit stared at him in horror, then at Louis-Pierre, whose hands were being tied behind his back while he gazed at his captors in consternation. He suddenly realised that this was, indeed, Annette's home.

'Louis-Pierre?' Toussaint asked. 'Can it be true?'

Suddenly, Richilde thought, he looked old. He had always *been* old, in relation to those he commanded, in his outlook on life. But it had been the age of wisdom, and authority. No suggestion of debility had ever entered into it. Even his short leg had never seemed anything more serious than a characteristic. But now his shoulders were hunched, and that brilliant brain seemed to have gone, if not dull, into retreat.

But then, she thought, are we not all dull, and tired, and old? I am old. I am thirty-four years old. I seek peace and domestic bliss, with my common-law husband, not another long season of trekking through the jungle. And even six and seven years ago, when she had crawled these treacherous paths, and had known the happiness of superb health and total optimism, she had yet dreamed of an end to it all, of the building period which would follow the expulsion of the British. The building period! Their greatest achievement had been the total destruction of Cap François.

Did Henry regret that? She did not think so, however he might have regretted her tears. But they had not affected his resolve. She was beginning to realise that nothing, save his own will, would ever affect Henry's resolve. But, as she watched him standing beside Toussaint and Dessalines, in a forest clearing as he had done so often in the past, even he looked tired. It was difficult to suppose that giant frame, those magnificent muscles, ever ageing. But he, too, was thirty-four. And he too had dreamed of building.

Unlike Dessalines. The bull-man was the only one of them who appeared utterly happy. *He* had been the one left adrift by the British evacuation, the speedy termination of the war with the mulattos in the south, with the Spaniards in the east. Fighting, murder, and destruction were the only arts he understood. They were his gods. She had a sudden, frightful sensation that in his arrival in St Domingue, only months before the rebellion had commenced, and on the very day that James Ogé had stepped off the ship on to the giddy path to destruction, he was perhaps an incarnation of Damballah Oueddo himself, come to exhort his people to fight, and fight, because he was the god of war.

'Bah,' he now said. 'Louis-Pierre is a fool. He always was a fool. Surrendering. How could he do that? Why did you not command him, Toussaint?'

'How could I command him otherwise?' Toussaint asked. 'Him, or any of them? Any of you? For ten years I have told them we fought for France. Now France has come to us. And we have rejected her.' His eyes, so full of sadness, rested on Henry Christophe.

'And you still think I was wrong?' Henry asked. 'After Louis-Pierre?'

'Henry was right,' Dessalines shouted. 'There can be no peace between us and the white people. I say, let us kill all the white people.' As usual when in his most declamatory style, his gaze rested on Richilde. 'Lead your people, Toussaint. Command us to war. We wait only the word.'

'What people?' Toussaint asked. He looked around the clearing, at the four hundred or so blue coated men who waited there. They were well armed, carried muskets and bayonets and filled cartridge belts; they were his personal bodyguard. There were perhaps another two thousand men, the regiments commanded by Dessalines and the garrison who had followed Henry from Cap François, scattered about the forest in various encampments. But there was only a handful of them, and they had no cannon. And a week in this forest would rip those smart jackets and breeches to rags, as Richilde well knew.

'Then make peace with the French,' she said.

Their heads turned.

'Spoken like a white woman,' Dessalines sneered. 'You wish to see us all hanged.'

'Why should LeClerc negotiate a peace with me now, madame?' Toussaint asked. 'He must know my forces are scattered, my people divided against themselves, between those who wish peace, and those who would fight.' Once again he looked at his men.

'Why must he *know* that?' Richilde demanded. 'He has not been a month in St Domingue. What can he have learned in that time? He has learned that Henry, your military governor of Cap François, Toussaint, preferred to burn the city and withdraw his men into the forest rather than surrender. And he has learned that another, small, body of your people *has* surrendered, and he has hanged a tenth of them. He must know that you are angry about that, and he must now be awaiting your attack. And he must expect that you can still muster ten, twenty, thirty thousand men to lead against him. He has Rigaud and Petion with him. They will have told him all about your defeat of the British. Dare he risk a campaign such as that?'

Toussaint stroked his chin.

'If you were to negotiate from strength,' she said.

114

'*Pretend* to negotiate from strength, at the least. Make him believe that you command a vast army out here, that the reason you have not yet attacked him is because you have been waiting for all your troops to assemble, that you are offering him one chance to make an honourable peace, or you will launch a war against him even more terrible than you launched against the British . . . he must agree to negotiate then.'

'She wishes us to surrender,' Dessalines growled.

'I am trying to save lives,' Richilde said. 'All of our lives.'

'And you are speaking sound sense,' Toussaint said. 'In any event, it is our only hope. I will go to this LeClerc, this brother-in-law of the great Bonaparte, and . . .'

'Never,' Henry said.

Toussaint looked at him.

'He would seize you and hang you, on the spot,' Henry said. 'If you are determined to negotiate, then I am the man to do it. I burned Cap François. I am the one with whom he first negotiated. He can resume negotiations, with me.'

'And do you not suppose he will hang *you*, on the spot?'

Henry shrugged. 'I am a soldier,' he said. 'I am *a* general, not *the* General. I expect to die, one day, in your service.'

'Neither of you will go,' Richilde said.

Once again the heads turned as they looked at her.

'*I* will go,' she said. 'They certainly will not hang me. And both my brother and my cousin are with the French. I will go, and speak with them on your, on our, behalves. I will be able to secure the best terms, and I will know whether or not they are to be trusted.'

'You?' Toussaint asked. 'But madame, those white people hate you more than they hate us.'

'I will go,' she said. 'And bring you peace.'

Henry had allowed her to pack a box before leaving Cap François, and thus she was able to dress herself with some elegance, but there was little she could do about her toilette save brush her hair very carefully – it remained very long, contained only the slightest wave – wash her face, clean her nails, and shelter the whole beneath a broad-brimmed straw hat. Shoes were obviously impractical for the journey she had to make, but she did not think she could approach the French army barefoot – so she wore her boots. If they made an incongruous adjunct to her gown, she supposed they could expect her to look incongruous. And she rode astride; it was too long since she had ridden side saddle.

Henry himself accompanied her and Aimee to the forest fringe, inside Vergée d'Or, whence they could see the white tents of the French encampment, even distantly hear the bugle calls. The young Negress had insisted on going with her. 'You are the General's woman,' she had said. 'You can't walk before them white folk without a maid.'

'If anything should happen to you,' Henry said, 'I will slaughter every Frenchman I can find, for the rest of my life. I swear this. You may tell them.'

She squeezed his hand. 'Nothing will happen to me, Henry. I will bring you peace.'

Yet her heart pounded as she rode out of the trees and on to the so well remembered road leading towards the destroyed city. Memory went back all of eleven years, to the day she and Annette had walked into Cap François, the only survivors of the Vergée d'Or massacre. Then they had been welcomed – but on the white people's terms. Now she was a self professed enemy of the French, Christophe's woman.

'Halt there,' came a shout, and she reined her horse, watched the blue-clad infantrymen starting up from their stand beside the road. She waited, as they approached her, in the beginning looking past her for

116

any sign of blacks, and only slowly taking her and her servant in.

'My God, a white woman,' someone said.

'No, a mulatto,' said another. 'White women don't have brown skins.'

The sergeant stood before her, frowning at her, appreciating her grey eyes. 'My God,' he said. 'It *is* a white woman. It is . ... you are the white nigger,' he accused.

'I am Madame Richilde de Mortmain,' she said carefully. 'I have come to speak with General LeClerc.'

'You have come to surrender,' he said.

'I have come to speak with General LeClerc,' she repeated, keeping her voice even.

'You'll get down,' he commanded.

She hesitated, then dismounted, covering her legs as well as she could. But not well enough. His eyes gleamed, and he licked his lips.

'She's the white nigger, lads,' he said to his men. 'She lies with the blacks. What do you think? Shall we see what she offers?'

Richilde stepped back, tension flooding her body in a deluge of sweat. 'I am an emissary from General Toussaint,' she gasped. 'If you touch me . . .'

They surged forward, two seizing her arms, the others reaching for her thighs to lift her from the ground, while the sergeant unbuttoned his breeches. Behind her she heard Aimee scream as she was dragged from the saddle. She wanted to scream herself, and could find no breath. This was August 1791 all over again – but these were white men.

'Stop there! Attention!' The voice was brisk, and hard . . . and most magnificently familiar. The hands grasping Richilde let her go, and she struck the earth with a thud which left her for a moment incapable of movement. But Colonel Boyer had already dismounted, and was reaching for her hand, while his

117

escort glared at the abashed guard. 'Madame de Mortmain,' he said, and gently pulled her to her feet.

She gasped for breath. 'Colonel,' she said, 'you have my utmost gratitude.'

'You took a grave risk,' he said. Then the hard, strong, handsome features suddenly smiled. 'You are a woman who likes risks. You have come to surrender?'

She shook her head. 'I have come to see General LeClerc, with a message from General Toussaint.'

He frowned at her. 'Toussaint sent *you*, to do his work? Christophe permitted this?'

Her chin came up. 'We are all one, in Toussaint's army, Colonel. And I am best suited for such a mission.'

'Even at risk of rape?'

Her turn to smile. 'At least I was sure I would not be hanged.' She looked round in alarm. 'My maid!'

Two of the soldiers still held Aimee's arms, but now they released her beneath Boyer's glare, allowed her to scramble back into the saddle, endeavour to straighten at once her bonnet and her gown. One of the men grinned at her as he handed her up her parasol.

Boyer's face remained sombre, as he assisted Richilde into the saddle, carefully looked away as she swung her leg across. 'I would not count on your sex, madame, to preserve you from *that*. Not in this army.' He remounted himself. 'Make way there,' he commanded.

The guard stood to attention, staring at Richilde, with hungry, unsatisfied eyes, while Boyer's staff fell in behind him.

'I had counted on the presence of my brother, and my cousin,' she explained, as they walked their horses down the road. 'Are they not here?'

'Your cousin is, certainly, madame. Your brother has departed.' His mouth twisted. 'He quarrelled with our commanding General. He could not stomach the hanging of men who had surrendered in good faith. Well,

118

neither can most of us. But we have taken an oath. Captain Hamilton had not. He also . . .' Another twist of the lips. 'Did not find General LeClerc's society to the best of taste. I am sorry, madame.'

Not half so sorry as I am, she thought, as they approached the camp. She had counted on Kit's presence, as a stabilising, non-emotional factor. Now she would have to rely on Etienne. Etienne, of all people.

But she had volunteered to carry out this mission, and it was her duty, whether she succeeded in it or not, to obtain as much information as she could for Toussaint. Thus she looked at the encamped army with interest: the orderly rows of tents, the men drilling, the horsemen practising charging and reassembling in the open space under the city walls. This was an immense, and well disciplined force, she realised. And an utterly confident one. It was certainly larger than the army the British had attempted their conquest with – and they had come uncomfortably close to success.

And supporting them, as with the British, was a fleet of war. She looked out at the three deckers and the frigates and the transports, riding quietly at anchor. At least a hundred of them, altogether. They would not be able to remain there once the storm season started. But that was not until June, and it was only March.

Closer at hand, she looked at the beach, and two armed sentries patrolling there, and the half dozen people swimming, and playing in the shallows, the morning sun gleaming from their crystal white bodies. Only black people had ever swum on that beach in the past. But these were . . . Her head jerked.

'The General's lady is very fond of sea bathing,' Boyer observed. 'Early in the morning, before the sun becomes hot enough to scorch her complexion.'

'The General's lady?' She stared. Because she realised that all of the six women were white, or at least pale-skinned mulattos, and that all of them were quite naked, and apparently unashamed – certainly they

119

could be in no doubt that from the road, however the sentries might prevent intruders approaching, every aspect of their femininity was clearly visible. 'My God!'

'Indeed,' he agreed. 'Should you choose to look closely, madame, you will also discover your cousin-in-law, the new Citizeness Mortmain, as well as several other wives of our officers. And mistresses, of course,' he added. 'As I said, your brother found this new French society distasteful.'

She looked at him as they rode past the swimmers and into the camp itself, immediately attracting stares, and gathering groups of men, and a great deal of comment. 'And do you not find it distasteful, Colonel Boyer?'

Boyer returned her gaze. 'St Domingue is my home, madame. I would sit down with the devil himself, or his succubus, to regain my place in it.'

They approached a cluster of tents, set apart from the main army, and very heavily guarded. Here Boyer dismounted, and assisted Richilde down also, before in turn giving his hand to Aimee. 'You'll remain here,' he said, and walked away from her, towards a cluster of officers seated or standing a few yards away.

'Man, but I am frightened,' Aimee confessed. 'You know that I am frightened, madame? You think they going hang us?'

'No,' Richilde said. 'Is my hat straight?'

'Well . . .' Aimee held the brim to tilt it back. 'That is better. But madame . . . you ain't afraid?'

I am terrified, Richilde thought. Terrified at the thought that I belong to such a race, such a nation – even half of me. 'Of course I am not afraid,' she said. 'They are human beings, like us.'

She looked up as Boyer returned, now accompanied by a tall, saturnine looking young man, who wore a moustache. 'You are Christophe's woman?'

'I am Madame de Mortmain,' Richilde said.

'This is Major Palourdes,' Boyer explained. 'The commanding General's aide-de-camp.'

Richilde inclined her head. She did not see any point in embarrassing them both by offering him her hand.

Palourdes looked her up and down, slowly. 'By God,' he said. 'I have heard much about you, citizeness. But perhaps none of the tales do you justice. The General will receive you.'

He turned to lead her. She glanced at Boyer.

'I will remain with your servant, madame,' Boyer said.

For which she supposed she must be grateful; she would have been happier had he remained at *her* side.

'I understand that my cousin, Monsieur de Mortmain, is with your army,' she said conversationally, hurrying to keep pace with Palourdes's long strides, terribly aware of the officers emerging from their tents to stare at her, and once again of the comments with which she was surrounded.

'Citizen Mortmain is out visiting the ruins of his old plantation,' Palourdes said.

'*His* old plantation?'

They had halted before the largest of all the tents, before which there were two guards, and a staff bearing the tricolour. 'You will wait here, citizeness,' Palourdes said, and ducked his head to enter the doorway.

Richilde reached into her reticule for a fan, became increasingly aware of the heat as the sun rose behind her.

'There's a handsome one,' the first guard remarked. 'Do you suppose she's for the General?'

'Wouldn't surprise me,' said the second. 'He never gets tired, does he?'

She flushed, and bit her lip, and turned away, to watch Generals Rigaud and Petion hurrying towards her.

'Madame de Mortmain.' Rigaud raised her hand to

121

his lips. 'A happier meeting than our last, I would hope.'

'So would I, General,' she agreed.

'Madame.' Petion also kissed her hand.

'Citizens.' Palourdes stood in the doorway of the tent.

Rigaud nodded, and Richilde went forward, having to duck her own head to enter, pausing just inside the doorway to look at LeClerc, who was seated behind a trestle table piled high with plans, mostly of streets and houses and churches – clearly he was already contemplating rebuilding Cap François.

She was immediately struck by his youth, and also by the coldness of his face, as he raised his head to look at her in turn. 'Christophe's woman,' he remarked.

Richilde decided against offering him her hand, either; besides, she was too afraid he might notice it was shaking. She stood before the desk. 'I am Richilde de Mortmain.'

LeClerc glanced at the two mulatto officers. 'I have summoned you,' he said, 'to give me your opinions on what this woman has to say. Have either of you ever met her before?'

'We have met Madame de Mortmain,' Rigaud said.

'And you have no doubt that this woman *is* Citizeness Mortmain?' LeClerc asked.

'Of course not,' Petion said, adding, 'sir,' as an afterthought.

LeClerc stared at him for a moment, then looked at Richilde again. 'I am informed that you have a message for me,' he said. 'From the black rebels.'

Richilde met his gaze; she was well aware that only boldness would serve her here – he must never even suspect the butterflies in her stomach. 'I have a message, General, from the Governor General of St Domingue.'

His head came up, and he frowned at her.

'General Toussaint,' she said, 'holds a commission as

122

Commander-in-chief of St Domingue, given him by Monsieur Santhonax, in the name of the National Convention in Paris.'

'The National Convention,' LeClerc said contemptuously. 'History has passed you by, citizeness.'

'Perhaps you would be good enough to let me finish, uninterrupted,' Richilde suggested. 'Or I had best return to my people.'

'*Your* people?' LeClerc commented. But as she would not lower her gaze, he shrugged. 'Continue.'

'Acting on that commission,' Richilde said, 'General Toussaint waged war on the British, and drove them from St Domingue. He then . . .' she glanced at the two mulattos, 'completed the reduction of those who would not recognise the authority of the Convention, and then evicted the Spaniards from the eastern half of the island, to complete the conquest of the entire area of St Domingue, for France. He then despatched letters to Paris, informing the government of what he had accomplished, and, as Monsieur Santhonax had died, further informing the government that he proposed to remain in command of St Domingue, as Governor General, until other arrangements could be made. The then government, to which I understand the First Consul was already a party, confirmed these arrangements.'

'The First Consul has now changed his plans,' LeClerc said. But he spoke more quietly, was obviously interested in what she had to say. She felt an almost exhilarating surge of confidence.

'As he is entitled to do, General,' she said. 'Although it would have been wisest, as well as more polite, to inform General Toussaint by letter rather than by presenting him with a series of ultimata, or by hanging his people.'

LeClerc leaned forward again. 'The so-called General Christophe, your *lover*, citizeness, began hostilities, by burning Cap François.'

She did not even flush, any more. 'General Christophe conceived your demand of him as an act of war. So does General Toussaint, just as he considers your hanging of General Louis-Pierre and sixty-four of his men as an act of aggression. The General is constrained, however, by his honour. He swore on oath to Commissioner Santhonax to uphold the government of France, and he considers himself bound by that oath. He therefore would be most reluctant to take up arms against you. If he were forced to do that, General, then be sure the entire country would rally to him. In case you are unaware of it, General Toussaint is regarded almost as a god by his people. Certainly as their hero. You may ask these gentlemen if that is not true.'

LeClerc glanced at Rigaud.

'That is certainly so, General,' the mulatto said.

'He also,' Richilde said, 'commands an army of fifty thousand well armed men.'

'*Fifty* thousand? That is impossible. How does he feed such a number, in those forests?'

Richilde shrugged. 'If you would care to mount your horses, General, and accompany me back to our encampment, I will show you.'

LeClerc glared at her, then again looked at Rigaud.

'There are certainly at least fifty thousand blacks capable of bearing arms, General,' Rigaud said. 'Logistics for such a force, in St Domingue, would be difficult, certainly. But by no means impossible. These people need very little to survive.'

LeClerc's stare returned to Richilde.

'General Toussaint,' she went on, beginning now to sense victory, 'has been assembling his people these last two weeks. But as you say, General Rigaud, feeding such an army is a difficult business. Therefore General Toussaint must present you with the following choices: one, that you recognise him as Governor General of St Domingue, his officers as appointed by the French government, through him, and his people as loyal subjects of the Consulate. This is all he asks. He will then be willing to retire from his position, handing it over to you, and his Generals will also retire, as will his people surrender their arms and return to their peaceful pursuits. It follows of course that you will give a guarantee for the lives and safety of the black people of St Domingue.'

'You mentioned two alternatives, madame.'

Another victory. She smiled at him. 'That you refuse the above terms, and therefore will have to be regarded as an enemy, and destroyed, as were the British destroyed.'

LeClerc gazed at her for several seconds, and then allowed his eyes to wander up and down her body. 'And suppose,' he said at last, 'that I make no reply at all, but merely hand you over to my men for their amusement, before I hang you?'

The crude threat did not even make her sweat. 'If I am not back at General Toussaint's encampment by this evening, with your reply, he will assume that you *have* replied, by a declaration of war.'

LeClerc continued to study her for several more seconds. 'You are a courageous woman,' he said at last.

Richilde waited. Now that she had won, her knees suddenly felt weak.

'Well,' LeClerc said. 'My mission is to pacify St Domingue, and return it to French control. Clearly if that can be done without waging a major campaign, the First Consul will be well pleased. Your General Toussaint may have his titles, as may his officers.'

'And his people will have their freedom.' Richilde insisted.

'May I point out that there is a great deal of reconstruction necessary, Citizeness?' He smiled. 'Rebuilding Cap François, for a start.'

'You have but to *employ* the Negroes, General.'

He nodded. 'As you say. They shall be free.'

It had all been so very simple, she thought. Too simple by far.

'Then you will draw up a treaty of peace, to this effect, General?'

'What, can this black fellow read?'

Richilde refused to lose her temper. 'Yes, monsieur,' she said. 'He can read. I would like to take the treaty with me, when I leave.'

LeClerc shrugged. 'You shall have your treaty. Major Palourdes, you'll summon my clerks.'

'I should also like the treaty, when it has been written out and I have had a chance to study it,' Richilde said, 'read aloud to all your people.'

LeClerc frowned at her. 'Citizeness? One would almost suppose that you do not trust me.'

'General LeClerc,' Richilde said, at last allowing her face to relax into the semblance of a smile. 'I do not trust you.'

126

Chapter 4

THE BETRAYAL

Toussaint agreed to an armistice, having secured for himself and his generals the preservation of their military ranks and privileges. He then handed over the administration to LeClerc and retired to his home on the west coast. French diplomacy and commonsense had accomplished what several European armies had been unable to do – except that it was never Napoleonic policy to rely on diplomacy alone. Commonsense, certainly; in the dead of night, hardly a month after the capitulation, Toussaint and his family were arrested by French soldiers and taken on board a waiting warship. They were carried direct to France, where the Negro leader was not even granted the privilege of an interview with the man who had outwitted him. He was confined in a prison in the French Alps, left a winter in an unheated, insanitary cell, encouraged to die.

'His Excellency, Citizen General Pierre Toussaint, and Citizeness Toussaint,' bellowed the major-domo.

Toussaint limped forward, Clotilde, several inches taller at his side. The huge meadow, which had so rapidly been converted into a lawn, was packed with French officers and their ladies, and with French soldiers, too, standing guard around the edges – for beyond the fencing there was a huge crowd of black people, gawking at the whites, and at their leaders, waiting to mingle on equal terms with these people from across the ocean. Almost they seemed to steam, for it was a very hot afternoon – and promised eventually to be a wet one, as enormous black clouds drifted in from the sea.

Richilde, standing next to Henry, felt her fingers sweating inside her gloves. She had naturally put on her very best gown – but it was in a fashion several years out of date, and had been run up by Negro seamstresses during her sojourn in Cap François as the Military Governor's lady. Just as her hair was loose. Now she was about to meet high society straight from Paris, dressed in the very latest creations, with their hair a mass of ringlets and oddly shaped chignons – and at their head would be the sister of the First Consul himself.

She kept her gaze fixed on the enormous back of Dessalines, immediately in front of her. But Dessalines was now moving forward.

'His Excellency Citizen General Jean-Jacques Dessalines,' the major-demo bellowed.

Richilde watched the bull-man facing LeClerc. Pauline LeClerc was just beyond her husband, and could not be clearly seen as yet. But Richilde wondered what she made of the grim figure in front of her – and what he, with his oft repeated chant to destroy all the whites, made of her.

'His Excellency Citizen General Henri Christophe,' the major-domo shouted. 'And Citizeness Mortmain.'

The field became an immense *rustle*, as heads turned and people, mainly women, crowded forward. This was the moment for which they had been waiting, their first sighting of the woman who had spent ten years living with the blacks. Richilde's knees felt weak, and she could only move by being carried along on Henry's arm.

LeClerc smiled at her as he bent over her hand.

'Well, citizeness,' he said. 'Your moment of triumph. I would have you meet my wife.'

Richilde was completely taken aback by the utter indecency of Pauline LeClerc's gown, for a moment could find no words. While the Frenchwoman looked Henry up and down before turning her glittering gaze on Richilde. 'The white Negress,' she remarked. 'But you are not *such* a fool, are you, Citizeness.' Another glance at Henry's giant frame. 'I look forward to having a conversation with you, Citizeness. And with your paramour, to be sure.' She smiled. 'I have already met your brother.'

'She has insulted you,' Henry muttered, in English. 'I should like to wring her neck.'

'I doubt she converses with anyone any differently,' Richilde pointed out, determined to have nothing spoil this afternoon. And now they were before Admiral Villaret-Joyeuse, who in the strongest contrast to the LeClercs was clearly a gentleman, before she was shaking hands again with Rigaud and Petion, and finding herself face to face with Major Palourdes.

'You'll take a glass of champagne, General, citizeness?' He ushered a girl forward. 'My wife wishes to meet you.'

Amazingly, Seraphine Palourdes gave a brief curtsey. Richilde was once again taken aback by the shapeless gown, as well as its transparency, which left nothing to the imagination, and revealed that Seraphine Palourdes was a remarkably beautiful young woman.

'It is my pleasure, Citizeness Palourdes,' Richilde said. 'And have you also an acquaintance with my brother?'

To her surprise, Seraphine shot her a quick glance, and a trace of colour appeared in those pale cheeks.

While Palourdes gave one of his sardonic smiles. 'My wife is acquainted with Captain Hamilton, citizeness. During his brief sojourn with our army, he made himself popular with the ladies.'

129

Richilde raised her eyebrows. She could not imagine Kit playing the gallant. But Madame Palourdes's flush certainly suggested that something had happened. And why not, she thought, she is a most delicious creature.

'Well, madame. General Christophe, I am sure we have met before, on Vergée d'Or.'

'Jacqueline!' Richilde cried. 'But how good to see you.' Her reaction was instinctive, for all the studied insult her old friend had just attempted to offer Henry. And the mulatto had clearly prospered; she was dressed after the fashion of her new white friends. 'How splendid you look.'

'As do you, Richilde,' Jacqueline acknowledged. 'The very picture of strength and health. When you begin to dress more fashionably, you will be the toast of St Domingue.'

'More fashionably? Oh . . .' she glanced at Henry. 'I do not think these modern gowns would become me.'

'What nonsense.' Jacqueline said. 'I am sure General Christophe would appreciate it.'

Henry merely stared at her. But her gaze was drifting past his left shoulder.

'Richilde! My dear Richilde.' Richilde turned, heart pounding, gazed at Etienne. An Etienne as florid and as prosperously dressed as she had ever known him, from snowy cravat to polished black boots, and with a plump giggle of a woman on his arm. 'Have you no kiss for me?' he asked.

Richilde realised that her right arm had been released. She looked over her shoulder, but Henry had already turned his back, and was walking into the throng.

'I observe that merely being called 'General' does not necessarily give a man manners,' Etienne remarked.

'For which you should be thankful, 'Tienne,', Richilde said. 'He has left, undoubtedly, to prevent himself from strangling you on the spot.'

'Eh? Eh?' Etienne lost some of his rich colour. 'Does

he still bear a grudge for a whipping? Are not those days gone forever, Richilde?'

'He mourns his only child,' Richilde said evenly. 'As do I. You have not introduced me to *Citizeness* Mortmain.'

'Because you already know her, my dear,' Etienne said. 'Louise, you remember my cousin Richilde?'

'Of course I do, 'Tienne,' Louise giggled. 'I was but twelve when you last saw me, madame. Citizeness,' she hastily added.

Richilde frowned at her. 'Not the child with the hot water?'

Louise gave another giggle.

'We have a great deal to talk about,' Etienne said. 'Of course it cannot be done here. But as soon as Madeleine arrives, and Annette . . .'

'Madeleine? Annette? Annette is returning to St Domingue?'

'On Kit's next voyage. He promised me. It is my intention to reunite the family, rebuild Vergée d'Or, recommence living, if you will. And of course, my dear, there is always a place for you there, if . . .' he paused, deliberately.

She gazed into his eyes, coldly calculating, as they had always been. 'If I divest myself of Henry,' she said. 'But I regard myself as married to him, 'Tienne. As you say, it is something we shall have to discuss.'

'Now, you listen to me,' Etienne began, and checked as a large drop of water fell on his hand. 'My God!'

The black cloud had arrived overhead, and a moment later the rain was cascading down, only less heavy than the storm which had overturned her coach on that ride to Rio Negro, so many years ago. Richilde gathered her skirts and ran for the few trees at the edge of the meadow, was rescued by Henry, who had taken off his uniform jacket to hold over her. She looked back, at Louise de Mortmain jumping up and down as her gown seemed to dissolve, and then beyond, at Pauline

131

LeClerc, gazing up at the heavens with a bemused expression, while rouge ran down her cheeks like a pink stream. Then the Commanding General's wife gave a peal of laughter, and with a single movement tore off her gown, to go dancing through the rain. Immediately she was joined by several of her ladies.

Richilde looked up at Henry, who held her closer; water dripped from his chin on to her face. 'Those,' he said, 'are the people who would rule us.'

'Cap François,' Annette de Mortmain cried. 'Oh, Cap François. How I have dreamed of returning here. How I have wondered if I ever should.' Tears rolled down her cheeks.

Kit had to leave her side to con his ship into the harbour, and find a berth amidst the French fleet which clustered at anchor. It seemed like only yesterday that he had left here, in a rage, to sail north. Because, in seafaring terms, it was only yesterday. Had he been in that much of a hurry to divest himself of the woman to whom he had volunteered his life? And in exchange for what? If he dreamed, it was of a whore, to whom all men were but playthings. In affairs of the heart he was surely the most unfortunate of men.

Yet he knew that he would be also the most relieved man on earth when Annette was finally returned to her brother's care. And there could be no conscience involved here; she had been overjoyed at the idea. That the French would eventually regain control of St Domingue had been *her* dream for eleven years; now that it had happened she had been almost sane on the voyage. He had feared, of course, her reactions as she had approached her homeland once again, but in fact she merely seemed delighted, and if he watched her carefully as they rowed ashore, she continued to gaze at the new city with rapt interest. And in truth LeClerc had done wonders in hardly more than a month rebuilding the city. Everywhere there were black labourers

132

scurrying to and fro, supervised by French architects and overseen by French soldiers. Here was the past coming back to control the present. Annette clapped her hands in delight. 'Of course,' she reassured herself, 'we could not hang them *all*, Kit. They are needed for labour.'

But LeClerc had done wonders in more than mere architecture. He had succeeded in his mission. How, Kit found it difficult to understand. Yet Etienne had been quite definite in his letter. Toussaint had accepted honourable terms of capitulation, and St Domingue was once again a peaceful French colony. Kit supposed that had to be one of the most extraordinary coups that history would ever record.

He found them a carriage for hire, and hurried Annette out of town. He had no wish to encounter either Pauline LeClerc or any of her minions, or any of his black friends. Not with Annette on his arm.

She peered out of the window as the coach rumbled towards Vergée d'Or. 'I did not expect ever to see it again,' she said, tears still rolling down her cheeks. 'Oh, how fortunate I am.'

Madeleine was there to greet them, as statuesquely and blondely beautiful as ever in her mid forties, embracing Annette tenderly as she gazed above her head at Kit, who could only shrug optimistically. While Etienne and Louise fussed.

'You will find it all rather primitive at the moment,' Etienne explained. 'We have only this wooden cottage, for the time being, and that is all. But it is quite comfortable.' He showed them up the steps and on to the shallow verandah; behind there was a living area from which extended a corridor to the three bedrooms. 'But of course our first priority is to harvest a crop and have it ground, to earn some income. Do you know, Kit, I have ridden over the plantation, and I think it is going to be a good crop. You've no desire to abandon the sea, and return to planting?'

133

Kit stood at the rail, hands on hips, looking out at the site of the chateau. Because it was no more than a site, now; Etienne had been busy here, too, and all the stone had been accumulated into a huge dump some yards away, while the skeleton of the grand staircase had been pulled down. Now only the foundations remained, and the cellars, like huge caves in the ground. And the work proceeded; even as he watched, a gang of labourers under the supervision of a white overseer were picking away at the loose stone on the patio. And the overseer carried a whip. Indeed had the past returned, except that surely . . . he turned to his cousin. 'How much do you have to pay these people to work for you?'

'Ah,' Etienne said with a grin. 'I am not actually paying them anything. They are a labour battalion lent to me by LeClerc.'

'You mean the government is paying them?'

'In kind. The government supplies them with food, and clothing where it is absolutely necessary.'

'But not money?'

'Now really, Kit, what would be the point in giving these people money? They would only buy strong spirits with it.'

'And they can leave this work whenever they choose?'

'Of course not. They have been conscripted as a labour battalion, as I said. To desert the battalion would be mutiny, and in the French army that is punishable by death.'

Kit stroked his chin. 'Then they are as much slaves as they ever were.'

'Well . . .' Etienne smiled. 'They know no other existence. And it is the only way to get them to work. The only way we are going to get the colony back on its feet.'

'What do the black leaders think about this?'

'I shouldn't think they think very much about anything.'

134

'The General did say that this Toussaint person made some remonstrances to him,' Madeleine said. 'But he was sent off with a flea in his ear.'

'Yes,' Kit said. 'And Richilde?'

Etienne and Madeleine exchanged glances.

'We have seen nothing of Richilde,' Madeleine said. 'She has not even come to call.'

'Perhaps she feels you should have called on her,' Kit suggested. 'And invited her to join you here. This is her home.'

'That is a debatable point,' Etienne said. 'I am Philippe's heir.'

'With a responsibility to care for his widow,' Kit said. 'I should have supposed it your duty to seek her out and offer her a home.'

'I'm afraid I take a different view. My responsibility towards Philippe's widow exists only as long as she remains a widow. Richilde considers herself married to this scoundrel Christophe, although they have certainly never entered a church together, except perhaps to loot it. There is no question of my having any legal responsibility towards her. But having made that clear, she is, of course, welcome here whenever she wishes, provided she comes alone.'

'I see,' Kit said again. 'Well, things seem to be working out for you very well, 'Tienne. I wish you success. But I do not think I wish to return to St Domingue to live. My home is in New York, my future is in America. Now I must leave you.'

'You'll not stay to supper, Kit?' Madeleine asked.

He shook his head. 'I have a deal to do.'

'Kit.' Annette held out both her hands. 'You are saying goodbye. How can I ever thank you.' But he was already an item in her past. What he might once have felt for her, what he might still feel for her, was irrelevant. He had kept her and fed her and clothed her for eleven years, against the moment she could resume her proper station. And that moment had arrived.

'But I should prefer you not to try,' Kit said.

'But you'll come to see me? Whenever you are in Cap François?'

'Whenever,' Kit agreed.

Etienne walked with him down the steps to the waiting gig. 'You are going to see Richilde?'

'She *is* my sister, 'Tienne.'

'Of course. I understand entirely. And I am glad of it. Kit . . .' he hesitated. 'I would not discuss this before the girls, but Richilde *is* more than welcome to make Vergée d'Or her home again.'

'On your terms,' Kit said.

'On the terms of the new colony of St Domingue,' Etienne said, gazing at him. 'It would be best if you could convince her of this, and convince her too that there is not too much time. Now is her last chance to make her choice. Either resume her proper station in life, or be condemned forever as a white nigger, doomed to suffer whatever . . . well, whatever vicissitudes of fortune lie ahead.'

Kit frowned. 'What are you saying, exactly?'

'What I have said.' He shook Kit's hand. 'As you value your sister, Kit, persuade her to come here, at the very earliest possible moment.'

Kit drew rein where the road – it was hardly more substantial than a cart track – sloped down to the little bay. He could hardly imagine anything so peaceful, the curving arms of white sand, built up against the ages old coral of the inner reef beyond, the swiftly changing colours of the sea, from white to a deepening shade of green before the blue was reached beyond the reef, the palisade of palm trees which separated the beach from the scrub behind, the breeze filtering off the ocean, and the little cottage nestling in the midst of the trees. Here he had left the hustle and bustle of the rest of the coast, that part nearest to Cap François, and thus more firmly under French control.

It was a scene entirely in keeping with his own mood.

He had only realised, these past few weeks, perhaps as late as last night, how all his life he had been straining, to be something or to escape something, or to possess something. Annette had been the end of that strain, as she had been the longest part of it, as her presence had dominated his life for ten years, as his love for her had slowly turned into bitter ashes in his throat. Now he, too, felt at peace.

As if he, or anyone in St Domingue, apparently, could ever truly feel at peace. What *had* Etienne been trying to hint?

A dog barked, and then showed itself from the far side of the hut, a large, shaggy mongrel. It kept its distance, but maintained its baying warning to its owners. Kit cupped his hands. 'Anyone home?' he shouted.

Richilde appeared on the little porch, drying her hands on the skirt of her gown. The true Richilde, he thought, wearing but a single garment, so that the morning sunlight outlined her legs, and with her hair loose and fluttering in the breeze – he had forgotten how long she had allowed it to grow. Just as he was inclined to forget with what strength and purpose she moved, what, indeed, strength and purpose flowed from her very being. He wondered what the reaction in New York or Boston would be were he to recommend to the good matrons that their daughters should all be sent into the woods in their early womanhood to survive as best they could, as a guarantee of future health and strength.

'Kit? Is it really you?' She hurried from the house. 'Down Beast. Away with you.'

Beast subsided, panting, and Kit dismounted to take his sister in his arms.

'Etienne told me you would be coming back,' Richilde said. 'Bringing Annette. I didn't believe him. I *couldn't* believe that Annette would really wish to come back here.'

He tethered his horse, walked beside her, hand in

hand, back to the porch. 'She wanted that more than anything else in the world.'

'So now at last you are rid of her.'

'Yes. I feel a strange sense, half of relief and half of, well . . . loneliness, I suppose. But also of distress, at what I see here.'

There was a hammock suspended from the porch uprights. Richilde sat down in it, began to swing, gently; Kit sat in the one straight chair. 'It is my fault,' she said.

'Your fault?'

'Well . . .' she shrugged. 'Henry wanted to fight them from the beginning, remember? I recommended peace. And I negotiated it for Pierre. I thought I was doing the right thing. Our people did not really wish to fight any more. Most important, Pierre did not wish to fight any more. And without him these people are nothing.' She sighed. 'But LeClerc outwitted me. All of us. Can you believe, that when he told us he intended to recruit a Negro force, we actually encouraged our people to volunteer? To be driven by whips to carry stones and plant cane.'

'And there is nothing you can do about it?'

'We have surrendered our weapons.'

'You did what you thought was best,' Kit said. 'You can have nothing to reproach yourself with. And you have at least stopped the killing. What does Henry think of it all?'

Again she shrugged. 'He fishes. He has built himself a boat, and goes fishing.'

'And leaves you here, alone?'

'What have I got to be afraid of, Kit? My notoriety does have some advantages. No one will ever lift a finger against the woman of General Christophe. But Henry . . .' she sighed. 'We had such dreams, Kit. Such dreams.'

'Of great armies, and splendid uniforms.'

'Of much more than that. Of making St Domingue

138

into a new country. Of showing the world what we could do, given the chance.'

'You identify yourself with these people?'

'They are *my* people, Kit.'

'Yet must you from time to time consider your own future. As you say, you had dreams. They were never practical, real prospects.'

'They were,' she said fiercely. 'They could have happened. If Toussaint had been ten years younger, perhaps. He is tired now, too tired. Or if Henry had somehow had some sort of an education.' She gave a twisted smile. 'That is our fault; he was our slave. If only one could have some glimpses, into the future.'

'It is not so opaque as all that,' he said. 'All the upheaval, the turmoil of the past few years, is now over and done with. Even in France it is done with. They may not have a king, any more, but they have a First Consul for life, who is more powerful than any king. And he has secured recognition by all the European powers, has ended the war ... Europe has reverted entirely to how it was twenty years ago, save that the old French aristocracy has been destroyed. A new one has already arisen. It is composed of people like LeClerc and his Pauline, but are they any more vulgar or indecent than the Mortmains or the Richelieus, or even the Bourbons themselves? So here on St Domingue too, it is over. The past has returned, and you may be sure its grip will be tightened, with every passing week.'

'Then that is a tragedy,' she said.

'All life is a tragedy, Richilde. We can only endeavour to make our way in its midst. It is your way that I want you to consider.'

'My way is Henry's way.'

'Sitting on an empty beach? You are not yet thirty-five years old. You have lived but half your life. You will spend the rest of it, here? Etienne offers you a home, and your proper place in society.'

'Etienne? I would rather be dead.'

139

He chewed his lip. 'Well, then . . . New York? I have a fine house there, Richilde. An empty house, now. And a fine, free life. An expanding one, too. Alexander is going to be Governor of the State, in a couple of years' time. And then, who knows. I think he even has the presidency in mind. He is handicapped, of course, by being born in Nevis, but I do not think that is an insuperable obstacle. Certainly he is well thought of. America is the country of the future, Richilde.' He held her hand. 'I sail at dusk. If you were to come with me, when you awake tomorrow morning St Domingue will be nothing more than a cloudbank on the horizon.'

'And Henry?'

Kit sighed. 'It will make things difficult. It will be difficult for him, as well, now he has had a taste of power, of being a general. But he is welcome, if he wishes to come.'

'He will never leave St Domingue,' she said. 'Or his people. The people he has led into battle, time and again. That is *too* difficult, Kit.'

'Well, then . . .'

'My place is at his side. He is my man, and where he goes, there will I go too.'

Yet she knew that Henry could not spend the rest of his life fishing. She waited on the beach to help him drag his pirogue up the sand. 'Kit was here today.'

Henry lifted a grouper from the bottom of the boat, walked towards the hut. 'A big one, eh? Food for two days. Kit? I'm sorry to have missed him.'

She walked behind him, bare toes sinking into the sand. He wore nothing but a pair of drawers; his uniform, carefully washed and pressed, hung on a hook inside their tiny bedroom. It was a memory of things past, of dreams once shared.

'As he was to miss you. He takes a gloomy look of the future.'

Henry sat in the hammock with a sigh. 'Don't we?'

140

'Well . . .' she sat beside him. 'Kit, as usual, is full of solutions.'

'He wants us to go to America?'

'Well . . . yes. Yes, he does. He does not trust the French. He feels we aren't safe, here. There is no slavery in New York, Henry. He will find you a place on board his ships, and we can be properly married, and . . .' she bit her lip as he looked at her. 'But St Domingue is your home.'

'I must stay,' he said. 'Because I too do not trust the French. I must stay, in case Toussaint once again has to call on me, and my soldiers.'

'And if he never does?'

He grinned. 'Then I will go fishing. And come back to you, to make love.'

But when they were finished, he looked deeply into her eyes. 'But if you wish to go, to America, Richilde, I will not stand in your way.'

'Do you wish me to go?' she asked.

'Half of my life would go with you.'

'Then I shall stay. And clean your fish. And make love. In any event, Kit has already left.'

Because what more, she wondered as she lay with her head on his arm, could a woman really want? A strong, resolute, utterly loving man, a quiet bay, no sound to disturb the evening save the ever present whisper of the surf, the rasp of the cicadas, the faint jingle of harnesses . . . she sat up, heart pounding, a tremendous gush of sweat pouring from her neck and shoulders, even as Beast barked.

Henry was also awake. 'Horsemen,' he said.

She got out of bed, ran to the window, peered into the night, saw the gleam of swords and muskets through the trees. 'Oh, my God,' she said. 'Oh, my God. Those are French soldiers.'

Henry was priming his pistols. 'I will drop two, at any rate.' By dint of constant practice he had made himself into a good shot.

She held his arm. 'No,' she said. 'They would kill you, eventually.'

'Have they not come to do that, anyway?'

'And you will give them what they want? Get out the back. Make the sea, and swim round to the next headland. Quickly.'

He hesitated, while Beast's barking grew more urgent, and the sound of men filled the night. Then he nodded. 'It is a slim chance. But the only one. Come.'

She shook her head. 'It is no chance at all, Henry, for both of us. They are at the door. I will talk with them.'

'You? But . . .'

'It is *you* they have come for,' she said. 'They have no cause to fear me, therefore they have no cause to wish my life. It is you they mean to destroy. I will come to you the moment they have left. Wait in the woods. You will know when I am there.'

Another hesitation. 'You would have me play the coward.'

'I would have you play the *man*,' she said. 'Don't you understand, if the French are moving against you, secretly, in the dead of night, they will be moving against Toussaint too, and Dessalines? Against every black man of any importance in St Domingue? Toussaint will have need of you, now.'

Henry hesitated, for a last long moment, then he kissed her on the lips. 'I will wait for you, in the woods,' he said, and ran for the back of the house.

'Christophe,' a man called. 'We know you are in there. Come out with your hands in the air.'

Richilde moved slowly towards the door. It was of course possible that they might open fire the very moment anyone appeared. But so many things were possible. She grasped the handle, drew a long breath, and threw the door wide. Instantly Beast brushed past her, leaping into the yard before the little house, feet spread, glaring at the men and the horses.

'Come forward,' the officer said.

Richilde blinked into the gloom, could make him out,

142

still mounted, although several of his men were on foot. But she was accomplishing her objective. They were all looking at her, rather than the beach or the sea. She moved forward, stood beside the dog.

'Citizeness Mortmain,' the officer said. 'Is your paramour hiding under the bed?'

'General Christophe is not here,' she said.

'Bah,' the officer said. 'Search the place,' he commanded.

Four of the dragoons came forward. Beast gave a low growl and leapt at the first one. There was the flash of a musket and an explosion, and the dog gave a howl, rolled over three times, and lay on its side, tongue lolling. Richilde restrained a scream with an effort. For suddenly she knew that all the years had rolled away and she was back in the hall of Vergée d'Or chateau, on 23 August 1791. Only then she had been twenty-four years old, had not truly believed it was possible for her to die.

'That was not necessary,' she said, forcing herself to speak quietly, to maintain the legend that she had become. 'Be sure I will report it to your commanding General.'

'Bah,' he said, and himself dismounted. Behind her she heard the sound of her house being torn apart. Well, she thought, this is not the first house of mine that has been destroyed. Will it be the last?

'He is not here, Captain,' the sergeant said.

The Captain stood before Richilde. 'Where is he? Do not play games with me, citizeness. We are not here to play games.'

'I do not know where he is,' she said. 'He went fishing, and has not yet returned.' She bit her lip, aware that she had betrayed herself.

The Captain smiled; she saw the gleam of his teeth. 'He went fishing, but his bateau is on the sand? So, you do wish to play games. This is your last chance, citizeness. Tell me where I can find Christophe.'

She became aware that the men who had searched

the house were standing immediately behind her, that the rest of the command, reassured that the dreaded Christophe was not about, had also dismounted and were crowding forward. An immense weakness seemed to fill her stomach, to seep upwards into her chest, making breathing difficult.

'If you do not tell me, citizeness,' the Captain said. 'I will give you to my men.'

Richilde inhaled. 'I do not know where General Christophe is,' she said. 'I have not seen him in days.'

The Captain stared at her, then he jerked his head, and she felt fingers close to her arm.

She walked, or rather was dragged, behind their horses, her wrists tied in front of her, and then secured to the sergeant's saddle. They had not allowed her to regain her gown, as if, torn to shreds as it was, it could possibly have provided any protection. And after a while it did not matter. She fell, and was dragged over the dusty earth, and was coated in mud to join the blood and the sweat . . . and the semen; her hair seemed stuck together in a solid mass on her back.

And she suffered agonies of fear, that Henry, who would certainly have watched what was happening from the trees, would attempt to rescue her, and be killed. But the trees remained silent; he was after all, a *man*, who knew where his primary duty lay. For that she was grateful, and yet, perversely, she wished that he could, in some way, have managed to raise sufficient force to attack her captors – or at least be able to let her know he was *there*.

So, am I a girl, an Annette, to go mad? she asked herself. Because a dozen men had rammed their evil selves into me, and even worse, have torn at my most private parts with their filthy fingers? I am Richilde de Mortmain, Christophe's woman. I have but to survive, to be avenged. And if I do not survive, then will I still be avenged.

Thus the woman, who had survived the past, who could keep the future in perspective. But beside her, always, was the woman who had to endure the present. The pain, some of it dull from the punches she had received, the tremendous pressure on her shoulders and back as she was dragged forward, some of it sharp, as each time she fell some new cut was ripped across the flesh, the agony of her bruised and bleeding toes, and all of it hideous as she inhaled dust, and worse, from the horses in front of her, as she listened to the laughter of the men. Occasionally one would lean from the saddle to poke her with his whip, and, as they had not actually tortured her as yet, and she had not told them where Christophe was, as yet, she dared not consider what might be going to happen to her in the next couple of hours.

She allowed herself the luxury of tears, but mostly they were tears of anger, and outrage. And she had not screamed once, nor had she begged for mercy. That had angered the sergeant. 'Scream, you nigger whore,' he had shouted, slapping her face to and fro, even as he had knelt between her legs. 'Scream.'

She could afford to weep, now.

Dimly she became aware that she was surrounded by increasing dust, and increasing noise, and thus increasing people. More horsemen, and foot soldiers as well, herding large numbers of black people towards the French encampment. It seemed as if all the Negroes in St Domingue had been arrested at the same time. All who *could* be arrested, anyway. All who had not escaped to the forest. LeClerc's way of honouring his promises. A treachery Kit had feared, because he knew these people. A treachery she had discounted, because they were white, like herself.

Not all the black people were bound. Most were just being herded along by the whips and the gun butts of their captors. Several saw her, and recognised her, and called out her name, and one man attempted to help

145

her back to her feet the next time she fell, only to be
driven away by the sergeant's whip. But they had
noticed one immense fact about her.

'Man,' they called to each other. 'That is Christophe's woman. But they ain't got Christophe.'

'They ain't got Christophe.' The whisper went across
the huge throng of prisoners. 'Christophe gone.'

'And Christophe going get *them*.'

Christophe would get their enemies. There was all
the hope they needed. All the hope she needed. She
could even smile at the sergeant, as they finally halted,
and she sank to her knees while he dismounted. 'Christophe is gone,' she whispered.

'And you will hang,' he said. 'And when you are
dangling, I will poke my bayonet up your cunt.'

'Christophe will get *you*,' she said, and did not even
turn her head away from his swinging fist.

She was dragged to her feet again, released from the
saddle now, to be pushed and prodded with the other
captives towards a vast wire enclosure which had been
prepared, again apparently very recently – but it was at
least a month since Richilde had last been near to Cap
François. Now it was already half filled with blacks. But
she was not going to be allowed to claim the anonymity
of the mob. As she was led towards the pen, she heard a
familiar voice.

'Citizeness Mortmain.'

Instantly she was jerked to a halt, pulled out of the
line. She raised her head, looked at Palourdes, lowered
it again. For the first time she was truly aware of her
nakedness.

'Where is your paramour, citizeness?'

'In the forest by now,' she mumbled through her
parched and bruised lips. 'Raising an army to strike at
you.'

'She is a devil, Major,' the Captain said. 'She fought
us like a she-wolf, in order that Christophe might
escape.'

'I can see that, from her condition,' Palourdes commented, drily. 'But the Commanding General would wish a word with her, I am sure. Bring her along.'

Richilde was pulled away from the other prisoners, and sent stumbling towards the officers' encampment, terribly aware that Palourdes was walking at her shoulder, and watching her, and now that other men were also gathering to stare at her, to congratulate the Captain, and to make the coarsest and lewdest of suggestions. But could anything they wished to do, or have done, to her be any worse than what she had already suffered?

LeClerc breakfasted outside his tent. Suddenly brought to a halt by the sergeant, Richilde's knees gave way and she sank to the ground, to her chagrin, while even more to her shame she was unable to keep from staring at the jug of iced water on the General's table.

'It seems that Christophe has escaped, Citizen General,' Palourdes said.

'The devil,' LeClerc said, delicately slicing a piece of bread, and conveying it to his lips. His gaze roamed over Richilde. 'Why was she not killed in resisting arrest?'

Richilde caught her breath. Up to this moment she had not believed she was actually in any danger of her life.

The Captain stood to attention. 'I supposed you would wish to question her further, Citizen General.'

'If Christophe has escaped, he has escaped,' LeClerc said. 'She will have no more idea where he is at this moment than do we. You were sent to arrest him, and you failed. No doubt through . . .' once again his gaze scorched Richilde's flesh. 'Dallying with this woman. You are reduced to the rank of sergeant.'

'Sergeant?' cried the Captain. 'But Citizen General—'

'And are dismissed my presence.' LeClerc finished chewing, swallowed, leaned back. 'Well, citizeness, it seems you and I are always encountering one another. Have you anything to say?'

'Yes,' Richilde said. 'I would like to ask why? In the

name of God, *why*? You had outwitted me, you had outwitted all of us, you held all of St Domingue in your hand, and now this. You must be mad.'

He shrugged, seeming to indicate that it did not matter how she insulted him. 'As neither you nor your friends are very intelligent, citizeness. Has it escaped your notice that we are now in June? The hurricane season, citizeness. Admiral Villaret-Joyeuse has informed me that he must take his fleet, the mainspring of my strength, back to France to be safe from these winds, and that he will not be returning until November. It thus became necessary to close that hand, and grasp St Domingue even more tightly, until a new fleet, with reinforcements, arrives. And this I have done.'

'By arresting me?' she asked contemptuously. 'And a few hundred, even a few thousand, blacks? What you have done, Citizen General, is convince even the most peaceful of our people that you are not to be trusted. That you *have* to be destroyed. And you *will* be destroyed, General. Because you will even have convinced Toussaint, and he above us all wished to give you a chance to make this peace into a permanency. But now . . .'

LeClerc smiled. 'I am sure you are right, and that I have convinced the slave Toussaint of my true intentions, citizeness. Look there.'

He pointed, and she turned to follow the direction he was indicating, to see a ship, standing out of the harbour, her sails filling beneath the offshore breeze as she made for the open Atlantic.

'Do you suppose he stands on deck, taking a last look at his homeland?' LeClerc asked. 'No, he will not be doing that, citizeness. He will be in the hold, weighed down by his chains, with his sons beside him. And he will remain chained until he reaches France, when no doubt the First Consul will know what to do with him.'

'You . . .' She could not believe it.

148

LeClerc smiled. 'So you see, citizeness, Toussaint did not escape. And without Toussaint, as you yourself will agree, we have to deal with nothing more than a slave mob. Believe me, I have my plans already made for destroying *them*.' His smile faded. 'And I will commence by demonstrating how I will deal with anyone, white, black or brown, male or female, adult or child, who seeks to defy my orders, who seeks to give aid or support to any rebellious slave.' He glanced at Palourdes. 'Take her away and hang her. Hoist her high above the battlements of Cap François that she may be seen for a good distance. Let the niggers understand that I will deal with them, no less harshly, if any one of them raises his hand against me.'

Richilde's knees gave way, and she would have fallen if Palourdes had not caught her arm. Despite everything that had happened, she had never seriously supposed that the French would ever seek to kill *her*. Desperately she licked her lips; her throat was suddenly more parched than ever before.

'I wish to protest against that order, Citizen General,' Palourdes said. 'Citizeness Mortmain is no traitor. She has made her loyalties clear from the beginning.'

'You wish to protest,' LeClerc sneered. 'But you wished to protest against this entire coup, Palourdes. What, are you afraid of upsetting a few blackamoors? My orders stand, and *you* will carry them out. Have *you* anything to say?' he asked Richilde.

'I . . .' But she was Richilde de Mortmain. And she was Christophe's woman. She could not beg this upstarted guttersnipe. At least, not for her life. 'I request the privilege of a gown, *Citizen* General,' she said, both surprised and delighted by the steadiness of her voice. 'In common decency.'

He allowed his gaze to roam up and down her body. 'Why should you wear a gown, citizeness?' he inquired. 'As you have appeared before *your* people often enough, I have heard, in your natural state. But I will have my men give you a *bath*, eh? So that you will be more easily recognisable.'

'You . . . you are surely not a *man*, monsieur,' she said. 'Are you not afraid that by the time you regain your hole, it will become blocked, by the filth which emanates from your mind?'

He stood up, his face suffused, and for a moment she thought he would strike her. Then he sat down again. 'Have it done,' he said to Palourdes.

The Major held her arm, turned her round. Her eyes were filled with a haze of tears, which she knew were about to start rolling down her cheeks. But surely a woman could weep, as the rope tightened about her neck?

'My God! The white nigger. And looking more like a nigger than usual. What are you doing with her, Palourdes?'

Richilde blinked her vision clear, experienced the greatest humiliation of the day, as she gazed at Pauline LeClerc, her scantily clad body shaded by an enormous parasol carried by an attentive Negro boy, and accompanied as usual by her two disciples, Seraphine Palourdes and Jacqueline Chavannes.

'She is to be washed clean, and then hanged, citizeness,' Palourdes explained.

'Hanged?' Pauline demanded. 'Oh, really, Palourdes.'

'Orders from the Commanding General, citizeness.'

'An example,' LeClerc said, having overseen the arrival of his wife, and left his table. 'Besides, she deserves it for her consistent defiance of us.'

'You are absurd, LeClerc,' Pauline remarked. 'And wasteful. I do not think hanging a naked white woman will advance our cause in the slightest. Hang some of the blacks. I will take Citizeness Mortmain off your hands.'

'You?' LeClerc stared at her. 'May I ask with what intention?'

150

You, Richilde thought, keeping her feet with an effort. Now waves of exhaustion were sweeping over her in company to the pain. But waves too of hope. And these she both hated and distrusted. She had not intended to allow herself to hope, ever again.

Pauline LeClerc was smiling. 'I wish to . . . observe her. I think she is a very interesting specimen. Do you not think she is an interesting specimen, Jacqueline?'

'Oh, indeed, citizeness,' Jacqueline said. Her face was expressionless. Could *she* really be meaning to save my life, Richilde wondered?

'It is impossible,' LeClerc said. 'My orders have been given.'

'Impossible? My dear Charles, I would have said that my brother the First Consul might well consider it impossible to hang a white woman.'

He bit his lip. 'And do you not realise, citizeness, that this man Christophe, once he understands that she is still alive, will wish to regain possession of her? She will be a constant encouragement to the Negroes to attack.'

Pauline gave a peal of laughter. 'And do *you* not realise, my dear General, that they are going to attack you anyway? In any event, could you wish for anything better than to lure Christophe into Cap François, looking for his mistress? I should have thought such a plan was obvious.'

Which was absolutely true, Richilde realised, with a pang of real horror. Henry would undoubtedly launch one of those all out and futile frontal assaults on the French position, once he knew she was alive. And he would lead the assault himself.

LeClerc was chewing his lip.

'So I will take care of her for you,' Pauline said. 'You may release her, Palourdes.'

Palourdes looked at his commander, and LeClerc shrugged and nodded. His fingers released Richilde's arm. Once again she nearly fell, had to transmit strength to her knees by a conscious act of will.

'She needs assistance,' Pauline said. 'You will help her, Jacqueline. She is an old friend of yours, is she not?'

'An old friend,' Jacqueline said, and took Richilde's arm. Seraphine Palourdes took the other.

'Do not worry, citizeness.' Pauline said, 'We will soon have you clean, and fed, and watered.' She gave a shrill laugh. 'And even housed.'

'I . . .' Now the tears were coming very fast. She had to force herself to speak, in view of what she had to say. 'I *am* a traitor, to France,' she said. 'You do wrong to interfere with your husband's sentence, citizeness. I will not thank you for it. I will hate you. And I will harm you, if I can.'

Pauline gazed at her from beneath arched eyebrows. She gave another of her shrill laughs. 'The poor woman is overwhelmed. She does not know how to thank.'

Jacqueline smiled at Richilde. 'There is nothing to thank *me* for, Richilde. I am but obeying Citizeness LeClerc.'

'As for me, my dear,' Pauline said. 'You will thank me by *amusing* me.' She looked over her shoulder at the scowling LeClerc. 'I will let her amuse you too, my dear Charles. From time to time.'

Chapter 5

THE KING

Unlike Toussaint and Christophe, Dessalines had been born in Africa, and knew all the horrors of the Middle Passage. Dark-skinned and dark-visaged, squat and repulsive, talented and terrible, he assumed command of what was now openly a war of extermination.

Kit Hamilton leaned on the rail of his ship, watched the bananas being hoisted on board. Here in Port Royal, in Jamaica, he was almost entirely surrounded by land, as the long sandspit of Los Palisadoes curved round from the mainland to enclose the bay. On the end of Los Palisadoes, close indeed to where the *Stormy Petrel* now rode to anchor, there had once been the town of Port Royal, the capital of Jamaica, and also of Henry Morgan's buccaneers, the City of Sin. Strange to suppose that the first Mortmain, who had certainly been with Morgan at the sack of Panama, must have trodden those long disappeared streets. Because on the morning of 7 June 1692, just a hundred and ten years ago, he realised, Port Royal had disappeared into the sea. The earth had opened up and swallowed the capital of every vice in the New World. Now it was only possible, by peering down through the translucent green water, to make out the rubbled remains of the buildings where once the pirates had roistered.

He wondered what history would say of St Domingue, of Cap François, in a hundred and ten years' time?

153

No earthquake there. But a man-made convulsion which in its pitiless intensity was far more vicious than any act of nature, however primeval. And which was still happening. He could not doubt that. The uneasy truce which existed between LeClerc and Toussaint could not endure, however honourable the intentions of the Negro leader.

He sighed, strolled across the poop deck to watch a ship standing round the end of the sandspit. He recognised her, of course; there were not that many trading vessels out of New York making the West Indian circuit. She was called the *Golden Star*, and he had left her anchored in Cap François when he had sailed from there, four days before. Like him, she would now be seeking a cargo in haste, in order to run back north to the safety of New England before the first of the hurricanes which ranged across these sunlit waters from June to October came tearing through the sky.

'Ahoy, the *Stormy Petrel*,' came the hail across the water. 'You've heard the news?'

'What news?' Kit shouted. Not another war, he thought.

Further conversation was rendered impossible for serveral minutes as the *Golden Star* dropped her anchor, the rasp of the chain through the hawsepipe sending the sea birds screaming around the bay. But the moment she was secure a boat was lowered and pulling towards the *Stormy Petrel*, Captain Lowery himself at the tiller. 'Toussaint has been arrested,' he called.

'Toussaint? But . . . whatever for?' Of all the men in St Domingue, Kit would have thought Toussaint the least likely to break the treaty.

Lowery came up the ladder, a small, swarthy, Nantucket Islander with a drooping moustache. 'It was a bit of skullduggery on the part of the French, if you ask me.' He shook hands. 'Must have happened the night you sailed, Hamilton. Seems his home was surrounded,

154

and he and his two sons placed under arrest while they were at table. That same night they were put on a ship for France.'

'Good God.' Kit led his friend into the cabin, set out a bottle of rum and two glasses. 'But what is LeClerc hoping to achieve?'

'A return of the colony to slavery, I would say.' Lowery drank deeply.

'He supposes arresting Toussaint will accomplish that?'

'Not just Toussaint. All the Negro leaders were arrested. Or at any rate, that was the French plan. Kit . . .' he leaned across the table. 'Your sister was certainly taken.'

'Richilde? But . . . she is not a Negro leader.'

Lowery flushed. 'She lives with one. Or she did. The word is that Christophe escaped, but that Richilde was taken. Dragged into Cap François with a lot of blacks, naked and beaten.' He bit his lip. 'That is what I heard.'

Kit gazed at him. 'Would not her cousin have looked to her protection?'

'I can but repeat what I have been told. I supposed you would wish to hear of it.'

'Aye,' Kit said. 'I thank you.' He gazed into his glass for several seconds. So once again he was being summoned back to that tortured island. And once again he had to attempt to rescue Richilde from the grave she had dug for herself. But there was nothing else he could do; certainly she could not be abandoned in a French prison.

Besides, if LeClerc had declared war on the blacks, as his action in arresting Toussaint would most certainly be considered . . . it was impossible to imagine what might be going to happen next.

He drained the drink, got up. 'There's a cargo of bananas, contracted for, and waiting for you, Lowery,' he said. 'I'm for Cap François.'

155

'Citizens. Citizenesses. I am sure you all know Citizeness Richilde Mortmain.' Pauline LeClerc smiled at her guests. 'At least by reputation.'

Richilde feared she knew them all too well. She had expected nothing like this. But then, the entire three days since her capture had been totally confusing. She had been kept a prisoner, certainly, but in the most luxurious of confinements, attended only by Jacqueline and Seraphine Palourdes, and by Pauline herself. Her cuts and bruises had been smoothed and ointmented, until they had all but disappeared, she had been fed the best of food and given the best of wine to drink. She had been kept in bed on a feather mattress and between linen sheets. In the beginning she had momently expected some sudden reversal of fortune, or at the least some obscene assault from these creatures whom she knew to be utterly amoral. Nor could she doubt that they loathed her. Jacqueline certainly – and she in addition sought revenge – and Pauline also, she thought. She could not be sure about the young one, Seraphine, who said little, and who went about whatever duties Pauline appointed her to with the same sad, resigned expression. Presumably, Richilde thought, she should be grateful to her in view of the way her husband had endeavoured to save her life. But then, should she not be grateful to all of them?

But today had been the greatest surprise of all, as she had been taken from bed, and bathed and perfumed, and had her hair dressed, in the fashionable chignon which all the French women wore, and then given this gown to wear, one of the transparently indecent garments which again seemed to form the main part of her new friends' wardrobes – because they were dressed hardly different.

'In France, my dear Citizeness Mortmain,' Pauline had explained with her invariable glittering smile, 'they wear flesh coloured tights beneath their gowns, because of the cold and the damp. Here, in this delightful climate, we have no need for such subterfuge.'

Yet Richilde could hardly feel less than utterly exposed, as she gazed at the faces of the other people who were attending this 'intimate' little supper party, in the great dining room of the Governor General's old residence, where Monsieur Peynier had once entertained, as had Henry and herself more recently. A fact which, mercifully, seemed unknown to the LeClercs. In any event, the burned out building had been rebuilt in so different a style as to be almost unrecognisable.

Present tonight there was LeClerc himself, of course, together with two other of his senior officers from the garrison, and their wives, and naturally, Palourdes. These she could have stood, and she was heartily relieved to discover that Etienne and Louise were *not* here. But to make up for the slight blessing, she found herself gazing at the mulatto General, Alexander Petion, and even more disturbing, at his aide-de-camp, Jean Boyer.

Boyer, indeed, was placed on her right during supper, while the wine flowed and the conversation became animated. And horrifying.

'How many did you dispose of today?' inquired General Morel.

'How many did we *marry*, you mean,' LeClerc said, with a shout of laughter. 'Oh, I suppose about a thousand. The difficulty is not the marriages themselves, my friend, but disposing of the bodies when they start returning to the surface.'

Richilde glanced at Boyer, saw that his face was rigid with distaste, and indeed with anger. As Pauline LeClerc, predatory eyes ever restlessly roaming the table, observed, just as she had observed Richilde's look.

'You do not know of it, of course, my dear Citizeness Mortmain,' she smiled. 'But Charles has devised a new method of dealing with blacks. Well . . . it is not new, I suppose. Did not Fouché practice it at Nantes, in '93?'

'There is nothing *new*, when you come down to it,' LeClerc grumbled.

'These blacks, you see,' Pauline said. 'These people

who were brought in with you, are told that they are going to be returned to Africa. Which presumably is what they wish. Thus they are yoked together, a man with a woman, the republican marriages, Fouché used to call them, when he did the same with the aristocrats in Nantes, and thus yoked, are marched on board the waiting ship, which is alongside the quay, you understand. A long line of couples, happily embarking. And once on board, would you believe it . . .' she gave one of her shrill peals of laughter. 'They are told to keep on marching, as they do, right across the ship, only to find that a port has been opened on the far side. Yet must they keep on marching.'

'Oh, my God!' Richilde clasped both hands round her throat.

'And so in they go, plop, plop, plop. While all the time the bands are playing on the quay for their embarkation on the other side, so their screams are not heard by the others waiting to embark. It is so droll.'

'It is mass murder,' Richilde said.

The LeClercs gazed at her.

'It is mass *execution*, citizeness,' the General said at last. 'And you may believe me when I tell you that when I lay hands upon that devil Christophe, I shall have the greatest pleasure in dispatching him, whether or not you accompany him. It is no simple matter, you know,' he complained at large. 'To dispose of so many people so quickly. Fouché at least had the Loire, which runs fast, and carried the bodies out to sea. Here there is not even any tide.'

'I cannot help but agree with the citizeness,' Major Palourdes said. 'The methods you are employing, Citizen General, not less than your attitude to these unfortunate people, is barbaric, and utterly unworthy of a civilised nation. It is indeed but lowering us to the level of the blacks.'

LeClerc turned his glare upon his aide. 'You oppose,' he said. 'You *oppose*. You are always opposing, Citizen

Major. You are not a soldier at all. You are some whimpering choirboy.'

Palourdes's face paled in anger, and he made to rise, but was restrained by Jacqueline's hand on his arm.

'Well, I am sick to death of your *opposing*,' LeClerc said. 'I need an aide-de-camp who supports me, not opposes me in everything. As of this minute you are relieved of your rank and your post. And of any post in this army. Consider yourself under arrest. You will take passage on the next ship bound for France, and there you may *oppose* the First Consul, and see how you fare with him.'

Palourdes hesitated, then threw off Jacqueline's hand and stood up, bowed to Pauline. 'You will excuse me, citizeness,' he said, and left the room.

Seraphine Palourdes promptly stood up as well.

'Oh, sit down, Seraphine,' Pauline shouted. 'Let the men do the quarrelling. It is the heat.'

'Yet might not Citizen Palourdes be right, Citizen General?' asked Petion.

LeClerc glared at him in turn.

'I had assumed your action in attempting to arrest all the black leaders was to make sure of your grip on the colony during the absence of your fleet.' Petion went on, refusing to lower his gaze. 'I cannot say that I approved of such treachery . . .'

'Treachery?' LeClerc shouted, jumping to his feet.

'That is certainly how it must seem, General, to the blacks. What word would *you* rather use?'

'It was a military necessity,' LeClerc declared.

'As you wish, citizen. As I was saying, I cannot truly approve of such military necessity, but I can understand its . . .' he smiled. 'Necessity. And it may well have succeeded. But to continue executing every black you can lay hands on, and in what is, after all, a barbaric fashion . . .'

'Barbaric?' LeClerc shouted. 'You talk to me of barbarism? What of that patrol of mine ambushed yester-

159

day? Every man castrated while still alive, and several with their buttocks cut off as well, as if they were intended for some cannibal feast.'

Richilde caught her breath. Could it be true? Could Henry have permitted such a thing, however great his rage and his grief?

'Yes,' Petion mused. 'I suppose it comes down to the chicken and the egg.'

'And now this fever,' LeClerc grumbled, sitting down again. 'Which strikes down my men, leaves them with ghastly yellow faces, and leaves even those who survive quite unfit for duty. You know of this fever, Citizen Petion?'

Petion looked at Richilde.

'It is called yellow fever, Citizen General,' Richilde said. 'Given time, it will kill all your men. Perhaps even you.'

He glared at her, then turned to his wife. 'You invited me to an entertainment, madame. I did not come to be plagued by insubordinate officers and insolent prisoners.'

'Dear Charles,' Pauline said. 'I apologise. But I did invite you to an entertainment, and an entertainment you shall have. May I suggest we all withdraw to those chairs over there?' The chairs had been arranged in a row, at the far end of the room. 'Oh, not you, Citizeness Mortmain,' Pauline said. 'You must remain at table.'

Richilde gazed at her, heartbeat suddenly quickening, then at Jacqueline – who smiled.

The guests walked away from her, sat down.

'Now,' Pauline said. 'We are going to watch a little play. There are no words, except those which will come naturally and involuntarily to the actors, and there is no scenario. Because we are going to re-enact the fall of the Chateau of Vergée d'Or.'

Richilde stood up.

'Stay there, citizeness, or I shall have you tied to your chair,' Pauline said. 'Although it would be better

160

for you to co-operate. Because, my friends,' she said to her guests. 'We are fortunate to have with us one of the very few survivors of that historic occasion. It has often been asked, *how* did Citizeness Mortmain survive? When all around her, her own husband, were being killed in the most horrible fashion. We know the facts, yet find them difficult to relate to what our imaginations tell us must have been the situation. So tonight we shall carry out a scientific investigation. There you have the citizeness. Her chateau has fallen, but she has managed to retreat to her boudoir, the most private apartment in the house. She knows what has happened outside, in general, but she does not know who is already dead, who may be suffering untold tortures; all their screams are merged in the general cacophony. See her there, pale of cheek, hands clasped about her throat, facing the door through which she knows her fate must come . . .' she clapped her hands, and the door burst open; six black men stood there. 'Now,' Pauline said. 'We must sit back and let events take their course.'

Colonel Boyer stood up. 'You cannot be serious,' he said.

'I assure you that whatever is going to happen will be entirely authentic, Citizen Colonel,' Pauline said. 'These fellows are under sentence of death. But I have promised them their freedom, if they successfully conquer Citizeness Mortmain. And of course entertain us into the bargain. They are thus in exactly the same position as the men who did burst into her boudoir on that unforgettable night eleven years ago. Where men, and women, are placed in exactly the same positions, it has long been my belief that they will act in exactly the same ways. Do not be afraid for her. They have my absolute command that no matter what they may choose to do to her, she must neither be killed nor mutilated, at least on this occasion.'

The Negroes were hesitating, looking from Pauline

161

to the mulatto officer, uncertain what might happen next. Richilde was aware of a feeling of rising horror, as if she was about to be sick – but it was a mental rather than a physical sickness. She would not vomit, but she would lie on the floor and shriek her brains into madness. Save that suddenly she was too exhausted even to do that.

'It is obscene, citizeness,' Boyer said. 'But then . . .' he might have been going to say. 'You are obscene.' But he controlled himself, bowed. 'You will excuse me.' He looked at Richilde. 'Will you accompany me, Madame de Mortmain?'

'Accompany you?' Pauline demanded. 'Accompany you where?'

Boyer stepped away from the chairs and the other guests, rested his hand on the pocket of his jacket, which was now seen to be sagging as if carrying a heavy weight. 'I have decided to resign my command in your army, Citizen General,' he said to LeClerc. 'I can no longer fight for a man who practices treachery and murder on so vast a scale. I cannot believe that the First Consul, your *brother-in-law*,' he said with heavy irony, 'commanded or indeed would authorise such uncivilised behaviour. You are driven, Citizen General, by an insensate ambition to equal the achievements of others greater than yourself. Well, you will do so without my aid.'

LeClerc stood up. 'You are mad,' he declared. 'I shall have you arrested. You *are* arrested.'

Boyer drew his pistol, presented it at Pauline. 'If anyone makes a move to stop me, I shall shoot Citizeness LeClerc.' He allowed himself a grim smile. 'Through the breast.'

LeClerc stared at him.

Pauline stifled a scream. 'Charles . . .'

'Come here, citizeness,' Boyer said.

Pauline looked left and right. 'Charles . . .'

162

'You had best stop that fellow,' LeClerc said to Petion.

Petion stood up. 'On the contrary, Citizen General. I think I shall accompany him.' He also drew a pistol.

'You came here tonight, armed, intending some treachery . . .'

'We came on our guard against *your* treachery, Citizen General,' Petion said.

'Yet are you committing treason, in time of war. I will have you shot.'

'When you may,' Petion agreed. 'Citizeness LeClerc, you will accompany us to the main gate. And we *will* shoot you, if we are taken. So my advice to you, General LeClerc, is to remain in this room . . .' he glanced at Jacqueline and the other ladies, 'amusing yourself, until your wife returns to you. She *will* be returned to you, I give you my word.' He smiled. 'And *we* are accustomed to keeping our bargains.'

'You cannot let them take me,' Pauline shrilled. 'Charles, you cannot. You cannot let them hand me over to Dessalines and Christophe.'

'I imagine you would enjoy that very much, citizeness,' Petion said. 'At least for a while. But I am not going to do that. Come.'

Boyer reached for Pauline's arm, pulled her against him. 'Now remember, citizeness, we are all going for a moonlight bathe. One of your favourite pastimes. Attempt to play us false, and we shall kill you without a moment's hesitation.' He looked at Jacqueline Chavannes. 'Are you coming?'

Jacqueline drew a sharp breath, glanced at LeClerc. 'No,' she said.

'It is your last chance,' he warned. 'If you stay, you are an enemy, from now.'

'I will stay,' she said. 'To see you hanged.'

'As you wish.' Boyer backed to the door, still holding Pauline's arm, while the other people in the room, including the black men, stared at him as if mesmerised.

Petion beckoned Richilde, who went to him, also feeling as if she were in a dream, that she must awaken, and find herself still Pauline's prisoner, confined to her bedroom.

Or had the whole last week been only a nightmare, and was she really sleeping securely, her head on Henry's arm?'

'Now remember,' Petion said. 'No one is to leave this room until Citizeness LeClerc returns. If you ever wish to see her again.'

'Wait,' Seraphine Palourdes said. 'I should like to accompany you.'

'You, citizeness?'

'If you will permit me to fetch my husband.'

'You would not be considering attempting to betray us, citizeness?'

She met his gaze. 'My husband has just been cashiered, *monsieur*. And is probably destined for at least prison. If he remains in Cap François.'

'Very well,' Petion agreed. 'You may go and fetch him. Meet us in the yard. But haste, citizeness. If you are not at the gate when we reach there, you must fend for yourself.' He bowed to LeClerc. 'If you will take my advice, Citizen General, when your wife is returned to you, contract your defences, call in your garrisons, and sit tight within the perimeter of Cap François. When your fleet returns in November, sail for France. You have not the talent, even at treachery, to win this country, much less hold it.'

'It is unwise to go too far from the city, citizeness,' said the captain of the guard. 'We do not know where the blacks are, but it is believed they are very close.'

'Yes,' Pauline LeClerc said. 'Yes, you are right. We had best turn back.'

'We are not going far, Captain,' Petion pointed out. 'Only to that beach down there. We are three men.

164

Three soldiers, as you can see. And believe me, we are armed.' He smiled at the Captain. 'We wish to bath. And you, you rogue, wish to oversee the ladies. Come along, citizens, citizenesses.'

The little cavalcade walked their horses past the guard. Boyer had found a shawl for Richilde, and this she kept wrapped around her hair and face, so that there was no risk of her being recognised; the Captain was confused enough by the presence of the three senior officers, together with the Commanding General's lady – dressed for the dining room but sitting astride horses.

'When you hang,' Pauline said, 'I am going to sit and watch you die. Every movement, every wriggle. I shall clap my hands in time to your writhings.' She looked at Seraphine. 'As for you, you treacherous little toad, I am going personally to flay you alive, and paint you in salt.'

Seraphine kept her eyes fixed on the road they followed, as she had done since leaving the gate. Like her husband, she had said nothing throughout the escape; both were overwhelmed by the magnitude of the disaster which had overtaken them.

'You are entitled to be angry, citizeness,' Petion agreed. 'But let me repeat the advice I gave your husband. Return to France, while you may. Or you may be the one to find yourself hanging, and I doubt it will be by the neck.' He drew rein, looked over his shoulder. 'Far enough. You may return, citizeness. Comrades, let us make haste.'

'Ride, madame,' Boyer shouted.

Richilde kicked her horse, sent it forward, and the five of them galloped down the road.

'To me,' Pauline was shouting back at the guard. 'Come to me. After them. Bring them down. Oh, bring them down.'

'I know not how to thank you. How can I ever thank you?' Richilde gasped, as they slowed their horses, now well beyond musket range. 'To risk so much . . .'

165

Petion smiled at her. 'Our decision to abandon the French cause was taken before tonight, madame. Almost the moment that LeClerc began practising his "military necessities". St Domingue is our country, and if we do not always see eye to eye with the blacks, we must oppose murder, as well. So it was merely a matter of when. It was Boyer's idea that we wait the opportunity to take you with us.'

'Colonel Boyer?' Her head turned.

'You are our passport to safety, Madame de Mortmain,' the Colonel said, gravely. 'To Christophe, we are renegades who fight for the French. He might well decide to treat us as enemies, before we could explain our change of allegiance. He is hardly likely to do so if we come under your protection.'

'I see,' she said, unsure whether to be relieved or chagrined. But she did not suppose he was telling the whole truth; she could remember how he had always looked at her, from the moment of their first meeting, that day in the forest that Santhonax had died.

'Then I think,' Major Palourdes said. 'That Madame de Mortmain had best commence protecting us.'

Petion drew rein, realising that they were surrounded by armed men.

'French soldiers,' someone said. 'Pull them from their horses.'

'And women,' said someone else.

'Pull *them* from their horses too.'

'Wait,' Richilde said, urging her horse forward. 'I am Richilde de Mortmain. My friends and I seek General Christophe. Would you risk his displeasure?' But as she spoke her heart gave a distinct pitter patter; she, and her companions, all supposed Christophe to be in command here. But they did not even know for certain if he was alive.

The black man came closer, put his hand on her bridle as he peered at her. He wore blue uniform and a cocked hat, and she saw to her inexpressible relief that he displayed the badges of Henry's personal guard. She even recognised his face.

'Good evening to you, Captain Gounod,' she said.

He frowned at her. 'Madame de Mortmain? We heard you had been executed.'

'Well, I have not, as you can see. Thanks to my friends here. You will provide us with an escort to General Christophe's headquarters.'

'Of course, madame. Of course.'

This time her heart lurched in relief, so much so that she felt sick, physically sick this time. She had not dared ask a direct question. But he was there, even if he thought *her* dead. And only two hours later she was slipping from the saddle to be in his arms. 'Richilde,' he said. 'Richilde! They told me you had been hanged.'

'White people,' Dessalines bellowed. 'Mulattos. You know what to do with the men.' He drove his fingers into Seraphine Palourdes's hair, pulled her against him. 'I will take the woman first.'

Seraphine gave a little gasp as the brutal fingers tore at her bodice, but her expression never changed as she gazed at Richilde.

'These are my friends, Jean-Jacques,' Richilde said. 'They saved my life. I promised them a welcome here.'

'No doubt you remember me, General Dessalines, General Christophe,' Petion said, ignoring the black soldiers who had seized his arms.

'We remember you,' Henry said. 'You fight for LeClerc.'

'Not any longer,' Petion said. 'I fight for St Domingue. I can tell you the French dispositions. There are also several thousand mulattos living in the south, who will follow my lead.' He looked around him at the black men. There were only a few hundred of them, gathered in the jungle clearing – always a jungle clearing for Jean-Jacques Dessalines, Richilde thought, it was his true metier. And for Henry?

'My men will be a valuable augmentation of your

army,' Petion was saying. 'Where *is* your army, General Dessalines?'

'Army?' Dessalines bellowed. 'Army?'

'It is assembling,' Henry said, quietly, his arm still round Richilde's waist. 'This treachery of LeClerc's has taken us by surprise.' Richilde felt his arm tighten. 'They still hold Toussaint.'

'Toussaint has gone,' Petion said. 'He has been sent to France.'

'To France?' Henry asked in dismay.

'He will not be coming back,' Boyer said. 'It is up to us, now.'

Henry looked at Dessalines.

Who gave a roar. 'Well, was he a god? He was a man. A man who did not believe in gods. And a man who was weak. Weak,' he shouted. 'He trusted people.' He stared at Palourdes. 'He trusted white people. Believe me, I will not make the same mistake.'

Richilde clutched Henry's arm. She dared not speak, dared not utter what was certain everyone, including the blacks, was thinking. But only Henry could say the words, because only Henry could offer himself as an alternative.

'*I* will lead you,' Dessalines shouted. 'I will drive out the French. I will make us free, as Toussaint never tried to do.' Now he too was staring at Henry, anticipating a challenge. 'I will beat the French,' he said. 'I will avenge Toussaint.' His gaze turned on Richilde. 'And all our other wrongs. I will make the French hate the day they ever landed here. I swear these things, or may Ogone Badagris strike me dead.'

Henry drew a long breath. 'Long live General Dessalines,' he shouted.

Richilde's stomach seemed to fill with lead.

'Shoal water ahead,' came the call from the maintopmast.

'Starboard your helm. Trim those braces,' bawled Mr Rogers.

168

Kit hurried from the cabin, where he had been completing his papers for landing, as Cap François was only a few miles away, ran up the companion ladder. 'What's the trouble, Mr Rogers?'

'Shoals, sir, dead ahead,' said the mate.

'That's not possible.' Kit took the telescope. He had sailed this course too often to believe a reef could suddenly have surged to the surface where his ship had passed but a fortnight earlier. He stood at the rail, levelled the glass, stared at what was undoubtedly broken water, spurts of white, leaping around what was equally undoubtedly a brown mass on the surface. Slowly he focused, his stomach rolling, his brain refusing to accept what his eyes were seeing. 'By Christ,' he said.

'I have altered course to give it a wide berth, sir.' Rogers said.

'Well, alter your course back again, and make haste.'

'Captain?'

'Those are dead bodies, Mr Rogers. Men and women. Being attacked by the sharks.'

The brigantine resumed her former course, every man on deck now to stare in horror at the huge mass of bodies, pushed together by the slow moving tide, which bobbed in the low swell, while the black fins, unable to believe their good fortune, carved through them like upturned knives, scattering blood equally with the foam of their darting movements.

'They're tied together, in pairs,' someone whispered.

Someone else, a seaman of ten years' experience, vomited over the side.

'The devils,' Rogers muttered. 'The black devils.'

Kit glanced at him. 'Do you suppose black men did this, Mr Rogers?' he asked. 'To their own?'

'Then who . . . you do not suppose the *French*?'

'It is certainly a method of execution used by the French before,' Kit said. 'I have read of it.' They were close now, and he stared into the seething brown horror. He sought white limbs, trailing brown hair, while his entire body seemed to contract into an angry vice.

He did not see her. But that did not mean she was not there.

Four hours later they were entering the harbour. It was like stepping back in time. When he had left here, only ten days before, Cap François had been the busy, bustling place he remembered from his childhood, more bustling indeed, *than* he remembered, as it had still been being rebuilt. There had been black people everywhere, as well as white, as well as ships, for the fleet of Admiral Villaret-Joyeuse had still been at anchor. Now the harbour was empty, save for two trading vessels, and the blacks were gone, just as the building had ceased and the bustle had disappeared. Now there were only French soldiers to be seen, patrolling the battlements, dragging guns into place. Moving slowly, and dispiritedly, and when he went ashore, the men who greeted him on the dock and demanded his papers were yellow-faced and trembling.

'Do you suppose, Citizen Hamilton, that General LeClerc has the time to speak with every sea captain who comes here?' inquired the captain of the port. 'We are in a state of war, as you should be able to see. Besides . . .'

'He will see me,' Kit said, and regained his papers, strode through the city towards the military headquarters, which had now been brought inside the walls. 1791, he thought, all over again, the shops shuttered and the houses too, with only frightened faces to peer at him through the cracks.

'Kit! Kit Hamilton!'

'Madeleine? Well, there is one relief, at the least. But what is happening here?'

Madeleine shrugged. 'The blacks, your friends, have broken the treaty and risen against us. They are in arms everywhere, and now we are told the mulattos have joined them. The whole country is in a state of war, all over again. It is quite terrible.'

Kit peered at her. She looked tired, but neither frigh-

170

tened nor deprived of any of the comforts of life; her clothes were new and recently laundered, and she smelt of perfume – her parasol was also new.

'And Vergée d'Or? Annette?'

'Well, we have had to abandon the plantation again, at least for the time being. We are using the house which used to belong to Louise's mother. You remember it, Kit. You will come to see us there? Annette ... well, it would be idle to pretend she has not been upset by what has happened. She wept when we left Vergée d'Or. But we are all upset. You *will* come to visit?'

'As soon as I may. I seek some information about Richilde.'

'Richilde?' Her brows drew together.

'I was told she had been brought here, a captive.'

'I believe she was arrested,' Madeline said. 'As part of the general counter revolutionary precautions. But of course the General released her, sent her back to her ... her paramour.' She pointed, long finger at the end of an outflung arm. 'She is out there. In the jungle. With her cannibal cousins.'

'They seek to defy me. They massacre my men. They *mutilate* them.' Charles LeClerc stood in front of his desk, waved his arms.

'As you drown them, by the thousand?' Kit asked.

LeClerc glared at him. 'You come here, with your foolish American ideas, having no concept of the true situation ...'

'I am trying to *discover* the true situation, Citizen General,' Kit said, patiently. 'I have been told it was you broke the treaty, by arresting Toussaint. By attempting to arrest Christophe and Dessalines. By arresting my sister.'

'Your sister is as much a nigger traitor as any of them,' LeClerc said. 'She should have been hanged. By God, I was weak there.'

171

'And Toussaint?'

'Toussaint will shortly be where he belongs. Behind bars. Where they all belong. And where I intend to see that they all go, by God. By . . .'

'With your permission, Citizen General, I should like to have a word with General Petion. Or Colonel Boyer.'

LeClerc's head came up. 'What for?'

'I but seek the truth of this matter.'

'You . . . a damned American, come here, trying to badger me, a general of France. Be careful I do not have you locked up as well. Or hanged.'

'Will you then resume war with the United States?' Kit demanded. For only a few years before French attempts to bribe American envoys had actually led to an abortive conflict, carried on entirely at sea. Peace had only been signed on 30 September 1800.

'Ah, bah! You are not worth the trouble. As for the mulattos, you are welcome to talk with them, if you can find them. Ha ha. Yes, indeed. They have run off as well. They are all niggers. They are all . . .' he was overcome with a sudden spasm of shivering, despite the heat, turned away from Kit, and fell to his knees. Instantly his aides hurried forward, attempted to raise him up. LeClerc waved them away, used his desk to drag himself to a standing position. 'Brandy,' he gasped. 'A glass of brandy.'

A servant hurried forward with a tray.

'You, General, had best go to bed,' Kit said. 'And pray.'

'Pray? A French soldier does not pray. I have work to do. Bed, what nonsense. I . . .' Another spasm seemed to tear through his system. The brandy glass dropped from his fingers and crashed to the floor, shattering into a thousand crystals.

'You,' Kit said, pointing at the servant. 'Put your master to bed.'

172

'But . . . what is the matter with him?' asked General Morel, hurrying into the room.

'He has yellow fever,' Kit said.

'What will you do?' Kit asked.

'Do?' Etienne stood in the middle of the small drawing room, hands tucked beneath the lapels of his coat. 'Why, wait for the position to be stabilised, of course, so that we may return to Vergée d'Or. My dear Kit, the illness of the Commanding General is of no real consequence. There are other generals.'

'But . . .' Kit looked at Annette, who sat as ever, with her interminable needlework, but now raised her head to smile at him.

'It cannot take long, Kit,' she explained. 'They are only blacks. General Morel will hang them all, soon enough.'

Kit looked at Madeleine, who refilled his glass with wine.

'I'm afraid I agree with Annette,' she said. 'About the length of time it will take. These people are only savages. I know you have a quite absurd regard for their potential, Kit, but you must confess it has never been realised. Not even Toussaint succeeded in making anything of them, and now he is gone . . . well, who is left? Not that absurd little boy Henry Christopher.'

Kit drew a very long breath. But there was absolutely no point in losing his temper with these people. They lived in a world of their own. A world which, he supposed, had lasted too long for them ever to regain touch with reality.

'And suppose the French decide to evacuate?' he asked, quietly.

'Oh, come now. Do you really suppose the French are going to walk away from their richest possession? Can you really see Bonaparte accepting such a blow to his prestige? Of course, I forget,' Etienne said. 'You

173

have never met him. I have, you know. He gave me an audience, when this expedition was first mooted. "My dear Citizen Mortmain," he said to me. "It is to people like you that we look to sustain the greatness of the French colonial empire. Do not fail me." And do you know what I said back to him? I said, "I shall not fail you, Your Excellency. Providing you do not fail me." Do you know, there was an absolute silence? I do believe everyone else in the room was terrified. This little Corsican is not used to being answered in kind. But he merely looked at me for several seconds, and then said, "I never fail, Citizen Mortmain. I sometimes change direction, but I never *fail*."'

'Yes,' Kit said. 'Well . . .'

'And having despatched such a force, thirty thousand of his best troops, his entire fleet, this is one direction he will not change. I do assure you of that, Kit. Far more likely . . .' he chuckled, 'that if LeClec does not end the matter quickly enough, Bonaparte will appear here himself, with the Imperial Guard at his back. That would show these blacks what warfare is all about, I can promise you that. He is a remarkable man, Kit. Of course, he is no gentleman. You can see that at a glance. And it is confirmed when he speaks. But still, a remarkable man. And who knows? The age of gentlemen may well be passing.'

'Yes,' Kit said, again, and equally sceptically. 'Well, my offer stands, of course. I sail tomorrow. You are welcome to berths if you should change your mind.'

'America,' Etienne said. 'What has America got to offer us, that St Domingue has not?'

It does not contain a few thousand black men all thirsting for your blood, for a start, Kit thought. But he did not say it.

Madeleine came to the door with him. 'And Richilde?'

He sighed, and shrugged. 'Like you, she regards St Domingue as her home. She has gone back to Henry.

174

She will not leave him. Believe me, I have tried often enough to persuade her in the past.'

She held his arm. 'You do understand, Kit, that it is now war to the bone?'

He nodded. 'I have seen some of the evidence of it. It sickens me, which is why I am leaving.'

'And you therefore understand that when the blacks are smashed, she will suffer with them? There will be nothing we can do to save her?'

He gazed at her. 'Would you even try, Madeleine?'

She did not lower her eyes. 'No,' she said. 'Not now. I think she would be better off dead. She is diseased.'

'Then, dear cousin,' he said. 'We can only hope and pray that she does not feel the same way about you.'

Kit adjusted his tricorne hat, looked up at the sky. The moon was just rising; in another hour it would be bright as day. Then why did he not leave Cap François tonight? There was nothing to remain here for, now. The colony was inextricably caught up in a downward spiral, which would probably, so far as he could see, leave it once again deserted. Save that it had never been deserted, in the past. Not even the labour hungry Spaniards had been able to kill off all the aboriginal Indians; at least, not before replacing them with Negro slaves.

He sighed, walked towards the dock. And yet, Hispaniola exerted the most powerful charm. There was no wind – one reason for waiting for the dawn breeze to spring up before attempting to leave – and thus there was endless sound, shrouding the occasional challenge of a sentry, voices drifting across the empty rooftops; he listened to bull frogs croaking in the ditches, to the rasp of cicadas, the shrill cries of the nightbirds, even to the loud buzz of one of the strange insects called 'singers' by the black people, usually silent during the hours of darkness. While the air was filled with the fragrance of oleander and night blooming jasmine, where it should have contained only the stench of decaying corpses.

'Kit,' Jacqueline Chavannes said.

He turned, sharply, his hand dropping to the pistol he carried in his pocket. But she was alone, in the shadows, her head shrouded in a shawl. But for her voice he would not have known her.

'My . . . my mistress would speak with you.' she said.

'I am leaving Cap François,' he said. 'Nor am I in the mood for after supper parties.

'And do you suppose we are?' She came closer. 'You can spare her a few minutes of your time. It is most urgent.'

He hesitated, his brain calling out to him to shun these people, and flee their company. But his every male instinct was equally begging him again to weaken, just for a few minutes. Because here in St Domingue was every feminine charm he had ever loved, or desired. As he had learned on his last trip home, there was naught but an empty house in New York. And once he went this time, he would not be coming back. Quite apart from Richilde, he would never again see Annette, to whom he had devoted so much of his life, in such futility. And he would never again see this woman, who had first introduced him to the desires and the mysteries of her sex. He doubted he would truly miss either of them. But he would also never again see Seraphine Palourdes. There was a strange admission. He had *seen* her but once in his life, but as every single occasion he had held a woman in his arms had been equally attended with an overwhelming guilt, he could at least remember that night as the most memorable of such adventures. Since then he had avoided her. And to her, he had obviously been nothing more than an itinerant penis, one of her mistress's toys.

Yet now he was leaving St Domingue forever, he thought he would like to see her for one last time.

'A few minutes,' he agreed, and walked beside her.

'You will return to New York?' Jacqueline asked.

'That is my home.'

'You will not try to see Richilde again?'

'There does not seem much point, now.'

'But you will return here?'

He shook his head. 'There does not seem much point in that either, Jacqueline. Perhaps, when the war is over, it may be possible to re-open trade with Cap François. But I see nothing ahead but savagery and barbarism. It is difficult to trade with barbarism.'

They had reached the Governor General's palace, and were challenged by the guard. Jacqueline gave the password, and they were allowed up the steps. 'And have you no thoughts, no regrets, for anyone you may leave behind?' She gave an almost nervous smile, strange in so self-possessed a woman. 'I mean, apart from your sister?'

She had paused, in the upstairs hall. Such servants as they had passed had hastily turned and scurried away. No one was obviously allowed to overlook Madame Chavannes escorting a man to her mistress's pleasure. Even when her husband lay dying, no doubt in this very house.

Jacqueline opened the bedroom door, showed him in. It was a room he had never entered before, but he realised with something of a shock that Richilde and Henry must have slept in here, during those brief summers when their revolution had seemed to have succeeded, when their horizons had been bright with promise.

'Captain Hamilton! Kit!' Pauline LeClerc sat in the centre of the huge tester bed, arms outstretched. She was, he observed, entirely nude – and possessed a figure, superbly delineated by the flickering candlelight, which put even Seraphine Palourdes to shame.

'Citizeness.' He remained standing by the door, became aware that it had softly closed, as Jacqueline had left them alone.

177

'Will you not come closer?' Pauline asked. 'I can hardly see you, over there.'

He approached the bed, and she held her hand towards him. Cautiously he took the white fingers, kissed the knuckles.

'It is good of you to come,' she said. 'So good.'

'Madame Chavannes said you wished to discuss an important matter.'

She withdrew her hand. 'Am I not an important matter?' She gave a twisted smile. 'I had intended us to know each other better, long before this. That Palourdes bitch was merely to be an appetiser. I had not realised she would upset you.'

'She did not upset me,' he lied. 'May I ask where she is?'

Pauline uttered a peal of laughter. 'What, do you still hanker after that cunt? She is gone, Kit. Gone to the blacks.'

'To the . . .'

'She accompanied your sister.'

'Good God,' he said.

Pauline realised she might have made a mistake. 'She went with her husband, of course. He is a traitor, like Petion and Boyer. They are all scoundrels.'

'Or patriots and honest men, citizeness. It is all a point of view.'

She gazed at him for several seconds. 'I did not invite you here to talk politics.' She cupped her breasts, one in each hand, held them up. 'Can you truly stand there, as if turned to stone? Or do you have to be *told* what I am offering you?'

'Citizeness,' he said. 'Your husband is dying.'

Once again the stare. 'Do you not suppose I know that?'

'But it does not interest you?'

'He was Napoleon's choice. My brother has this habit of dictating other people's lives for them. But *I* do not intend to die.' She moved, suddenly, rising to her knees to seize his hand. 'You are leaving Cap François. Take me with you.'

'Eh?'

'Kit,' she said. 'I hate this place. I loathe and abhor it. It is nothing but disease and death. If I stay here I shall die. I know it. No fleet will return for us until the autumn, and it is only June. I cannot stay here. Take me with you. I will pay you. I will pay you in gold coin, and I will pay you with my body. I will be *your* slave, Kit. Just take me with you.'

Her plea was so desperate he nearly softened. He reflected that she was but a woman, young and beautiful and full of life. There was no reason to condemn her as he condemned her husband and his people.

But there was every reason. He had seen enough of her to know that she was possessed of a heart as cold as a block of ice, that her own desires and her own ambitions were the driving force behind LeClerc's absurdities, that she was probably the most vicious person in Cap François.

As she was proving by attempting to desert her dying husband, whether she loved him or not.

She frowned at his expression, understanding her fate. 'I saved your sister's life,' she said. 'Don't you understand that? I saved her life. LeClerc would have hanged her, publicly. He had already commanded her execution. And I intervened.'

Kit frowned at her in turn. 'Is that true?'

'How do you suppose she managed to leave the city? She is Christophe's woman. She was an invaluable hostage. But I stepped in, because she was a woman, like myself, and because she was your sister.'

Kit hesitated, his brain swirling.

As she saw. She squeezed his fingers. 'You owe me a debt. You, owe me. But yet will I surrender myself to you. I will be your slave, Kit. Just take me from this living hell. Listen to me. Come to bed, now. And I will make you the happiest man in all the world. Then we can leave this place.'

'If you are coming with me,' he said. 'You had best come now. I sail at dawn.' He turned away to avoid looking at her, stared out of the window at the sleeping city. He certainly could not refuse to take her, if she had indeed saved Richilde's life. Her desertion of her husband must be between her and her conscience. He would never have believed her tale, but for the simple fact that Richilde *had* been arrested, and had been let go again. Because Pauline had certainly been right about her value as a hostage.

But what tangled path was he now allowing his feet to explore?

Pauline got out of bed, began to dress.

'I will put some things in a satchel for you,' Jacqueline Chavannes said.

Pauline and Kit turned together; she had re-entered the room by another door, so quietly they had been unaware of her presence – and she already carried a satchel.

'I can manage, thank you, Chavannes,' Pauline said.

'But I must play my part,' Jacqueline said.

'Your part? Your part is to remain here, with my husband. Your lover. Keep his brow cool,' Pauline said contemptuously.

'Stay here? While you go off to safety with Kit? You must suppose me demented.'

'Do you seek to defy me?' Pauline demanded.

'I seek my rights, Citizeness LeClerc. Do you suppose I have any more desire than you to remain in this pit? Do you suppose I wish to be hauled before Dessalines, and subjected to his lust? And do you suppose I intend to let you take Kit? I have a greater claim on him than you, citizeness. I was the first woman he ever knew.'

Pauline gazed at Kit with her mouth open.

180

'Which is perfectly true,' he agreed. And shrugged. 'So you both come. But make haste. And do not suppose I intend either of you as my mistress in the future. I am repaying a debt. Nothing more.'

But oh, to be sure he would keep that resolve, when exposed to nothing but their company.

'No,' Pauline said. 'I will not share my exile with this . . . this creature. I know her for what she is, Kit. A crawling thing. A nigger. I am her mistress. I have commanded her to stay, and she will stay. I think you had best tie her up.'

'You listen to *her*?' Jacqueline cried. 'You believe *her*? You are a fool, Kit Hamilton. You have always been a fool. You believe that she saved your sister's life? Oh, she stopped her from being hanged, but only to keep her as a plaything. She would have had her raped, time and again, by twelve black men, just to amuse her after dinner guests. Until eventually she would have had her murdered, for the same sport.'

Pauline drew a sharp breath as Kit's head turned. 'That is a lie,' she said. 'That is a *lie*.'

'You have but to ask the Captain of the guard,' Jacqueline said. 'If, a week ago, this *citizeness* did not go riding one night after supper, with General Petion and Colonel Boyer, and Major Palourdes and his wife, and Richilde. Even the Palourdes fled her miserable company. And they took this *thing* as a hostage, to secure their escape. You have but to ask the guards, Kit. It was to them she went wailing for assistance when she was finally released.'

'Why, you . . .' Pauline hurled herself at the quadroon. Although she was considerably the smaller woman, she was also much the younger and at least as strong, and far more vigorous. The force of her attack sent Jacqueline sprawling, and Pauline knelt on her chest, tearing at her face with her nails. 'Wretch,' Pauline snarled. 'Foul thing from the pit of hell. I shall have you whipped, from one end of Cap François to the

181

other. No, better than that. I will have you bound and delivered to Dessalines, as a present from me. That is what I shall do. I shall . . .'

Carefully Kit opened the bedroom door and stepped through it, closed it behind himself, and hurried down the corridor towards the street.

'Gone,' Jean-Jacques Dessalines said. 'Gone,' he shouted. He raised both hands high in the air. 'Gone,' he bellowed, his voice reverberating.

'Gone,' the black soldiers, and their women, and their children, shrieked in unison. They crowded the beach outside of Cap François, roamed the empty battlements, stared in disbelieving joy at the French fleet, already hull down on the horizon.

That fleet had re-appeared a week ago, after a long, hot summer of vicious warfare, surely bringing, the Negroes had supposed, fresh troops to prosecute the war. But instead it had only remained anchored off Cap François just long enough to embark those fever-ridden survivors of LeClerc's expeditionary force.

'Gone,' Henry Christophe said. 'We have won, again.'

'Gone,' Alexander Petion said, and looked at Jean Boyer.

'Gone,' Richilde de Mortmain whispered, and looked at Seraphine Palourdes. They had become friends, by force of circumstances, and yet she knew the young Frenchwoman very little better now than during her three days as Pauline LeClerc's prisoner. Seraphine spoke little, moved through life with a cautious suspicion, as if attempting to discover in advance from whence the next blow would be delivered. She had reason for her scepticism, this much at least Richilde had learned, from her husband. Both her mother and father had perished in the Terror, her father on the guillotine, her mother torn to pieces by the mob on that dreadful August night in 1792 when the Parisians had

182

supposed themselves about to be conquered by the Prussians.

Just a year after our own holocaust, Richilde thought.

Thus tainted as a royalist, or at least an enemy of the state, for all that she had only been nine years old, and although her father had been a reputable merchant rather than an aristocrat, Seraphine had been destined for at best a Parisian brothel. From that fate she had been rescued by Palourdes, but only on account of her beauty and innocence. Albert Palourdes was, in his own way, an honest and even an honourable man – Richilde had good cause to thank him for being those things. But he was also a revolutionary, who hated all hereditary wealth or privilege, and as a career soldier, a harsh and grim and loveless man. Certainly he was so to his wife, his harshness increased by his inability to discover what went on behind that lovely mask.

The orbit of the LeClercs into which they had drifted had not improved their relationship. As a soldier Palourdes had considered it necessary to be loyal and subservient to his appointed chief, as his wife had been commanded to adopt the same attitude to that chief's wife. But Palourdes must have found Pauline's excesses difficult to stomach from the very beginning. It was less easy to be sure, about Seraphine. She had been in the prison whence her mother had been dragged by the mob, and undoubtedly she had been forced to watch her die. No one could say what else she had been forced to endure before encountering Palourdes. In many ways, Richilde thought, her life had been very like Annette's, save that she had been half Annette's age when the catastrophe had occurred. And save that she had twice Annette's strength of mind, in that she had not gone mad. Or was her quietness, her constant self communion, but a form of madness?

But certainly she was sane enough to understand what had happened. The French had sailed away, like the British, after eight futile months of murder and

183

bloodshed, and yellow fever. They had left their Commanding General behind them, and more than a third of his original invading army. For the second time in five years St Domingue had proved only a burial ground for a European army. So once again the black people were going to be granted an opportunity to make something of themselves. To become a nation. Or were they? Seraphine Palourdes, now even more of a renegade white than Richilde de Mortmain, must doubt that more than anyone.

Jean-Jacques Dessalines was also looking around him. 'They have gone,' he said, speaking loudly, so that he could be widely overheard. 'We have driven them out. We have driven them out because I, Jean-Jacques Dessalines, determined that they should be opposed, that they should be driven out. Where Toussaint wished only to deal with the white people, to remain subservient to them, I said, death to all white people. That is the only language they understand. And that is the language of victory. Was I not right?'

The Negro soldiers had crowded round to hear him. Now they shouted, 'Yes,' with a great voice.

'So now I tell you this,' Dessalines shouted. 'There will be no more white people. No more colony. From today we are free of that. We are independent. We are a nation of free men.'

'Yes,' they shouted.

'General Dessalines has spoken well,' Petion said. 'And truly. We will show the world how we can live, as free and equal people. We shall be the Republic of St Domingue, and we shall have a president, as they do in the United States . . .'

'President?' Dessalines roared. 'President? A president is the white man's way. We are black men. We are not ruled by presidents, who are elected and then discarded. Who sway people by oratory. Why, Monsieur Petion, the people might even choose *you*, as president.'

184

Richilde clutched Henry's arm, but Petion decided not take up the insult.

'You have a better suggestion, General?' he asked, speaking quietly.

'We are black people,' Dessalines shouted again. 'We wish to be ruled by strength, that we too may be strong. We seek a king. The strongest, the most able man amongst us shall be king.' His gaze swept them, and he jerked his head at one of his aides, who had obviously been previously coached.

'Long live King Jean-Jacques,' the man shouted.

'King Jean-Jacques,' the cry was taken up.

'Long live King Jean-Jacques.'

'Monsieur?' Dessalines inquired of Petion.

Who looked at the men surrounding him, and shrugged. 'Long live King Jean-Jacques the First, of St Domingue.'

Dessalines looked at Henry, Richilde at his side. But she could say or do nothing. Henry remained what he had always been at heart, a soldier, faithful to the ideals that Toussaint, and perhaps even herself, she realised, had instilled in him. And Dessalines was his superior officer. Toussaint had made that clear.

'Long live King Jean-Jacques the First,' he shouted, and now the cheers became general – Richilde realised that there had been a considerable number of the blacks waiting on Henry's response.

But it was too late now. Jean-Jacques was beaming on his people, and preparing himself for his new role. 'Now let us see what the French have left behind them,' he said.

'This woman,' they shouted, and Richilde's heart constricted as she saw Jacqueline Chavannes, naked and with her hands bound behind her, her glorious hair a dishevelled mass clouding across her face, her body showing the marks of mistreatment and the emaciation of starvation, being dragged forward.

'Who is this?' Dessalines demanded.

'We found her beneath the palace,' they said.

'She is, or was, General LeClerc's mistress,' Boyer said.

'I have been a French prisoner,' Jacqueline said, her voice as strong as ever. 'For four months they have kept me locked up in a cell. They are fiends. I hate them. I have prayed for your coming, Great King.'

'You are a traitor,' Dessalines said. 'Where is the General?'

'He is buried,' one of the captains said. 'We have found his grave.'

'Then open it up,' Dessalines said. 'Let us gaze upon his corpse.'

Jacqueline looked at Richilde, her face seeming to collapse as she realised what was going to happen to her. 'Mercy,' she said. 'For the love of God, Richilde, *help* me,' she screamed.

Richilde made to step forward, and was restrained by Henry; now was not the time to challenge the new king.

'And then we will bury him again,' Dessalines said, with a roar of laughter. 'With his mistress in his arms.'

Chapter 6

THE TYRANT

Dessalines was a grotesque misfit as emperor of a nation. He thundered forth pronunciamentoes, mostly intended to inflame his countrymen against white people in general and the French in particular; he complained bitterly about the tiresome aspects of government; he spent long hours changing from one magnificent uniform to another and attempting to learn how to dance the minuet. His brutalities indicted every Negro in the West Indies; his absurdities made a black skin an object of ridicule.

The surgeon raised his head. 'He is dead.' The men seemed to take a step forward together, but Kit was in front of them all, looking down on the body of his cousin. The most brilliant man in America, Alexander Hamilton had been considered. Shot to death.

He raised his head, looked across the bed at Aaron Burr. The dapper little man, Vice President of the United States – and he could, Kit remembered, have achieved the Presidency itself had he not disclaimed his rights to a fresh vote after tying with Thomas Jefferson in the election of 1801 – flushed, but would not lower his eyes. 'You were there, Captain Hamilton,' he said. 'It was a fair fight.'

'Between a good shot and a poor one,' Kit said. 'Oh, aye. It was a fair fight.'

He left the room, was followed by the President himself. 'It *was* a fair fight, Kit. God knows we would all have wished Aaron to fire in the air once your cousin missed. But he was not obliged to.'

'Because they hated each other.'

'Had they loved each other, would they have fought in the first place?'

Kit sighed, his shoulders slumped.

Jefferson embraced him. 'I have been told he was your only living relative.'

Kit shook his head. 'I have other relatives.'

'But none so dear?'

'I have a sister,' Kit said.

'A sister? Now that I never knew.'

'And cousins. Although where they are I have no idea.'

'But you know where to find this sister of yours?'

'Oh, aye, Mr President. I know where to find her.'

Jefferson hesitated for a moment. 'It might be best for you to take a holiday, Kit,' he said. 'You are angry, and that is no proper state for a man to conduct business. You are also a better shot than Aaron . . .' he smiled. 'I cannot afford to have another member of my administration brought down. Not even if, perhaps, he deserves it. In a few months' time, things will look different.'

Kit went down the stairs to his horse. A holiday. But was that not what he wanted to do more than anything else in the world? Where he wanted to go, more than anywhere else in the world?

It was two years since he had sailed from Cap François, leaving Pauline LeClerc and Jacqueline Chavannes wrestling on the bedroom floor. Two years in which he had heard nothing precise of what happened to all those people who had played so large a part in his life. He knew merely what was common knowledge. That the French had been evacuated by their fleet the moment it could return to their rescue, and that the

Negroes had declared their independence, and chosen the bull-man, Jean-Jacques Dessalines, as their first king. He knew too that Bonaparte, in offering to sell the entire vast hinterland of Louisiana to the United States, had definitely turned his back on the New World as a goal of French expansion, and that therefore St Domingue should be left in peace to pursue its own salvation – the British, having had their fingers so badly burned in the nineties, were not likely to interfere again.

Just as he knew that Pauline LeClerc, pursuing her self-interested way through life, and having after all survived the yellow fever, had remarried, an Italian prince named Camillo Borghese, and was now no doubt indulging her doubtful pleasures to the total scandalisation of Rome.

And he knew too that Toussaint l'Ouverture was dead, technically of lung disease following a winter confined in a damp Alpine cell, but more truly of a broken heart. Had he been allowed to remain in St Domingue, then indeed would his people have pursued their salvation. But he had been succeeded by an altogether different man. With whom Henry and Richilde, and Seraphine Palourdes, would have to make their way as best they could. If they had even survived to try.

And he no longer had anything to keep him in New York. As Jefferson had said, things would look different in a few months' time.

'It doesn't seem to have changed a great deal,' Rogers the mate said, peering through his telescope at the houses of Cap François. 'Do you suppose we'll find a cargo worth shipping?'

For Kit had not told the mate that he might be in command on the way back. It was not a decision he had yet taken himself. Nor could they suspect his motives in any way. During the last two years he had confined his West Indian trading to Kingston and San Juan and

Havana, but those routes had necessitated sailing past Hispaniola often enough, and he had never failed to peer at those green clad peaks through his glass. It had been his childhood home, and his crew knew that. What could be more reasonable than that he should wish to revisit it at the first opportunity?

'If they wish to trade,' he said. 'But you'll keep the guns loaded, Mr Rogers, just in case.'

The anchor plunged into the still blue water, clean now, at least of corpses, he supposed. The jollyboat was lowered, and he was rowed ashore, happy to recognise the blue uniformed officer who commanded the guard. 'Captain Gounod,' he said.

'Captain Hamilton,' the Negro acknowledged. 'We had not expected you. You'll salute His Majesty.'

'Eh?' Kit turned, sharply, half expecting to see Dessalines standing behind him, looked at the wooden carving resting on a stone plinth at the end of the dock. There had been a stone statue there once, of Louis the Fifteenth, as he remembered. This had been torn down and replaced by the wooden sculpture, like all West African art a strange melange of the grotesque and the exquisite, purporting to represent a man wearing European uniform and carrying a sword, but with heavily Negroid features.

Gounod saluted, waited for Kit to do the same. 'There will be a proper statue in due course,' he explained. 'When we can find a stonemason to carve it. You are visiting General Christophe and Madame de Mortmain?'

'Why, yes,' Kit said, feeling the tension oozing from his mind as he learned that they at least had survived the storm.

'Then I will give you an escort.' Gounod snapped his fingers, and one of his men hurried forward, to lead Kit through the streets, in the direction, he realised, of the old Governor General's palace. Where he had left Jacqueline and Pauline to wrestle. But as Pauline had fal-

190

len so thoroughly on her feet he supposed Jacqueline had also prospered; she had risen from the ashes before.

It was reassuring, however, to learn that Henry was once more military commander of the port, and indeed the entire north coast, and that Dessalines had not apparently turned out to be quite the mad tyrant he had expected. But yet, things were very different to when he had visited here during Toussaint's brief reign. He looked at groups of Negroes still employed in rebuilding the partially destroyed town, and at others being marched off, clearly to do some field work, as it was still early in the morning. They were marshalled like any slave gang, and were driven by the whips and shouts of overseers, like any slave gang – but the overseers were black men wearing army uniforms. He glanced at his companion, but the soldier did not seem disturbed by the sight, or even interested in it, so he decided against asking any questions.

He climbed the steps of the palace, heart pounding, remembering the occasions he had visited here in the past, and indeed, the occasions on which he had fled here, his heart fit to burst. But there was Richilde . . . and Seraphine Palourdes? He stopped, quite unable to proceed.

'Kit!' Richilde hurried down the steps to embrace him. He had seen her in so many guises he never knew quite what to expect of her. Today she was in what he might disparagingly have called, had he wished, her white Negress role, wearing a very simple housegown, her feet bare, and with her hair concealed beneath a bandanna; she had obviously been engaged in her domestic chores. Yet was she, in her tall vigour, the health of her delighted flush, the clarity of her eyes, the firmness of her grasp, the same intensely healthy woman as he had ever known, even at the age of thirty-eight.

But his gaze kept drifting to Seraphine Palourdes.

191

As Richilde saw. 'I think you have already met Seraphine,' she said.

Kit gave her a quick glance, but she was clearly innocent of any double meaning. He kissed Seraphine's hand. 'I had heard you had elected to remain in St Domingue, madame,' he said, inhaling her scent, once again enjoying the velvety texture of her flesh, remembering so much. 'And yet had not expected to meet you, so soon. Your husband . . .'

'Is adjutant to General Christophe, monsieur,' she said, quietly as ever.

'But Kit . . . to have you back . . .' Richilde linked arms with him as they went inside, past black servants who stood respectfully to attention. 'I would have written, but . . . is all well with you?'

'Alexander is dead,' he told her.

She stopped, her face aghast. 'Alexander? He was hardly older than you.'

'He did not die of a disease, Richilde. He was shot to death in a duel. By a man called Aaron Burr.'

'Oh, Kit.' Her distress was clearly genuine, although she had never laid eyes on Alexander, that she could remember. 'I am so sorry.'

'But Henry is well?'

'Henry is always well. Even if he works too hard. There is so much to be done.'

'I had observed.'

She gave him a quick glance. 'It is His Majesty's determination, Kit, to restore the prosperity of St Domingue.'

'With whips?' Kit inquired. 'You approve of this? Henry approves of this?'

'In St Domingue, Captain Hamilton,' Seraphine Palourdes observed. 'It pays to approve of what His Majesty decrees.'

Kit looked from her to his sister.

Who shrugged. 'He is at least ruling. We see little of him, thank God. He has made a capital for himself, in

192

the forest. We hear rumours, but he leaves Henry much to himself, to get on with the task of restoring Cap François, and restoring the sugar crop, too. He will be so pleased to see you. Shipping is hard to come by, since the French left.'

'There is so much that I wish to know,' he said. 'So much I have to understand, obviously. Etienne? And Annette?'

'They left with the French army, so far as we know. Certainly they are no longer here. Vergée d'Or is a government sugar plantation.'

'Poor Annette,' he said. 'How she must have hated leaving again. Jacqueline Chavannes? Did she also leave with the French? I had gained the impression that she and Madame LeClerc were no longer exactly friends.'

The two women exchanged glances, and then Richilde looked at the door in relief. 'Here's Henry,' she said. 'He will be so pleased to see you.'

'Alive?' Kit asked. 'They buried her *alive*?'

'It was terrible,' Seraphine Palourdes whispered. 'How she screamed, and begged. But she was bound, and placed in his arms. Can you believe it? He had already mouldered to a skeleton.'

Kit looked at Richilde. There was so much to be remembered, about the three of them. More than either of them knew.

More than Henry knew, certainly. But he also could remember. 'She was a tragic figure,' he said. 'All of her family were doomed, it seemed almost from birth. But yet . . . do you remember your first night in St Domingue, Kit? How your cousin . . .' His sombre gaze rested on Richilde for a moment. 'Had a man torn to pieces by dogs? To impress you, I think, with his terrible power.'

'I remember,' Kit said.

'Well, I think His Majesty had some such idea in mind, as he had just been elected king.' Henry half smiled, a rare lightening of his grim features. 'You must also remember, Kit, that my people are for the main part simple and uneducated. They believe what they see, and can remember. Hence this.' He shrugged his shoulders. Because his jacket was certainly one of the most gorgeous Kit had seen: blue, faced with red, but with gold braid at every button hole and also composing his epaulettes, and with a white cross belt to support a silver hilted sword. Henry's eyes twinkled. 'I can promise you that His Majesty's uniforms are far more brilliant. But you will have the opportunity to see for yourself, soon enough. I will have to report your arrival, and he will certainly wish to see you. He is greedy for news from the outside world, as he is, indeed, for trade with the outside world. And there are few traders who come to St Domingue, now. They think we have reverted to savagery.'

Kit looked down the sweep of the dining table, at the crystal and the silver cutlery. And then thought of the work gangs outside. 'I would say you have reverted entirely to the St Domingue of twenty years ago. As you say, your king is but a reincarnation of Philippe de Mortmain.'

Henry frowned, and indicated the door with his head, to suggest that not all the footmen were necessarily loyal to *him*.

'But can you seriously support such methods, Henry?' Kit persisted. 'You?'

Henry sighed. 'His Majesty is right, in that our people must work, Kit. We must restore St Domingue to prosperity. Then perhaps it may be possible to allow them more leisure, more choice. We do not imagine the path ahead of us will be an easy one, or a brief one. There is, as you may suppose, much discontent, which means we must sometimes deal harshly with men and women who have fought for us, and supported us, faithfully and long. Yet must the work be done. If you have any better suggestions, then believe me, I will be happy to listen to you, and to present them to His Majesty. Or indeed, as I say, you may present them yourself.'

Kit looked at Richilde, and then back at Henry again. 'But you support him, and will continue to do so.'

'He is my king,' Henry said simply. 'Chosen by my people.'

They rode through a jungle roadway, a squad of hussars first, brightly clad in new crimson uniforms with yellow braid on their breeches and across their chests, then the General's party, with his ladies, then their wagon, for it was a two-day journey and there was no food to be had on the way, and then a rear guard of more hussars.

'By whom do we expect to be attacked?' Kit asked.

'It is His Majesty's orders that we always travel well protected,' Henry explained. 'It is his opinion that the more people see of the army the better. Besides, if we are prepared to be attacked, by anyone, then we stand less risk of being attacked, by anyone.'

Warfare, bloodshed, the necessity to be constantly on the alert, had clearly entered his blood. And perhaps Richilde's as well, Kit thought, watching his sister, wearing a sky blue habit, riding sidesaddle as she might have done as Philippe de Mortmain's wife, followed by her maids and even one of her cooks. She looked from left to right, at the trees which clustered close, certainly watchfully, but equally certainly without apprehension at anything which might be about to happen. She and Henry were the new aristocrats of this savage, unstable world, and they moved through it with the utmost certainty.

And what of Seraphine Palourdes? She rode just behind Richilde, as was her place. She was doomed, it seemed, always to be the inferior. But could she so quickly have become accustomed to this new life? He felt *she* was more nervous than she pretended, kept casting anxious glances into the trees on either side. How the sight of her, the knowledge of her presence, made him remember that night on board the *Bucentaure*, and then remember so much more. Jacqueline, being interred alive in the arms of a corpse. Was it possible to imagine a more horrible fate? And it had been at the whim of a man who could so command the execution of any person in his kingdom, and who had never made any secret of his hatred of white people.

And who was supported faithfully by Henry, and therefore by all those who supported Henry, because that was his nature.

He longed to ride beside the French girl, to engage her in conversation, to discover if she also remembered that night, or anything particular about it. To discover, in fact, if it might be possible to seduce her again? Because suddenly he was aware of desire, where he had almost supposed it dead.

But that way led both to madness and dishonour. So instead he rode beside Albert Palourdes; he had last done that, he remembered, the day after the French had landed, three years before. The day LeClerc had made his intentions so terribly clear.

'Will you make your home here now?' he asked. 'I mean, in St Domingue?' he added, as the soldier's sombre face turned towards him.

'I cannot return to France, monsieur,' Palourdes pointed out. 'Not as long as Bonaparte rules. And now that he too is an emperor, that may be for a very long time. Besides, I will prosper here. This brother-in-law of yours, this Christophe, is a man of many parts. But he is to be trusted.'

'And the King?'

Palourdes's face seemed to close. 'I do not know His Majesty as well as I know General Christophe,' he said. 'I serve General Christophe.'

Kit would have continued the conversation, probed further, but his nostrils were assailed by a dreadful stench. He looked at the ladies, saw that each of them

196

was holding a perfumed handkerchief to her nose. They rode round a bend in the track and sighted the imperial citadel. But before the gate there was a row of gallows, to either side of the road, and from each cross bar there hung the naked body of a man, or a woman, some freshly dead, others already decomposing, all surrounded by a cloud of red headed crows, who cawed angrily and flapped their wings as they flew away from the intruders.

'His Majesty guards himself with the bodies of his enemies,' Palourdes observed. 'Or his suspected enemies.'

Kit urged his horse forward beside Richilde's. But there was nothing he could say to her, and nothing, apparently, that she wished to say to him. He studied the approaching village, for it certainly could not be described as a town, was reminded of the drawings he had seen of African kraals. Here was the same circle of wooden palisades, with a single gate, and inside, the same accumulation of huts. The roofs were of troolie palms rather than more securely thatched, and the guards wore brilliant uniforms and carried muskets and bayonets rather than spears and bows, but the differences were of degree rather than fact. Dessalines was clearly reaching all the way back into his West African heritage, in creating this refuge in the jungle after the only pattern he knew. But he was carrying his people with him, backwards.

General Christophe's party was allowed through the gate, but once within the hussars were relieved of their weapons and their horses, and led away to barracks apparently reserved for visiting soldiery. The main party then had to submit to a search, which included even the women, while the men also were disarmed. Richilde stood very straight, and with her eyes closed as the Negro captain slid his hands over her body, raised her skirts to make sure there were no poignards strap-

197

ped to her thighs or calves. Seraphine Palourdes, submitting to the same humiliation, breathed deeply and could not prevent her cheeks from glowing.

Kit looked at Henry, who shrugged. 'His Majesty does not yet feel secure, Kit.'

But it was easy to see that he did not enjoy watching his womanfolk manhandled.

They were given no chance to discuss the matter further, however, being immediately escorted, almost as if they were prisoners, up the central walk towards the largest of the thatched houses. To either side there were gaily uniformed soldiers, and their women and children, all clad in the most splendid new clothes: the little boys with satin knee breeches in a variety of colours and white stockings with buckled shoes, their sisters also a mass of satin and silk, with brightly coloured bonnets and parasols and a rustle of frilly underskirts. But they remained, just simple children, picking their noses and gawking at the white skins, just as they were also obviously sadly undernourished.

At the palace, for such it was obviously intended to be, they were admitted through a small door into an ante-chamber, which was crowded with men, and women, all wearing the very best, jostling about to obtain a position nearest the inner door, protected by two enormous green-jacketed hussars, each carrying a drawn sabre, and beyond which there came the most peculiar of sounds, certainly intended, Kit supposed, to be musical, but hardly recognisable as any tune or rhythm he had ever heard before.

He went forward, with Henry and Richilde, to look past the guards into the reception room, and at King Jean-Jacques the First who, together with half a dozen men and an equal number of women, was dancing what was obviously intended to be a minuet, guided and instructed by an elderly mulatto woman, while on the far side of the room half a dozen musicians scraped at unfamiliar fiddles. All of the people in the room were elegantly uniformed or gowned, with Dessalines himself, in a pale green frock coat over white knee breeches, quite the most spectacular person present. But there was something irresistibly amusing about that huge, bull-like figure being so dressed in any event, much less cavorting about the floor in the centre of what was really nothing better than a large hut. Kit could only suppress a smile with an effort.

And just in time, for Dessalines had looked across the room and seen the new arrivals. Instantly he clapped his hands, and the music ceased. 'Henry,' he said, beckoning him in. 'It is good to see you. Richilde!'

Henry bowed, and Richilde sank into a deep curtsey.

'Major Palourdes. Madame.' Dessalines's eyes lingered on Seraphine, also curtseying, then he looked at Kit. 'The American sea captain.'

'Your Majesty.' Kit followed Henry's example, and bowed.

'By God, but I am hot. Hot,' Dessalines shouted, his voice rising into a bellow. 'Fetch me something to wear.'

Two valets immediately hurried into the room to remove his green jacket; Kit saw with surprise that he wore nothing underneath; another valet stood by with a towel to dry that mighty torso. And two more were waiting with a fresh uniform jacket, this one in crimson with black facings.

'You,' Dessalines said, pointing at Kit. 'May be useful to us. Has Petion come yet?' he demanded of the major-domo.

'Not as yet, Your Majesty,' the official replied, in a deep bow.

'Ha! Trust him to be late. Out,' the King shouted. 'Out!'

The ladies and the courtiers hurried for the door.

'That mulatto whore does not know anything about dancing,' Dessalines announced. 'And she used to teach it, mind. She is a cheat and a swindler and I will

199

have her flogged. You, Richilde, you will teach me to dance.'

Richilde gave a quick glance at Henry. 'If you wish it, Your Majesty.'

'I wish it. You, and Madame Palourdes. You will teach me. Tomorrow. But now . . . Henry, I have received no money from you this last month.'

'There is none to be had, Your Majesty,' Henry said.

'That is nonsense. There is always money to be had. People must have money. There is a consignment of clothes and uniforms arriving at Port-au-Prince from Jamaica, next month, and I must have money. The confounded Englishman will not even enter the harbour. I have to send the money out to him. If I had a navy . . . even a sloop of war. But I am surrounded by cheats and traitors. You, Captain Hamilton. You will bring clothes for me from New York? I will show you what I wish.'

'They will also have to be paid for, Your Majesty,' Kit pointed out.

'I know that. That is why I have summoned you here, Henry. And Petion. Where the devil is Petion? I will have him flogged. He thinks generals cannot be flogged. I will show him how wrong he is. Damned mulatto scoundrel. All mulattos are scoundrels. They are only one degree better than white people . . .' He stared at Seraphine Palourdes. 'Scoundrels. But black people are scoundrels, too. They will not work. Henry, you do not make them work enough.'

'They are working very hard, Your Majesty,' Henry said, patiently. 'Too hard. Perhaps if you were to give them something more worthwhile to work for . . .'

'Bah. They will not work. And I will tell you why they will not work.' His enormous forefinger stabbed through the air. 'It is because they do not understand that I am their King. Too many of them remember me, as they remember you, as mere slaves. We must correct that, Henry.'

He paused, but no one said anything.

'Because I *am* King,' Dessalines insisted. 'And if I am King, then I am chosen by Ogone Badagris himself.' He glared at them. 'Do you deny that?'

'I am sure that is true, Your Majesty,' Richilde agreed.

'Then I *am* Ogone Badagris. His spirit has entered my spirit, and we are as one. Is that not right?'

Richilde hesitated, but how often had that very thought occurred to her? 'It is certainly possible, Your Majesty.'

'Well, I shall prove it to these scum. I shall prove it,' he shouted, and Kit almost expected to see him beat his chest. 'I am the lord of the voodoo. I am the *hougan* of all *hougans*. Summon my people from all over the country, Henry. Call them here. Their *hougan* would demonstrate his power to them.'

'Voodoo,' Alexander Petion said in disgust. 'A nation, governed by voodoo. Is that not the very edge of madness?'

But, like everyone else, he stood in the vast crowd in the clearing outside the royal kraal, watching King Jean-Jacques. And his aides. Richilde was taken back all of the twenty years and more to that night outside Vergée d'Or, perhaps the most important night of her life. But not one she had ever expected to repeat. She glanced at Kit, standing beside her, and at the Palourdes, standing just beyond him. They were the only white people present. And they had no idea that she had ever stood in the darkness and the wind before, just as they had no idea what was about to happen. They stared at the tethered, frantic cockerels, listened to the beat of the rada drums, with fascinated attention, watched a young man, tall and strong, but sweating with apprehension, who was being led forward to sit cross legged on the earth, his handmaidens waiting attentively at his side.

And stared at their King, shrouded in the red robe of

his sacerdotal office, who now waved at the drummers to lower their cadence, while he stopped forward.

Madness, she thought, But is that not what has overtaken this country, this people . . . this woman? She had grown to love the Negroes, as she had fought with them and laughed with them and lived with them and cried with them, and all but died with them. Besides, they were Henry's people. But she was always aware that she was living in the midst of an uncontrolable emotional force, which would somehow have to be harnessed before any real progress could be made. She still thought that Henry possessed the strength to do that, still dreamed, of the day which had to come, when Henry would rule St Domingue with her at his side to guide and advise him, and had been foretold in the prophecy. Without her dreams she was nothing. But in reality she often found the future quite impossible to contemplate. These last few weeks she had for the first time really appreciated having Kit at her side. Because they were all growing older, even Henry, while they obeyed a madman.

Because Dessalines did not *wish* to harness the unstable power he pretended to rule. He sought to release it.

'Hear me, oh mighty one, Ogone Badagris, Lord of the skies and the earth, of fire and water, and of the souls of men,' he shouted, his voice echoing over the trees. 'Hear me, oh Damballah Oueddo, oh Dreadful One, master of the passions that make us men. We are your people, chosen by you, and led by you to victory. I am your King, chosen by you. Guide me so that I may lead my people to greatness and prosperity. Inspire me that I may know what must be done and that I shall do it. Show my people the way, that lies through me, that they may be humble in their hearts, and obedient in their actions. These things we ask of you, oh mighty ones, as we live and work in your sight and at your bidding.'

He paused, his mighty chest rising and falling, while the drums swelled in noise, booming their message across the forest, undoubtedly taking hold of the minds of those who heard them, as once they had taken hold of her own mind. Once again she stole a quick glance at the people beside her. Seraphine's eyes were almost closed, and she breathed slowly and regularly. Palourdes and Kit were both staring at the King, certainly caught up in the mood of the moment. Henry also stared at Dessalines, his face hard. But like her, he was not affected this time. He felt her glance, and returned it, then gave her hand a quick squeeze of reassurance.

The ceremonial sabre was brought forward, gleaming in the flickering light. Dessalines held it high, while the drumbeat rose into a tremendous roar of sound, and then he uttered a great shriek and swung it around his head, slicing cleanly through bone and muscle and arteries, throwing away the sword and grasping the head between his hands as he did so, expertly, holding it high, while the two girls fanned the blood spouting neck. Seraphine gave a gasp and sank to her knees – but she still watched, as Dessalines replaced the head, as the blood red cloth was thrown over the young man, as the cadence of the drums changed to the rhythm of the dance.

And as the young man slowly toppled forward to sprawl on the earth, his severed head rolling away from his dead body.

'He *is* mad,' Petion said. He walked with Kit and Boyer and Henry, in the garden of the palace, listened to the music emanating from the reception room. 'You must admit that, Christophe. To execute one of your own people, without reason . . .'

'He had his reasons,' Henry said. 'He explained them to you. He did not expect that boy to die.'

'Now, Christophe, you know and I know that these

voodoo ceremonies where the dead are brought back to life are all illusions. Dessalines merely has no knowledge of how it is done. Possibly he believes in it himself. That only confirms his madness.'

'Then you are condemning our entire nation to madness,' Henry said.

Petion stopped walking, stared at him. 'You do not believe in this nonsense yourself, surely?'

'What I believe is my business,' Henry said. 'And you are talking treason.' He gave one of his rare, grim smiles. 'That is not a very sensible thing to do, when actually inside the palace, and without even a sword at your side.'

'I am saying what I must because we are all here. You must realise where his madness is leading us. Where it will certainly lead us in the future. We have had people at Port-au-Prince, visitors from the United States, and from England, and France, and Germany, good people who wish us well, who have come all this way to see what the black man and the brown have made of their independence, only to be repelled by the poverty of the people, by the primitive conditions under which most of them are forced to exist, by the death sentences which are handed out as freely as the planters used to inflict the lash . . . God knows what the world would say of us were it to know this charnel house, where the stink of rotting flesh is never absent, much less attend one of His Majesty's voodoo ceremonies.'

'There is no hope for our economy,' Boyer put in, on a less emotional level, 'while His Majesty spends every cent he can scrape together on uniforms for himself and his soldiers. Why does he need to keep so many men under arms? Who are we going to fight?'

'The French will come back,' Henry said. 'Bonaparte does not forget. The very presence of a Negro nation where once was a French colony will bring him back. It is a mortal affront to his prestige.'

'If Bonaparte ever intended to return to St Domingue, he would not have sold Lousiana to the Americans,' Petion said. 'Is that not true, Captain Hamilton?'

'I cannot say,' Kit said. 'He is well on the way to becoming absolute master of Europe. And with Pitt and Nelson both dead, it is difficult to see who is going to oppose him. He certainly has the *power* to return here.'

'It is not practical,' Boyer said, 'while the British navy rules the oceans.'

'Nor does it alter the fact that we are living, if that is a reasonable word to use, at the mercy of a grotesque tyrant,' Petion said. He cocked his head to listen to the music. 'A man who dances the minuet one minute, and cuts off the heads of his subjects the next.'

'What are you proposing?' Henry asked, quietly.

'That he be deposed. That we collect our forces and put an end to this farce. Your people from the north will follow you, Christophe. Certainly mine in the south will follow me.'

'And His Majesty's will follow him,' Henry said. 'And we will start a war all over again. A war which will be fought to the last man. There is no fleet going to evacuate any of *us* who decide we have had enough.'

'Dessalines's men can hardly follow him, if he is not there,' Boyer said, also speaking very quietly.

'You are proposing to assassinate your King,' Henry told him.

'For God's sake,' Petion exclaimed. 'The man was a slave but fifteen years ago. And since then he has been nothing more than a soldier. *We* chose him King. Well, it is time we realised our mistake.'

'Yet is he the King,' Henry said. 'I will not rebel against my King.' He gave another grim smile as the two mulattos exchanged glances. 'I shall not betray you, either, gentlemen. I believe you have nothing but the good of St Domingue at heart. But I will tell you this: if

205

you raise the standard of revolt in the south, I will fight beside His Majesty against you, and you will bring upon your peoples the most dreadful calamity.'

'And you will stand there and do nothing, the next time *His Majesty* decides to attempt a voodoo ceremony?' Petion demanded. 'Suppose he were to choose as his victim someone dear to you? Even Richilde, perhaps?'

Henry stared at him, brows drawing together. 'You may consider His Majesty to be mad, General Petion. I certainly do not consider him to be a fool.'

He walked away from them.

'What is this?' the King bellowed. 'Papers? Papers? I have no time to read papers. Tell me what they say.'

Richilde and Seraphine exchanged glances; they were well aware that Dessalines, like Henry, could not read.

The manservant bowed low. 'It is a petition from the people of Morne Rouge, Your Majesty,' he said. 'They beg to be excused from next month's tax collection, because of a rain storm they have suffered. Rain such as no man has ever seen before, Your Majesty, which has washed away all of their crops, and flooded their homes, causing great damage.'

'Rain storms? Rain storms? What do I care about rain storms? I *send* rain storms,' Dessalines shouted. 'To remind my people of my power. For am I not Ogone Badagris, come to life to rule over them? They have been punished, for thinking evil thoughts of their King. Their taxes next month will be doubled. Tell them that. And if they are not paid, I will personally go and collect them. With my soldiers. Tell them that.'

The secretary bowed, and withdrew. Richilde patted a bead of sweat from her temple. As it was still early in the afternoon it was extremely hot, and she was also overheated by the endless dancing. She was also worried. Because Henry was not here. She always worried when separated from Henry, but never before had she been forced to remain in the royal palace while he had been despatched on some entirely unnecessary investigation of a reported uprising in the east. Only the presence of Kit, who had been invited to remain a while longer, in order to discuss trading projects with the King's ministers, was the least reassuring. But Kit was not Henry. He had no faithful regiments at his back. Had even Petion and Boyer remained, she would have been reassured, but they had returned to Port-au-Prince in the south. And Albert Palourdes was a negligible quality in the affairs of state.

So she remained, with Seraphine, to entertain a madman, and teach him to dance. There could be no doubting the fact of Dessalines's madness, now. When he had cut off that unfortunate boy's head, and been unable to restore him to life, he had gazed at the corpse in utter disbelief for several seconds, then he had thrown back his head and given an almost animal like howl of anguished dismay. He had, of course, very rapidly recovered himself. Whatever the twisted mental processes he endured, his was a sharp and active brain. He had laughed at the horror around him, taken the credit for the disaster as his own decision, to reveal to them his power. It was difficult to be sure whether or not anyone had been convinced, as they had dispersed to their villages to repeat what they had seen. What was certain was that Dessalines himself had been severely shaken. He now pronounced himself a reincarnation of the god on every possible occasion, almost as if he was trying to convince himself.

But what would happen when he attempted the feat again?

And indeed, what would happen before then, as his brain sought some other remedial action? There could be no doubt, for instance, that he had always desired her, had been restrained from reaching out for her only because he feared Henry.

207

There could also be no doubt that he desired Seraphine. And now he had them both, with Henry sent away. Being Henry, he had obeyed without question, saying only, 'I leave Richilde in your care, Your Majesty, until my return.'

But he had gone. And suddenly, for the first time since the early days of the revolution, she was afraid he might not return.

The door had closed behind the secretary, the ladies and gentlemen were taking their places again, Richilde and an equally perspiring Seraphine at their head, while the musicians struck up their tune . . .

'Stop that noise,' Dessalines bellowed. 'Stop it. Do you think I wish to be driven deaf with your scrapings? Out. Out. Get out. All of you. Get out.'

The musicians ran for the door. The ladies and gentlemen curtsied and bowed, and followed them.

'Not you, Richilde,' Dessalines said. 'You will stay. And you, Seraphine.'

They hesitated, again exchanging glances. But the door had already closed upon the others, and they were alone, with the King.

'I am wearied,' he said. 'With all of this dancing. All of this business. I should not be wearied. I am Ogone Badagris.' His huge forefinger stabbed the air. 'Do you not believe me, Richilde? Speak, woman.'

Certainly lies cost nothing. 'I believe that, Your Majesty,' she said.

'Well, you are wrong,' he shouted. 'If I were truly Ogone Badagris, I would not be weary. I would be able to dance. I would have restored that boy to life. Can you deny that?'

'No man, Your Majesty, can understand the intentions of the gods.'

'Ah, but they can,' Dessalines said. 'The gods make their intentions plain enough. It is the blindness of men which leads them into error. I have been a fool, all of these years. Can you deny that?'

Richilde drew a long breath. 'Your people would not agree with you, Your Majesty,' she said. They would not dare, any more than I would dare, she thought.

'Well, I can tell you that I have. Is it not true that many years ago there was a prophecy, made by the great *mamaloi*, Céléste, on Vergée d'Or?'

Richilde stared at him, her heart beginning to slow. Seraphine looked from one to the other, in bewildered apprehension, aware that there were forces swirling about her which she did not understand, but which might well encompass her destruction.

'I know of no prophecies, Your Majesty,' Richilde said.

'Do not lie to me, Richilde,' Dessalines shouted. 'I know all about this prophecy, and so do you. It has been a beacon, guiding Henry and yourself for twenty years. Can you deny this?'

'Your Majesty . . .'

'Black he shall be,' Dessalines intoned. 'Black as the night from whence he comes, and into which he will sweep the whites. And big he will be, a man of greatness apparent to all. Yet will his might be surrounded by beauty, and his blackness surrounded by light. By this beauty, by this light, shall you know him.' He threw out his right arm, finger pointing. 'You always supposed that it referred to Henry, and yourself. Do not deny it. Many people have spoken to me of it, have shown me how Henry, alone of the leaders of the first revolt, alone of Toussaint, and Boukman, and Jean François, has survived, unharmed. But I have also survived unharmed, Richilde. And I am as mighty a man as Henry.' He grinned. 'And as black. Why should the prophecy not apply to me? Have I not stumbled all these years through the darkness, waiting only for the white beauty to come to me?' He held out his hand to Seraphine Palourdes.

Seraphine took a step backwards, licked her lips, looked from Dessalines to Richilde in stark fear.

'I will make you my queen, pretty Frenchwoman,' Dessalines said. 'I will let your white beauty surround my black strength. I will do it now.' He unbuttoned his jacket.

'Oh God, oh God,' Seraphine gasped. 'Help me, Richilde. *Please!*'

'Your Majesty,' Richilde said urgently, realising that the moment she had for so long feared had finally arrived. 'You cannot take Madame Palourdes to wife. She is already married.'

'Ha,' Dessalines shouted, throwing his jacket on the floor and releasing his breeches in turn to show them a hugely erected penis. 'What do I care for marriages? I will make you a widow, eh?' He gave a bellow of laughter. 'And then a wife.' He reached for her, and when she tried to duck away, drove his fingers into her hair, dragging her towards him. 'Now,' he said. 'Now, I will make you a goddess. I . . .' his other hand was peeling down her bodice, ripping away the layers of material as if they had been paper, to bare her from the waist up. Seraphine's reaction was perhaps instinctive. She swung her hand, and Dessalines gave a howl of rage and pain and released her as he jumped backwards, blood streaming down his cheek where her nails had torn the flesh.

'Oh, my God,' Richilde said. Her legs seemed to have turned to stone. She simply could not move.

Seraphine stared at the King, and saw him staring back, saw too the enraged anger in his eyes, knew that she was about to die. She threw back her head and screamed, a high pitched wail which reverberated through the palace and took even Dessalines by surprise. He tossed his head like the angry bull he was, about to charge, and the door burst open, to admit several of his aides, but also Kit and Albert Palourdes, who stared from the women to the King, understanding in a moment what had happened, and what more had been about to happen.

'You have assaulted my wife,' Palourdes cried. 'You

210

black savage. You . . .' his voice trailed into a wheeze and blood frothed through his teeth as he fell to his knees and then forward on to his face. One of the guards withdrew his sword from the dead man's back.

'Albert,' Seraphine whispered, and slowly sank to her knees in turn, beside her husband. Everyone else in the room seemed to have been struck dumb by the suddenness and finality of the execution. Kit was first to recollect himself, sprang forward, knocked the guard sideways with a single sweep of his fist, catching the sword which fell from the man's fingers, and seizing Seraphine by the arm to jerk her to her feet and push her towards the inner doorway.

'Richilde,' he snapped. 'Haste!'

Richilde found that she was panting, her mind clouded with the certainty of the catastrophe which was about to overtake them all. She made herself move forward, and had her arms seized by two of the guards. Kit, already at the door, and still half carrying Seraphine, hesitated, facing the crowded room.

'Ha,' Dessalines roared, having recovered himself. 'A plot, by God. You would assassinate your King. But you have failed, as all will fail who dare to pit themselves against Ogone Badagris. Throw down your sword, white man, or I will cut your sister's throat.'

'Run,' Richilde shouted. 'Leave Kit, leave. He will not harm me. He fears Henry.'

'Not even Henry will protect a traitor against her King,' Dessalines said, and himself took a sword from the other guard. He stood beside Richilde, dug his fingers into the hair to pull her head back, presented the blade to that pulsing white throat. 'I will do it now, and mount her head on a stick.'

Kit gazed at his sister, breast heaving as she gasped for breath, body sagging as she was supported by two of Dessalines's aides. Then he looked at Seraphine, whose eyes were shut as she seemed to have fainted. Then he threw his sword on the floor.

Richilde's hands were bound behind her back, and she was marched outside into the sunlight, down the ceremonial walk, surrounded now by almost everyone in the kraal, whispering their excited comments. She was taken through the gate, and on to the road, to look at the hanging bodies; here men were already erecting a large new gallows, a simple affair of two uprights with a cross beam some eight feet from the ground.

Up to this moment she had been so shocked by the rapidity with which catastrophe had followed catastrophe she had not been able to think. Now she realised that she was about to be hanged, her heart seemed to slow and she wanted to vomit. She had lived for so long in danger of her life, had experienced so much, had seen so much death and destruction, it was not the thought of actually dying herself that frightened her. But she had never anticipated such an end, far from Henry . . . and with Kit as company. She turned her head, and looked at him, as he had been marched out beside her. She opened her mouth, but could frame no words. Neither, it seemed, could he.

The guards stripped her by the simple method of ripping the cloth from her shoulders down. They looked embarrassed, preferred not to meet her eyes. Many of them had campaigned with her, and Henry, in the forests, against the British. And all of them knew there would have to be a reckoning, for this day's work.

As did she. If only she could survive to see it. But that was an impossible hope. The sunlight played on her flesh as she was pushed forward, to stand beneath the gallows, and a rope was thrown over the cross bar. She realised that it was too long since she had prayed, because she had not been sure, in twenty years, to whom she *should* pray. And now it was too late. The rope came down and struck her in the face, and the Captain of the guard stepped forward . . . but to release her wrists. She stared at him in horror. He could not mean to leave her dangling, and strangling, slowly, able to use her hands to hold herself up on the rope until her strength gave way?

And then she realised that he did not even mean to hang her, at this minute. He retied her wrists, in front of her, then raised her arms and secured them to the drooping rope. Four of his men pulled on the standing part, and she rose to her tiptoes, and then from the ground altogether, to hang from her wrists, swinging several inches above the earth.

The pain in her arms was excruciating, but she was alive. And for every second she remained alive, no matter what torments Dessalines had in mind for her, there was hope. She looked at Kit, who had been similarly suspended opposite her, and even attempted a smile. But there was no response, as he watched the other preparations being made.

For the soldiers now produced the cut down branch of a casuarina tree, stripped of its leaves and bark to become a long, powerful stake. This stake they shaved down at one end, to make a sharp point, then the blunt end was embedded in the earth, beneath the cross bar of the gallows, and exactly equidistant between Kit and Richilde. Above it another rope was looped over the bar. Then they waited, while the afternoon sun began to decline, and the mosquitoes rose in their thousands from the forest, to nip and tear and bite at their defenceless bodies as they gazed at the hideous weapon of destruction which was waiting, for its victim.

Who was at last dragged from the gate of the kraal by two soldiers, each holding a wrist, naked white body bumping and writhing on the earth. It was impossible to decide whether or not she could have walked had she been given the chance; there were welts and bruises, cuts and bite marks, scattered all over her flesh. And behind her walked the King, wearing only a pair of drawers, his face still twisted with angry venom.

Behind him was dragged the body of Albert Palourdes.

213

Richilde found herself nearly choking from a combination of pain and horror as she watched Seraphine being pulled to her feet beneath the gallows. Her eyes were closed and she hardly breathed as her wrists were bound and carried above her head, and a moment later she was swinging, long hair brushing her thighs, and opening her eyes as her hips touched the sharp point of the stake, which kept seeking to get between her legs.

'Ha, ha,' Dessalines said. 'Raise her higher.'

Two soldiers pulled on the rope, and she was raised another inch.

'That will do,' Dessalines decided. 'Hang there the night, pretty Frenchwoman, and reflect on the fate of those who defy their King.' He stood immediately in front of her, and spat in her face. Her head jerked, and her eyes opened again. Dessalines smiled at her. 'Tomorrow,' he said. 'We will *lower* the rope. Just an inch or so. But you will feel it, stroking your pretty slit, as you swing. And the day after that, my little chick, we shall *insert* it, and lower you another inch. Then you will beg for death. You will beg and scream and pray for death. But you will not die. Not for at least a week, as we lower the rope, just a little every day. Think about that, pretty Frenchwoman.'

Seraphine said nothing, Obviously, if she opened her mouth, it could only be to scream her misery.

And now her husband's body was laid at her feet, beside the stake.

'Is that how a mighty King behaves, Jean-Jacques?' Kit asked. 'To a defenceless woman?'

Dessalines grinned at him. 'And defenceless men. Ha ha. You plotted against me. Do not worry. Your turn will come. You will hang there, and watch her die. Then you will watch your sister die, slowly, the same way. Then you will die yourself, the same way. Sleep well, white man.'

He walked away from them, followed by his people, and they were alone, in the darkness, with the dead, and the mosquitoes.

214

There was no sound, above the humming of the insects, the gentle soughing of the breeze. Richilde thought the girl's courage almost superhuman, in that she did not even appear to weep, much less howl her agony, her apprehension of the quite unimaginable torture which would be hers tomorrow. Yet she too was hanging silently, in the darkness. But she had lived in this atmosphere of vicious violence for too long, was too used to it.

To be reconciled to being impaled, slowly, for day after day? There was madness lurking at the edges of her consciousness.

Would it ever end? Would it end, when Henry returned, and found her corpse, spitted on a stake? Henry's anger would be frightful, of that she had no doubt. But she could also now have no doubt that Dessalines anticipated this, had deliberately provoked the entire episode in order to force a showdown with Henry. And the King retained sufficient sense to know that the first overt act must come from the General. Well, he could be sure of that, when Henry found her.

But Dessalines had sufficient supporters, and there would once again be war, and destruction . . . and even after he had won his war, for she did not doubt he would, could Henry accomplish any of the things of which he dreamed, without her at his side, to guide and encourage him?

Would he even wish to?

'Kit,' she said. 'I am terribly sorry.'

'You did your best for these people,' he said. 'Your very best.'

Almost she thought he was about to say something more, about Seraphine perhaps, or even to the French girl. But he did not, and speech was difficult in any event, because of the pain. If her wrists had now become numbed, the pain stretched down into her arms and forearms, and she could not stop herself giving a convulsive twist or jerk every so often as a mosquito sucked her blood. She wished there was something she *could* say or do to Seraphine, to relieve what must be the girl's much greater agony, just as she wished she could have conveyed more to Kit, of her sense of the horror and injustice of *his* fate, that in merely returning to see her and reassure himself as to her welfare, he should have come to such an end. But she could think of nothing, so she hung in silence, and in time, remarkably, even seemed to sleep, a sort of coma, out of which she awoke to the coming of daylight, and the sound of jingling harnesses, and opened her eyes to look at the dawn, and the red jacketed hussars who formed the escort of Henry Christopher.

'Dessalines,' Henry said, his voice only a little more than a whisper.

'As I foretold, Christophe.'

Richilde blinked past Henry, saw Petion. And a whole host of soldiers, waiting on the forest road. And Jean Boyer? She hoped not. Somehow, to dangle naked before Petion, before an entire army, seemed unimportant beside the shame of dangling naked before Boyer.

'Take them down,' Henry commanded. 'Take them all down. And be careful the Frenchwoman does not fall on the stake.'

He himself held Richilde in his arms while his men cut the bonds holding her wrists, and she could lean against his great chest, weeping with pain as the blood slowly felt its way back up her tortured arms, yet able to allow herself to relax, until her head jerked in terror as she heard the bellow of the bull man.

'Christophe? You dare to interfere with my justice? These people . . . these white people . . . conspired against me.'

'Oh, my God.' Richilde whispered. 'Do not let him take us alive, Henry. Please.'

Henry squeezed her a last time, then handed her to Petion. He stepped past her, faced his King, who was accompanied by most of his guards, and most of his courtiers, too, come to see Seraphine's impalement.

216

'I left Richilde in your care,' Henry said.

'Ha. And she conspired against me. Be careful, Christophe, that I do not include you in that conspiracy.'

'You have already done so,' Henry said, and took off his uniform jacket to throw it on the ground, and stand before Dessalines, naked from the waist up, huge torso swelling in the morning sunlight as he breathed.

'Are you mad?' Dessalines demanded. 'You seek to defy *me*? Over a woman? A *white* woman? An *old* white woman? Here, take your pick from amongst any of my girls. They are young, and strong, and know how to make a man happy. They will give you *children*, Christophe.'

Henry pointed, turning his head from left to right to look at his men, and Petion's, and Dessalines's. 'This man is unfit to rule,' he shouted. 'He is unfit to live. He is unfit.'

'I will hang you beside them,' Dessalines bawled. 'You, seek to defy me? I, who am the incarnation of Ogone Badagris? I will crush you like a nut. I will impale you before I impale the white people. Seize him and string him up.'

The guards moved, restlessly, aware of the mass of Henry's troops, and of the waiting mulattos.

'If you are Ogone Badagris,' Henry said. 'Then I am Damballah Oueddo. Come, oh mighty one. Come and pit your strength against me.' He drew his sword, threw away the scabbard. 'Come and cross swords with me, oh Lord of the Tempest.' He threw the sword away as well, and placed his hands on his hips, huge muscles rippling. 'Or come, and wrestle with me, bull-man, that I may break your neck in ten places.'

Dessalines stared at him, tongue slowly circling his lips.

'Come,' Henry shouted, his voice reverberating like a peal of thunder. 'Or crawl away forever into your burrow like the snake you are.'

Richilde's breath was almost painful to draw, and she

wanted to close her eyes. But she could not. So she watched, as Dessalines gave a tremendous roar and charged forward, drawing his sword as he did so. And Henry had thrown away his weapon. But, almost like a trained matador, he swayed his body to one side as Dessalines reached him, avoiding the sword thrust, and then bringing his hands together to club Dessalines on the back and send him sprawling in the dust.

'Come,' Henry shouted. 'On your feet, oh Great King. On your feet.'

Dessalines seemed to be gathering his wits and his strength, while the watching people were so silent they might have been turned to stone. Then with a bound he reached his feet again, and ran, not towards Henry, but to the nearest hussar. He swept the man to the ground with a stroke of the sword which he still held, vaulted into the saddle, wrenched the animal round, and rode for the trees, swinging his sword left and right.

Christophe's hussars watched him go. Even Christophe watched him go. But his way took him past the mulatto escort of Alexander Petion.

'Bring him down,' shouted Colonel Boyer, his voice crisp and clear.

The muskets exploded. Dessalines reeled in the saddle, almost regained his balance, and then tumbled over the horse's head, to hit the ground and lie still.

PART TWO

The Emperor

Dessalines's successor had obviously to be Henry Christophe, but because of mulatto opposition he was elected president for a four-year term only. The youngest of the three great revolutionary leaders had for too long lived in the shadow of the other two. He was known and loved in his own, northern half of the island, but not elsewhere. In the south Petion held sway, and in 1810 Christophe was forced to acknowledge that a separate and independent regime existed there. Meanwhile, the Spaniards had regained control of the eastern half of the island. Christophe was left with the north; soon he followed the example of his predecessor, and became the Emperor, Henri I.

Chapter 1

HENRI I

Haiti, under [Christophe's] rule, was a surprising phenomenon. To the east the Spanish colony of Santo Domingo basked lazily in the sun; to the south the light brown followers of Petion groped in search of an ideal social structure and slid perilously from corruption to national bankruptcy; in the north there was unceasing activity as the Emperor stormed around his kingdom exhorting, demanding, encouraging, driving his people to work as they had never worked before, even as slaves and above all, building.

Could it really be over? All of the years of striving and agony, of hopes and disappointments?

Richilde stood beside Kit, with Henry on her other side. She and her brother were the only white people present in the crowded reception hall of the late King's kraal; Seraphine was in bed, suffering from shock as well as her injuries. She was going to be a problem for the future. But now, Richilde knew, all the problems were going to be solved.

Alexander Petion addressed the assembly. He stood next to Jean Boyer, smiled at the black men and the brown. 'As General Christophe said,' he declared, 'Jean-Jacques Dessalines was unfit to rule us, unfit to have authority, unfit as a man, but also, my friends, as an institution. Free men do not have kings. The very word is indicative of a subservient nation. But we *are* free men, my friends, my comrades. We will model ourselves upon that other republic which has declared its freedom, here in the Americas: the United States of North America. We shall be the United Peoples of St Domingue. No, as of this moment St Domingue no longer exists. We are the United Peoples of Hispaniola. We shall be ruled by a president, who will be responsible to his people, and will rule for four years, and four years only, and then peacefully step down from his power, and acknowledge the rule of his chosen successor.'

He paused, to glance at Henry. But Henry's face remained expressionless.

'To have a president,' Petion continued, 'we need to have an election, to choose one. We must have an election in which every adult man in Hispaniola has his say. But that will take time, and until it can be done, we must be governed. I have therefore a proposal to make to you all. My proposal is that we here today elect ourselves a provisional president, who will rule us until the plebiscite can be held. We shall hope that the plebiscite confirms our choice here today as the first President of Hispaniola. But if it does not, then whoever it is we choose will step aside, and hand over power to his successor. I pledge myself should I be elected to abide by the result of the election, whenever it can be held.' He looked at Henry.

'I will abide by the election results,' Henry said.

'Well, then, it but requires us to choose our provisional President,' Petion said, and looked at the men. That he claimed the position for himself could not be doubted. Just as that he had the necessary qualifications could not be doubted, more qualifications indeed than anyone in the room, save perhaps his own aide, Boyer. He had fought since the very commencement of the revolution, for his mulattos in the beginning, but at the end for all the coloured peoples, and he was educated, well travelled, knew Europe as well as America, and was most certainly a civilised man, with no trace of the savage in his character.

But also no trace of the magic power that Henry exuded, no great deeds of daring in his past. And above all, no connection with the prophecy. And yet, Henry, secure, as Richilde now understood, in his faith in that prophecy, would step aside again, prepared to wait, for his day to come. Uncaring that too many days had already passed him by.

Desperately she squeezed Kit's hand. He glanced at her, and understood.

'Long live President Henry Christophe,' he shouted.

The cry was taken up. 'Long live President Henry Christophe.' The black men outnumbered the mulattos in the room by two to one. Petion hesitated, looked at Boyer, and then shrugged.

'Long live President Henry Christophe,' he cried.

'Long live President Henry Christophe,' Richilde said. 'Oh, long live President Henry Christophe.'

He looked down at her, and half smiled. His face remained solemn, however, there was not even a gleam of triumph in his eyes. He walked away from her, to stand in the centre of the room, and wait there, for the tumult to die. He made an immense, dominating figure, in his red hussar uniform, with his sword dangling almost like a dagger at his side. Now he took off his busby, held it under his arm, looked around him.

'I thank you,' he said. 'I thank you all. You have placed much confidence in me, and I will do my best to honour that confidence. But do not suppose I can promise you any easy life. We are an infant people, and we are beset with troubles. Our men and women are starving. The Spanish seek to re-establish themselves in the west. The French await only the opportunity to launch themselves once again at our throats. And . . .' he glanced at Petion. 'There will undoubtedly be other

222

problems. So, if you will have me as your leader, then you must be prepared to work, as I will be prepared to work, to bring peace and prosperity to this great country of ours. Will you give me that promise?'

'We will follow you, President Christophe,' they shouted.

Petion said nothing.

'Well, then,' Henry said. 'I will make you a promise back. I will promise you that I will not fail you, and that I will deal justice to all, and injustice to none. Now listen to what I would have you do. In the first instance, I wish those dead bodies out there taken down from their gallows, and buried. Then I wish a state funeral arranged for King Jean-Jacques . . .' He held up his hand as there was a mutter of objection. 'He was our King, and he must be buried as a king deserves. And then . . .' he drew a long breath. 'Then I would have you burn this place. Burn it until no trace of it remains, until its ashes can be stamped into the dust.'

'Burn the King's palace?' Even Petion was amazed. 'But . . . where will you live?'

'Not in the jungle, and that is certain,' Christophe said. 'I will live at Cap François, where I have always lived, until I can think of somewhere more suitable. And it is to Cap François that we must all repair as soon as the King has been buried. I wish a meeting, of all our leaders, all our generals and all our mayors. This is necessary, to tell them of the election you wish to hold. It is also necessary to tell them what they must do, what *we* must do, to make our country great.'

'As you must tell me,' he said to Richilde, as they lay together that night, under the canvas roof of their tent, deep in the forest, with the flames of the royal kraal still lighting up the western sky.

'Me?' She sat up, tried to see his face in the darkness.

'You have waited long for this moment,' he said, with a half smile. 'Do not pretend that you have not. Well,

223

so have I, Richilde. But I am a soldier, and I was a slave. I know nothing but fighting.'

'And now you have no one left to fight,' she said.

This time his smile was grim. 'There are always people to fight,' he said. 'The French will be back, soon enough. They will have to be fought.'

'I do not think the French will ever come back, Henry.'

'Well, I think they will. Or if not them, some other European power. This is too great and fertile a land to be ignored by the white people. The Spaniards have already returned to the west, because Dessalines would not immediately march against them.'

'And will you now march against them? Have you not more important things to do here? Send one of your generals. Send Petion to deal with the Spaniards.'

'Before I have to fight him as well, you mean? But I am waiting for you to tell me of these more important things I must do.'

There were so many, she was not at all sure where to begin. So she temporised. 'You must allow me time. I had supposed I would be advising a king, who could command. Not a president, who must persuade.'

'You will be advising a king,' he said.

She frowned into the darkness. 'But you have just been chosen President.'

'Petion dreams these dreams of his. But republics will only work, real republics, with peaceful elections every four years as he wishes to happen, will only work where every man in that country can read and write and understand what his betters are talking about. Where there is total illiteracy, or even part illiteracy, men cannot understand the issues and the principles their leaders are concerned with. Thus they cannot choose. And indeed I do not believe that my people wish to have to choose. They wish only to be led.'

The simple profundity of what he had just said left

224

her speechless for a moment. Then she said, 'But will Petion ever agree to another monarchy?'

'Do I have to wait for Petion's agreement?' he asked. 'I *will* wait to be elected President. Then you will be able to work out what proportion of my people wish me as their master. If it is a sufficiently large number, as I think it will be, then I will take the opportunity as it comes, to declare myself King.' He waited for her comment, and receiving none, hugged her against him. 'There is so much that needs to be done,' he said. 'So much that cannot be accomplished in four years. You know this.'

'I know this,' she said.

'So tell me of them, these things that have to be done.'

'Your people must be adequately fed,' she said. 'That is the most important thing. For that you must make them clear land to plant corn, and you must tame some of the wild cattle in the interior and make them breed, and give milk, and you must set up organised fleets to bring fish in from the sea. You must also arrange some means of distribution. I do not think you should give food away, because your people are by nature indolent, and if they are *given* food they will not work at all. I think you must set up a succession of great markets, as Toussaint did, but on a larger scale. I know there is no money in Hispaniola, but you must encourage your people to barter, one man's vegetables for another man's fish, and so on, and you must appoint inspectors to supervise the markets and make sure that every man deals fairly with his neighbour. The inspectors should have the power to set a price on all goods. But they too will have to be carefully watched by your ministers, to prevent corruption.'

'What you have just said is the strongest of all arguments for a monarchy,' he pointed out. 'I must *make* them cultivate land. I do not take issue with that,

Richilde. I know I will have to make them. But I must have the eternal, the everlasting, the unceasing authority to do that. Just as I must have the unopposable authority to appoint these inspectors, and to punish them when, as you say, they are found to be corrupt.'

'Yes,' she said. 'I think you are right.' Because he was right, and in more ways then he knew. Henry understood nothing of the arts of dissimilation or persuasion. He *could* only command.

'Now let us speak of the palaces we shall build,' he said. 'The fortresses. The fleet.'

She sighed. 'Such things cost money, Henry.'

'Then we must get money. I told you and them that the road would be hard. Only one third of the people, less the army, of course, can be set to food production. Another third must be set to re-cultivating the canefields, that we may have an export crop. I will invite Kit to charter his vessel to us, as the nucleus of our merchant fleet. I shall also ask Kit to act as our agent in America, and attract other ships to come here to trade. He may give whatever guarantees for their safety or their eventual payment he chooses. I will support him. Will he accept such a task, do you think?'

She hardly heard his proposition beneath the enormous impact of what he had just said, apparently without realising it. The scale on which his thoughts roamed. Hispaniola was to be divided into the army, and the workers for domestic consumption, and the workers for export. And the rest? Because that he had plans for them as well could not be doubted.

'Yes,' she said. 'Yes, I am sure he would wish to help us. You have only spoken of part of your people.'

'The last third will build,' Henry said. 'A palace. A palace worthy of you.' He smiled in the darkness. 'And of me.'

'Henry,' she said. 'I do not wish a palace. There are more important things to do first.'

'There can never be a more important thing than building a palace. Did not Frederick the Great build a palace?'

She sighed. 'Yes.'

'What was it called?'

'Sans Souci. But Henry . . .'

'What does that mean, Sans Souci?'

'It means what it says, without care. But Henry, Frederick came of a long line of kings, and he ruled a country which was already peaceful and wealthy. You are starting from the very bottom.'

'Which is all the more reason why I must have a palace,' he explained. 'Because that is where Dessalines made his mistake. He was quite right when he said that the people did not properly respect him. But it was not merely because they remembered him as a slave, like themselves. It was because, having been chosen to rule them, he did not sufficiently rise above them in stature and prowess. He lived in a kraal. A kraal is the biggest house they have, in Africa. But these people here can remember Vergée d'Or chateau, and Rio Negro chateau and even the Governor General's house in Cap François. How can they ever look up to a man who calls himself their King, but lives in a house inferior to those?' He thought for a moment. 'And there is another thing. A king must live *with* his people, where he can be seen and his greatness understood, every day. He must not bury himself away in the jungle, as if he was afraid of them.'

'Then let us live in the Governor General's palace, in Cap François,' she said. 'I was happy there.'

'We shall live there, while Sans Souci is being built.'

'Sans Souci? You mean to call your palace Sans Souci?'

'Why not?' he asked. 'Frederick the Great is dead. He will not mind if we borrow the name of his house. It has a ring to it. Sans Souci! We cannot remain in Cap

François, Richilde. We have seen too often that Cap François is indefensible. We must remove ourselves from the coast, and we must be close to the citadel.'

'The citadel? You will build a fortress, and call it Sans Souci?'

He laughed. 'No, Sans Souci will be the palace. The fortress will be something else again. When the French come back, I intend to meet them with a fortress not even *they* can conquer.'

He paused, as if expecting her to comment, but she could no longer argue against his fixation.

'Do you remember?' he asked. 'That day in the forest, so many years ago, when we saw the redcoats climbing up towards us? I said then I would build an impregnable fortress, where they were climbing. This I shall do. It will be the greatest fortress ever built. The fame of it will reverberate around the world.'

'A fortress? In the jungle? But Henry, that will be too expensive . . . it will cost lives, as well as money. It is just *impossible*.'

'Nothing can be impossible, to the man who would rule Hispaniola,' he said. And frowned into the gloom. 'Hispaniola. That is a Spanish word. How can I be King of a country named by the Spaniards?'

'It is its name, Henry.'

'Well, then, we will change the name. We will call the country . . . Freedom. What do you think of that?'

'Henry . . .'

'Yes,' he said. 'The white people will laugh at the King of Freedom. But we must have a name, Richilde. A name which has nothing to do with the white people, whether they be Spanish or French or English. A name we can call our very own. Tell me of such a name, Richilde.'

Her brain seemed to have gone blank. Then she remembered . . . 'I have read,' she said. 'That the Indians who lived here before the Spaniards came, called this land, Haiti, the High Place.'

228

'Haiti?' demanded Alexander Petion. 'That is barbaric. No one will ever know how to pronounce it.'

'Then they will have to learn,' Henry said. 'I wish a flag designed for the country of Haiti. It must have black in it, and red, for the blood that has been shed to bring this miracle about, and gold, to represent the light and the glory that lies ahead of us.' He gazed around the group of officers, gathered in the old gubernatorial council chamber in Cap François. 'Now, here are my first orders as President of Haiti. I will give every man in the country a choice, up to a point. I am told there are approximately five hundred thousand men, in Haiti.'

'You are told,' Petion said. 'By whom?'

His gaze drifted to Richilde, seated with several other women, in the far corner of the huge room; but the other women were clearly intended to make the fact of her presence less obvious.

'Five hundred thousand men,' Henry repeated, refusing to lose his urbanity. 'Between the ages of twelve and sixty. They will all have to go to work. We have fifty thousand men under arms. That still leaves four hundred and fifty thousand. These I wish divided into three groups. One third will cultivate the land and catch the fish and in general provide for our domestic needs. One third will grow sugar cane, under the supervision of appointed officers, and thus create an export crop. And one third will build. I wish you all to return to your respective towns and villages and districts, and seek out all of these men. You may ask them, in the first instance, to volunteer for one of those three services. But as soon as we reach the required number in any one of the three, then we will have to appoint men, to whichever of the three is short handed.'

They stared at him, unable for a moment to take in the immensity of the manner in which he was summoning the nation to work.

Petion, as usual, was first to recover. 'You need one

229

hundred and fifty thousand men, to build?' he demanded. 'To build what, President Christophe?'

'To build a palace,' Henry said. 'The palace of Sans Souci. I have already chosen the site. It will be by the village of Millot, that is at the foot of the mountains, and yet not far from Cap François. It is close, too, to Vergée d'Or, where our revolution began.' He smiled at them. 'My palace will make Vergée d'Or chateau look like a village hut.'

'*Your* palace?' Petion inquired.

'The Presidential Palace,' Henry said. 'But I will build it. And I will turn Millot itself into a great city. A city worthy of the capital of Haiti.'

'I see,' Petion said. And looked at Richilde again. 'This also has been recommended to you. Told to you, perhaps?'

'This has been decided,' Henry said, still retaining his smile. 'And when the palace and the city are built, then my workers will build a citadel, up in the mountains. They will build the most impregnable citadel the world has ever known, that the world may know that Haiti will never again be conquered, not even by the French.'

Petion stared at him, then looked at Boyer, then seemed inclined to tear his hair out by the roots. 'And in pursuance of these fantastic schemes you would devote the labour of one third of your people? I should have thought it was the duty of the army to build your fortresses. They have precious little else to do, and there are far too many of them. How can we have one man in ten under arms? Who have we to fight? Who *can* we fight?'

'The army is going to fight the Spaniards, to begin with,' Henry declared. 'I will make that your task, General Petion. The Spaniards must be expelled from the west of the island. Haiti must be re-united.'

Petion shook his head. 'I decline your invitation, Mr President.'

At last Henry frowned. 'You refuse to lead my armies into battle?'

'I refuse to lead them because there will *be* no battle. We shall be commencing yet another interminable bush war. And with what? Are you aware, Mr President, that your fifty thousand soldiers muster hardly a hundred thousand cartridges between them? Two bullets for every man, and they are going to fight a battle? You have perhaps fifty cannon balls, for all of your artillery. King Jean-Jacques spent all his money equipping his soldiers with uniforms, not with bullets. Or do you now propose to arm your men with bows and arrows? Because if you do, Mr President, then you must take command of them yourself. I know naught of prehistoric fighting.'

Christophe stared at him for some seconds, then looked at Richilde, then he got up and left the room.

Henry walked up and down the floor of his private office. 'That man is my enemy,' he stormed. 'He has always been our enemy. The mulattos are not for Haiti. They are for the mulattos. I should have him . . .'

'No, Henry,' Richilde said.

He paused in his perambulation, to glare at her.

'You swore on oath, to your people,' she said. 'To deal justice to every man. Even Alexander Petion.'

Henry's huge fingers curled into fists. 'So I must be opposed,' he growled. 'Constantly. You . . .' he pointed at Captain Gounod, waiting with Kit by the door. 'You knew of this state of affairs? Why was I not informed sooner?'

'I did not know that it applied to the entire army, President Christophe,' Gounod protested. 'I knew that *our* people were short of shot, but I supposed it was part of King Jean-Jacques's policy, to prevent us from opposing him.'

'Ha,' Henry said. 'Who is that?' he shouted, as there came a rap on the door.

The door opened, to admit Colonel Boyer, who stood stiffly to attention.

'Well?' Henry demanded. 'You have brought a message from General Petion?'

'No, sir, Mr President,' Boyer said. 'I wish you to know, sir, that General Petion's attitude does not reflect the opinions of the majority of his officers. If you wish to repeat your command, sir, I will willingly lead my men against the Spaniards. I hold the opinion that every moment they remain in possession of their old colony will be disastrous for our hopes of regaining it.'

Henry stared at him. 'This is some trick?'

'Henry,' Richilde protested, and flushed as Boyer glanced at her.

'It is no trick, Mr President,' the mulatto said. 'You have but to issue the command.'

Henry regarded him for several more seconds. Then he said, in a quieter tone, 'I thank you, Colonel Boyer. Be sure that when I am ready to march against the Spaniards, you will have a command. But your General did me no disservice by bringing to my attention the condition of the armed forces. This I propose to remedy before undertaking any offensive action at all. I thank you.'

Boyer hesitated, then saluted, gave Richilde a brief bow, and withdrew.

'That man,' Henry said, 'is far more dangerous than Petion could ever be. He has a resolution that Petion entirely lacks.'

'A resolution which could be a great asset to you, Henry,' Richilde said.

'To you, perhaps,' Henry said. 'Not to me. Never to me.' He beckoned Kit. 'Can you get me ammunition for my men, Kit?'

'I can try, Henry,' Kit said. 'But it will be difficult, without money.'

'And I have none, until after the next sugar crop,' Henry mused. 'But can we not pledge the crop?'

Kit hesitated, glanced at Richilde.

'Yes,' Henry said. 'They will not take the word of a black man. But you must try for us, Kit. Invite them to come here and see for themselves what we are trying to do. Pledge the crop. Pledge whatever is necessary. But return to me in haste with a shipload of guns and ammunition. Can you do that?'

'I will try,' Kit said.

'Then leave, immediately. The matter is most urgent. And bring back as many ships as you can, too. And people. We are not afraid to receive people. Not now. You will be well rewarded, Kit. You may have anything you wish, that is in my power to give.' He grinned. 'You may have Madame Palourdes.'

Kit's head jerked.

Henry gave a roar of laughter, and slapped him on the shoulder. 'Do you suppose I have not seen how you look at her? You desire her. And so you should. She is a fine looking woman.'

'What makes you suppose that she will desire me?' Kit asked.

'That is important? She is a lonely widow woman, in a strange land. She cannot spend the rest of her days just staring out of a window. She must have a man, and it is better that she should have a white man, one of her own kind, than a black. I am the only black man who can be allowed to have a white woman, eh? Or someone else may suppose he is the hero of the prophecy. But you are afraid, that she will have gone mad, like Annette de Mortmain. I do not think she has gone mad, Kit. She is not a Mortmain. She is made of sterner stuff. Do you not think so, Richilde?'

'I do not think she is mad, Henry,' Richilde agreed, and gazed at her brother.

'Then go to her, Kit,' Henry said. 'I allow you this night with her, and tomorrow you will sail for New York. She will be here for you when you get back. But for this night, why, you may discover what you can look forward to. Go to her, Kit. Your President commands you.'

Kit hesitated at the bedroom door. Richilde had offered to come here before him, and prepare her. But he had declined. He wished to know her true reactions, not those she would present after she had had the time to consider her situation.

Was he excited? He supposed he was, in a subdued, almost subconscious fashion. He had certainly wanted her, for several years. He wanted her more than ever now, knowing what she had suffered, what more she had so nearly suffered. And it was exciting to know that she was to be his. Yet he also knew that he would never force her, *could* never force her. And whatever his feelings, she had never revealed the slightest indication of any affection for him. So once they had been forced to make a public display of love, a display which haunted him, as much for his shadowy memory of the woman as for the humiliation of it. But she had never suggested any memory of it at all, as it must have been only one of many.

He drew a long breath, and knocked.

'Yes,' she said, her voice as quiet as ever.

He opened the door. She had been sitting by the window, looking down at the city. This was the room she and Palourdes had shared when Pauline LeClerc had lived in this palace. He had thought it a mistake to return her to such familiar surroundings, where every object must remind her of happier times. Richilde had thought that such familiarity was essential. Besides, she had pointed out, there had *been* no happier times. Seraphine Palourdes had never been happy in her life, certainly not since her childhood.

That must be his first objective. Her happiness.

She had turned her head to discover the identity of her visitor. Now she stood up, little patches of colour

234

filling the pale cheeks. Copying Richilde, she wore a simple housegown, in green. It was made of thick material, Richilde having absolutely forbidden any of the current French fashions in Cap François, but it was simple to decide that she was wearing nothing underneath. And her feet were bare. While her magnificent black hair hung in a straight shawl past her shoulders.

'Captain Hamilton,' she said. 'You have come to say goodbye?'

He wondered how she had known that. And if it bothered her.

'Only for a season,' he said. 'President Christophe wishes me to return to New York, and do some business for him.'

'Of course,' she said, and sat down again. She looked away from him, out of the window. 'I do not suppose . . .' she hesitated, biting her lip.

'I cannot offer you a passage, madame,' he said. 'Much as I would like to. President Christophe would not permit me. And I must return here.'

'Of course,' she said. 'President Christophe is your friend, and Richilde is your sister.' She forced a smile. 'It is merely that I cannot help but wonder what his plans are for me.' Her head turned to give him a quick look. 'To anticipate them, perhaps. I . . . I cannot contemplate the future without a shudder. I have not the fortitude of your sister.'

'Richilde loves,' he said. 'And thus does not need fortitude.'

'And I cannot love,' she said. 'At least, a black skin. But I have never loved a white skin, either. I have never loved.' Now she looked directly at him. 'And yet I must *belong*, it seems. Because I have a woman's attributes.'

Perhaps a cue? 'Is there no one you *could* love?' he asked.

'No one I have ever met,' she said. And gave a half smile. 'I do not think I have been very lucky in the men I have met.'

He bit his lip in turn, and her smile became genuine, if sad.

'You must not take that as a reflection upon yourself, monsieur. Circumstances . . . I should rephrase what I said. Circumstances have never been fortunate, in my encounters with your sex.' She held out her hand. 'It is good of you to come, to say adieu. I am sure I will prosper here, with Richilde's friendship to sustain me.'

Kit drew a long breath. But she was so lovely, so desirable, if he did not speak he thought he would burst.

'President Christophe has already selected the man,' he said. 'To whom you must belong, as you put it.'

Her head came up, pink spots flaring in her cheek. 'So soon? And you know who it is?'

'It is I.'

She stared at him, while the colour deepened, and then faded. 'You?' She spoke in hardly more than a whisper.

'Yes.'

'And you agreed to this? You, who know me for what I am? Who have seen what I have had done to me?'

'I, who know you as the most desirable woman I have ever met.'

Seraphine sat down. Kit had the impression that her knees had simply given way. 'You,' she said. 'Desire me?' She raised her head again. 'I am flattered, monsieur. Even if you mean merely to amuse yourself with me. Shall I undress now, or will you take a glass of wine, first?'

He could not be angry with her. She knew only such treatment, could envisage nothing better.

'I will marry you,' he said. 'As soon as I may. As soon as I can discover a priest.'

A faint frown gathered between her eyes. 'What has marriage to do with desire, monsieur?'

'In our cases, surely, a great deal. I will love you,

Seraphine. I am sure of that. I would like to feel that one day you will love me back.'

'Love,' she muttered. 'I know nothing of love.' Then her head raised again. 'But if you love me, if you desire me, if you will marry me, then you will take me away from here. Take me to America with you.'

He shook his head. 'I cannot.'

'I see.' Her head bowed again, her shoulders sagged.

'I cannot, because President Christophe wishes you to stay here,' Kit explained again. 'He is my friend. He is virtually the husband of my sister. And he is the man I have sworn to help as far as I can. He trusts me, I think, and yet he has known so much treachery, white treachery, in his life, he cannot bring himself wholly to trust anyone, save Richilde. I must prove to him that I, too, am wholly trustworthy.'

'So I am to remain here, as a prize, for when you return,' she said.

'You will not be harmed, or insulted. As you say, you are Richilde's friend, and you may be sure that she will care for you. And I will not be gone a moment longer than I have to.'

'Should that consideration make me happy, monsieur? In view of my fate when you return?'

Her coldness, her rejection of him, was inspired more by a resentment at the way she was being treated, as if she were a slave herself, rather than any absolute dislike of himself. Of this he was certain.

'I would hope the idea would grow upon you, madame,' he said. 'As you consider it.'

'And I shall consider it,' she promised. 'As I have nothing else to consider.' She stood up again. 'As he sent you to me, no doubt President Christophe commanded you to take at least a memory with you on your voyage. To discover if I have changed, perhaps, from our last . . . meeting. I would but ask you to be gentle with me.' Her mouth twisted. 'The King left me bleeding in many ways.'

237

'When I take you, Seraphine,' Kit said. 'You will be smiling. I will see you, in two months' time. Think of me, if you can.'

'Heave,' came the command.

'Heave,' shouted the work gang.

'Heave,' bellowed the soldiers standing behind them, in a tremendous roar which went up to the skies.

'Heave,' said Henry Christophe.

There was a sound like that of a whistling wind, and the huge tree came crashing to the ground, slicing through other, smaller trees, leaving a swathe of destruction behind it. Instantly the men with axes swarmed over the fallen monster to hack it into manageable pieces, while others went on to the next tree, where the ropes were already being secured – the immense tap-tap of the axe-blades sounded like an entire forest of woodpeckers, Richilde thought.

She sat in a tent, before a trestle table, overlooking the site, but more concerned with the pile of returns and the mass of figures before her. Henry had chosen already to take up residence under canvas at Millot, regardless of heat and rain and mosquitoes, to drive his men onwards, day after day after day, to the completion of his palace – even if they had not yet completed clearing the site. His energy was insatiable. And Richilde knew, whatever Petion might think, that this was no mere vanity, the fulfilment of a lifelong dream. It was an act of deliberate statecraft. Henry, not less than Dessalines, was aware of the importance of outward show to his people; he merely, as he said and as she hoped and believed, intended to put more substance behind the show than had ever occurred to Dessalines the bull-man. And he was thinking not only of impressing his own people. He looked forward to receiving foreign ambassadors, and even more, foreign financiers, and to meeting them in circumstances as splendid as ever they might have known in London or Paris or Berlin.

But Petion did not only think. He also spoke, ranging the country to raise his voice in criticism of the wasteful extravagance of the President. This he was entitled to do, as he also was a candidate for the Presidency, but Richilde knew that Henry, for all his promises, had no intention of laying down his authority were he defeated at the election; the only hope of avoiding another outbreak of civil war was for him to win, and win overwhelmingly. Thus the returns which were now being laid on her desk were of vital importance to the whole nation.

And they were exactly what she was looking for. She raised her head to smile at Captain Gounod as he laid another pile of papers on her makeshift desk.

'These are the last, madame,' Gounod said.

'Have copies of all these returns been sent to Port-au-Prince?'

'Indeed, madame,' Gounod said. 'With instructions for General Petion to attend us here in the north.'

'And with absolute guarantees for his safety?'

Gounod's eyes were hooded. 'Of course, madame.'

She gazed at him for a moment, and then returned to her sums. She checked and re-checked. But there could be no doubt of the verdict of the people of Haiti. The black people, at any rate, and they outnumbered the mulattos by some eight to one. She did not suppose every black man would have wished to vote for Henry Christophe, left to himself. Henry had lived all of his life in the northern half of the country, had never even visited Port-au-Prince, and did not appear to have any wish to do so. When she had suggested it might be politic for him to make a tour of the country he had shaken his great head, and pointed out that he had too much to do here. But with Gounod riding from town to town, with a regiment of hussars at his back, and summoning the people into the market square and telling them that they must vote, there and then, for either President Christophe, the hero of the revolutionary war, or General Petion the mulatto renegade, who had

239

once fought for France against them, it would have had to be an exceptionally bold or foolhardy man who would have dared raise his hand for Petion.

Hardly an election, she supposed, as it would be regarded in England or America. But necessary, for Haiti, as Henry had explained to her on the night of Dessalines's death. And she did not suppose there truly was any large number of black men who would have preferred a mulatto president to Henry.

She assembled her papers, put on her straw hat – it was very hot – and went outside. Her grooms held her stirrups for her as she mounted, riding side-saddle because that was how Henry liked to see her ride, and trotted over to where Henry and his officers over-looked the work of clearing the forest. 'All the election returns are in,' she said.

Henry turned his head.

'You have received over four hundred thousand votes, President Christophe,' she said.

'And Petion?'

'Just under a hundred thousand.'

'Long live President Christophe,' Gounod shouted, and threw his bicorne in the air.

'Long live President Christophe.' The shout was taken up. The workers laid down their tools to cheer.

'A hundred thousand men voted for Petion?' Henry demanded. 'You told me there were no more than fifty thousand mulattos in all Haiti.'

'I do not think there are many more than that,' Richilde said.

'Then I have been betrayed, by my people.'

'That is not so,' Richilde insisted. 'Perhaps those black men in the south who voted for Petion were forced to do so. In any event, your people have not betrayed you, Your Excellency. They have voted for you by a margin of more than four to one. There can be no doubt of the choice of the majority, the vast majority, of the people of Haiti. The future is yours, Henry. To

240

do with as you please. But Henry, you must remember your promises, of justice to all men, black or brown. You must rule, not merely bully.'

Henry looked at her for several seconds, then he smiled. 'I shall rule,' he said. 'I shall rule, my Richilde.'

'Kit!' Henry Christophe stood on the terrace of the Governor General's palace in Cap François to welcome his friend, arms outstretched. 'Oh, welcome back.' He gazed out at the harbour, the *Stormy Petrel* riding to her anchor, the lighters already swarming around her to unload her cargo. 'You outsailed the others, eh? That is good. That is what I like to see.'

Kit glanced at Richilde. 'There are no other ships, President Christophe.'

'Eh? No other ships? How can that be?'

'May we go inside? I would speak with you in private,' Kit said.

Henry frowned at him, then turned and walked into his study. Richilde followed the two men. 'You have failed me,' Henry said.

'I'm afraid I have. In New York they regard you, well . . .' he hesitated.

'As a savage,' Henry said. 'Why are you afraid to speak the truth?'

'They are businessmen,' Kit explained. 'They will not advance money on a sugar crop which may never be reaped because of some new civil war. They have the opinion that the wars of the past twenty years have completely destroyed everything of value in the country. I could not persuade them otherwise.'

Henry gazed at him. 'Then you have brought me nothing?'

'I have brought you a ship filled with arms and ammunition, with powder and with ball, as you requested me to do.'

Henry's face lit up. 'Your ship is filled with arms? For me? But . . . if you had no money . . .'

'I sold my house, everything I possessed,' Kit said. 'And thus paid for them.'

Henry got up, slowly, while Richilde's eyes were filled with tears.

'You did that, for Haiti?'

'I did that, for you, Henry,' Kit said. He gave a twisted smile. 'You are my President now, as well.'

'You did it, for Haiti,' Henry said. 'Yours will be a forever honoured place amongst my people. I will make you rich, and famous.' He smiled. 'Whenever that can be done. But first, you shall have your reward.' He pointed. 'I am told you spent but half an hour with Madame Palourdes, before departing for New York, and that you did not share her bed.'

'I did not consider the time was right, Your Excelency,' Kit said.

'You do not desire her?'

'Of course I desire her. But . . .'

Henry turned to Richilde. 'Fetch her here.'

Richilde left the room.

'Guns, and ammunition. Powder and ball,' Henry said. 'That is splendid. Yet it is but a start. What must I do, Kit, to find more money? To make people understand, that I am no savage, but a king.'

'A king?' Kit asked.

Henry glanced at him. 'That is my intention. It is a secret, and you will not repeat it. But now I know what my people want. Yet if I am going to do everything I must, for Haiti, and my people, I must have money, and recognition. What must I do, Kit? What must I do?'

His anguish, his determination to achieve his ambitions and his dreams, was almost frightening to behold. Kit sighed. 'You, we, must practice patience, to begin with,' he said. 'We shall reap a crop of sugar, in only a few months, and I will ship it for you to the United States. When they see that we can deliver, then they will change their attitudes.'

'You cannot ship the crop we will produce in a single ship, Kit,' Henry pointed out.

'I know that. I will return to the mainland, and endeavour to interest other shipmasters in our business. I but felt I had to return here as soon as possible, to deliver the munitions, and to acquaint you with the situation.'

'Yes,' Henry said. 'Yes, you are a good and faithful friend, Kit. But I never doubted that. And the munitions are important. Now I can carry forward at least the first part of my plans.'

'There are other things you can do,' Kit said. 'You must prove to the world that you are *not* a savage, but a leader of your people. You must prove that you can be trusted, and that you will deal with white people as well as with black.'

'Have I ever done otherwise?' Henry demanded.

'You must be positive. Petion knows this. That is why he is inviting the French émigrés back to the south. To Port-au-Prince. This is the best way . . .'

Henry's brows drew together. 'Petion is bringing the French back to Haiti?'

'Did you not know? He has his agents in Jamaica, and in Savannah and Charleston, attempting to convince the blancs that with Dessalines dead and Haiti now a constitutional republic, it is safe for them to return.'

'No,' Henry said. 'No, I did not know of this. How can he do this, without referring to me, his President?'

'I am sure he means to inform you,' Kit said. 'But I consider it a good move. Nothing will more speedily restore international confidence in you and your government, than a spirit of letting bygones by bygones; of encouraging the planters, who are, after all, mostly Haitians themselves, by birth, to return. And I may say, Henry, that they are the people to give you the very best sugar crop.'

'French people?' Henry asked. 'Planters?' he

243

shouted. 'People who supported the French invasion, and who will certainly support the next French invasion as well? You expect me to allow such brutes and traitors back into my country?'

'You are the President of Haiti,' Kit said. 'You must inspire confidence. You must not carry personal hatreds forward into the affairs of government. You must rise above such things. I know that you hate Etienne, for instance. But Etienne is a capable planter. If you were to restore him to Vergée d'Or, he would soon have a crop . . .'

'Etienne?' Henry asked, his voice again low. 'Etienne de Mortmain is in Haiti?'

'He has written to me to say he is going to Port-au-Prince,' Kit said. 'At the invitation of General Petion, governor of the city.'

'Oh, my God,' Richilde said. She stood just inside the doorway, holding Seraphine Palourdes by the hand.

'Etienne de Mortmain,' Henry growled. 'Is invited back to Haiti, by that mulatto swine? By God . . .' His huge fingers curled into fists.

Kit looked at his sister in bewilderment.

'Etienne had Henry flogged, once,' she explained. 'After you had left.'

'I heard of it,' Kit said. 'But that was a very long time ago, Henry. Twenty years ago. And he will return here as your inferior. As your subject.'

'He also murdered my son,' Henry said.

'I doubt he really had anything to do with that,' Kit said. 'That decision was undoubtedly taken by his sister Madeleine.' He bit his lip, and looked at Richilde again, realising that he might have said too much. 'And that was a time when fears and passions were running high. Nothing would more thoroughly convince the world of your stature were you to bury that particular hatchet.'

'*I* will convince the world,' Henry said. 'I will convince them by my deeds, by my strength, by my power. But I cannot convince the world if I cannot convince my

244

own people. If I cannot convince myself. I have sworn that no Frenchman shall ever set foot in the land again. And I have sworn that if I ever set eyes upon Etienne de Mortmain again, I shall kill him with my own hands. These oaths I shall keep, and if the world does not like it, then the world will have to put up with it. I will not rule to please the world. I will rule, for Haiti, as I am its King.' He glared at the three white people, and then suddenly allowed his face to dissolve into a smile. 'But we are not here to quarrel. We are not here even to discuss affairs of state. We are here for a much happier occasion. For a marriage. Come here, Madame Palourdes.'

Seraphine approached him, slowly, face flushed, breathing heavily.

'And you, Kit,' Henry commanded.

Kit also went forward, had his hand seized, and placed on top of Seraphine's.

'By the authority I possess as President of Haiti,' Henry said. 'I now pronounce you man and wife.'

'You do not look happy,' Henry said. 'Why do you not look happy? Do you not wish to be married to her, Kit?'

Kit glanced at the woman. 'We had thought to be married in a church, and by a priest.'

'Bah. The vault of heaven is your church, or should be. As for a priest, we have none. None in your religion, anyway. But, as President and King of Haiti, I am a priest, a *hougan*.' He smiled at their expressions. 'Do not worry, I am not going to chop anyone's head off to prove it. Yet do I have that authority. As for the priests of your religion, we will have them back, soon enough. But will it not be me who will appoint them? Therefore any authority that they can have, must come from me. Therefore anything they can do, I must be able to do better. Richilde, let us have some wine, to toast the happy couple.'

Richilde filled four goblets with red wine, offered Kit and Seraphine one each.

Henry raised his glass. 'I drink to your future happiness. And to yours, Madame Hamilton.'

'As do I,' Richilde said, and kissed Seraphine on the cheek. 'Kit will make you happy, my dear. I know he will.'

They gazed at each other.

'And now, a feast,' Henry said. 'Tell the cooks, Richilde. Tell them we wish a banquet, and send for Gounod and his wife, and Labalastierre and his wife, and Foucans and his wife. We shall have a party. We have much to celebrate. Kit has a wife, Seraphine has a husband, and I have powder and ball for my soldiers.'

Kit did not doubt that this last was the real cause for the celebration. It was, indeed, unusual to see Henry so thoroughly determined to enjoy himself, just as it was unusual to see him take more than a single glass of wine. But this evening he laughed, and joked with his officers, and even kissed Richilde before them, and allowed the huge power of his personality to flow over them.

'Because it will happen,' he said. 'It is *there*. We have the power, now. The power to do what we wish, what we seek. The power to rule.' He brooded down the table. 'The power to punish.' His head turned, as he could feel Richilde's eyes. 'I swore an oath. To destroy that man. If a man breaks his oath, if a man does not avenge his dead son, then he has no right to call himself a man.'

Richilde said nothing. Kit could only marvel at her obvious adoration of this man. So why had Henry never married her? Why did he not marry her now, as he was in a marrying mood? Could it be, that after all of these years, something of the relationship between slave and mistress still remained? It was difficult to doubt that he loved her.

But, married or not, aware or not, as Richilde

undoubtedly was, of the immense angry power her patient love so barely restrained, they were happy. She was happy. He looked at the woman seated beside him. She had eaten almost nothing, and had just allowed the wine to brush her lips.

As Henry had noticed. 'Your bride is impatient,' he said. 'And we are showing no manners, in keeping her waiting here. Do you retire, Kit, to the reward you have earned so well.' He pointed. 'And do not fail to accomplish your duty this night, eh? I will personally have the situation investigated tomorrow morning. See to it.'

Seraphine stood up. Kit hesitated but a moment, and then followed her from the room, pausing only in the doorway to bow to the party.

She walked in front of him down the corridor, black hair swaying; this night she had been given no time to prepare herself, even by dressing her hair.

She opened the bedroom door, went inside. The covers on the bed had already been turned down.

Kit closed the door. 'He means well,' he said. 'Henry. It is just that he is impatient of custom and habit, of tradition and manners. You cannot blame him for being those things. He was born and lived a slave for the first twenty years of his life.'

'And you support him, because you knew him then.' She did not look at him, even removed herself from the line of the mirror, so that she could not see herself, as she released her gown, shrugged it from her shoulders.

'I knew him from the moment of his birth,' Kit said. 'But I do not support him for that reason. Sometimes I do not *know* why I support him. Save that I believe he is a great man, in his instincts, his ambitions, what he would do, and that he is the leader these people want, and need, and must have, if they are not to revert to savagery.'

He watched the beauty unveiling itself before him. He had, in fact, not remembered her with any accuracy, he discovered. He had not been able to see her prop-

247

erly, as she had hung in the darkness outside Dessalines's kraal, even had he wished to look. But now he wished to look. The too thin girl had become the most perfect woman. The breasts were larger than he had remembered, and the thighs more perfectly shaped, as the legs remained long and slender, delicately muscled at thigh and calf, muscles which revealed themselves as waves of tension swept through her body.

And through his own. He had not touched a woman in too long. But she was not smiling. Her mouth was tight, as if she was holding back an immense desire to scream. Memories of Annette swept through his mind.

'He will not really investigate us tomorrow morning,' he said. 'There is a bolster on that bed, if you wish to place it between us.'

At last she turned, inhaling. 'I am not afraid of you, monsieur,' she said. 'If I am anxious, it is a fear of being hurt. Albert often hurt me. And Dessalines ... Dessalines savaged me.'

'I will not hurt you,' Kit said.

'Then take me now, monsieur, and love me. Show me that it is possible to love, and not to hurt.'

He swept her from the floor, laid her on the bed, undressed, took her in his arms. H's own desire was swelling, overwhelming, unquenchable. Yet he would have prepared her, loved her, made her desire him as much as he desired her. But her lips remained closed to his kiss, her body made no response to his fingers. So in the end he could only take her as she had feared, and as he had done once before. Even that was a joy, just to feel her body against his while he surged into her in a paroxysm of passion. But it was a selfish joy, which faded the moment he was spent, and he could raise his head, and look at her, and watch the tears rolling down her cheeks.

'We offer our congratulations to the President on the ratification of his election by the people of Haiti,' Alexander Petion said. 'We speak on behalf of all our people in the south.' He stood before his delegation of half a dozen officers, headed as usual by Jean Boyer, facing Henry, who was seated at the head of the council table in the gubernatorial palace, surrounded by *his* officers; but he had some thirty men around him. Richilde sat with the wives, on the right of the room.

'I thank you, General Petion,' Henry said, his face hard.

'We wish you a happy and prosperous, and successful, four years in office,' Petion went on, and turned his head, as if looking for someone. 'May we inquire, Mr President, if the American sea captain has yet returned? We observed no ships in the harbour.'

'He has been, and he has left again,' Henry said. 'His business is trade. The trade of Haiti.'

Petion allowed himself a slight smile. 'But there is no trade here in Cap François, Your Excellency.'

'There is trade in Port-au-Prince?'

'We are visited by ships,' Petion said. 'And people. There are people would do business with us, can we but promise them a profit.'

'French people,' Henry said, his voice deceptively quiet.

'People of French descent, certainly,' Petion said. 'As they speak the same language as ourselves, they find it most convenient to represent their less fortunate countrymen. They are largely from New Orleans. That is a city in the American territory of Louisiana, Your Excellency, and like Haiti, belonged to France but a few years ago.'

Henry refused to rise to the bait of becoming angry at the implied slight on his knowledge of the outside world. 'I know where New Orleans is,' he said, quietly. 'But you are also receiving back Frenchmen from Haiti. Planters and the like.'

Petion inclined his head. 'I am negotiating with them for their return, on behalf of your administration, to be sure. We need their skills, as I am sure you appreciate,

Your Excellency. You are finding difficulty in attracting American resources, even with an American to negotiate for you. But they will be more prepared to trade with us when they know that we are making a multiracial society here, that white people, even those who . . .' his gaze drifted to Richilde, 'are not especially privileged, may yet live at peace and in prosperity in our midst.'

Henry pointed. 'No white people, unless, General Petion, they are especially privileged by reason of their services to the state, are welcome here. Or will ever be welcome here. I am displeased that you should have undertaken such a course of action without reference to me. That is tantamount to an act of treason.'

Petion's head came up. 'A president rules with the aid and advice of his cabinet, and ultimately, with the consent of his people, Your Excellency,' he said. 'I am not aware that you have yet formed a cabinet.'

'What do you suppose this is?' Henry asked.

Petion gave a contemptuous shrug. 'This is some sort of a council. To which you read lectures. This has no aspect of democracy in it. This is an absurdity. I have put forward a serious proposition which in my opinion, and in the opinion of my advisers, is for the good of the state. Of Haiti.' His lips curled as if he still found the name distasteful. 'It is not to be turned aside merely because of personal hatreds felt by you and a few others. Nor am I to be lectured as if I were some clerk. I am Vice President of Haiti.'

'I doubt you will remain Vice President of Haiti very much longer, if you continue to defy me,' Henry remarked, his voice a low growl. And Richilde suddenly realised that he was choosing this moment for his coup d'etat. Without confiding his intention to anyone. Not even to her. Her heart began to pound, and she was aware of a rush of sweat on her neck and shoulders. But no fear. It was impossible to fear, when Henry decided to act.

Petion stared at him. 'Do you suppose you can dismiss me, Christophe?' he demanded. 'I have been elected by the people.'

'By less than a quarter of the people.'

'Nonetheless, I have been constitutionally elected. I have rights. I have the right to put forward certain policies, and have them debated by the entire council, not dismissed out of hand, as if you were some monarch, and I some puling courtier.'

Henry stood up. He had donned his red hussar uniform for this occasion, and now his immense presence seemed to fill the room. 'I am a monarch,' he said. 'As of this moment. I declare myself to be a monarch. My people have chosen me. I declare myself to be Henry, King of Haiti. No! this is a great land, and will be greater. I declare myself Henry, *Emperor* of Haiti.'

Even the black officers seemed taken entirely by surprise, while the mulattos seemed to move insensibly closer together, except for Boyer, who, Richilde discovered to her embarrassment, was looking at her. He well knew the influence she possessed.

Petion continued to stare at the huge figure in front of him in total consternation. 'That is not legal,' he said at last.

'What do I care for legality?' Henry thundered. 'I make the laws, as of now. I *am* the law.'

'You . . . you are another Dessalines,' Petion shouted. 'A tyrant and a murderer.'

'I am your King,' Henry said. 'Chosen by his people.'

'Not a single mulatto cast his vote for you, Your Excellency,' Boyer said, quietly. And Richilde caught her breath. Somehow she did not really care what happened to Petion. But Boyer, so courageous and so courteous, and so reliable, she thought, as a man . . .

'No doubt they were confused,' Henry said, also now speaking quietly again. 'Or coerced. But you gentlemen have the opportunity to make amends for the shortcomings of your people, here and now. On your knees, to swear allegiance to your Emperor.'

'You . . . you . . . ' Petion seemed temporarily to have lost the power of speech. But he recovered himself quickly enough. 'Swear allegiance to you? *Henry*. You are supposed to be ruling a French speaking nation, not an English speaking one. You do not even have the right name.'

Henry considered the point, without either haste or anger, without even the confusion which might have been expected. 'You are quite right,' he said at last. 'I will change my name, for the sake of my people. I am the Emperor Henri, of Haiti. On your knees.'

'I'll be damned if I will,' Petion shouted.

'You'll be hanged if you don't,' Henry said.

Petion gazed at him. 'You . . . do you suppose my people will stand idly by and watch this happen? Do you suppose your savages have any chance against my trained soldiers? Your *hussars*, with their two cartridges a man.'

'You are mistaken,' Henry said. 'Captain Hamilton did not *altogether* fail in his attempts to bring me supply. He brought me powder and ball, General Petion. I have fifty thousand men under arms, and I can raise many more. And arm them, and give them bullets to shoot with. This is your last chance to save your people from destruction. On your knees.'

Petion struck a pose, hand thrust into his coat. He had, Richilde remembered, been in Paris during the Convention and the Terror, had no doubt witnessed the deaths of Robespierre and Danton. Yet there *was* something heroic about the little man, defying the might and power of Henri Christophe. 'Never,' he shouted.

Henry's brows drew together. Then his hand came up, again pointing. 'Take that man outside and hang him,' he commanded. 'And all of his people with him.'

252

Petion gasped, and looked right and left as the red uniformed guards moved forward. Richilde drew a long breath, and stood up.

'Your Majesty,' she said.

Henry's head turned, sharply. It was the first time he had actually been addressed in such terms.

'I would but remind Your Majesty,' Richilde said. 'That General Petion and his officers came here under a guarantee of safe conduct, issued by yourself. A guarantee you must honour, if you are truly to prove yourself worthy of leading your people to peace and prosperity, and international recognition.'

Henry glared at her for several seconds, while again she held her breath. Indeed, everyone in the huge room might have been holding their breaths.

'And will these scoundrels not conspire against me, the moment they are safely back in Port-au-Prince?' he demanded at last.

'Then you may arrest them, and execute them, Your Majesty,' she said. 'Without in any way contravening your honour. Their future existence is in their own hands, once they leave Cap François on this occasion.'

Henry turned away from her, 'Madame de Mortmain has interceded for you,' he said. 'And reminded me of my honour. So be it. But as of this moment you are dismissed from your privileges and prerogatives, either as Governor of the south . . .' he looked at Petion. 'Or as officers in the army.' This time he looked at Boyer. 'Captain Gounod will accompany you to Port-au-Prince and disband your puerile militia. And my advice to you, General Petion, and your people, is to think very carefully. Those who do not serve their Emperor are his enemies, and the enemies of Haiti. They will be exterminated. And you can tell your French friends that every one of them that sets foot in Haiti will be shot.' He leaned forward, resting on his hands. 'And Etienne de Mortmain, should *he* ever dare to return

here, will be flayed alive. Tell him that. Now get out.
Crawl back to your holes, and stay there, lest I tread on
your necks.'

Petion gazed at him for a moment, and then turned
and left the room. His officers followed him. Boyer
alone hesitated to salute, before bringing up the rear.

And the council chamber was silent. But that Henry
was deeply angry could not be doubted. His entire torso
seemed to swell as he breathed. He had been challenged, and as ever when challenged, his instincts had
been to seize his antagonist and squeeze the life from
his lungs. Now his frustration was plain to see.

But he had taken the most important step of his life.
Could he but be reminded of it. Richilde stepped away
from the women. 'Long live the Emperor,' she shouted.
'Henri, of Haiti. Now is the prophecy fulfilled. Long
live the Emperor.'

Chapter 2

SANS SOUCI

Christophe's palace of Sans Souci outside his capital city of Millot was unashamedly a copy of its European namesake, a fabulous accumulation of halls and marble pillars, of ballrooms and reception rooms, built around a staircase which even when surrounded by a hundred and fifty years of decay takes away the breath.

Richilde sketched the crown, taking her inspiration from the several pictures of crowns to be found in the few books which had survived the destruction of the library when Henry had burned Cap François in 1802, but keeping the design as simple as possible, merely a circlet with six prongs. A blacksmith made it out of iron, polished the metal to a brilliant shine, and then Henry faced his people in the main square of the city.

They had come from far and wide, abandoning farms and villages and fishing boats to converge on Cap François, until Richilde estimated there must have been well over a hundred thousand people jammed into the square and the approach streets, restrained by the soldiers in their reds and blues and whites, steaming and chattering in the midday sun. In the centre of the square, facing the site of the old Hotel de Ville, a platform had been erected. It stood close by the gaol, and brought back a flood of memories, at least to her, of the night Ferrand de Beaudierre had been torn to pieces by the mob, that night, she had no doubt, when the sequence of events which had led to this revolution had truly started.

And the night of the day when Henry Christopher, for the first and only time in his life, had been suspended from the triangle and flogged. And now, not quite twenty years later, he stood alone on the dais, surrounded by the people who had chosen him to be their Emperor. It had been his decision to mount the platform by himself. His Generals formed a cluster at the foot of the steps. Their women, and his, stood together, just in front of the main crowd, Seraphine Hamilton, as sad faced and resigned as ever, shoulder to shoulder with Richilde. There was no point in feeling disappointed, however, Richilde knew. However much she might have dreamed of standing beside him when he achieved the greatest moment of his life, as she had stood beside him on so many other occasions, tragic as well as happy, horrific as well as famous, she understood that this had to be *his* moment. The people of Haiti wished to observe no human weakness in their Emperor. And how could they, she asked herself, when Henry had no human weaknesses?

That he was their choice, and that he was carrying out their will, however subconsciously it might be expressed, could not be doubted. They laughed and they cheered, and they called his name, and the roar when he mounted the dais sent the birds scurrying out to sea and into the jungle.

'Henri,' they roared. 'Henri,' as if they had been waiting for twenty years to call him by his, to them, proper name.

He made a magnificent figure, for over his red hussar uniform, surmounted by its black busby, and with his gold hilted sword hanging by his side, he had thrown the red cloak of the *hougan*, which swirled about him as he climbed the steps, and turned to face the crowd. His face was solemn, even hard, but his eyes glinted with triumph. Of them all, who had dreamed, and fought,

256

and died, out of Toussaint and Jean François, Céléste and Boukman, James Ogé and Jacques Chavannes, Louis-Pierre and Dessalines, he alone had bestrode the revolution from its beginning, and still survived, to reap the rewards of victory.

He raised his arms, and silence slowly crept across the square. 'My people,' he shouted. 'I come before you, as your Emperor. Tell me straight, would you have me as your ruler, to be henceforth obeyed without question?'

'Yes,' they bellowed with a tremendous shout.

'Then be it so,' Henry said, and pointed, down at General Labalastierre, who now came slowly up the steps, bearing the iron crown on a red velvet cushion. Henry took off the busby, handed it to the General, then grasped the crown and raised it above his head.

'Kneel,' he commanded.

The entire concourse settled themselves on their knees. The square rustled and thumped and sighed, and then sank into an immense silence.

'In the name of Ogone Badagris,' Henry shouted. 'And of Damballah Oueddo, great lords of the heavens, and of the lords Loco and Agone, and the great mistress of the skies, Ezilee the gentle, and of the Prophets Jesus Christ and Mohammed, and of all those who claim to speak in the name of the eternal ruler of heaven and earth, wind and water, men and beasts, but most of all, in the name of the people of Haiti, whose chosen king I am, I proclaim myself, Henri, Emperor of Haiti.'

'A staircase,' Henry said. 'I wish a central staircase. It shall be of iron, and it shall reach up and up, to the very roof of the palace. It will be wide, and yet it will curve, and spiral. It will make the grand staircase at Vergée d'Or look like a ladder. Design me such a staircase, Richilde.'

An entire bedchamber of the palace in Cap François

had been cleared of furniture, and covered with sheets of paper. In their midst Richilde crawled, or sprawled, with ruler and pencil. With her were several black draughtsmen. But none of them truly knew anything of the principles of architecture. Richilde was reaching back into her memory, of pictures of Frederick the Great's palace of Sans Souci at Potsdam, and forward into her imagination, to create a fitting home for an emperor.

Who stood above her, looking down at the drawings.

'You will have a grand staircase, Your Majesty,' Richilde promised. 'It will go here . . .' she marked the plan. 'And it will ascend for four stories.'

'Four stories?' Henry demanded. 'That does not seem a very large palace.'

'Vergée d'Or chateau was only three stories high,' she reminded him. 'We shall have great galleries extending from it, on four sides. It will be the focal point of the entire house. Now here, on the ground floor, will be the reception rooms. One for receiving foreign ambassadors. Not large, you see, Your Majesty, but sufficient.'

'Foreign ambassadors,' Henry said, gloomily.

'They will come,' Richilde promised him. 'And then, on the other side, will be the great ballroom, for when you wish to have a Court occasion. Behind that will be the kitchens and the wine stores.'

'There is no dining room,' Henry protested. 'We must have a dining room.'

'The dining room is here, on the first floor.' Richilde showed him another piece of paper.

'It does not look very large,' he grumbled.

'I have deliberately not made it very large,' she explained. 'I think that dining with the Emperor should be a great privilege, and should be confined to small groups of people at a time. That is the way to get to know your people, to understand what they are thinking, what they are trying to attain. During small and intimate dinner parties.'

'Should *they* not be trying to attain what *I* am trying to attain?' he demanded.

'They will hold opinions of their own,' she said. 'You must always allow them to do that, and to tell you those opinions. You do not have to do everything they suggest. Or anything they suggest, for that matter. But it must be for the good of the nation that you sift the ideas of other men, and choose the best.'

'Ha,' he said. 'Where do I make the grand entry? I wish there to be a grand entry.'

'Down the staircase, Your Majesty.' She indicated the plan again. 'This hall extends the entire width of the building and reaches as high as the ceiling also. It is a vast vault, down the very centre of which will flow the staircase. Thus, when you leave your apartments on the top floor, and begin to descend, you will be seen coming down, by everyone gathered in the great hall. I would suggest that you leave your apartments attended only by . . .' she glanced at him, but his face was expressionless, 'your lady, and a few attendants, and that your lords and their ladies should be waiting to join you on each level, so that when you start upon the final spiral of the staircase, you will be leading an assembly of all your most eminent men and women.'

'Lords and ladies,' he said, thoughtfully. 'I have no lords and ladies.'

'You must create them, Your Majesty. You are Emperor of Haiti. You must have a nobility. Napoleon created his own nobility, out of his Generals.'

'A nobility.' He walked to the window, looked out at the city. 'A nobility. Yes, I shall have to consider that.' He turned, and gave a shout of laughter. 'You! Richilde de Mortmain! Rise! I will commence my nobility with you. As of this moment . . .' he frowned. 'What is the highest rank I can give you?'

Richilde drew a long breath. 'The highest female rank in the land is obviously that of Empress, Your Majesty.' She hesitated, but he merely gazed at her. 'The next below that would be Duchess, I would think.'

259

'Duchess. Yes. That is a fine sounding title. As of this moment you are Duchess.'

'I must be Duchess of Something, Your Majesty.'

'Of course. You are the Duchess of Sans Souci. Come here and embrace your Emperor, as the first Duchess of the realm.'

She went forward, and was squeezed in that giant embrace, while the draughtsmen stood with bowed head.

'And are you happy, my Henry?' she whispered against his chest. 'Now that you can make all of your dreams come true?'

'Happy,' he said. 'How can an emperor be happy, my Richilde? How can I be happy, until I hear from Petion?'

General Gounod stood with bowed head. Behind him in the square in front of the palace his men also waited, dishevelled and undisciplined, many without even their weapons, their uniforms torn and tarnished.

The Emperor stood before them, his hands on his hips, his head seeming to toss with anger as he looked at them. 'Independence?' he inquired. 'They have declared independence?' he roared. 'And you let them? You let yourself be defeated?'

'We were outnumbered, Majesty,' Gounod protested. 'And they were led by Boyer. A skilful commander, Majesty. It was all we could do to fight our way clear, and make our retreat into the mountains. There I left a strong force, to guard the passes and protect the plains, before returning here. But they did not march in pursuit. They themselves were busy fortifying the passes, against us.'

'To guard the passes, and protect the plains,' Henry said contemptuously. 'You are a failure, Gounod. I should have your head. No doubt I *will* have your head, soon enough. Protect the passes.' He turned away, stamped into the palace. 'General Labalastierre, you will order a general mobilisation. Every man who can carry arms, and for whom we can find a weapon. Send a messenger to General Faucans in the west. Tell him I wish his troops to concentrate, south of Millot, in one week's time. Tell them we go to war, and that this time we shall exterminate these half breed scum.'

'Yes, my Emperor,' Labalastierre said, and left the room.

Henry looked at Richilde, waiting at the top of the stairs. 'You have done me an ill service, madame,' he said. 'In begging lenience for Petion and Boyer and their crew. No doubt you consider that you owe them your life. I understand that, and I forgive you, this time. But do not beg for their necks when they are dragged here before me.'

Richilde came down the steps. 'I sought the preservation of your honour, Your Majesty,' she said. 'Rather than the settlement of any debts of mine. And again I must beg Your Majesty to practice patience, and forbearance.'

He frowned at her. 'What are you saying?'

'And even commonsense,' she said. 'Your Majesty, Henry, I beg of you, where is the sense in going to war against a handful of mulattos? They hold one city, and a small strip of land beyond the mountains. The south is a place in which you have never even been sufficiently interested to visit. They have not attempted to capitalise on their victory over Gounod. They know their weaknesses. Yet will they be difficult to conquer. Boyer and Petion know how to fight this kind of a war. They have practised the art, often enough, at your side, my Emperor. So you will launch this tortured land once again into ten years of conflict, and destroy everything you have set out to achieve. Has not Kit been here, and with seven ships, to load our sugar? Is it not the finest crop we have had since the revolution? That is because your people have been at peace, instead of war. And because of that, have you not been promised credits,

261

and even recognition? Have you not Sans Souci to complete, and your nation to raise to prosperity? Have you not the Citadel of La Ferriere to build? Would you squander all of those achievements in the pursuit of some bush feud against a totally unimportant group of men?'

'You would have me do nothing?' he roared. 'Those people, those mulattos, set upon my army and my governor, and defeated them, drove them out. They have killed my soldiers. And now they declare themselves an independent republic. And you would have me do *nothing*? That is honour? That is how an emperor behaves? That is how Napoleon would behave?'

'Napoleon's mistakes have only arisen when he has allowed his heart to rule his head, Your Majesty,' Richilde said. 'You must never make that mistake yourself. I am not saying that you should never settle with Petion, that you should never reclaim the Spanish half of the island. I am begging you to arrange your tasks in a proper order of priority. Here, in the north, you have the heart of Haiti. Here you have the richest canefields, the most cattle, and the most people. And here you are absolutely certain of the love and respect of your people. This is your base, your rock, upon which you must build. I am but begging you to make this part of Haiti, the true Haiti, an impregnable fortress, before you undertake the reconquest of its outer fringes. And it must be impregnable not merely in the size of its army, in its castles and its guns, but it must be impregnable in the wealth and prosperity of its people, the respect in which they are held by the rest of the world. Accomplish that, Your Majesty, because that is the greatest task before you, and let Petion and his friends wriggle away to themselves, and I will make you a prophecy: when Haiti is so strong that dealing with Petion will be but the work of a week, then will you no longer have to deal with him at all, because he will no longer be able to stand against you.'

Henry stared at her for several seconds, then looked

at Gounod, still waiting in the doorway. The Emperor chewed his lip, the savage in him still wrestling with the would-be statesman. Then he pointed at one of his aides. 'You,' he said. 'Recall General Labalastierre.'

'It will be quite a building.' Kit Hamilton sat his horse beside his sister, gazed at the walls of Sans Souci, gleaming white in the afternoon sunlight, rising out of the huge park which had been cleared by Henry's workmen. '*They* are certainly impressed.'

Together they looked at the group of white men, American merchants and bankers, whom Kit had at last persuaded to accompany him on an all expenses paid visit to Haiti, to view for themselves the potential and also the orderliness of the new country, and who were now being taken on a guided tour by the Emperor himself, Generals Labalastierre and Gounod at his side, their height and breadth and brilliant uniforms dominating the sombre browns and blacks worn by the white men.

'What will he do next?' Kit asked, as they turned away.

'He plans a city, around the palace. And of course, after that he plans his citadel up in the mountains. He has had that dream for so long I do not know if I will be able to dissuade him of it. But at least it is several years in the future, and I would not have you suppose he deals only in grandeur. He is already implementing a tremendous cattle ranching programme in the plains, rounding up the wild animals there and domesticating them. He is projecting a great extension of acreage under cane, here on the coast. And he has created a huge fishing fleet.'

'But he still dreams of going to war.'

'Well . . .' she glanced at him. 'He *is* a soldier, by instinct.'

'It is quite a source of wonder, in New York, that he has not yet fought it out with Petion. Some say it is because he knows his own weakness.'

'Now you know that cannot be true, Kit,' she protested. 'In cold terms. But he understands that it will be a long and bitter war. That Petion and Boyer will fight the sort of defensive campaigns against him that he and Toussaint and Dessalines fought so successfully against the British. And he understands more that it will cost all the money he is so hardly accumulating, and mean the end of his plans for the country. So he is content to wait.'

'You persuaded him to understand these things?'

She flushed. 'He sometimes gets so *angry* he just cannot see the wood for trees.'

'Why, do you help him so?' Kit asked.

She frowned. 'Should I not? He needs my help. And he is my . . .' she hesitated.

'Quite,' Kit said.

'I love him,' she said, defiantly. 'And through him, I love the people of Haiti. They have the capacity to be a good people. Even more important, they have the capacity to show black people the way to go, the way to take their proper place in a white man's world. Can you deny that more and more of them will soon be given the chance? Great Britain has abolished the slave trade. So have most of the countries in Europe, save for Spain and Portugal. And that will follow. Even the United States will follow. And the next logical step after the abolition of the trade is the abolition of slavery itself. And that too will follow.'

'I don't doubt that you are right, Richilde,' he said. 'There is already a strong movement towards that in England. When the war with France ends, if it ever does, I think Abolition may well come about. And I think this is a splendid experiment, if you like, even if I doubt that either Britain or France will follow Emancipation by allowing any other black kingdoms, or mulatto republics, to spawn, here in the West Indies. But I cannot think of a better man than Henry to make it happen, here. With you at his side. In fact I can think of no other man who *could* make it happen. Not even

264

Toussaint, because Toussaint was too broad-minded, too willing to see the other man's point of view. He lacked the iron that Henry commands in his mind and his will. But he, even he, could not do it without you. You have stood at his shoulder for twenty years. And what is your reward? To be made the Duchess of Sans Souci. Hardly a compliment when you consider some of the other titles he has bestowed.'

'He has an imagination,' she said, 'which is wholly uninstructed, uninformed. He is not truly aware of what may be considered ridiculous. You brought him some marmalade, which he happened to enjoy. But he liked the word better. It rippled off his tongue. Marmalade. So he made Gounod the Duke of Marmalade. Is that any more ridiculous than having the Duke of some little island or county in England? And he knows and values sunshine. If he recognises anything in heaven or earth as being actually greater than himself, it is the sun. So he has named Labalastierre the Prince of Sunshine. These things do not seem absurd to him.'

'Yet do they tell the world that he is nothing but an unlettered savage.'

'Let the world of *lettered* men equal anything that he has accomplished before they jeer,' she said, angrily.

'And you are content, to remain his mistress, because you love him.'

'Because he makes me happy,' she said. 'As I make him happy. Are you happy, Kit?'

His head turned away, and she instantly regretted her words.

'I am sorry,' she said. 'I did not mean . . .' she sighed. 'Is there nothing you can do?'

'Do?' he asked bitterly. 'I sometimes wonder if she is actually aware of my presence, even when I lie on her. I am cursed, in my relations with women, and there it is.' His fingers curled into fists. 'I sometimes think that perhaps I am wrong, to be gentle with her. Perhaps I should flog her, or kick her. It would at least awaken some reaction. With Annette, one was at least aware of hatred. With Seraphine there is nothing. She could be a painting hanging on the wall, save that she moves and breathes.'

'Perhaps she is afraid to feel,' Richilde said. 'Because whenever she has felt in the past it has meant pain, either mental or physical.'

'Then, as I have said, she is just as mad as ever Annette is, and I am the most misbegotten of men.' He sighed, glanced at her as their horses picked their own way down the road towards Cap François. 'Did you know they are all back in Haiti?'

She frowned at him. 'Etienne?'

'And Annette, and Louise, and even Madeleine.'

'My God. But . . .'

'Aye. I wrote to him, and warned him of Henry's implacable hatred, and he returned a cold answer. He has been given a plantation, by Petion, and dreams of rebuilding the family name and the family fortune. As he has always dreamed.'

'But to bring them back here,' she said. 'Madeleine . . . does she not wish to be with her own?'

'Her children have grown up, and are too English for her, I think. Certainly they find her too French for them. But do not suppose Madeleine is the cold fish she pretends, beneath that composed exterior of hers. She hates, just as strongly as Etienne or Annette. She remembers the destruction of her family, and looks to see the Negroes restored to their proper servitude. Nor do they doubt for a moment that it will happen, that the blacks are so incapable of enjoying freedom or of managing their own affairs that Henry's kingdom must collapse in civil war, and soon. That is why I think you were wrong to restrain him from immediately invading the south, and settling the matter once and for all. There can never be peace in Haiti, while people like Etienne and Madeleine and Annette are whispering in Petion's ear.'

266

'There is peace now,' she said. 'And that is what Haiti needs. And would you have had them destroyed? Your own cousins? Together with countless others? I would rather let nature take its course. Etienne, Madeleine, Annette, they will not live forever. All the generation which remember August 1791, and which hates, will fade away in time.'

'As will Henry, you know. How old is he now?'

She gazed at him. 'He will be forty-eight years old this December,' she said. 'As will I. I know we are growing old.' Even if she found it an impossible fact to accept. But she was still thinking of Kit and his problems . . . and remembering her own, as a girl. What had been done for her could surely also be done for Seraphine.

'Would you have me help you?' she asked. 'To make your wife respond to you?'

It was not difficult, through the good offices of Anjelica, the wife of General Labalastierre, and thus the Princess of Sunshine, to discover a *mamaloi* of repute. For however much the Emperor might appear as a sceptic, in the absence of Christianity as imposed for so many years by the French, voodoo was fast becoming the sole religion of the superstititous black people. But was it not, Richilde thought, a religion that in many ways she believed in herself? It reached back into the human subconscious, could not be so very different to the old European beliefs in Pan and Dionysius, Aphrodite and Artemis, which appealed perhaps to the baser instincts of humanity, but were none the less valid for that.

Of its power, there could be no doubt at all. And undoubtedly it could be used for good as well as ill, for white equally with black magic.

Anjelica Labalastierre had prepared the way, told her when the time was ripe. Up to that moment Richilde had kept her own counsel, but this night she visited Kit and Seraphine, found them sitting silently and sadly in the house given them by the Emperor, Kit checking the accounts of his last voyage, Seraphine's fingers entangled with her endless and pointless needlework.

'I have come to take you for a short journey,' Richilde said, wrapping her cloak in a cowl over her head.

They stared at her in amazement, much as she, she remembered, must have stared at Jacqueline Chavannes, so many, many years ago. But Kit at the least had an inkling of what she had in mind. He stood up. 'I have just returned from a long voyage, Richilde. I doubt we feel like society this evening.'

'I do not offer society,' Richilde said. 'And you will soon be away on another lengthy voyage, will you not? But as you are here, I have come to offer you a glimpse of happiness. Should you not come, then you are a fool, and you are both damned forever.'

Seraphine glanced from one to the other, in bewilderment.

Kit hesitated, then shrugged. 'Fetch your cloak, Seraphine,' he said.

Richilde had had the horses saddled and brought to the door, and the three of them rode out of the city, challenged on the gate, but allowed to pass the moment it was established that it was the Duchess of Sans Souci, and her brother, wishing to ride abroad, however much the commander of the guard might shake his head at the absurdities of the white people.

Richilde led them along the coast road, and then followed a fork into the interior, skirting the back of Vergée d'Or as she plunged into the jungle, following the directions given her by the Princess. Soon the track became hardly more than a path, and branches and forest creepers threatened to sweep them from their saddles. It was here she had come, again with Seraphine, but also with Petion and Boyer and Albert Palourdes, that night in 1802 when they had fled the

Cap François of the LeClercs, in search of Henry, and safety. Now she searched for something far less honourable, aware that her heart was pounding and her flesh was clammy with sweat. Here she was dabbling in things she had sought to put behind her. No, she realised, that was not true. She had never sought to put voodoo behind her. She had wanted to know more of it, to understand it, perhaps even to use it. And had never been allowed the opportunity. How strange that she had never realised that as the mistress of Henry Christophe, even when he had been no more than the General in command of Cap François, all the mysteries of obeah and the worship of the Snake God were hers for the asking.

And tonight she was going to ask. But not for herself. She would not dare that, any more, because she dared not risk knowing the answer. She could only observe, and remember.

The little hut suddenly loomed in front of them, and Richilde drew rein. 'We have arrived.'

'Here?' Seraphine had not lived in Haiti for ten years without understanding something of the society in which she moved. 'That is the house of a *mamaloi*.'

'Who is expecting us.'

'Voodoo is unspeakable,' Seraphine declared.

'I had not supposed you would sink to black magic,' Kit said. 'I doubt we can benefit from that.'

'And I promise you that you can,' Richilde said, and dismounted.

'Who comes to visit Elaine?' came the whisper.

'The Duchess of Sans Souci. And Captain Hamilton and his wife,' Richilde said.

'You are expected.'

'I do not believe in voodoo, Highness,' Seraphine said. 'Therefore it can have no effect on me, either for good or for evil.'

Richilde held the curtain for her. 'Enter,' she commanded.

Seraphine hesitated, then stepped past her into the

269

gloom, paused to inhale, the incense, the other smells, attractive and repulsive, which filled the room, and to stare at the *mamaloi*, crouching on the far side of the fire. Richilde's heart nearly stopped beating. It could have been Céléste, all over again. But that was the red robe, and the gnarled features, the age of the woman.

'Welcome, Madame Hamilton,' Elaine said. 'I have long waited for you to visit me.'

'I am not visiting you,' Seraphine said. 'I was brought by the Duchess.'

Elaine smiled, and stood up. 'It is still a visit, madame, and you are welcome. Come.'

Another curtain, at the back of the room, was swept aside, and Elaine led them into an inner chamber. Here it was utterly dark, save for the inevitable fire glowing in the centre of the floor, doubling the heat. Richilde felt sweat trickling down her face. Because now memory was surging through her mind, awakening her body, her every sense, making her feel every urge of her womanhood, making her dream of the tumbling ocean rollers which had finally sated her surging desire, that night thirty-three years ago.

Elaine stooped, a taper in her hand. When it glowed, she straightened, handed it to Richilde. 'Light the candles, Your Highness,' she instructed.

Richilde could see them now, set into the wall. She stepped away from Kit's side, lit each wick in turn. The room glowed; the candles were scented. She could hear Seraphine breathing. Perhaps she had anticipated a bedchamber. But it was not. It was a *love* chamber. Against the centre of the far wall – the room revealed by the flickering light was larger than it had appeared – there was a mattress, laid on the earthen floor, reaching almost as far as the fire. In the wall, above the mattress, were two rings, to which were attached buckskin thongs. At the foot of the mattress, beyond each corner, were two stakes, to which were also attached buckskin thongs. Seraphine gave a gasp, and turned, but Elaine had remained behind her.

'You practise witchcraft,' Seraphine whispered.

'In this case, white magic, madame,' Elaine said. 'Undress.'

'I will not.'

'Then you will be stripped.' Elaine stretched out her hand, stroked the material of Seraphine's collar. 'It will be a pity, to destroy a beautiful garment. And you will be humiliated. We may need to call others. Undress, Madame Hamilton. Then your secrets will belong only to this room.'

Her voice seeped around the chamber.

'My secrets?'

'You will have secrets, madame. I promise you. What, are you afraid to be naked before your husband, who would also be your lover? Before the Duchess of Sans Souci, the most famous woman in the realm? Before me? I am an old woman, Seraphine. I have seen many naked woman, many naked men. Many more beautiful even than you.'

Her quiet voice filled the room, yet seemed to echo. It made thought difficult, when combined with the heat, and the incense. Seraphine's fingers were already at the buttons of her gown.

But she looked at Richilde. 'I will not be bewitched, Highness,' she insisted. 'You have no right to make me suffer this.'

'We do not seek to bewitch you, Seraphine,' Richilde said. 'We seek to help you.'

'We would release you from your prison,' Elaine said.

'My prison?' Perhaps without her being aware of it, Seraphine's gown was sliding past her thighs, and to the ground. She wore no stays, in the informal society that Richilde had established in Cap François. A moment later her shift joined her gown. She wore no stockings, either. Only her soft skinned riding boots.

'The prison of your mind,' Elaine said. 'Now lie down.'

Again Seraphine hesitated, glanced at Kit, and for

271

the first time that he could remember since their wedding night, flushed with embarrassment. Or was it only the firelight, flickering in her cheeks?

She lay down.

'Arms above your head,' Elaine said, reassuringly, and gently secured the young woman's wrists to the buckskin thongs. 'Will you not remove your wife's boots, monsieur?'

Kit knelt, unlaced Seraphine's boots. She gave an involuntary little kick, and then lay still.

'If you intend me no harm, madam,' she asked, 'why bind me?'

Elaine smiled at her. 'To keep you *from* harm, child.' She secured each ankle in turn, leaving the girl spread-eagled on the mattress. Then she rose, slowly, with the faintest rustle of material. 'You must also undress, monsieur, and stand at the foot of the bed,' she said. 'Your woman must gaze upon you, throughout the ceremony.'

Kit obeyed; the heat of the fire scorched his back, made his blood run the more quickly. But no doubt this was what the *mamaloi* intended. He glanced at Richilde, but Richilde was almost invisible in the darkness, pressed against the far wall. Now memory was almost painful in its intensity.

Elaine removed her red robe; she wore nothing underneath, possessed a younger and more heavily muscled body than her withered features had suggested might be possible. She left the bedside, stooped by a chest in the corner of the room, turned and straightened, suddenly, and rose at the same time, throwing both arms outwards, fingers extended. Drops of liquid scattered through the flickering light, brushed Kit's cheeks, fell on Seraphine's belly. The scent was at once erotic and intoxicating, sending Richilde's mind, and no doubt Kit's and Seraphine's as well, she thought, whirling into space.

Elaine began to dance, a slow movement, of belly

and thighs and groin and stomping feet, accompanying herself with clapping hands in time to the tune she sang. She moved around them, and her sex, her song, served to envelope them, to fill the room. Kit felt himself panting, felt he would explode long before he could enter the woman.

Elaine swept round the room, pausing by the chest to seize a bottle. Her movements stopped, and it seemed the entire night had stopped with them. The only sound was their breathing.

Elaine knelt before Seraphine's feet, her back touching Kit's penis, brushing it from time to time. She uncorked the bottle, poured a little into the palm of her hand, and commenced to massage the woman's toes, slowly and gently, humming the same little tune. The scent, vaguely sweet, the tune, mind-consuming in its erotic cadence, kept his mind swimming, and obviously Seraphine's as well. Richilde wished to escape the room and the enormous power of suggestion which was present here, but she could not move. She watched Seraphine staring at Kit, her breathing, which had been heavy with distaste and anticipation of discomfort when she had first lain down, subsiding until her breasts did no more than flutter.

Slowly Elaine worked, from time to time pouring more fluid into the palm of her hand. She came up Seraphine's body, from calf to thigh, from thigh to groin. Now Seraphine scarcely breathed at all, and her mouth sagged open; she was so still she might have been asleep. But her eyes remained wide, staring at Kit. And as Elaine reached her belly, her breathing began again, slowly, building up, as was his own.

Elaine's song grew louder, as she worked. Up from the belly to caress the ribs, to seek the breasts, to leave them and stroke neck and armpit, before returning, once again to stimulate the nipples into erection. Now Seraphine panted, and her ankles strained at the buckskin cords as she attempted to bend her knees. And still she stared at Kit, mouth wide, tongue circling her opened lips.

Elaine stopped, sitting astride Seraphine's thighs, picked up a fowl feather which had lain unnoticed at the side of the mattress, and very gently drew it across Seraphine's right nipple. Seraphine's body jerked, and she uttered a huge sigh, while Elaine threw back her head and gave a gigantic shout, and then leapt up, as if she were a girl.

'Now,' she screamed. 'Now, now, now.'

Kit obeyed. Could this be different to any of the others? Seraphine had never once attempted to resist him. She had always lain beneath him, in perfect submission. She could not possibly be any more submissive merely because she was secured. The difference had to be in him, that he was kneeling between her legs, before a strange woman and his sister, without feeling any embarrassment or reluctance, concerned only with the pulsing white flesh beneath him.

And Seraphine was no longer secured. Even as he reached his own climax her legs came free, to wrap themselves around his body, as a second later her arms came free, the cords loosened by Elaine, to allow her fingers to close on his back, to eat into his flesh. Jacqueline Chavannes had screamed her ecstasy. Seraphine Palourdes reached hers in silence, but her entire body tightened on his, seeming to suck him against her.

Elaine touched Richilde on the arm, and jerked her head. The two woman stepped through the curtain, into the front room of the hut, gazed in consternation at Henry Christophe.

'Did you not suppose I would know where you had gone?' he asked. 'Did you not know I would be told, immediately, that you had left the city?'

Richilde looked past him, at the hussars waiting in the doorway. 'I had no wish to deceive you, Your

Majesty,' she said, aware of a curiously empty feeling in her belly. It was the first time that he had ever appeared truly angry with her. 'I did not suppose that you would be interested.'

'I should not be interested, when you visit a *mamaloi*, to seek spells to cast across my bed and my person?'

'That is not why I came, Henry,' Richilde said, and looked at Elaine, who seemed quite undisturbed by her Emperor's anger. Quietly she drew the curtain again, and allowed Henry to look into the inner chamber, before closing it.

'The Duchess sought love for her brother, Christophe,' she said. 'That can be no crime.'

'You should have confided in me,' Henry grumbled, somewhat embarrassed.

'As she says, she did not suppose you would be interested,' Elaine said. 'But I am pleased that she has brought you to visit me, Great King, however inadvertently. I am pleased to be able to look upon your face, and into your eyes. I am pleased to be able to warn you.'

'Warn me?' Henry demanded. 'Of what can you warn me, if there is no conspiracy?' He looked left and right, into the shadows, as if expecting to discover Petion and Boyer, lurking with drawn swords.

'I would warn you of yourself, Great King,' Elaine said. She stepped forward, until she stood immediately in front of him, and reached up to stroke his cheek, tracing her finger right down his face and then across the pulsing arteries of his throat. 'You ask too much, of yourself, Christophe,' she said. 'You are killing yourself, with effort, with overwork, with endeavour. And sometimes, with anger.'

'You speak nonsense, old woman,' Henry said. 'How can I be working too hard, when I am taller, and stronger, and more able than any man in my kingdom?'

'Thus your heart has more work to do than most,' Elaine said, quietly. 'You must allow it to rest, from time to time, to beat more slowly. To enjoy some of the peacefully pleasurable things in life, and not be constantly seeking things to do, and people to fight, and ideas to excite. Hear my words, Great King, or you will not see your allotted span, and there will be a sad day for your people.'

Henry looked from her to Richilde, waiting in the shadows, scarce daring to breathe.

'You are talking nonsense,' he repeated. 'I have much to do. Time enough to rest, when I have accomplished all I must.'

Elaine sighed, and shrugged. 'You are the Emperor. You must do as you see fit. But at least let me help you to survive the envy and the hatred of mortal men.'

Henry frowned at her. 'You can do this?' he asked.

'I have that power,' she said. 'If you will believe in it.'

'Show me,' he commanded.

Elaine knelt before another of her chests, in a corner of the room, opened it, and reached into the interior. When she rose, she carried a shining object in her hand. 'Take this, Great King.'

Henry peered at it. 'A bullet? Why does it gleam?'

'Because it is a very special bullet, Great King. It is made entirely of silver.' She raised it by the cord which had been passed through its base to turn it into a pendant, allowed it to swing, gently, to and fro before him. 'I took it from the body of a French officer, during the war,' she said.

'Ha ha,' Henry remarked. 'A *dead* French officer.'

'But he died of yellow fever, Great King, despite having been in the forefront of several battles. Not a single shot could harm him while he wore this talisman.' She smiled, for Henry had involuntarily stepped backwards. 'It carries no disease, now. Take it, Great King, and wear it, and believe in it.'

Henry hesitated, then slowly stretched out his hand, and took the bullet from her fingers.

'If I believe in this, I can never be killed by mortal man?'

'If you believe in that bullet, Great King, then only that piece of silver can ever harm you, from the outside. So wear it always. Never let it from your sight, and you may enter battle without fear.'

'I have never feared, before,' Henry said, and slowly hung the silver bullet around his neck. 'What payment do you require?'

'Merely the satisfaction of knowing that I have pleased my Emperor,' she said. 'But you will remember, Great King, that that bullet only protects you from the weapons of mortal men. It will not help you against the harm that you do yourself, every minute of every day, by your unceasing labour.'

'Bah,' Henry said. 'I am the strongest man in Haiti. Only an assassin's bullet can bring me low, old woman. But I am grateful for your charm. I will wear it, as you suggest.' He held out his hand. 'Come, Richilde. You may let Kit find his own way back to Cap François. When he is ready!'

A vast crowd waited outside the palace of Sans Souci, stamping and shuffling, coughing and spitting, causing little dust storms to eddy upwards into the still air. There were farmers and their wives and children, and their chickens and their goats and their dogs, come in from the surrounding country; there were sailors from the coast; there were merchants from Cap François, together with their wives; there were soldiers, in variegated uniforms, and there were the members of the new nobility, wearing even more gaudy uniforms, with cocked hats and masses of feathers, with their ladies in silks and satins. And there was even a handful of white traders, Americans, who had come to Haiti at the invitation of Kit Hamilton, and who had remained to manage their factories. But there were no mulattos in the crowd.

Everyone present was aware that he or she was witnessing a famous occasion, as Emperor Henri solemnly

277

cut the blue ribbon draped across the huge wooden doors, and the major domos threw them open.

Few people truly knew what to expect, whatever the rumours which had flown from mouth to ear throughout the land these past two years. Now there was a gigantic gasp, as the watchers gazed at the entry hall, the largest expanse of polished stone they had ever seen, and then at the huge curving staircase, which rose out of the centre of the hall, and then clung to the balustrades of the galleries on each floor as it slowly and gracefully mounted upwards.

This was all that the peasants were allowed to see, as they were restrained by the soliders. The nobles, and the white people, were permitted inside the building itself, to gape at the marble pillars supporting the upper floors, at the great wide galleries stretching away in every direction, at the high ceilings, and most of all, at the great dome of a roof rising sixty feet above their heads. Perhaps there was as yet insufficient furniture, and perhaps not all the pieces, garnered far and wide, from the length and breadth of the land, from the ruins of every great house which had not been entirely destroyed during the years of the revolt, truly matched. This was not a point to disturb the black people. It was the size of the palace that took away their breaths, and even that of the Americans.

'It is quite splendid, Kit,' Seraphine said, and squeezed his arm, as she so often squeezed his arm nowadays – they seemed to be perpetually honeymooning.

While the Emperor, having mounted to the very top of the staircase, could look down on the concourse, and smile. 'Is it as it should be, my Richilde?' he asked.

'Not yet,' Richilde said, seriously. 'It will be more complete when the drapes arrive from New York, and the rest of the furniture. And the walls are too bare. We must have paintings on the walls.'

'Can they not be bought in New York, also?'

'Indeed they can, Your Majesty,' she said. 'But I doubt pictures obtained in New York would be appropriate for Sans Souci. Should this palace not contain scenes of Haiti, and portraits of you and your people?'

'Of course you are right,' he agreed. 'We will have Kit find us an artist in America.'

She shook her head. 'Let you and me find us an artist, from amongst your own people, Henry. I am sure there will be some who have a natural gift with a brush. That I think would be more fitting.'

'I marvel at the scope of your mind, my dear, dear Richilde,' he said, and held her hand, to draw her from the stairs on to the gallery, and thence along a wide corridor, from off which, as she well knew, the doors opened into his own apartments. And *they* were most certainly fully furnished; the palace in Cap François had been looted for that purpose.

'Henry,' she protested, looking back at the amused black people. 'Not now. And here. We have guests.'

'I have something to show you,' he said, leading her the length of the corridor, to open another pair of double doors, and take her into a magnificent apartment, hall, reception room, bedchamber, with a pantry and kitchen secluded to the side, the whole facing the mountains and receiving a glorious fresh breeze through its opened windows. Richilde ran on to the balcony, and looked down at the grounds below, cleared for the laying out of the imperial gardens, although as yet little had been done.

'It is magnificent,' she said.

'It is yours,' Henry said.

'Mine? Oh, but . . .' she bit her lip. It had not occurred to her that she would not be sharing the imperial bedchamber, as she had always shared Henry's bedchamber. 'It is magnificent,' she said again. 'I will be able to see out over the city. Because we can commence that now, Henry. I have drawn up plans, for streets, and sewers, and . . .' She was talking, wildly, anxiously, to prevent him from uttering the words she had always feared to hear.

'We cannot commence the city now,' he said. 'Which

is not to say it cannot be built. I have given instructions that anyone who wishes may build in Millot. Providing he keeps to your street plans, of course. It will be something for you to occupy yourself with.'

'Something to . . . Henry, why cannot we build Millot, ourselves? Now? It was what we always planned to do next, once the palace was completed.'

'We start work on the citadel, tomorrow,' he said.

'The citadel?' She looked up at the mountains, rising above the palace.

'That has become necessary, now,' Henry said. 'Urgent. I should have built that before, even before this palace.'

'But why?' she cried. 'Why is it urgent now, when it was not so urgent, two years ago?'

'Great Britain has gone to war,' he said sombrely. 'With the United States. The news arrived yesterday.'

'England? And America? But why? England is still fighting Napoleon.'

'Great Britain is very powerful,' he said. 'You have told me so, time and again. As to the war with America, that appears to be a nonsense. It is apparently about the British right, which they claim, to seize ships on the high seas, and to impress some of their crews. This is what Kit has told me. But that has to be nothing more than an excuse. It is but a pretext, to launch fleets and armies once again into the West Indies. Against Haiti.'

She shook her head. 'That cannot be, Henry. I am sure of it. The British will never return here. Certainly not until they have beaten the French. Or been beaten by them.'

'You will see,' he promised. 'They will invade us again. I know exactly how they will go about it. They will treat with Petion, and he will happily treat with them, the scoundrel. Thus they will have a secure port and even allies when they begin their march to the north. Thus the citadel must be built, and in a hurry. Did I not tell you, in the forest, years ago, that I would build the most impregnable fortress the world has ever seen? A fortress to which we could always retreat, when we were attacked? And did you not reply, that if I built such a fortress, then no one would ever dare attack us? If it were there now, then we would have nothing to fear. The work commences tomorrow.'

She sighed. 'Yes, Henry.' She sat on the bed.

He stood above her. 'Do not be sad. Millot will still be built. Everything we have set out to do will still be done. We have just had to alter our priorities, that is all.' He smiled at her. 'You do not believe any of that nonsense that *mamaloi* spoke of me?'

She raised her head to gaze at him. 'Of course not, Henry.' How can I, she wondered, when you are so tall and strong and dominant, and so obviously as healthy as you have ever been in your life?

But then she thought, why *should* I not believe her, as you so obviously believe in that silver bullet?

Henry turned away from her, walked to the window, looked out at the afternoon. 'There are so many plans I have had to alter, since I became Emperor. It is sometimes hard to remain true to one's real interests, one's real path. I love you, Richilde.' He half turned, and then changed his mind, continued looking out of the window. 'I have always loved you. Have you ever doubted that?'

'No, Henry,' she said, scarce daring to breathe.

'Ever since we were children together,' he said, as if she had not spoken. 'I have loved you. I would have been content to live the rest of my life, with just you, in that little hut on the coast, fishing, and lying with you. But the French would not let us do that simple thing. And now I cannot go back. I love you, but I can never marry you. I, the black Emperor of Haiti, would betray his people were he to marry a white woman. Can you understand that?'

'I have always understood that,' she said.

'Yet must I marry. The Emperor must have an

Empress, to sit at his side on great occasions, and that he may have children, to continue his line.' Now at last he turned.

Richilde gazed at him. 'I understand that, Henry,' she said.

'Do not doubt,' he said. 'That I shall continue to love you above all other women, above life itself. These apartments are yours, and I swear that I will visit you at least once a day. I will still rely upon you, utterly, for help in the many things I must do. But I must have an Empress.'

'I understand that, Henry,' she said again, and wished he would leave before the tears came.

'You will not attempt to flee Haiti?' he asked. 'I would not allow that.'

Because the prophecy required her presence.

'I will not attempt to leave Haiti,' she said, and stood up.

He gazed at her. 'I feel this more than you,' he said. 'Were I not the Emperor . . .' he sighed, and his right hand clutched the breast of his jacket, beneath which, she knew, the silver bullet lay against his chest. Because he most certainly had come to believe in the efficacy of the talisman, even if he had never been engaged in battle since receiving it.

But it was his talisman. Not hers.

'Well, then,' he said, attempting to smile. 'I have commanded all my Generals, and all my senior citizens, to bring their daughters to the reception this evening, that I may choose one, as my Empress. They will be waiting for me, now.' He held out his hand. 'Will you come with me, and help me choose, the Empress of Haiti?'

Richilde looked at him for several seconds. Then she shook her head. 'No, Henry,' she said. 'This is one decision you must make for yourself.'

Chapter 3

THE COURT

Haiti became a showpiece of what could be accomplished by the Negro. Like the ministers of Catherine the Great's Russia, Christophe could present to the world a reasonable façade of power and prosperity provided he could keep his visitors in the halls of Sans Souci or beneath the rising shadow of La Ferriere. Many were impressed; many more came only to sneer at Negroes wearing caricatures of European uniforms and mincing about a ballroom with European airs and graces, at upstart noblemen with titles such as the Duke of Marmalade.

'Kit should have returned by now,' Seraphine said, anxiously, standing on the balcony of Richilde's apartment in the palace of Sans Souci, from whence it was possible to see the rooftops of Cap Françis in the distance, and beyond, even the ocean. 'Something has happened to him. The British . . .'

'Now, Seraphine,' Richilde said. 'The war with the British ended months ago. And the weather has been fine all year. There is nothing can have happened to Kit. He has just been delayed, that is all.' Gently she removed her finger from the babe's mouth, the chubby little hand having seized her flesh and inserted it before she had really noticed, in order to give her a hearty bite. 'I do believe little Alexander has cut another tooth.'

'No doubt.' Seraphine returned into the room,

scooped the child from her sister-in-law's lap, gave him a kiss, and then brought him against the breast exposed by the unfastened nursing bodice. 'He is always cutting teeth. One day I swear he will remove a nipple.'

'Then we should find you a wet nurse,' Richilde said.

Seraphine shot her a glance. 'No,' she said. 'No, I should prefer to continue feeding him myself.'

Richilde made no reply, picked up her needlework. Seraphine had now lived in Haiti for a dozen years and more, and for most of that time as a part of the people, rather than as an alien. Yet she would never overcome her repulsion for black skins, would not allow her child to feed from a black breast. Whereas I, she thought, would give half of my life to have a brown skinned babe at *my* breast, were such a thing possible for a near fifty-year-old.

She looked out of her window, and up into the mountains, at the towering scar which represented the citadel, rising out of the forest and the craggy escarpments. Henry was up here, superintending the building of his monument. He spent most of his time up there, left affairs of state largely to Gounod and Labalastierre, busily pursuing his dream. In fact, she knew, he had so organised his kingdom that his presence here was hardly needed. All of his people knew what he required of them, and they knew too that he *was* there, huge and terrible, if ever opposed, gigantically reassuring and rewarding, when they carried out his wishes. Undoubtedly they grumbled. Perhaps they even remembered the less hectic lives they had lived under Dessalines, or even under the French – certainly they worshipped the memory of the comparatively lazy days under Toussaint l'Ouverture. But then, they worshipped Toussaint himself, and were encouraged to do so, by the Emperor. He could explain, to her, that this was an act of policy. A nation had to have heroes, and dead heroes were safer and more reliable than live ones. But it was also, she knew, because he himself worshipped Toussaint, more than a little. The lame old coachman, whose life had been such a triumph and a tragedy, was one of the only three creatures he had ever loved in *his* life.

His mother had been the second. And she was undoubtedly the third. She might have felt more pride in belonging to such an elect group had she not always been aware of it, and had she not known that just as his worship of Toussaint had not prevented him from burning Cap François, in defiance of what he had known would be Toussaint's wish, or that his love for his mother, who had always believed it was right and proper for the black people to work for the white, had not prevented him from leading a slave revolt, so his love for her had not been allowed to interfere with his triumphant march onwards, in search of his destiny.

In many ways, she thought, not having to share his bed nightly was a considerable relief. It was not that, at forty-eight, she felt any less of a woman, that her sexual urges had in any way diminished. In fact, now that the transition to infertility had been completed, she was able to enjoy sex more than ever before, and she sought no other man but Henry. But inevitably their old intimacy had vanished. She did not think he ever repeated anything they said, or related anything they did together to the Empress Honeybelle. But he certainly related to *her* the conversations of the imperial bed, as usual seeking her comments, her ideas. As if she could possibly comment on his marriage, with any honesty. He did not love Honeybelle, she knew. Honeybelle was an extraordinarily lovely girl, tall and slender, with all the exquisite grace of her people. She had a bright and sunny disposition, and if she seemed quite unable, at eighteen, to understand the dignity that should accompany her exalted position, this unawareness certainly increased the attractiveness of her personality. She remained on the best of terms with Richilde. Like everyone else in Haiti, she knew that the Duchess of Sans Souci had been Henry's woman since the revolution, twenty-four years ago, and thus long before she had been born. And again like everyone else in Haiti, she was happy to accept the situation. Besides, Richilde sometimes thought, as she found the girl staring at her with enormous brown eyes, Honeybelle clearly found it quite impossible ever to be jealous of a woman very nearly three times her age.

Just as she found it impossible to be jealous of a girl young enough to have been her own granddaughter. Rather did she fear for her. For after more than two years of marriage, Honeybelle had not yet become pregnant. The fault was undoubtedly with the Emperor. But not even the Duchess of Sans Souci would dare tell the Emperor Henri that fact. Yet would he seek to remedy the situation soon enough, she was sure of that.

But for herself, life had settled into a very even tenor. Sometimes she managed to recall the tensions of being Philippe de Mortmain's child bride, the deluge of the revolution itself, the long days and nights in the forest, the nausea of LeClerc's administration, the constant awareness of the looming and irrational fury of Jean-Jacques Dessalines, with something like nostalgia. But on the whole she wanted only peace, and the feeling that her life had not been entirely wasted. Certainly it was not being wasted at the moment. She remained in charge of the growing township of Millot. This was, in fact, not a happy duty. There were many people who wished to live in the shadow of the palace, as Henry had prophesied, and there was no one in Haiti prepared to argue with her dispositions, with the streets she had laid out, the simple rules of sanitation that she imposed. But there was also no one in Haiti with the resources of Henri the Emperor, or even one tenth of them. So where she had dreamed of a city of marble and statues, of fountains and perhaps a flowing stream, of gardens and shade trees – a recreation, perhaps, of Cap François as she remembered it from her first morning in this

286

strange, passionate land – she looked down on nothing more than an overgrown village of mud huts, with troolie palm thatched roofs, only occasionally enhanced by a building made of wood. But even the wooden buildings, as they reflected the whims of their owners, and particularly in regard to paint, were but garish excrescences, hurling the sunlight skywards from a variety of pinks, and pale blues and browns, and favourite of all, bright yellow walls.

The Emperor had said, let them build, and the Emperor's word was law. The most disturbing thought was that, when he had completed his fortress, he would certainly then turn all his mighty energy on his capital city of Millot, and carelessly order the destruction of all these houses, which, however poor, were still the loved possessions of a man and a woman, and have them replaced with stone according to the original plan.

But, as La Ferriere remained no more than a scar in the trees, a costly, bloody scar, the rebuilding of Millot had to be some years in the future. If it were ever to happen at all.

She listened to trumpets blaring, the thudding of hooves, laid down her work. Seraphine was already on her feet, her son clutched in her arms, staring at the door as she always did whenever there was a disturbance. She could never overcome the fears which still lurked at the back of her memory.

Richilde also gazed at the door, knowing that if Henry had returned in haste from the citadel – he had not been due at Sans Souci for another week – then some crisis was at hand, and his visit to her would not be long delayed. In fact, she realised, listening to the boots hitting the stairs and the corridors, swelling closer, he was coming to her before anyone else.

Her heart began to pound. She could think of no occurrence quite so urgent – save perhaps that something *had* happened to Kit. She glanced at Seraphine, but the Frenchwoman might have been turned to stone, scarce seemed to breathe; she had even neglected to refasten her bodice.

The double doors burst open, and Henry strode across the hall, blue uniform jacket stained with sweat, and brow as well, fingers of his left hand nervously clutching the hilt of his sword, white gowned maids scurrying to get out of his way, anxious aides remaining in a huddle on the gallery. Yet he did not look unhappy. Merely thunderstruck. 'Richilde!' he shouted. 'Richilde! There is an English ship in the harbour. Kit has brought it in.'

'Kit?' Seraphine shouted, and bit her lip as Henry glanced at her. Little Alexander began to cry.

'Kit?' Richilde asked. 'A prize, you mean? But there is no war between us.'

Henry waved his hand. 'No prize. A great warship. A ship of the line. Seventy-four guns, it has; he has seen them. And it has an admiral on board. It has come from the English King, King Regent, to present credentials at the court of the Emperor Henri. An ambassador, Richilde. An ambassador, at last. And from England.' He strode across the room, held her in his arms. 'An ambassador, at last.' Then he released her, and stood back, whole body seeming to droop. 'What must I do, Richilde? Tell me what I must do?'

From her balcony, Richilde could look down on the procession as it slowly approached Sans Souci. It was incongruous to see the naval officers mounted on horses, their legs encased in flawless white stockings rather than boots. But there could be no denying the glowing hilts of their swords, or the shine of their leather shoes, the perfect cut of their blue jackets, the jaunty angles of their tricorne hats. They were the representatives of the greatest navy in the world, a navy which ruled unchallenged over the seas, despite the gallant efforts of a few Yankee frigates.

And at their head rode Vice-Admiral Sir Home

Popham, Knight Commander of the Bath, Fellow of the Royal Society, probably the most talented if one of the least famous of all the remarkable group of officers who had come to maturity under Jervis and Nelson. His features, as seen through her glass, were curiously soft and open, for a sea captain who all his life had possessed absolute power of life and death over those who sailed beneath his command. And that he was interested in what he saw could not be doubted; his head turned from left to right, looking at the houses of Millot, asking questions of Kit, riding at his side, and then gazing up at the palace itself, before which, as she knew although she could not see them, Henry and his nobles would be waiting; once again she had declined to take her place with the ladies. She was not one of the sights to be gawked at, any longer.

Beneath her, the band struck up, as best it could, but she almost thought the Admiral, used to his own superb musicians, winced as he disappeared from her sight. She wondered what he would make of the guard of honour. At her recommendation, Henry had dismissed all of his soldiers save for his own regiment of hussars. They were the best disciplined of his men – it was possible to say they were the *only* Haitian soldiers who had the least concept of timing or orderliness in their manoeuvres – but even they were not greatly better than an armed rabble, for all their brilliant red uniforms. As Popham would very readily discern, she had no doubt at all.

Then she could only wait, for Kit and Seraphine, who had attended the official banquet, to join her.

'Oh, it was grand,' Seraphine said. 'Barbaric, but grand. If only the Empress hadn't eaten that fish with her fingers.'

'I think Popham carried it off very well,' Kit said. 'He immediately followed her example.'

'But His Majesty was displeased,' Seraphine pointed out. 'He was frowning most severely.'

'Did he remember to say King George?' Richilde asked, anxiously. 'And not King Regent?'

'He did,' Kit said. 'He was very good. And he spoke with Popham in English, which impressed the British no end. Popham is apparently this new Commander-in-Chief in Jamaica. That means he commands the entire West Indies. I think we may have a good friend there. And you'll never guess what news he's brought.'

'Not another war?'

'The end of one,' Kit said. 'After all of these years. The end of the war with the French.'

'Oh, my God,' Richilde said. 'That will set Henry to preparing to resist a French invasion, all over again.'

Kit laughed. He laughed so readily nowadays. His transparent happiness, and that of Seraphine, was perhaps her greatest achievement, Richilde thought. 'Not any more. It has ended not in a truce, but in the total defeat of the French. Napoleon has been abdicated and been sent off to some remote island. There is a Louis back on the throne, the Eighteenth, I think. Henry can at last stop worrying about the French.'

'If Bonaparte has finally been driven from power,' Seraphine said wistfully, 'perhaps we could go back. I should love to go back, at least for a visit.'

'Well, it may be possible,' Kit said. 'We shall have to persuade the Emperor to spare us for a season. Certainly I have never seen him looking so pleased. He has even accepted an invitation to dine on board the warship, tomorrow. I am to accompany him. There will be a famous occasion.'

Richilde awoke to the sound of her doors opening, sat up. Her maids had turned down the candles, and the apartments were dark, save for the moonlight streaming in the opened windows and across the floors; four stories up, and in the cool period of the year, she suffered little from mosquitoes or sandflies. And despite the gloom, there was no doubting the giant figure who stood beside her bed.

Midnight passion was unusual, between them, after so many years. 'Henry?' she asked. 'What is the matter?'

He sighed, and sat on the bed. 'I have come from the warship,' he said.

She waited.

'I never knew,' he said. 'That there could be anything so perfect in the world. I have never seen such clean decks. And the guns . . . my God, Richilde, if I had even half of those guns I could wipe Petion off the face of the map, tomorrow, And the men. They call them marines. Have you ever seen marines on parade, Richilde?'

'No, Henry,' she said.

'They wear red jackets, with silver braid, and tall hats, and white pants, and black shoes, and they carry muskets and long bayonets. And they stand, like statues, not even a wink, staring straight to their front. They are the finest men I have ever seen. How may I match such men?'

'You matched them once, do you not remember? You and Toussaint matched them, and beat them. You have naught to fear from them.'

'Fear from them?' he asked. 'You do not understand. I do not fear them. But I must *match* them. I looked at these men, these magnificent creatures, and this Admiral Popham could see that I was impressed, and he said, "My master, the Prince Regent of England, commands regiment upon regiment of men such as these. It is the finest army in the world, Your Majesty." And then he waited, for my reply. I had to reply, Richilde, as best I could, without you at my side. And so I said, "As he is a prince, Admiral, he should command many men. And he should be proud of them. But I, I am an emperor. My soldiers are as the sands of the

291

sea. Their discipline is that of black men, severe, to be sure, but more concerned with ardour and courage, than with the stoic virtues. And their weapons are the finest in the world." I boasted to him, Richilde. I could not be rendered inferior to a mere prince.'

'What did he say?' Richilde asked.

'He thought for several moments, and then he said, "I should like to see your army, Your Majesty. I have heard much about it. I should like to see it very much." And do you know what else he said? He said, "I should also like the privilege of meeting the Duchess of Sans Souci, of whom also I have heard so much."'

'And what did you reply?' Richilde asked, softly.

'What could I reply? I said, "Then you shall see them both, Admiral. Tomorrow afternoon, you and I shall hold a grand review of my soldiers, and at that grand review, the Duchess of Sans Souci shall be present, and you may talk with her." Oh, Richilde, my Richilde, what am I to do? I have but five thousand men here in Millot. And of those, four thousand have no discipline, and their weapons are old and rusty. This Popham, he will look at them, and he will sneer at their numbers, and he will laugh at them as they march past. All the world will laugh. All the world will laugh at me, and my puny army.'

Richilde got out of bed, and stood beside him. His arms went round her waist, and he kissed her breasts. 'What am I to do, my Richilde?'

'You have in store in Cap François,' she said, 'all of the uniforms accumulated by Dessalines for the army he never had.'

'That is true,' he said. 'But I have no men to put in them. This Popham is not a fool, Richilde. He will know the difference between a soldier and a farmer dressed up in uniform. The only men I have who I can possibly set against those marines are the Imperial Guard, and they are scarce a thousand strong. I have promised him untold legions.'

292

'I am sure Admiral Popham is not a fool,' Richilde said. 'But he is certainly a white man, and I have heard it said that to a white man, all black faces look alike. Send to Cap François for those uniforms, Henry. And then summon the Prince of Sunshine to meet us, to discuss our plans for tomorrow. For what you have promised, you must deliver. The Duchess of Sans Souci, and the finest army in all America.'

She wore a white lawn gown, and a feather boa, tucked her hair out of sight beneath a huge straw hat, decorated with hibiscus blossoms. She was well aware that her clothes, and the style of them, were considerably out of date, but at least she would appear like no white savage. She came down the great staircase, behind Henry and the Empress to be sure, but accompanied by Seraphine and Kit, also dressed in their best, and very well aware that she was the cynosure of all eyes, and not merely those of the British officers – the black courtiers were sufficiently unused to seeing the Duchess of Sans Souci attending a state occasion.

'Your Grace,' Sir Home Popham bent low over her fingers, and spoke in English. 'I have waited for this moment with the most keen anticipation.'

'I wonder why, Sir Home,' she said. 'I am but a woman.'

'A very famous one,' he pointed out.

'Am I, famous? Outside of Haiti?'

'Indeed you are. They have written about you, poems and even a novel. But I am afraid those gentlemen scribblers knew very little about what they described.'

She smiled, 'No doubt I am depicted as a naked savage.'

'Very much so,' Popham agreed. 'With your hair down to your ankles and a bow and arrow ever at your side.'

'Well, sir,' she said. 'I do have hair which stretches a long way, when loosed. And there have been occasions

293

when I have longed for a bow and arrow readily to hand. But I think that at my age running naked through the forest would be tiresome. I should like to read one of these stories. Would that be possible?'

'I shall obtain one for you, and send it to you, you have my word,' Popham promised.

'The parade is about begin,' Henry said, also speaking English. 'The Duchess will sit with you, Sir Popham, and you may continue your conversation.'

He was anxious, and would indeed have preferred Richilde to be able to engage the Admiral in conversation throughout the review. But Popham, although the soul of politeness, and alertness, quick to reply to any of her remarks, was also an acute and interested observer, of the troops which now began to pass before him.

'You will understand, Sir Home,' Richilde explained, 'that His Majesty has ordered but one company of each regiment to appear today. To review the entire army would be most tedious, and besides, as you will know, we are in a state of war with the south, which could erupt into actual fighting at any moment, thus a considerable proportion of our troops are already deployed in the mountains.'

'Indeed I understand that,' Popham agreed. 'And it is very good of His Majesty to take so much time to show me his strength. But you know what humanity is, Your Highness. Our politicians and so-called diplomats back in England are inclined to rate the value of an ally, or the importance of an enemy, entirely by the size and capability of the army he can put into the field. Now these fine fellows, these are the Imperial Guard, am I right?'

Richilde nodded, as the red coated hussars rode by, emerging from beyond the left wing of the palace, walking their horses in review order past the dais, and then disappearing round the right hand palace wing.

'Those are, as you say, the Imperial Horse Guards,' she explained. 'These are the Imperial Foot Guards.'

Bright yellow jackets, smartly sloped muskets and gleaming bayonets, impeccable discipline.

'Fine fellows. Oh, fine fellows,' Popham commented.

'The Imperial Marines,' Richilde said.

Popham gazed at the sky blue jackets, the tall shakos. 'Bless my soul,' he said. 'I had no idea Haiti possessed a navy.'

'It doesn't,' Richilde said with a smile. 'Except for coastal protection. But that is no reason not to have a regiment of marines, is it, Sir Home?'

'Why, no,' he agreed. 'I suppose not.'

He looked back at the parade, but after the Marines had passed there was a hiatus. Richilde was aware of beads of anxious perspiration rolling down her back and filling her gloves. 'Now we will have the first of the regiments of the line,' she said, hopefully. 'Oh, there they are.'

Dark blue jackets, these, white breeches, gaiters, gleaming muskets, tall shakos, led by their drummer-boys, who wore red sashes and beat time as they tramped past, dust eddying from their feet. There were three companies of these.

'All from the same regiment?' Popham asked.

'Oh, good heavens, no,' Richilde said. 'Those are the first three regiments of the line. You will observe that although they all wear the same uniforms, their regimental banners are different. There are twenty-seven regiments of the line altogether, arranged in brigades of three regiments each.' For once again, the three companies having disappeared round the right wing of the palace, there was a break in the procession.

'Each regiment is eight hundred men. You are, as I said, just seeing the lead companies here. So each brigade is approximately two thousand four hundred foot soldiers. His Majesty combines these with two

295

regiments of cavalry, of three hundred men each, and a battery of artillery, to make a division. I know these are smaller divisions than in your European armies, but His Majesty has discovered that such small tactical units are best suited for jungle warfare.'

Popham scratched his ear in astonishment, as much at her detailed knowledge of such military matters as at the implied size of the army being displayed for him. He watched the next company appearing from the left. As Richilde had prophesied, these wore the same blue uniforms as their compatriots, but carried different banners. And behind them came two more. And then more and more, in groups of three companies, until all twenty-seven has passed, and Richilde could listen to the excited murmurings of the junior British officers who stood behind the Admiral, and were clearly most impressed.

'Now we have the cavalry,' she said, and with an effort had to prevent herself from twisting her fingers together. Sir Home Popham might not know the difference between one black man and another, but as an English gentleman he would surely be an excellent judge of horseflesh. Yet had everyone remembered her instructions. As company after company of horse rode by, each company in different uniform jackets and flying different banners, there could be no doubt that the horses on the inside rank, and therefore the only ones which could be accurately inspected by the Britishers, were entirely different beasts.

'Twenty-seven regiments of the line, twenty regiments of horse, plus the Imperial Guard,' Popham remarked, half to himself. 'And such splendid fellows. Why, Your Grace, your Emperor could hope to do battle with the best of European armies, and on an open field. If he were as well served with artillery.'

'It is approaching now,' Richilde said, as the first battery of six guns came round the corner. 'We have thirty of such batteries, as you will see.'

Popham removed his tricorne to wipe his brow; he had been seated in the hot sun for three hours already.

But it was a case of maintaining his composure, as cannon after cannon rumbled by, sending dust swirling upwards to be flicked into their faces by the afternoon sea breeze, and at last sighing with relief as the final caisson disappeared around the side of the palace. He got up, saluted, and then held out his hand to Henry. 'Your Majesty, I congratulate you. That is the finest army I have seen in a long time. Truly, sir, I am impressed.'

Henry smiled at Richilde. 'It is time for tea,' he said. 'The Duchess will entertain us all to tea.'

The meal was served in the ballroom, where a hundred officers, and their ladies, could be comfortably accommodated, and where the palace had already reached perfection, in its huge crystal chandeliers, its monogrammed silk drapes, and in the paintings which adorned the walls: portraits of Henry and his principal generals, in most cases grotesque caricatures, but filled with the colour and the exuberance of the African.

It was a buffet meal, so that the throng could keep moving as they talked, an ever changing kaleidoscope of colour and animation. Popham stayed very much at Richilde's shoulder, throughout the afternoon, allowing her to introduce him to the Negro Generals and their wives, and in turn introducing her to his flag captain and lieutenants. And eventually managing to stand beside her at one of the south facing windows, with Christophe temporarily stranded on the far side of the room and the crowd.

'Is that La Ferriere?' He pointed at the white scar high in the mountains.

'Yes,' she said. 'Would you like to visit there?'

'Indeed I would. But unfortunately I must get on to Jamaica, and write my despatches.' He smiled at her. 'May I ask what those walls are made of?'

'They are made of stone, Sir Home,' she said. 'And they rise one hundred feet out of the rock, and are more than thirty feet thick at the base. It is the most marvellous thing ever built by human hand. And it has, literally, been built by human hand. And human blood.'

He glanced at her. 'You disapprove of this?'

'I disapprove of the shedding of human blood, Sir Home, whatever the reason. I have seen too much of it.'

'Indeed you must have, Your Grace. But I have been told that the Emperor relies upon your advice in all things. Yet you do not approve of the citadel?'

'I do not approve of the citadel, Sir Home. I do not think it is necessary, and I think the cost is far too high. As for relying upon me, His Majesty follows his own council, and relies on no one.'

Popham was still smiling. 'Yet he is not above drawing upon your wits and your imagination, I think. Your very fertile wits and imagination.'

She shot him a glance. 'La Ferriere is real, Admiral. I would suggest that if you doubt that, you make the time to look at it.'

'I believe that it is real, Your Grace,' he said. 'And I beg of you not to take offence. As I have not taken offence at the . . . shall we say, the masquerade, which was presented for my entertainment, this afternoon.'

She frowned at him, while her heart gave a great lurch. 'I do not understand you.'

'There is a sergeant in the Imperial Guard, who I noticed at the very beginning of the review,' he said. 'Because he has a scar on his right cheek. But of course I am mistaken; in *every* regiment, certainly in every third company in His Majesty's army, there is a sergeant with a scar on his cheek. I have no doubt that it is the result of some initiatory duel, as in Germany.'

She stared at him. 'What will you do?'

'Do, Your Grace? Why, I shall write my report.'

'And say?'

'That His Majesty, the Emperor Henri, is one of the most resourceful men I have ever encountered. And Your Grace, in war, resourcefulness of the sort I have witnessed this afternoon often does make up for lack of numbers.' His eyes twinkled. 'However, purely for the gratification of my own curiosity, and with the word of an officer and a gentleman that what you tell me will go no further ... how many men *does* His Majesty command?'

Richilde met his gaze. 'His Majesty commands all of the thirty thousand odd that were represented here today, Sir Home. Unfortunately, not all of them have the discipline or the bearing of your marines, whom he wished to match. But I will tell you this: in their own jungles, and led by a general with Henry's genius, they are the finest troops in the world. As both the British and the French have discovered.'

'Indeed, Your Grace,' Popham said. 'I do not for one moment dispute what you are saying. Believe me, ma'am, I regard Haiti as full of promise for the future, and with you at His Majesty's elbow I am even more confident than I was before.'

'You are monopolising the Duchess, Admiral,' Henry said, joining them. He was in a tremendous good humour since the success of the review.

'I am but attempting to convince her how much I admire what I have seen here,' Popham said. 'I look forward, on my next visit, to inspecting your fortress, in the hills.'

'You will do that,' Henry said. 'And I will have more to show you than that. I will have a united country to show you, when next you come here, Sir Popham. Tomorrow I lead my armies south, to settle with Petion.'

'But *why*?' Richilde cried. 'Why now?'

'Because now is the time,' Henry said. 'I know it. I feel it in my bones.'

299

He stood in the centre of her private drawing room rather like a defiant schoolboy hauled before the headmistress.

'Henry,' she begged. 'Nothing has changed. The citadel is still not completed. You have no more men or guns than yesterday. What we showed Popham was a sham. Don't you understand that? It was the same thousand men, again and again and again, only changing their uniforms at every circuit of the palace. Why . . .' she bit her lip. She dared not tell Henry that the British Admiral had seen through their subterfuge.

'I know that, Richilde,' he said, with gentle patience. 'But a great deal has, in fact, changed. Bonaparte has been defeated. The power of France is in the dust. We do not know for how long it will remain there, but we must take advantage of it while we can. Popham has told me that there is a great revolt going on against the Spaniards in South America. Spain has no men to interfere with us here in Haiti. This is another factor we must take into account. And he has reassured me that at the present, at any rate, the British have no desire to extend their possessions in America. They have sufficient, for the time being. These are all factors we must consider. And of which we must take advantage. For the first time since August 1791 we have absolutely no fear of a foreign invasion. But these things will change. Other kings will come to power, other policies will prevail. Of course I had not intended to move against Petion until La Ferriere was completed. But that was when I had European intervention to fear. Now that is no longer a problem. Now we *must* move against him, and complete the unification of Haiti, while we may.' He threw his arm round her shoulders and gave her a squeeze. 'As for the citadel, work will of course continue on that, for the sooner it is completed the happier I shall be. I am placing it in your care.'

'My care?' she cried. 'That is impossible.'

'Why is it impossible? You know my requirements.'

300

'I also know that I could never drive men to their deaths the way you have been doing.'

He held her shoulders. 'You can, and you will. This is the backbone of Haiti that we are creating. You will do it, my Richilde, as you have done so many things in the past. Because I have asked you to. Because I need you to. Because it must done.'

Her resolution was leaking away like water from a holed bucket. 'But why me?' she asked. 'Why *me*?'

'Because in all Haiti,' he said. 'There is no one else I can trust, as I trust you.'

Chapter 4

LA FERRIERE

On a mountain top towering above his country, [Christophe] erected La Ferriere, the Citadel, the eighth wonder of the world and the architectural marvel of the Western Hemisphere, an impregnable bastion with walls several feet thick and rising a hundred feet and more from base to battlement, guarded by three hundred and sixty-five cannon, an engineering phenomenon, for each block of masonry, each cannon, each ball and each sack of food had to be carried by man muscles up the precipitous face of a mountain.

'There, Highness,' said Colonel Laborde. 'You can see it now.'

All the previous day they had walked their horses through the forest, along a cleared roadway, to be sure, a track trampled by the feet of thousands of men, with their horses, and the enormous weights they had carried, marked in an almost continuous row beside the road – and already becoming overgrown by the vengeful jungle – by the graves of those who had fallen.

But all the time they had been climbing, too, and now suddenly there was a break in the trees, and she could follow the direction of Laborde's pointing finger, and gape at what appeared, from below, as the sharply pointed bow of an enormous ship, jutting out of the mountainside several hundred feet above her. A ship made of stone, and greater than any vessel ever launched.

Seraphine was equally amazed. As Kit spent so much time at sea, ceaselessly ferrying Haitian sugar to America, and guns and ammunition back to Haiti, she had refused to remain by herself at Sans Souci, had opted instead for the ride through the forest and into the mountains, her son in her arms. It was the first time she had undertaken such an expedition, and everything was a source of wonder, or a source of fear. For Richilde, everything was a source of memory. Because at the end of it, after twenty years, nothing had truly changed. She was again making her way into the heart of the island, and Henry was again away campaigning. Only that immense stone monstrosity, looming above her, was a symbol of the years that had rolled away, the dreams that had faded, and the men who had died.

Another night camp, with the mosquitoes whirring about them, and the horses moving restlessly in the picket line. And then another dawn, the brilliant red sunlight scorching out of the Atlantic Ocean, far beneath them now, and immediately glinting from the walls of the fortress. But now they were coming closer, and it was a matter of arching the back and the neck, and staring straight upwards, at the bicorned heads peering down at them, and at the gaping mouths of the cannon, glaring over the forest. Henry's plan called for three hundred and sixty five cannon, one for each day of the year, just as his supply requirements called for sufficient food for one thousand men a year. The final, impregnable bastion.

A wooden drawbridge was lowered, and their horses' hooves clattered over a ravine some hundred feet deep, out of which the immense walls rose sheer. Then they were in a courtyard, as large as a village in itself, all hewn out of the living rock. At the rear were the barracks and living quarters, to the right the stables, to the left the storerooms. Richilde was taken to see the well, which stretched down through the rock for several hundred feet, to tap the resources of an inexhaustible

303

jungle stream. She had not been up here since the work had first commenced, and her blood had curdled as she had watched men and women being flogged like any slaves she remembered, as they had carried and dragged the huge blocks of masonry upwards. It had been nauseating and hateful – but she could not help but marvel at the results that had been achieved. She had been born and bred and lived all her life in the West Indies, where the works of man are meaningless compared with the immense and creative architecture of nature; she had only ever read of the Pyramids or the Hanging Gardens of Babylon, the Colossus of Rhodes or the Temple of Diana, but she could not believe that the Pharaohs or the monarchs of Chaldea, the Greeks or the Persians, had ever built anything to equal the Citadel of La Ferriere.

Which she was charged with completing. There was actually little left to be done to the fortress itself. Henry was more concerned to use her brains to establish the storerooms and the interior arrangements. He saw his fortress as the last retreat of himself and his people, or at least a selected few of them, where they would retire were they ever assailed by overwhelming force, and in which they would live, as in a town but with complete security, while yellow fever and hurricane winds gradually destroyed the invading army, as had happened twice before.

But the remainder of the cannon still had to be dragged up from the coast and hoisted into place along the immense battlements. The work continued as soon as Kit returned, and all along the coast from Cap François and through the forest the sweating labourers dragged and tugged and cursed and fell, and were crushed beneath the unceasing wheels and were buried by the roadside with so many others. While the cannon were slowly emplaced, each with fifty twenty-pound iron balls stacked beside it.

And *I* am doing this, she realised. Me, Richilde

Hamilton, daughter of a colonial shipping agent, sometime wife of the last of the Mortmains, and now mistress of the Emperor of Haiti. I am driving people to their deaths because Henry would have it so. While he fought and killed and hacked his way into the mulatto stronghold of the south. And yet found the time to continue government. Thus they received a messenger a week, with news of the campaigns, which were necessarily inconclusive, as she had always known they would be, with queries as to the progress of the citadel, with demands for more men and munitions, and with odd pronunciamentoes, as they occurred to him to make. Thus there was suddenly no more Cap François, but instead Cap Haitien, which Henry had decided was far more suitable. And with that there were orders for changing the uniform of the Imperial Marines, who alone had been left to guard Sans Souci, from pale blue to deep green, orders which Kit had patiently to carry out, and orders to change the imperial monogram to HC, and orders to seek the offices of a suitable *mamaloi* to discover why the Empress had not yet become pregnant, and inquiries as to why the food supplied by the north-west area was down a few per cent this year, and instructions for Richilde to take care as the hurricane season approached. Henry's energy bubbled out of the forests and drove everything before it, as if he were some gigantic volcano, rumbling away in subterranean splendour.

Yet it was a curiously happy time. However much Richilde hated having to drive the labourers to the very limits of exhaustion, she knew that she was creating a monument which would stand as long as time itself. And however much she waited with anxious dread to hear the reports of the unceasing campaigns in the forest, there could be no doubt that Henry *was* slowly squeezing the life out of Petion's small armies, slowly gaining the victory of which he had dreamed, and that he was happy too, happier campaigning than he was doing anything else. Nor could she truly feel apprehensive for his safety, as long as he continued to wear and trust the silver talisman. He had never been seriously wounded in his entire life.

There were domestic joys, too, as Seraphine gave birth to her second child, and as Kit came up to La Ferriere to spend Christmas with them, while the winds howled around the battlements and far below they could see the seething whitecaps of the ocean. It was a stormy winter, normally the best time of the year, and with the spring there was no lack of those who muttered that this coming summer would bring a hurricane. Richilde had never actually experienced a hurricane. The storms roamed the West Indies every year, but there were so many islands that it was possible to spend a lifetime, as indeed she had done, without ever encountering anything more severe than a gale. But this year she at last knew that the real thing was coming close, as she watched the great banks of cloud building to the south and east. It was a time for Kit to locate a land-locked 'hurricane hole' in which to hide his ship until the worst was over, and then to arrange berths ashore for his crews, which suited them well enough. And then it was a time for waiting and watching, as the cloud formations built and dispersed, and then immediately rebuilt again. But the storm had not yet arrived when the Emperor returned from the wars, and with him, his prisoners.

Richilde was down in the huge subterranean vaults, like everything else in La Ferriere hewed out of the solid rock by man muscles, supervising the rotation of the sacks of grain which were always stored here, when she was summoned by Colonel Laborde, who commanded the garrison.

'Haste, Your Highness,' came the call. 'The Emperor approaches.'

Henry! She had not seen him in more than a year.

And she wore an old gown and was dripping sweat and coated with dust. She gathered her skirts and ran up the stone steps, emerged into the courtyard as the draw-bridge went rumbling down, and listened to the horses' hooves clattering on to the wood. She pushed hair from her eyes, moved away from where Seraphine and the other women waited, stood by herself as Henry came into the courtyard. He had clearly not bathed or changed his clothes in several days, but she had seen him returning from a campaign often enough in the past. What struck her now were the deep lines of fatigue which were etched in his face, the unutterable weariness with which he slipped from the saddle and threw his reins to the waiting groom.

'Your Majesty.' She sank into a deep curtsey. 'We had no prior warning of your coming, or I should have prepared myself. And the fortress.'

He raised her and embraced her. 'I like you well enough with honest sweat on your brow, Richilde,' he said. 'And the fortress is always prepared, is it not?' His gaze swept the battlements. He could not count beyond ten, but he could see where additional cannon had been emplaced.

While Richilde waited, aware that there had been a distinct lack of real warmth in his greeting.

'The campaign goes well?' she asked.

'The campaign is over, for a season,' he said. 'We have had a great triumph, and taken one of Petion's fortified towns.' At last the grim face broke into a smile. 'He does not have very many of those. But my men need to rest, and the storm season is upon us. I wished to see the citadel again, and you. And besides, I have a task to perform. A duty to complete.' He turned, and Richilde's heart gave a great leap before seeming to slide all the way down into her stomach, as she watched the prisoners being pushed forward, stagger-ing, falling to their knees as they tripped. They had clearly been forced to walk, all the way from the battle-

307

field, after having been stripped of their clothing and their boots, so that their feet were a mass of blood and sores, and their flesh was lacerated, as much from thorns and swinging branches as from the whips of their captors.

Their white skins.

Richilde found herself on her knees as well, gazing at the man before her, head drooping, white hair and beard a tangled, matted mass. Etienne would be, she realised, sixty-four years of age, and had not worn well. Even the last time she had met him, fifteen years ago at Charles LeClerc's garden party, she had noticed that he had put on a great deal of weight. Now the rolls of flesh hung uneasily, and he shivered, despite the afternoon heat.

'Richilde,' he whispered. 'For God's sake, help me, Richilde. Help us all.'

She had to bite her lip to stop herself from crying out as she looked past her cousin, at Louise, also on her knees, plump white flesh discoloured with blood and bruises, and then beyond her, at Madeleine, who had remained on her feet. Madeleine was but two years younger than Etienne, and was therefore sixty-two. But she was still tall, and slender, and upright, her beautiful features a mask of cold reserve, for all the whip marks on her shoulders and buttocks. Beside her there was a girl, perhaps twelve or thirteen years old, Richilde thought, with the soft Ramlie features of her mother curiously juxtaposed with the big nose of the Mortmains. The *very* last of the Mortmains. She had not even been aware that Louise had had a child.

But there was no Annette. Thank God, she thought. Annette would have been more than she could bear.

'Stand, Duchess,' Henry said. 'It is for them to kneel before you.'

Slowly Richilde rose to her feet.

'Your other cousin, the woman of whom Kit was fond, took poison when we entered the town,' Henry

308

said. 'These lacked her courage. They begged for their lives. *He . . .*' he thrust out his riding crop and tapped Etienne under the chin to make his head jerk, 'begged for his life. His life, not theirs.'

'And you have granted them that, Your Majesty,' she whispered, scarce daring to hope.

Henry's smile was terrible. 'No,' he said. 'I will keep my oath. I have brought them back to die, here at La Ferriere, where the whole world will hear their screams.'

Richilde gazed through the window at the huge black storm clouds building out to sea, slowly filling the afternoon sky. They seemed no more than a complement to the mood that hung over La Ferriere. She wished that Kit were here. He had experienced hurricane force winds before. He knew how to cope with storms.

But Kit was in Cap François. Correction, she thought; Kit was in Cap Haitien.

'The storm will be upon us by dawn,' Henry said. 'I am glad to be here, and not in the forest. Will Sans Souci withstand the storm? Is it strongly enough built?'

His Empress was down there. But he was more interested in the palace itself.

'Yes, Your Majesty,' Richilde said. 'The palace is strongly enough built to withstand a storm. But they should remember to shutter the windows, or there may be some damage.' She turned away from the evening, looked at him. He sat in his hip bath, soaking, while the maids scurried to and fro, bringing fresh pitchers of warm water to pour over his back and head. His face was starting to relax as some of the exhaustion left his muscles.

'Would it do any good for me to beg?' Richilde asked, speaking English. 'For me to throw myself on the floor at your feet?'

'I will not have you beg,' he said. 'I swore an oath,

309

and you knew of this. They knew of it, too. Yet have they come back, time and again, always with my enemies, with the enemies of Haiti. They must die, that the world will understand how the Emperor Henri deals with his enemies.'

She sighed. 'Even the little girl? She has never harmed you.'

'She has Mortmain blood in her veins. She has Etienne's blood in her veins. That is a measure of her guilt.'

'Then let it be quick,' Richilde asked. 'Please, Henry. That they should all die is terrible enough. But let it be quick. Behead them, and have done with it. There is surely revenge enough.'

'No,' he said, and stood up, water rolling from his shoulders and down his legs. The girls hastily wrapped him in towels.

'Henry . . .' her shoulders sagged. 'What will you do with them?'

'Etienne will be flogged. Slowly. One stroke of the whip every five minutes, from dawn until dusk, until he dies. I think it will take several days. Perhaps a week. And while he hangs and suffers, and screams, his women will be spreadeagled before him and raped by my men, one after the other, until *they* die. It will be the last memory, the last sight his eyes will carry, as he goes down to hell.'

Richilde clasped both hands about her throat. 'You cannot be *serious*.'

'My people are erecting a triangle now, with a bed before it.'

'You . . . I had supposed you a man, not a beast, like Dessalines.'

His head came up, and then his hand, pointing. 'Beware, woman. You are not so far removed from a Mortmain yourself.'

'I *am* a Mortmain,' she shouted. 'The same blood runs in my veins, through my mother, as in any of theirs.

And I am white. And I was married to a man who ill used your people, and allowed you to be flogged. Because that is what you are avenging here. Your flogging. Not the death of your child or the enslavement of your people. You are avenging your flogging. Well, why do you not send me down with Madeleine and Louise and the girl. My God, she is my cousin and she is about to die and I do not even know her name. Why do you not execute me as well? Are you afraid that I will not scream? Do not be afraid of that, Henry. I will scream. I will scream more loudly than any of them. Because I will not only know pain, and fear, and humiliation, I will know the horror of failure, the horror of knowing that a man to whom I have devoted my life, to whom I have given almost every minute of my life, is at the end of it nothing more than a savage monster. Dessalines at least acted in rage. But you . . . your hatred is something cold, and malignant. It is the hatred of a snake, lurking in the weeds, waiting, year after year, to accomplish its . . .' His huge hand slashed through the air, and although she saw it coming and jerked her head, she could not avoid the blow. For a moment she lost her senses, and then she discovered herself sprawled on the floor, her scalp seeming to be made of steel and constantly rising and then slamming back again on her brain.

She gazed at his feet, as he stood above her. 'I did not wish to hurt you,' he said. 'I have never wished to hurt you, my Richilde. You are more precious to me than life itself. But you would make me into a woman, or a priest. I am a man and an emperor. There are things I have to do, for the sake of my people, of my fame, of my immortal memory. You have known this, always. You will not turn me aside now.'

He walked away from her, and she sat up. She had to hold her jaw between her hands to speak. 'Then do not ever approach my bed again,' she said. 'Or I will scratch out your eyes.'

He stopped, and turned, while the maids, huddled in the corner of the room, stared from one to the other in utter terror. Once again the Emperor pointed. 'Go,' he said to Richilde. 'And bid your cousins farewell.'

Outside in the courtyard, the wind had already risen. It came in squalls, accompanied by teeming rain, which pounded on the beaten earth, splattered from the battlements, drove the soldiers from their labours; the triangle stood only half completed, awaiting its victim, as the mattress awaited its occupants, slowly turning into a soggy mass.

The guards stood to attention, but did not query her as she went past them, opened the door to the cell, stood at the top of the stone steps and looked down at the huddled figures beneath her. They had not been secured in any way, sat on the cold earth floor, starting to their feet as they saw her.

'Richilde,' Etienne shouted. 'You have saved us.' He ran forward, reached for her as she descended the steps. 'I knew you would. I told them . . . did I not tell you, Louise? Richilde will save us. Henry but means to frighten us, and humiliate us. But if he is taking us to see Richilde, we will be saved.'

She said nothing, resisted his embrace, and his face slowly changed.

'Why should *she* save us?' Madeleine demanded. 'Is she not the white nigger herself?'

To speak, to unclench her jaw, was to send rivers of pain gushing through her head. 'I would save you if I could,' Richilde said. 'I have begged for your lives. But he is adamant.'

'You have begged for us?' Madeleine sneered. 'Have you any concept, any idea, of what we have suffered?'

'I know what you have suffered,' Richilde said. 'I have suffered it myself. I suffered it because Etienne ran away, when he could have stayed and fought with us, and perhaps shown us how to win. But I suffered. And I survived.'

'Because you are a white nigger,' Madeleine spat. 'You were always a white nigger.'

'Because my crimes were not so great as yours,' Richilde said. 'I had never murdered a child.'

Madeleine refused to lower her eyes. 'A mulatto bastard,' she said. '*Your* mulatto bastard. Christophe's spawn. The only mistake I made was is not strangling you with it. My God, there was another. I held you in my arms, within ten minutes of your birth, and I let you live.'

Richilde gazed at her. 'I begged for your life,' she said. 'But I regret that. Henry has made the right decision, after all.'

'But me, Richilde,' Louise cried. 'I have never harmed you. Marguerite here was not even born when all that happened. Are we to die, too?'

'Henry hates everything named Mortmain,' Richilde said. 'I am sorry.'

'But can he not let us live?' Etienne begged, kneeling at her feet, fingers entwined in her gown. 'He hates me, that I know. Let him flog me. For God's sake, Richilde, let him castrate me, but just let him be merciful, and allow me to live, as his slave.'

He was a despicable object, she thought. But then, he had always been a despicable object, even before the night he had galloped away and left her to die, with his mother and father, his wife and his children, his brother and his sisters.

'You are going to be flogged,' she said. 'To death.'

He stared at her, his mouth slowly drooping open.

'So you had best prepare yourself,' she recommended. 'As you must die, I beg of you to do so like a man.'

Still he stared at her, and then he burst into tears, and fell to the floor at her feet.

'And us?' Madeleine asked. 'Are we also to be flogged to death?'

'No,' Richilde said. 'You will be . . . the army will have you, until you die.'

Madeleine's head jerked. Louise gave a shriek of horror. The girl Marguerite, so like her grandmother in looks, just stared at her with wide opened mouth.

'And you will stand aside and watch this?' Madeleine asked in a low voice.

'I have no say in the matter,' Richilde said.

'Yet have you more say than you suppose, Richilde,' Henry said.

Their heads turned, to look at him, standing at the top of the steps, wearing his red hussar uniform.

'Mercy,' Etienne screamed. 'Mercy, Great King, oh mercy. Grant us our lives and we shall be your willing slaves forever more.'

'You must die,' Henry said. 'I have sworn this. And you.' He pointed at Madeleine. 'As I have sworn to avenge the death of my son.'

Madeleine said nothing, just stared at him. Etienne gave a tremendous shriek of agony, and once again collapsed to the floor.

'You . . .' Henry again pointed, this time at Louise. 'You are but an accident. You will leave this place, with your daughter.' He turned to Laborde, who waited at the top of the steps with several soldiers. 'You will provide Madame de Mortmain and her daughter with an escort into Cap Haitien. Give them clothes to wear, and make sure that the captain of their escort understands that they are not to be molested or harmed in any way. In Cap Haitien, they are to be kept under guard until a ship can be found to take them away. Captain Hamilton will attend to it. He is in Cap Haitien.'

Laborde saluted.

'Thank you, Henry,' Richilde said. 'Oh, thank you.'

'You . . . are sending us out into a storm?' Louise shrilled. 'You are sending us to our deaths.'

'For God's sake, Louise,' Richilde snapped.

'Take them away,' Henry commanded. 'They turn my stomach.'

314

The guards came down the steps, pulled Louise and her daughter to their feet, pushed them up towards the door. Madeleine remained standing against the wall, face rigid. Etienne was on his knees, whimpering and weeping, but raising his head as his wife reached the top of the stairs.

'Louise,' he cried. 'Have you nothing to say to me?'

Louise looked over her shoulder, briefly, and was then pushed out into the night.

'Your cousin has begged for you,' Henry said. 'At great personal risk. You should know this, and remember it, as you die. And I am listening to her prayers. I am being as merciful as I may. Bring the woman,' he told Laborde. 'And the man. He will watch.'

The door was opened again, and the wind leapt inside, swirling around the cell, causing Madeleine's hair to flutter. The guards came towards her, and a tremor seemed to run from her neck down to her toes.

'Henry,' Richilde said.

'Be quiet,' Henry said. 'Have I not promised to be merciful?'

The soldiers came towards them, half carrying Madeleine between them. She gazed at Richilde as she drew abreast. There were no tears in her eyes.

The rain was now falling heavily, and the thunder was rumbling, following the savage streaks of lightning which cut across the sky. The drawbridge was just being raised again, after the departure of Louise and Marguerite. And the entire garrison, with their wives and their children, and even their dogs, seemed to have been paraded for the occasion, crowding the courtyard, lining the battlements. No doubt, Richilde thought, Seraphine was somewhere in the crowd.

Madeleine looked left and right, at the black people, and gave another shudder, and then her head jerked with real interest as she realised that she was being pushed and dragged, not towards the soaking mattress set beneath the gallows, but towards a flight of steps leading to the east facing battlements, from where the drop was sheer for a hundred and fifty feet.

'Oh, my God,' Etienne wailed. 'Spare us, oh Great King. Spare us.'

'I will remain down here,' Richilde said.

'You will accompany me,' Henry said. 'You will stand at my side throughout. Or the original sentence stands.'

Richilde drew a long breath, walked at his side across the courtyard, aware that the rain had plastered her hair to her scalp and her gown to her back, and was thudding on to her skin as if she were being stoned. She watched Madeleine's white body being pulled up the last of the steps, and pushed across the firewalk, to the first of the huge embrasures, where a cannon protruded its long barrel into the night.

'Go out there, Madeleine de Mortmain,' Henry said. 'And jump.'

Madeleine realised that her arms had been released. She turned, to look at him, to look at Richilde. Her hair, too, the gold heavily streaked with grey, lay plastered on her shoulders. She watched the crowd surging up the various stairs to crowd the battlements, and stare down into the blackness. Richilde wondered what she thought, as she stood there. Did she remember her English husband and her estranged children, the long, lazy days in St Kitts? Or her girlhood, when she had been the toast of that small island, when with her name and her beauty and her French charm she had lived and laughed and loved like a queen?

Did she wish she had never abandoned that small but secure niche to follow her brother in his insensate search for revenge and reinstatement? Or did she hate too much ever to regret?

Madeleine turned away from them again, held on to the stone of the embrasure, and stepped into the open-

316

ing, leaning against the cannon. She looked down, into the darkness, and made the sign of the cross. She turned again, standing straight now, swaying as the wind struck at her. She pointed. 'I will see you, in hell, Henry Christophe,' she said, and seemed to fall backwards. Her misery tore a despairing wail from her mouth as she realised she was lost, and then that too was swallowed up by the wind and the darkness.

Madeleine's scream was echoed by Etienne, now grovelling on the soaking stone as he realised that his own moment had finally arrived.

'Bring him,' Henry said, and went back down the steps. He led them across the courtyard to the far end, where although the battlements had been completed, the powder store beneath was still being worked. Here torches were lit and set in the walls, to send their light flaring into the darkness. Richilde stood at Henry's side, feeling the water rolling down her legs to gather in a pool between her feet, listening to the whine of the wind and the growl of the thunder, watched Etienne being carried in; he could not even walk, such was his terror; watched too, against the farthest wall, soldiers who had already embedded iron rings into the stone – clearly acting on orders given more than a few hours previously – now fixing them with mortar.

Etienne was dragged across the rubbled floor and set against the wall, each wrist secured by an iron cuff to keep him from falling. His eyes were tight shut, but yet the tears seeped out and rolled down his cheeks, and now, as his feet touched the earth, he could not stop himself from opening his eyes, and looking around him in bewildered terror.

'Are you in pain?' Henry demanded. 'Are you in agony?'

Etienne stared at him, lips trembling; his whole face seemed to have been reduced to a jelly by his fear.

'Richilde begged for you as well,' Henry said. 'And

so I struck her. Now I grant her wish. You will suffer no pain, Etienne de Mortmain. You will merely have the time to think, of all the evil you have done, of all the sunshine you will no longer see, of the pit of hell which awaits you, with so many souls eager to lay their hands on your body.'

Etienne looked at him, mouth agape, then he looked at Richilde. Such was his fear he still did not understand what was about to happen.

'Commence,' Henry said.

The stonemasons came forward from the gloom at the back of the room, set the first bricks in place. The mortar had already been mixed, and waited in buckets for their use.

Etienne stared at the men for a moment, then raised his head again. 'No,' he shouted. 'No,' he screamed, and commenced to writhe against the wall, a terrible sight.

'What, would you *rather* be flogged to death?' Henry demanded. 'Would you like to be castrated by my women? Would you prefer to be fed to the ants? Be quiet, man, and try to die like a human being, and not an animal.'

Etienne wept and screamed and attempted to kick at the wall, but he could not reach it. And it was already two feet high.

'Perhaps, in a thousand years,' Henry said, 'someone will knock down that wall, and find your skeleton, and wonder what crime you had committed to have been so executed. Perhaps they will know, Etienne.'

The wall had reached three feet.

'Richilde,' Etienne begged. 'Sweet Richilde. Help me, Richilde, help me, for God's sake.'

'I would like to leave,' Richilde said, in a low voice.

Henry glanced at her.

'I am cold, and wet,' she said. 'And my head aches. I would like to lie down, Your Majesty.'

'You will lie down, when we are finished here,'

Henry said. 'You will wait, until the last brick is in place. It will not take long.'

It took, she supposed, several hours for the wall to be completed. Several hours in which Etienne screamed and howled and begged, and thrashed against the wall. When the last brick was in place, his screams could still be heard.

Richilde threw herself across her bed, soaked as she was, shivering as she was. The wind howled, and the lightning sent vivid flashes across the sky, each accompanied by unending peals of thunder. Almost it was possible to imagine the citadel was shaking, as perhaps the entire mountain, or all of Haiti, was shaking.

Equally was it possible to imagine that Madeleine was still falling, white body twisting through space, falling forever, into a bottomless cavern of hatred and despair.

Her door opened, and then closed, and a candle flared. She hugged the mattress closer, suddenly feeling the pain in her jaw where before it had been fading.

'You will catch cold,' Henry said. 'Lying there like that.'

'I will not die,' she said.

'No,' he said. 'You will not die, Richilde. You and I will never die. We will live forever. We are immortals, you and I. We are the favoured creatures of the gods.'

She preferred not to reply.

He waited, for several seconds, then he said, 'But you will not share your bed with me, ever again.'

'I will not share my bed tonight,' she said. 'I am in too much pain.' She did not specify whether the ache was in her heart, or her belly, or her jaw.

Another brief silence, and then she heard the door close again. That was Henry Christopher. A gentle, thoughtful giant, capable of remorse and sadness, of regret and even compassion. But where did Henry Christopher leave off, and the Emperor Henri of Haiti

319

begin? There was a boundary which was becoming more uncertain with every year.

Eventually she slept, and was awakened by a sort of moaning sound, which cut across even the howl of the wind. And then by another noise, a shouting, a fierce, angry bellowing.

It was still dark, although she supposed that it must be near dawn, and the wind still howled as the rain still cascaded over the stone of the fortress, as the lightning still cut across the sky with its accompanying booms of thunder. Her clothes were almost dry, her flesh clammily damp and her muscles stiff. She opened the door, went outside, reached the courtyard. This was as packed as it had been last night, when Madeleine had been hurled to her death. The entire garrison was here, with their women, and their children. Seraphine was here, holding her babe in her arms, while little Alexander clutched her skirts and screamed his terror.

But he was afraid of the storm. The watchers were afraid of the man, who wore the red robe of the *hougan*, and strode the battlements above them, clenched fists waved at the heavens as he defied its anger.

'Come to me,' Henry shouted. 'I am Henri Christophe, Lord of this land. Come to me, if you dare. Come hither, Ogone Badagris, and match me, god to man. Dare your muscles against mine, great Damballah. Face me, if you can. Come to me!'

Richilde found she was holding her breath, as he strode up and down, seeming to shrug away the bolts of lightning, tossing his head to defy the rain.

'He is mad,' Seraphine whispered. 'Like Dessalines, he has gone mad.'

'No,' Richilde said. 'No, he is not mad. He is guilty, and miserable.' She left the shelter of the doorway, once again walked through the rain to the foot of the steps, then slowly climbed them, *feeling* the thousand and more eyes which were staring at her. She reached the top of the steps. 'Henry,' she said.

He turned, fiercely.

She held out her arms. 'Come downstairs, Henry. Come to bed.'

He took a step towards her, and then suddenly every muscle in his body seemed to collapse; and he fell headlong at her feet.

A great wail arose from the watchers, as Richilde knelt beside their Emperor. Feet pounded on the steps, and General Labalastierre and Colonel Laborde reached her.

'He has been hit by a thunderbolt,' Labalastierre shouted. 'He has been struck down by the gods.'

'No,' she said. 'He has been struck down by exhaustion. Carry him to bed.'

Soldiers were summoned, and tenderly six of them raised the huge body of their King from the ground, carried him down the steps.

'He does not breathe,' Laborde whispered. 'He is dead. What is to be done?'

'He is not dead,' Richilde said, watching the mighty chest flutter. But a great lump of lead seemed to be forming in her stomach, as she remembered the *mamaloi's* words, remembered too the utter exhaustion which had been etched in his face yesterday afternoon.

They carried him into his bedchamber, laid him on the bed. 'Leave us,' Richilde commanded.

Labalastierre hesitated, glanced at Laborde. They both feared witchcraft.

'He will be well, once he has rested,' Richilde told them. 'I will stay here with him, and watch.'

'His Majesty is ill,' Labalastierre said. 'We must send for the Empress.'

'By all means send for her,' Richilde agreed. 'By the time she gets here he will be well. But only if he is left, to rest. Help me get his uniform off.'

Between them they stripped that massive, inert frame, and then they wrapped him in a blanket.

'Now go,' Richilde said. 'Go, and His Majesty will be well.'

They hesitated a last time, and then left the room. Richilde closed and locked the door, and then stood above him, looking down on him. She held the fingers of his right hand, found they could move quite easily. But the fingers of his left hand were stiff, and his mouth was twisted, the left side rigid.

She sat on the bed, and stared at him. Her knowledge of medicine was inadequate, but she could tell that he had had some sort of a seizure, as Elaine had foretold. The question was knowing how long it was likely to last, and what he would be like afterwards, and what might be done to prevent it happening again. Only rest would do that. But would Henry ever rest?

And for the moment, she realised, she was in command, of him and of the fortress. Labalastierre and Laborde would obey her, if she acted in the Emperor's name. She stood up, biting her lip in a sudden irresoluteness.

'You will leave him,' Henry said. His voice was hardly more than a whisper.

Richilde stared at him.

'You will leave him because he deserves to die,' Henry said. 'And because he will not again secure so easy a death as starvation.'

She knelt beside him. 'Thank God,' she said.

'That I should condemn your cousin, twice?'

'That you are speaking, so soon,' she said. 'I had feared . . . so much.'

'Who struck me down?' Henry asked. 'I felt no pain, and I saw no one. Who struck me down?'

'No one struck you down, Henry,' she said. 'You have had what the surgeons call a stroke. It is . . . I do not know for sure, but it is to do with the heart, when it becomes overtired.'

'A stroke?' he asked. 'I cannot move my arm.'

'Raise your right hand,' she commanded.

Slowly his right arm came up.

'That is the important one,' she said. 'The other will soon be well again.'

The right arm fell, across his chest, the fingers seizing the silver bullet which lay there.

Richilde smiled. 'You still have your bullet, Henry. All will be well. Now you must rest. Just rest. And all will be well.'

'You will not leave me,' he begged.

She hesitated, then nodded, and lay down beside him. 'I will not leave you,' she said. Because as you have said, Henry, she thought, Etienne does not deserve to live, and he will not again find so pleasant a death.

When Richilde awoke, the rain had stopped, and the wind had dropped. It still soughed, and when she went to the window, set high in the wall of the citadel, and looked down at the forest, she saw that the trees still swayed and bent. She saw too that several had been uprooted, and that great swathes had been cut through the bushes. But the storm itself had gone, and Haiti could resume its normal life. As if Haiti would ever have a normal life.

'What do my people say of me?' Henry asked.

She returned to the bedside, looked down at him. Much of the tightness had left his face.

'That you were struck by a thunderbolt, from heaven,' she said.

He smiled. 'A thunderbolt, from heaven. That is good. Yes, I was defying the gods, and Ogone Badagris struck me down. They will understand that. You will not deny this tale, Richilde. You will confirm it.'

'If that is what you wish, Henry.' She sat beside him. 'They have sent for the Empress. She will be with you in a few days.'

He frowned at her. 'She must not come here.'

'Not come here? But Henry, she is your wife.'

'My Empress,' he corrected. 'She must not see me like this. She must not. Send her back.' He rolled on his side, away from her, faced the wall.

Richilde rested her hand on his shoulder. 'By the time Honeybelle reaches La Ferriere, Henry, you will be nearly as healthy and as strong as ever before in your life.'

He rolled on his back again. 'Nearly?'

'You have just rolled over,' she said. 'Last night you could hardly move your arm. You are recovering moment by moment.'

'Nearly?' he asked again. 'Will I not regain *all* of my strength?'

Richilde sighed. 'You will regain all of your strength, that any man can know, Henry. But your heart, your mind, has given you a warning, that you are overtired, that you can no longer work as hard as you do, and fight as hard as you do, and demand so much of your body. You are over fifty years of age, Henry. I am over fifty years of age. We are not children any more. We must recognise that fact.'

'Bah,' he said. 'My heart gave me no warning. My heart obeys me, not I it. I was struck down by a thunderbolt, sent by Ogone Badagris. Do you not understand that?'

Richilde would not lower her gaze. 'If you do not heed me, Henry, you will have another stroke, and from that you may not recover at all. Why do you not spend a month here, with me, and Honeybelle? Or better yet, let us all go back down to Sans Souci. There you can rest, and go fishing, as you did before you came to power. Surely you can spare the time to do that?'

'No,' he said. 'Because I *have* come to power. If I rest, the whole country will rest. If I rest, Petion will recover from his defeats, and regain the territory he has lost. He may even invade the north.' He smiled, and picked up her hand. 'Believe me, Richilde, my dear,

dear Richilde, there is nothing I would like better than
to remain here with you and go fishing. But I cannot.'

She sighed, and left the bed, and stood by the
window.

'Have you forgiven me?' he asked. 'For executing
Etienne and Madeleine?'

'No,' she said. 'No, I have not forgiven you. Not for
executing them. But for acting the savage. But I understand what you did, and why you did it.'

'Understanding,' he said. 'That is your greatest gift,
Richilde. The gift of understanding. My people do not
have that gift. You must teach it to them, before we
die.'

She turned back to smile at him, through her tears. 'I
shall at least endeavour to teach it to you, Henry.
Before we die.'

By the time the Empress arrived, three days later,
Henry was, as Richilde had promised him, as well as
ever before in his life. And by then, too, the legend of
how he had challenged the gods, and been struck down
by them, had spread beyond the fortress, to add to the
legend of Christophe himself. And, as he had foreseen,
he gained only credit from it. Because the gods had
been unable to kill him. They had done nothing more
than knock him senseless, as one man might do to
another. He had survived the thunderbolt, and now, as
he displayed to his people by himself hefting cannon
balls, two in each arm, and carrying them up to the
battlements, he was stronger than ever before. When
next he sought to oppose Ogone Badagris, the god
would not find it so easy to gain even so limited a
victory.

Richilde knew that it was useless to attempt to
restrain him. She could only wait, and watch, and try to
get him to bed for a rest from time to time. But even
that was difficult, for Honeybelle had a tale of her own

to tell, of the great waves which had pounded the beaches, and driven across the coast road into the forest; of a tidal wave running through the streets of Millot, sweeping away houses and people, and even pounding at the doors of Sans Souci itself.

'My palace?' Henry shouted, in real alarm. 'What has happened to my palace?'

'It still stands, Your Majesty,' Honeybelle said. 'There has been a little damage. But Millot . . .'

'And Millot belongs to your people, Your Majesty,' Richilde reminded him. 'They are *your* people.'

'Yes,' he said. 'Yes, you are right. We must get down there, right away, and discover what has happened, and what must be done.'

So once again, a trek through the shattered forest. But for Richilde, a happy escape from the gloomy terrors of La Ferriere, where she could still hear Etienne's screams. As he had only been walled up for six days when they left, he could indeed still be screaming.

And I have acquiesced in this, she thought. As I stood by and watched Madeleine being hurled from the battlements. They had been guilty of everything Henry had accused them of. Yet had they also been her cousins. But Henry was her man, whatever his growing loss of any sense of reality, or proportion. And these were her people. Where he, and they, went, so must she.

Certainly there was enough to be done, down on the coast. Millot was indeed shattered, but now at last she could persuade Henry to give the orders to rebuild the town, and create the city of which she had always dreamed. In that sense the hurricane had turned out to be a blessing. Just as the destruction of Vergée d'Or, further along the coast, was a blessing. She rode out there, with Seraphine, and looked at the beach, almost totally gone, now, gouged out by the huge Atlantic rollers to leave only rock, even the little stream diverted and buried. Just as the foundations of the chateau itself had been ripped and torn, and the factory chimney had finally fallen, to wreck the remainder of the building and the machinery. Henry was furious. It would take a great deal of time, and money, to re-create Vergée d'Or as a prospering plantation. Richilde was content, that this strongest of all links with her past should finally be nothing more than a scar on the earth. The beach would return, she knew; the chateau with its lawns and terraces, its staircases and its portraits, its galleries and huge rooms, where so many people had died, would never rise again. It was a sobering reflection on the irrelevance of man when compared with the might of nature, that even had there been no revolution, Vergée d'Or might still have been wiped off the face of the map, by the hurricane. The chateau had been at least as strongly built as that of Sans Souci, but had been so much nearer the beach. Certainly it would have taken a terrible pounding.

But what then had happened to Cap François? Seraphine was naturally concerned about Kit, so they obtained permission from Henry to go into the city. But Cap François had withstood hurricanes before. Several of the wooden docks had been severely damaged, and the seas had risen far enough to wash right across the road and into the town, yet their force had been absorbed by the shoals lying off the beach, and the damage itself had been slight. Kit had put the necessary repairs in hand, and was on the point of setting off with Rogers and the crew to discover what had happened with the *Stormy Petrel*, but he already knew that all of the merchant ships which had been in the harbour at the approach of the storm, and had been securely tucked away in a shallow lagoon protected by a bank of mangroves a hundred years thick, were perfectly secure.

He was also able to reassure Richilde that Louise and Marguerite had arrived, safely. He had placed them in a house, under guard, and would despatch them to Jamaica as soon as the weather improved. Richilde decided against visiting them. She had nothing to say to them, and they would only have hate to express to her. The Mortmains were finished; their bloodstained saga at an end. She was content that it should be so; it was time also for Louise and Marguerite to find their way back to France, and their Ramlie relatives, and forget the tumultuous years during which they had followed Etienne blindly to destruction.

And it was time for her to return to Sans Souci, and Henry. Kit would be joining them in a few days. Somehow, knowing that Henry had at last expiated his hatred and his desire for vengeance, even knowing that he had been struck down, and recovered, made her feel more relaxed than she had been in a long while. Because he *had* recovered. And he was, however reluctantly, obeying her and taking life somewhat more easily. They had, she realised, suddenly entered upon the second half of their lives together. A time for coasting gently downhill, rather than constantly making the effort to mount the slope that lay ahead of them.

But as she saw the cavalcade approaching them on the road from the palace, her heart lurched, and then sank. Because Henry was there, with Labalastierre and Gounod, and his hussars, clattering towards her, bristling with warlike determination.

'Richilde!' Henry shouted, catching sight of her party and giving rein, and then remembering his dignity. 'Duchess! Great news! The very best. Petion is dead.'

She could only stare at him. 'Petion? But how?'

Henry shrugged. 'Heart failure, or some such thing. He must have been struck down the very same moment as I. But I recovered, and he died. There is a measure, eh?'

'What will you do?' As if she did not already know, what he would do.

'Do? Why, recommence the war. With Petion dead . . . there is only that boy, Boyer, to command the mulattos now. Now we shall wipe them from the face of the earth. Now the victory will be ours.'

Chapter 5

THE SILVER BULLET

*Christophe, the magnificent warrior, had no claims
to power beyond his physical stature and the living
memory of his accomplishments against the French.
When age had begun to sap the strength of those
giant muscles, and the memories of his followers,
Christophe had no promises, no development plans
with which to revive their loyalty. The ex-slave
could only become a tyrant, and stand whip in hand
over a resentful people.*

Richilde stood on the battlements of La Ferriere,
and listened. She did this every morning, at dawn,
had done it, every morning at dawn, for the past year
and more. At dawn the land breeze swept down from
the mountains, brought with it the sounds of the mountains, and even, perhaps, the noises of the plains
beyond. Sometimes it was possible to hear, or imagine
she heard, the roar of cannon, and the cries of dying
men.

The Emperor continued his war, now to the exclusion of all else. But he fought with no greater success
against Boyer than he had ever fought Petion. Haiti was
an offensive general's nightmare, as had been proved so
often in the past. Pitched battles could only ever be
fought by mutual consent. Retreating armies could
never be overtaken and routed by fast riding cavalry,
where they could melt into a jungle so thick that a man
on horseback was forced to travel even more slowly

than one on foot. And defensive positions could not be surrounded or flanked, where they were situated above impregnable precipices, from which uncrossable ravines stretched in every direction. Henry's victories against Petion had been gained where victories *could* be gained, by the capturing of towns and villages and sugar plantations. Boyer, who had lived and fought in these conditions all of his adult life, knew better than to offer such hostages to fortune, and long before the Negro host could reach his civilised outposts they had been burned and evacuated. And he kept on fighting, kept on campaigning. He had a soldier's ruthlessness, beneath the charm she remembered so well. And besides, he had an educated man's vision of the present and the future. He calculated that no matter how many skirmishes he might lose, no matter how many villages he might be forced to burn, he would still eventually win the war. Because Henry just fought. It was what he liked doing best. To campaign, in the midst of his soldiers, to expose himself to enemy fire, glorying in the immunity from harm granted him by his precious silver bullet, to plan and then to execute, the kill and to savour the glory of triumph, these were the true delights of life, to Henry. She realised that they always had been.

He expected his people, all of his people, to feel the same. All Haiti, every man, woman and child in the country, was in his opinion born with but a single simple purpose in mind: to support and sustain their Emperor in his determination to conquer the entire vast island. That each of his people might have an ambition of his or her own, that most of those ambitions were simply to till an acre of land and catch a net of fish, and raise a family, was incomprehensible to him. To express such a wish was an act of treachery. And, tucked away in his forest as he was, in the midst of his faithful soldiers, he was unaware of the deep resentments, the deep discontents, which were seeping through the life of his nation.

Richilde herself was not entirely aware of them. She spent most of the time, nowadays, at La Ferriere, protected by the cannon and the walls and Laborde's garrison, and by the immensity of the forest as well. The fortress, so high and so impregnable, so free from mosquitoes and from heat, had ceased to frighten and depress, was her own little sanctuary; its mood suited hers. That it contained the bones of Etienne, and that somewhere at the bottom of the east facing ravine there lay the bones of Madeleine, was no longer a disturbing factor; all sugar plantations, for example, had possessed their own cemeteries, and these usually very near to the house. She had been brought up to live close to her ancestors – and not very many of those had died peacefully in their beds. And besides, to leave La Ferriere, and go down to the coast, *was* to become aware of the gathering discontent. It meant watching the, as yet, unfinished city of Millot, suspended between drama and achievement by the requirements of the Emperor's war. It meant listening to the grumbles of the labourers and the farmers and the fishermen, a tithe of whose meagre earnings were gathered by the tax collectors, to pay for the Emperor's war. And it meant visiting Sans Souci, where the paint peeled and the wood rotted, and the Empress Honeybelle danced and played her way through life, uncaring of the misery beyond her front door.

La Ferriere was the place to be, until Henry came home. If he came home. Because she remained obsessed by a nameless dread, a certainty that that paralytic attack *had* been but a warning of what the future would hold for him, should he not be capable of slowing down, and accepting life more as it came, instead of perpetually attempting to mould it to his own pattern.

And today, at last, she knew he was coming. As the

dawn breeze whispered across the morning, she could hear the clank of wagon wheels, the rattle of accoutrements, drifting towards her. Others heard it too. Both Seraphine and Laborde heard it, and came to join her on the battlements.

'The army returns,' Laborde said. 'That is strange, Your Highness. We have had no messengers to tell of the victory.'

Good, honest, faithful Laborde, she thought. He cannot conceive of Henry ever returning, unless he has gained a victory. But now she could see the red uniforms of the hussars, winding their way along the forest track beneath her. And now too, she could see the horse litter, on which there lay the body of the Emperor.

Desperately Richilde looked for blood and bandages. Blood and bandages, evidences of a physical wound, were things she could cope with, and if he had survived them so far, he would survive them always.

But there was no blood, and no bandages.

She stood in the doorway as the Emperor was carried into his quarters and laid on the bed. His eyes were open. That was the most terrible thing she had ever seen. His eyes, so intelligent, so evident of his will and his determination, glared at her as if he would communicate his thoughts, for he had no other means of expression. His lips were rigid, and his entire face twisted. And he could barely twitch the fingers of his right hand.

'He just fell from his horse,' Labalastierre explained. 'As we were going into battle, His Majesty just fell from his horse. There was no thunder, Duchess. He just fell from his horse.'

'The battle?' Richilde asked. 'What happened?'

Labalastierre sighed. He looked exhausted, and his uniform was caked with sweat and dust. But so were all their uniforms. 'We lost the battle, Duchess. When our soldiers saw what had happened to the Emperor, they fled.'

Richilde discovered she was holding her breath. Christophe had never lost a battle. It was impossible to suppose that he could ever do so.

'Our men scattered,' Labalastierre went on. 'Shouting that the Emperor was dead. I knew he was not, and I sent messengers after them, but they would not return. So I brought His Majesty here, with the Imperial Guard. But Duchess, the soldiers will come back, as soon as they know His Majesty is not dead, that he is again well and strong. Duchess, you restored him to health the last time. You must do so now, again.'

Richilde chewed her lip, and stared into Henry's eyes.

'You must do this, Duchess,' Labalastierre said. 'And quickly. Boyer will not wait for long, when he learns what has happened.'

'Yes,' she agreed. 'I must do this, and quickly.'

He waited, but she did not continue. 'Shall I send for the Empress?' he asked.

She shook her head. 'No, not this time. It were best no one sees him like this.'

Labalastierre groaned. 'The whole army has seen him, like this, Duchess.'

'And they will see him again,' she said. 'When he is well.' But would he ever be well again? Could he?

Labalastierre hesitated, then turned for the door. 'You must tell me what you wish done. It will be done.'

Richilde's shoulders sagged. And then she squared them again. Were she to despair, then there was truly nothing left. 'Yes,' she said. 'I wish you to summon Captain Hamilton, the moment he returns to Cap Haitien. And I wish you to find a *mamaloi*, named Elaine. Your wife knows of her, Prince. Find her, and bring her here. Those are the people I need.'

Kit arrived a week later, to Richilde's very great relief. Because by then she knew that Henry would be a long time recovering, if he ever would. She spent her days massaging his arms and legs, and had achieved a measure of success, in that he could move the fingers of his right hand. His brain was also certainly unaffected. He understood everything that had happened, everything that was happening, everything that she said to him. And she wished he couldn't. The agony in his eyes was horrible to watch.

And Elaine had vanished into the jungle, her hut deserted. She had prophesied the illness of the Emperor. She had not waited to be arrested by his angry soldiers.

'How long?' Richilde asked Kit. 'You must have seen seizures like this before.'

She asked the question in a corner of her own bed-chamber, where they could not be overheard.

Kit's face was grim. 'It is a very complete paralysis. He may regain the partial use of his limbs. But he will never sit a horse again, or draw a sword.'

She stared at him in stark horror.

'Will you tell him?' he asked.

'No,' she said. 'That would be to kill him. We shall tell no one. We cannot tell *anyone*.'

'Are you sure you know what you do?'

'Yes,' she said fiercely. 'As far as his people, as far as the world is concerned, he is recovering. He is getting better, every day. Do not fail me, in this, Kit.'

'Because they will turn against him, when they know,' Kit said. 'And you, and Seraphine, and myself and the boys. Richilde, that is bound to happen. You cannot stop time. You cannot pretend, forever. Listen to me. You have done everything for Henry that you can. All of your life you have done that. Now you can do no more. Surely now is the time to think of yourself, just for once? I am due to sail again in a week. Come with me. It need only be a journey to Cap François, as

334

far as anyone knows. You and Seraphine have been to Cap François before. There will be nothing unusual in that. In Cap François you will come on board to say farewell, and we shall sail away. It will be as simple as that.'

She gazed at him for several seconds, then she turned away. 'You will be sailing from Cap *Haitien*, Kit. And I would like you to come to me, and wish me goodbye, before you leave. I doubt we shall meet again.'

Now she never left Henry's bedroom at all, had her meals served in there, tended to his needs, continued her massaging of his limbs, forced his mouth open to pour soup down his throat, waited for him to be able to move his lips. If he could but utter a word, then she would know he was recovering. But his lips could not even twitch.

The Empress arrived. She had been told nothing but rumours. Now she stood in the doorway of the bed-chamber, and gazed at her husband, who gazed at her. She did not advance to the bedside.

'It was his wish we did not send for you immediately, Your Majesty,' Richilde said. 'He wished you to wait until he is well again. But as you are here, I know he will be grateful for your comfort and support. It will not be long now. He will soon be well.'

Honeybelle's nostrils dilated. 'I will return to the coast,' she said. 'His Majesty is right, and I should not have come. I will see him in Sans Souci, when he can travel.'

The door closed, but Labalastierre had remained on the inside.

'How much longer, Duchess?' he asked.

'Soon,' she said. 'Soon, all will be well. Every day, his strength returns. I can feel it, and see it. Soon.'

'How soon?' he insisted. 'Tomorrow? Next week? We have heard that Boyer is on the march, Duchess. We must know, how soon.'

Richilde bit her lip, and Labalastierre gazed at her

335

for several seconds. Then he turned and left the room.

She slept, in the bed beside him, listened to his breathing. She doubted *he* slept. She doubted he had truly slept since his return, on the litter. And awoke, with a start, unable to decide for a moment what had disturbed her. Then she realised that it was the absence of the sentry's boots, hitting the stone firewalk above her head.

She sat up, looked left and right. Nothing had changed inside the room, and it was just dawn. But there was sound outside, an immense rustle. She dropped her gown over her head, ran to the door. Here too there was no sentry. She ran along the corridor, stood in the doorway, gazed at the courtyard. It was full, of people, soldiers, and their women, and their horses, and their dogs, and their children, and their bundles of precious belongings. And the drawbridge was slowly being lowered.

Richilde ran forward, found Labalastierre, at the head of the garrison, Laborde at his side. 'You cannot leave him now,' she said. 'You cannot desert him. He is recovering. Every minute, he is recovering.'

'You have said that every day, for the past month, Duchess,' Labalastierre pointed out.

'Perhaps I have been optimistic. But it will happen. It *is* happening,' Richilde insisted. 'I will swear to it.'

'It is happening too slowly, Duchess,' Labalastierre said. 'We have received a message from General Boyer, summoning us to surrender. He has taken possession of Cap Haitien, Duchess. The entire island is in his power, save only for this fortress.'

She stared at him, unable to believe what she had just been told. But they had to stay. They *had* to.

'And is that not what this fortress was built for?' she cried. 'As a retreat for our people, after invasion? It is stocked with food, and munition, for a thousand men for a year.' She pointed, at the cattle and the chickens, which had been taken from their pens. 'There is more livestock than on the entire coast. Boyer cannot hope to carry the citadel by assault. And he cannot besiege us here, either, for a year, without food. We must win in the end, if we defend the citadel.'

Labalastierre's face was stony. 'General Boyer has offered us our lives, and our ranks, if we surrender,' he said. 'He has promised us death if we continue to fight. We have agreed to surrender. You would do well to accompany us, Duchess. He has stated that he will execute *every* human being he discovered inside La Ferriere.'

'Are you men?' she shouted. 'Or cowards? Who do you think made you what you are? Who made you a prince, General Labalastierre? It was Henri Christophe, not Jean Boyer. Would you desert him now, when for the first time in his life he needs you, instead of you needing him?'

Labalastierre kicked his horse, and the animal moved forward. Richilde had to jump out of the way to avoid being trodden on. But she threw herself forward again to grasp Laborde's bridle.

'You at the least, Colonel Laborde,' she begged. 'Will stay and defend the citadel. You were placed in command. It is your fortress. Colonel . . .'

He wrenched her fingers free, threw her hands away. 'I must obey General Labalastierre,' he said.

She stood, hands hanging at her sides, as the garrison slowly marched out. They would not look at her, gazed in front of themselves as the dust eddied from their hooves and their feet, hung on the still morning air. Even when the last had gone through the gateway, she continued to stand there, unable to believe that it had happened, unable to believe they would not turn round and come back, to man these battlements, from which no shot had ever been fired in anger, against which all the muskets and cannon in the world could be fired, could they ever be brought to bear, without result. It was only when the sounds of their progress down the hillside began to fade, that she turned, to look at the houses – and at Kit and Seraphine, standing there, with their children.

'Have you not gone too?' she demanded. 'Did you not hear what Labalastierre said? Boyer will execute everyone who remains in the fortress.'

'Are you leaving?' Kit asked.

She stared at him. 'No,' she said. 'No, I will stay with Henry.'

'Then we will stay with you,' Kit said.

Her mouth opened, and then closed again, as tears sprang to her eyes. And then her head jerked, as from within the Emperor's apartments there came a crash.

Richilde ran into the house, gasping for breath, pulled open the door of the bedchamber, half fell beneath the enormous weight of Henry's body, leaning against it. Kit, at her shoulder, grasped the Emperor's arms, pulled him upright.

Richilde gazed at Henry, unable to believe the evidence of her eyes. His face remained rigidly twisted, his left arm hung useless, it was apparent there was little strength in his legs – but he had got out of bed and crossed the room.

'Easy, now,' Kit said. 'Easy now, old fellow. Let's get you back to bed.'

He half pushed, half carried Henry across the room, laid him on the mattress.

'My soldiers,' Henry whispered, his voice seeming to issue from the very pit of the grave. 'Where are my soldiers?'

'Kit!' she cried. 'To horse. Ride after them. Bring them back. Bring but one back. Just Labalastierre will do. Let him see for himself. Let him hear the Emperor speak. Let him know that all will be well. Oh, bring them back, Kit. Bring them back.'

Kit ran from the room.

Richilde knelt beside the bed, held Henry's head in her arms. 'Oh, Henry,' she said. 'Oh, *Henry*. How I have prayed. Oh, Henry.'

'My people have deserted me,' he said.

'They were afraid. How could they not be afraid, with you lying here, so stricken?'

'But you were not afraid, my Richilde.'

She smiled. 'No, I was not afraid, Henry,' she lied. 'And neither will they be, when they come back.'

He said nothing. but his eyes closed, almost for the first time since he had returned to the fortress. Then they opened again. 'It is good of Kit to have remained. My two old, faithful friends. It is good.'

'You have other friends, Henry,' she said. 'You will see.'

He sighed. 'I have no friends. Only followers. Who will follow me no longer.' Almost his lips smiled. 'I equipped this fortress, for a thousand men, for a year. How many years may two men defend it, my Richilde?'

'Five hundred years, Henry. But there are also two women. We will defend La Ferriere for two hundred and fifty years.'

Now he did smile, then his face grew solemn again. 'But one of the men is a cripple. Tell me straight, Richilde . . . will I ever sit a horse again?'

She hesitated. 'Yes,' she said. 'Of course you will, Henry. All you need is time.'

But the hesitation had been fatal. His face closed again, and his eyes remained open.

She fed him. Then she said, 'Kit will be on his way back, by now, with Labalastierre. I must go and look for them.'

'Load a pistol for me,' Henry said.

She frowned at him.

He smiled. 'I am lying here, helpless. I can but use my right arm. I have never been like this before, incapable of defending myself. Fetch me a pistol, Richilde. Just the feel of it will make me stronger.'

She chewed her lip, tempted to remind him that there was no one in the fortress for him to defend himself against. And that she knew too the despair which was lapping at his mind. But it was essential to keep him from becoming agitated – and she need take no risks. She went to the guardroom, primed a pistol, but removed the ball. She gave it to him, watched his huge fingers curl around the butt.

'Now I will grow stronger,' he said. 'By the minute. You watch.'

Richilde raised her head, gazed at Seraphine, who stood in the doorway.

'Kit has returned,' Seraphine said. Her features were once again the calm, composed mask Richilde first remembered of her. The same features which had hung beneath the gallows outside Dessaline's kraal, waiting for death.

Richilde ran outside, and into the courtyard, watched Kit dismounting, looked past him at the empty gateway, the empty forest.

'They would not come?'

'They *could* not come,' Kit said. 'They had already encountered Boyer. Can you not hear?'

She listened, to the sounds of an army on the march. She gathered her skirts and ran up the steps to the battlements, looked down on the forest, saw the gleam of swords and bayonets amidst the trees.

'They will be here in half an hour,' Kit said.

Seraphine stood at his side, waiting.

'We must raise the drawbridge,' Richilde said. 'The three of us can do it. Then we will defy them. No man can take this fortress, if but a single cannon is mounted. And we can do that too.'

Kit looked at Seraphine.

'We must,' Richilde shouted. 'We must. Come on.' She ran for the steps, checked at the sound of an explosion. Her heart lurched all the way down to her belly, and then rose as rapidly. The gun was unloaded. He

340

would be lying there in total mental anguish. She raced down the steps and into the house, opened the bedchamber door, and gazed at Henry Christopher, his right hand, holding the pistol, still slowly sliding away from his opened mouth.

She sank to her knees, aware that Kit and Seraphine were standing beside her.

'The silver bullet,' she whispered. 'I forgot the silver bullet.'

Jean Boyer stood above the body of the Emperor, slowly removed his cocked hat. 'He had greatness,' he said. 'The greatness of strength, and determination, and ambition. Had he also possessed the ability to harness those things, the education to understand what had gone before, to conceive what might come after, who knows what he might have accomplished?' He raised his head. 'No tears, Duchess?'

'I think I have shed them all,' Richilde said. 'Your Majesty.'

'But you stayed with him, to the end. With Captain Hamilton. There is faithfulness.' His lips twisted into the ghost of a smile. 'I am not a majesty, Madame de Mortmain. I think Haiti has had its fill of emperors, and dukes, and princesses. I promise you that His Majesty will have an emperor's funeral, however.

Richilde scarce dared breathe. 'And me, General Boyer?'

'Captain Hamilton's ship waits in Cap Haitien. I would suggest you accompany him to the United States, madame. I would invite you to stay, and grace our society as you have done for so long, but . . .' Once again he looked at Henry Christopher's shattered face. 'You will not look upon his like again, and you, madame, above us all, have too much to remember. I give you, those memories, of the greatest black man the world has yet known'.

Epilogue

Boyer ruled Haiti for twenty years, in which he reconquered the Spanish half of the island, and saw the French admit his sovereignty. As dictators go, he has not often been bettered, but also, as dictators go, he was at last driven into exile by a revolution, and the Spanish half of the island reclaimed its independence as the Dominican Republic.

Scarcely one of Boyer's successors – in either half of the island – has been allowed to retire. For a hundred years after Christophe Hispaniola remained a dark word and a darker blotch on the map, occasionally restored to some semblance of unwilling order by American influence, more often relapsing into revolution and anarchy. For most of the world the island became synonymous with the practice of voodoo, a religion more often than not confused with obeah, the primitive black magic of the West African Negro.

Even dictatorships move with the times. The last thirty years have seen both Haiti and the Dominican Republic developing into modern and even prosperous states. But they remain at the mercy of ambitious generals. And remembering how Ogé and Toussaint fought and died, and the century and a half which has elapsed since the declaration of independence, Haiti must be considered an experiment which failed.

The future was not revealed to Richilde de Mortmain. She knew only of Boyer's successes, and from the window of her house in New Rochelle she could look past the garden where Seraphine played with her children, at the East River, as it made its way towards the ocean which separated her from Haiti, and know, that she had had a share, in those green clad mountains, in those drums, and in the triumphs and the failures, and the love, of Henri Christophe.